EYES OF THE GODDESS

Book Two of the Fianna Cycle

First Edition

Written by
Janine De Tillio Cammarata

Highland Mountain Publishing
Rexford, New York
2010

Anita,

Enjoy the
magic of
Books.

Keep reading!

Janine DeTillio Cammarata

Published by
Highland Mountain Publishing
PO Box 217, Rexford, NY 12148
http://www.highlandpub.com

Library of Congress Control Number: 2010905858

ISBN 978-0-977-69121-0

Printed in the United States of America

Cover Design by
James Russo, Channel One Design, Inc.
www.channelonedesign.com

Interior Illustration and photo of eyes on cover by
Samantha Nichole De Tillio

Once in a lifetime
The world gets to see
A star that shines the brightest of all.

Once in a lifetime
A gift so precious
Makes the world a good place to be.

Once in a lifetime
A smile radiates so much love
That its warmth heals all pain.

In his lifetime
Nick was a shining star
Whose smile was a gift that changed my life.

This book is dedicated to my son, Nick

10/7/95-10/26/08

A portion of the author's proceeds from this book
will be donated to
Nick's Fight to be Healed Foundation

The mission of Nick's Fight to be Healed Foundation, Inc. is to support pediatric blood cancer patients as well as serve the young adult blood cancer community. We strive to improve quality of life by promoting well-being, reducing stress within the entire family, and providing resources to help children with blood cancer lead fun and fulfilling lives.

www.fighttobehealed.org

Acknowledgments

Special thanks to readers: Joe Mancini, Rita De Tillio, Joan Weiskotten (Clifton Park-Halfmoon Public Library), Julie Guzi, Caroline Guzi, and to Karen Knowles who edited the very first draft. Special gratitude to Penelope Jewell for editing the final version and bringing Reiki into my life. Thanks to Robert Moss for teaching me conscious dreaming. My amazingly artistic niece, Samantha De Tillio, is responsible for taking the photo of the eyes on the cover and for drawing the fantastic illustration of Natalie in the book, where she is intent on weaving her energy. Thank you for all you have done to support this book. Thank you to Amanda Distin for being the model for the eyes on the cover. The martial arts' fighting scenes would not be possible without the dedication and amazing teachings of Professor Ronald Malone (Chief), who brought the Hawaiian style of Kenpo Karate to the east coast. I appreciate everyone who has read my first book and kept encouraging me to write the second one.

The idea of the Fire Lord and the powers of fire, ice, and water came from my son, Nick, whose imagination exceeded mine. My other son, Stephen, designed Lon's sword with the protruding flames on each side. Thank you to my husband, Lucas, for always encouraging me to follow my dreams.

Special Note to my Readers

This book is a work of fiction combining my love of Celtic folklore, history, martial arts, and dreams. This is not historical fiction, although I have based some of my characters on historical figures, such as Cormac mac Art. Other characters like Fionn mac Cumhail are based on the Fenian Cycle, which is one the Irish mythological cycles. I have added my own twist to these stories and characters, so enjoy this book for what it is—a story of perseverance, standing up for what you believe in, and action-packed fight scenes.

Glossary

Achton (AK tun): Cormac mac Art's mother

Aiménd (Aw mend): Goddess of the Sky and Light and mother of Akir the Fire Lord

Akir the Fire Lord: Son of two Tuatha Dé Danaan gods, Manannán mac Lir and Aiménd. He spent two hundred years in captivity until he gathered enough spirits of Faery Folk to return to his human form and regain his god status.

Alba: Celtic name for Scotland

Amergin, Finnius: Chief Druid of the High King of Eire, father to Niachra

Awen Crystals: The Awen Crystals symbolize the Three Realms of the Celtic worlds. The crystals are worn as a trio and are attached by a leather band. The first ray on the right symbolizes the male force, the left symbolizes the female force, and the center symbolizes the balance between the two. Without this balance, the Upper World (sky), Middle World (land), and the Under World (sea) cannot exist together. Maecha and Kelan are given these crystals as a gift from the Lord and Princess of the Otherworld. When the crystals glow red, one will know that the other is in danger; black means that one has died or the crystal has been lost. If this happens all powers are broken. Green means that the Otherworld needs help and the crystals will glow yellow when Maecha's and Kelan's bond is complete.

Beltane (BEL tayn): Midpoint in sun's progress between spring equinox and summer solstice. Celebrated in the beginning of May.

Great bonfires marked a time of purification and hope for a good harvest.

Bendrui (BUN-drooee): Female druid

Broch: Dry-stone tower with about 15' thick wall surrounding a circular space usually 30' in diameter. Walls were 20' high. Entrance pierced the broch wall. Only found in Scotland.

Cada'me: A style of martial arts, which includes practicing katas (fixed forms of fighting) and the tonfa stick. Maecha combines her sword fighting with this style.

Cave of the Warrior: Entrance to the Otherworld where warriors travel to become candidates for the elite Fianna. It is found in the county of Roscommon. The cave is a portal that leads into the side of a hill. Warriors must venture through the portal to the realm of the Otherworld and successfully complete challenges.

Conchobar, Osgar: Leader of the Fianna of Leinster

Cruithne (Kruth nee): King of Alba, leader of the Picti

Each-Luáth: Member and leader of the Fian of the Otherworld

Eibhin (ay – LEEN): means light. She is the future daughter of Maecha Ruadh mac Art and Kelan mac Nessa.

Eire: Celtic name for Ireland

Eithne (Eth NÁY): Healer priestess from ancient Eire who time traveled with Finnius Amergin to the twenty-first century and disappeared there.

Fianna: Elite group of warriors led by Fionn mac Cumhail. The warriors were sworn in by their leader's authority and often lived outside the realm of normal society. Their purpose was to protect the king of Ireland and all his lands. Stories about these warriors can be found in the Fenian Cycles, one of the four major cycles of Irish mythology.

Imbas Skye: Maecha's sword, which she named after the Isle of Imbas Skye – the isle where Scathach trains warriors, including Maecha's mother, Queen Deirdre. Only a woman who is deemed worthy by the previous owners of the sword will be allowed to wield it. However, if she is killed by her own sword, then her killer will own the sword.

Leann-cha'omh (Leann-cha OM): Cormac's bendrui and healer.

Lon, son of Liomhtha (Lee óm tha): Master craftsman and teacher of smiths to the King of Lochlann in Bergen.

Mac Art, Cairpre (KAIR pree): Son of High King Cormac and High Queen Deirdre. Maecha's younger brother.

Mac Art, Cormac (kawr-mak): High King of Ireland from 227-266 A.D., son of Art O'enfher or "Art the Lonely," grandson of Conn Ce'tchathach of the Hundred Battles. He is known as Ireland's first lawmaker and is responsible for setting up the elite band of Fianna.

Mac Art, Maecha Ruadh (mac Art, Ma AY ka Ruath): Daughter of High King Cormac and High Queen Deirdre. Heiress to the throne of Tara through matriarchal sovereignty.

Mac Cumhail, Fionn (mac cool, Finn): Historical leader of the Fianna in the third century celtic Ireland.

Macha (mah ka): Celtic Goddess of War

Mac Morna, Goll: Was originally an enemy of the Fianna, but then became its most loyal member. His original name was Aed, which means "Red," but he changed it to Goll, which means "One-eyed" when he lost one eye in a battle.

Mac Morna, Treasa (tree AY sa): Queen of Roscommon of Connacta; leader of the female band of warriors in support of Maecha.

Mac Nessa, Kelan (mac Náyssa, Kay lan): Maecha's Champion and Fianna warrior. They are bonded through their challenges in the Cave of the Warrior and the blessing of the Mother Goddess.

Mac Ronan, Caoilte (mac ronan, KWEEL ta): Fianna warrior, Fionn's nephew.

Manannán mac Lir: God of the Sea

Naoise (Na ó see)

Niachra (Nee a Kra): Known as Natalie in the twenty-first century. She is daughter of Finnius Amergin and Eithne. She is prophesied to be a powerful druid and will guide and protect the daughter of Maecha and Kelan.

O'Dobhailen, Murtagh (O'Dub Haylin, Murtaug): Lon's second in command.

Rath (ráth): Irish ringfort

Ring of Mercy: This ruby ring is worn by Maecha and was a gift from her mother. When the ruby shines bright then the wearer will give mercy to one who has done her wrong. If its light is dim, then the Mother Goddess will set forth her punishment.

Samhain (sow-en): Name for the Celtic New Year celebration on November 1. All the farm animals were gathered together and those which were not needed for breeding in the following spring were killed for food. Because Samhain did not belong to the old year or the new, it was thought to be a time of magic. Spirits passed into this world to mingle with their loved ones.

Scathach (skaw-thach): Warrior Goddess. Trained other women, and sometimes men on the Isle of Imbas Skye. Her name means 'the woman who strikes fear.'

Sennight: Seven days and nights

Sidhe (shee): Faeries who live in underground magical mounds of the Otherworld.

Sommers, Michaela: In ancient Ireland, Michaela's name is pronounced 'Mikala.'

Tir-nan-og (Tir na nóg): Otherworld that is ruled by the Lord and Princess. Roughly means 'Land of Youth.'

Ton-fa: A wooden weapon that has a handle protruding from its side at a right angle. Can be used singly or with a pair and is effective against bladed weapons. Spelled with a hyphen and in italics, because it is foreign to Maecha and Kelan.

Tuatha Dé Danaan (thoóa-haw day dáh-nawn): People of the
Goddess Danu in Irish mythology. They are the fifth group to settle
Ireland, conquering the Fir Bolg.

Uatach (OO tak): Scathach's daughter.

Fianna Celtic Trinity—
"Trust in your soul, believe in your heart, have faith in your mind."

Chapter 1- Celtic Eire

"Open the gate!" Maecha called to the guard. She rode through the gates of Tara into the moon-streaked night. Men on horseback carried torches, their glow illuminating her enemy. Maecha Ruadh mac Art, daughter of High King Cormac mac Art, paused to observe the warrior wearing the Picti helmet. Boar tusks protruded from the top of the helmet, reflecting menacingly in the moonlight. Her enemy's eyes were hidden behind the face plate, but she heard him snarl. The helmet had been her father's, taken from the son of King Cruithne, a Pict who dared to invade their land. It was her father's prized possession and she would take it back for him.

"Come and get me, you coward!" Maecha screamed. Maecha sensed her champion, Kelan mac Nessa, just behind her. She was filled with love and strength. Together, they rode forward to kill her brother.

In the open field, Cairpre raised his sword and yelled, "Attack!" His men swarmed toward his sister.

"By the light of the Mother Goddess, I beseech you to protect what is right!" Maecha called. She swung her powerful sword, Imbas Skye, and didn't stop to watch the limbs fall from the men she took down.

The enemy attempted to surround Maecha. She protected her left side with her *ton-fa* and destroyed on the right with her sword. Feeling the power of the sword, she tightened her grip as the blue eye on the weapon's crossguard lifted its metal lid and

1

surveyed the enemy. Its light flashed. The first scream erupted from the man whose middle was torn open by the eye's flame.

More men were sent to attack. Instead of openly challenging her, he hid behind others. Well she would fight her way to him and erase any questions about her abilities to rule and protect her land.

Kelan's anger at Cairpre's actions resonated through Maecha's body; it revitalized her. A large warrior slammed his axe toward Maecha's head. She blocked it with her *ton-fa*, the impact numbing her arm. She squeezed her legs to stay on her horse. Encouraged by her struggle, the man shoved closer and fought to kill the acting queen. Kelan scooped her up and swung her onto his stallion, her back to his. They attacked in unison. Kelan maneuvered his horse toward the enemy. His stallion tore through their defenses.

Maecha searched for Cairpre. She found him inching his horse back from the raging battle. Fury filled her. Kelan, sensing her urgency, knew what she had to do. She slid off the back of Octar and sliced a path to her brother.

Kelan reached him first. One hard swipe of his flail knocked Cairpre off his horse. He scurried to his feet and was face to face with his sister. Their warriors moved back to watch the siblings fight for sovereignty. Maecha swung her sword at the side of Cairpre's head. He limped out of its path. Spinning toward him, Maecha clashed her sword with his and rammed the head of her *ton-fa* into his side. Cairpre stumbled onto his back. As her sword flew down toward his head, he rolled out of the way.

Maecha felt her sword come alive. Imbas Skye held the spirits of its past warriors, including her mother's. Only one who was deemed worthy could wield the sword. When Maecha had pulled the sword from its sheath, she had the blessings of its spirits and of the Mother Goddess. Only a battle to the death could take it away from her. Maecha would not let that happen. The Mother Goddess had other plans and so Maecha let the great goddess have her way with her brother. She held it so that the closed eye faced him. Celtic knots decorated the blade of Damascus steel that shimmered in the cool winter night. Maecha's fist was protected by a gold guard in the shape of a hand, which held a ruby ring. The Ring of Mercy did not ask its owner to be merciful. It was quite the opposite. So be it. Maecha stood strong as the blue eye opened and blasted its magic at Cairpre. Cairpre yelped and managed to block the attack with his sword. He dropped his severed blade to the ground.

"That sword should be mine!" Cairpre yelled. He raised his palms toward Maecha and bellowed, "By the power of the Fire Lord, you will die!"

A red flash appeared on his palms and fire glowed upon them. Surprised by her brother's ability, Maecha hesitated. Her trousers caught on fire. The blue eye of her sword retaliated, but missed its mark. While Kelan threw Maecha to the ground to douse the flames, Cairpre used the distraction to mount his horse.

"Beware, Sister! The Fire Lord will rule! You will regret the day you went against him!" Cairpre and his remaining men rode off into the woods.

"Forget them!" Kelan yelled to his men. "See if any of these fools are alive to be questioned. I must get Maecha to Finnius to be healed."

"I am fine, Kelan. Help me up," she said.

Kelan placed his hands under her arms and lifted her tall, slim frame to meet his face. He stared into her gray eyes, placed her on her feet, and said, "He wore your father's helmet."

She kept her hands on his chest that heaved with exertion and worry. Her father. Her heart broke each time she thought about how the Picti invaded their land and kidnapped him. She wondered if he had been tortured or was even alive. She forced herself to picture him strong and in control, as he always had been. Maecha's clearest picture of him was when he prepared for battle. When she was a little girl, his horse had stood like a giant next to her, but her father had matched it. He was, no is, a towering man. His silver helmet had glinted in the sunlight as the spikes protruded along the top like a rooster. He had long red hair braided along the sides of his head with the rest falling down his back. The long mustache that trailed down along his jowls past his chin had often been braided. His eyes could be the calmest clear blue and then in the next instant would turn a battle-axe gray. She remembered his eyes of steel, and how they would soften when focused on her. He loved his daughter, but he had trained her relentlessly once he knew that the warrior within her would not be quelled. Maecha shook the picture from her mind hoping that it would not be the last image of her father.

"Cairpre is the one responsible for the Battle at Gabhra where my father was taken. The deaths of so many of the Fianna are on his soul." Thinking about the large score of Fianna warriors who had been killed numbed Maecha's mind. The Fianna were Eire's elite band of warriors. Only the best men who were capable of surviving the challenges in the Cave of the Warrior were allowed into this group. They upheld the laws of the land, protected their sovereign, and their shores. Maecha hadn't understood how they could have overlooked such a large attack from the Picti who crossed from the highlands of Alba. But now she knew. Her treacherous brother had betrayed them all. She sighed. "And now I must leave to save our father while he stays to ravage our home."

Kelan pulled her into a tight embrace and gazed back at Tara. Its towering walls stood tall on the magical hill that was also an entrance to the Otherworld. It was Maecha's home and had been his for so long he often forgot that he wasn't of the sovereign's blood. Its stone walls could withstand the harshest attacks and indeed had done so numerous times. But they wouldn't be there to protect it.

Chapter 2 - New York City

Natalie Fischer smiled to herself as she walked holding hands between Michaela Sommers and Vince Cardosa. They had just finished seeing *The Adventures of Rocky and Bullwinkle*. At ten years old, this was the first movie that Natalie had ever seen in a theater and she didn't want it to end. She also didn't want the evening to end, because she dreaded bedtime. Oh, she loved the apartment where she stayed with Michaela and her sister, Shannon, and they even bought her a bed that was in the living room.

Benjamin Walker, the police officer who was Shannon's boyfriend, told them that everything would be fine. He said he would put those bad guys in jail if it was the last thing he did. Natalie hoped it wasn't the last thing he did, because when Jack Sommers tried to help her, he had been killed. Natalie felt bad that Michaela and Shannon's dad died protecting her, but they didn't blame her. Their dad only did what he had done every day—protect those who couldn't protect themselves. Well, Natalie had protected herself for ten years until she found out what a bad man Ricky Cartillo was. Then she had been running for her life.

Natalie's bed may have been in the living room, but it was like a mansion compared to the rat infested warehouse that she had been forced to live in for most of her life. It felt like a dream come true, until it was time for bed. Then the nightmares would return: all the death, drugs, and violence. Thankfully, the nightmares would recede and visions of a magical land would surface and she would be visited by a tall willowy man whose long white hair and beard would tickle her face when he bent over to comfort her. His bright eyes would reflect her own and she wanted to call him father, but knew that horrid beast of a man, Ricky Cartillo, was her father. She didn't know who this man was, but he was a blessing. Sometimes she would catch glimpses of him and a young woman she knew was her mother. Natalie didn't understand what it meant, but she also knew that she could see visions of the future, so maybe this was a vision of the past? She didn't know, but she was grateful for the reprieve from her nightmares.

But that night, after she had been tucked into bed by Michaela and Vince, her dreams changed just a little.

She sees the man dressed in his robes and she knows he is a druid. On her hands and knees she searches for something in the grass. He is closer and she sees it in his hand, held toward her. On a thin silver chain hangs a pendant—three interlocking lines connected within a circle with three blue gems lined vertically from the top to the bottom. It sways in the air and her breath catches at its simplicity and beauty. She feels the warmth of the sun's heat within her. The man places the chain around her neck as they face her enemy.

Donned in a black robe with a hood covering his face, he raises his hands and flips through the air as he throws bolts of lightning just inches from her person, showing that he can hurt her at any time. Natalie waits with the druid's hand on her shoulder. Natalie raises her hands over her head and tilts her face to the sky to absorb the energy of the sun. Bringing her hands together in front of her chest, she reaches forward, palms up. A blue sphere appears in her left hand and her body rises gently off the ground. She encircles the sphere with her right hand and a blue mist rises around the sphere. It heats her hand as its energy flows through her. She feels the love of the Goddess Brigid; her healing force as she releases her battle cry. She is strong and protects her own. She has the power to see, the power to heal, as well as the power to destroy.

He backs away in surprise. Natalie lowers to the ground and brings her hands to her chest; her body and mind are quiet once more.

Natalie whimpered in her sleep.

"Natalie, wake up," Michaela whispered. She pulled the small girl onto her lap and rocked her. "Shh. It's all right. Wake up and tell me what you saw."

Natalie shifted and wiped the tears that had escaped from her closed eyes. Then she wrapped her arms around Michaela's neck and held on.

"What's going on?" Shannon said sitting next to her sister and Natalie. She rubbed Natalie's back. "Another bad dream?"

Natalie nodded her head. "Someone's after me," she sobbed.

"Natalie, you are safe here with us. No one will ever hurt you again," Shannon said. It broke her heart to see Natalie still so hurt. It had only been a few months since the young girl had come to them and it would take much longer to heal the scars that were deeply embedded in this child's heart and mind.

"He's not here," she said, "but in here." Natalie pointed to her head.

Michaela placed Natalie between her and Shannon. Natalie held onto each of their hands and, even though the dream had scared her, she thought about how much she had come to cherish them both in such a short time. She loved Shannon's curly red hair that was similar, but longer than her own. People actually thought they were sisters or that Natalie was Shannon's daughter, since they also had blue eyes and freckles. Michaela and Shannon looked like sisters in the shape of their face and their actions, but Michaela's hair was a reddish brown, long and wavy. She now had a white streak through it and golden eyes instead of her gray ones. Natalie shivered thinking about the story she had been told about how Michaela almost died in ancient Ireland, but was saved by the champion, Kelan mac Nessa. He gave her the marrow from the tooth of the green serpent, which had healing powers. But, by doing so, it had unleashed some powers in Michaela that they didn't even know about. Michaela could speak Gaelic and had a close connection to Maecha Ruadh mac Art, the warrior she had time traveled to help in third century Celtic Ireland. If Natalie hadn't always had her own visions of this land, she would have thought Michaela was nuts.

"What do you mean?" Shannon asked, reminding Natalie that she was the reason they were all up in the middle of the night.

"I keep dreaming of this man who I feel is my father. He's old though, so I don't know how he could be."

"What does he look like and how do you feel when you are with him?" Michaela asked.

"Well," Natalie began as she sat straighter, less scared. "He has long white hair and a long mustache that connects to his flowing beard and wears a white robe. He's awfully nice and comforts me when my visions get a little hard to handle. I like being with him."

Both Shannon and Michaela were aware that Natalie could see into the future and had dreamt of both of them before they had met. But the visions came more often now and they knew that one day the reasons for them would become apparent. It had been the same for Michaela when her dreams of ancient Ireland became daydreams that led to her leaving her time and traveling to third century Celtic Ireland.

"Go on," Shannon coaxed.

"I've seen a woman. She's beautiful with long straight blond hair. Past her butt! Her eyes sparkle when she talks and she is tall and thin. She seems so fragile to me and sad. No matter

8

how much I walk, I can never get as close as I want. I know this may seem weird." Natalie giggled because their whole conversation would sound weird to an outsider, but here she was a normal girl having a bad dream. Michaela and Shannon were smiling so she said, "Her presence comforts me."

"Do you know where she is?"

"I'm not sure, but I see a lot of water and very cloudy skies. She lives in a simple cottage surrounded by flowers. She seems very alone. I'm afraid that he'll get her."

"Who?" both sisters asked in unison.

"The bad guy in my dream. He jumps all around and throws flaming balls at you, just because he can. He's a big bully and I think he wants to hurt this man with the long hair. I don't know why, but I am important to him and he seems a little afraid of me."

"Why would he be afraid of you, Natalie?" Shannon asked.

She took a deep breath and continued, "Well, when he was done with his fancy magic, I conjured up a misty blue ball. He seemed surprised that I could do that. Oh, and I was lifted into the air like I could fly. It was really awesome. I also thought of the goddess Brigid, but I have been reading a lot of Irish fairy tales, so that may be why she came up."

Michaela peered at Shannon over Natalie's head. She knew that, along with being a powerful warrior, Brigid was also a healer.

Michaela rubbed Natalie's head and said, "That may be true, but if it were my dream I would research Brigid and the color blue. Maybe it will give us some insights on how you should honor your dream. Okay?" Natalie nodded. "Now whose room would you like to sleep in?"

"Could I just have Max sleep with me? He's so cuddly and I know he'll protect me."

Describing her one hundred pound Rottweiller as cuddly

brought another smile to Michaela's lips. She didn't even have to call Max because, at the mention of his name, he was off her bed and onto the cot.

"Traitor," Michaela said.

Max picked up his head, his tongue hanging out the side as he panted innocently at Michaela. "Yeah, just because you're cute, you think I'll forgive you?"

He barked. "Well, all right." Michaela kissed his head and then Natalie's. "Pleasant dreams."

Shannon kissed Natalie as the young girl rested her head on Max's shoulder.

Shannon followed Michaela into her bedroom and closed the door. They sat on Michaela's bed and pulled the covers up as they leaned against her wrought iron headboard.

"So what do you think?" Shannon asked.

"The man that she describes sounds like Finnius Morgan, the man who owned the house that I disappeared in and who is also Finnius Amergin, a powerful druid from third century Celtic Ireland."

Shannon rubbed her temples because once again she really had to push her mind to think outside the box. Ever since she discovered that she could talk to her sister in her dreams and that her sister had really traveled to some other time nothing seemed impossible. But it still could get confusing. And the toughest part was figuring out what her role was in this whole thing. Sure she was a psychologist and had helped Natalie to adjust and begin to heal from her traumatic life, but that would take years to accomplish. Michaela had changed physically and emotionally and was the one who was connected to her ancient counterpart, Maecha. Shannon was more like the dock that everyone knew would be there when they came home. Not very exciting she decided. But then there was Ben Walker, the blond, blue-eyed police officer who had involuntarily become a part of

10

their group and a special part of Shannon's life. She smiled and sighed.

"Uh, hello?" Michaela said elbowing her sister. "Are you going to respond or sit there with that goofy grin on your face, making me think that you weren't listening?"

"Yeah sorry, my mind was drifting. If the man in her dreams is Finnius and Natalie thinks that Finnius is her father, then is it possible that Natalie isn't from our time period?" Shannon replied.

Michaela scrunched her eyebrows together. "Hmm, that's something to think about. Then how did she get here? She believes that Ricky is her father. Where is her mother? Did she come with Finnius or was she really some woman who died from a drug overdose?"

"If the woman did come with Finnius, how did they lose one another and end up in New York City?" Shannon wanted to know.

"Ugh! I don't know. Maybe we'd be better off sleeping on it and I'll see if Maecha has any answers for us," Michaela said.

"Sounds good to me," Shannon said as she rolled over to face the wall.

"Aren't you going into your own bed?" Michaela asked.

"No, your bed is cozier," Shannon said and closed her eyes.

"Just like when we were kids," Michaela said turning over with a grin on her face.

"Yeah, except we had separate beds with our dresser in between them. Remember how we would trace letters on the sides of the dresser and try to guess the words?" Shannon asked.

"I do, but Mom would always know that we were doing it." Shaking her head, Michaela got comfy and began to drift into her land of dreams.

"She seemed to know everything we did," Shannon said, yawning. "Goodnight, Michaela."

"Goodnight," Michaela said and she glided on the wings of her dream spirit.

"Block with sword, step forward and jab tip of ton-fa to solar plexus, uppercut to jaw, step back. Again," Michaela calls another form of cada'me to her student and ancient counterpart, Maecha. Michaela pushes the warrior to her breaking point and they finally rest.

"It's a wonder I will be able to make the trip to Alba. I'm so tired from fighting all night," Maecha says as they stretch their limbs under an oak tree.

"You do need to rest so I won't keep you much longer. But I do have some concerns about Natalie," Michaela says.

"What would they be?"

"She appears to be fighting some type of magical being in her dreams and she has described Finnius very clearly. She claims that he is her father. How can that be?"

Maecha ponders Michaela's words. "Finnius was gone from us for a long time. Perhaps he sired a daughter when he was in your time."

"That is possible, but then why does she think that Ricky Cartillo is her father? Plus, she keeps dreaming of a woman with long blond hair who she feels is her mother."

"I will ask Finnius if you feel this is important," Maecha says.

"I do. Whatever she is fighting in her dreamworld really wants to hurt her and I must know how to protect her until her destiny is revealed to me."

"We leave for Alba in the morn. I will speak to Finnius and then meet you tomorrow night."

"Thank you and good luck, soul sister," Michaela says.

Chapter 3 – Catskills

Vince and Michaela drove up the short driveway to the Little
Lake Inn in the Catskills. Vince had been renovating the house in
the woods that Michaela had inherited from the mysterious
Finnius Morgan. A long driveway had been paved leading from
that house to the parking lot of the Little Lake Inn, the quaint
bed and breakfast that Michaela and Shannon had visited last fall.
Emma and William Lansing hurried out onto their front porch,
letting the screen door slam behind them. As Max and Natalie
scampered from the back seat, Michaela hugged Emma and then
William. It felt like coming home to see grandparents, Michaela
thought.

"Emma, William, I'd like you to meet someone very
special. This is Natalie. She will be staying with us," Michaela
said.

"Hi there, Natalie," William said, waving while Emma
gave her a grandmotherly hug. Emma and William had lived in
the Catskills all their lives and had purchased the bed and
breakfast when they were in their forties. They were busier than
ever twenty years later.

"Oh and there's good ole Max," Emma exclaimed and
bent down to rub Max's big hard head. "He's looking much better
than when I saw him last."

"We had his stitches removed and he's moving around
fine," Michaela said as she bent down to give her hero a big hug.
Michaela didn't remember much of the time when she was
attacked in the house that she now planned to live in. However,

she did remember how her faithful dog had bitten the nasty man named Boris who tried to kill her. That heroic act had given her the time she needed to reach for the glowing wall that had called to her. Then she had time traveled to ancient Ireland but, instead of being in another place physically, she had been trapped in Maecha's dreamworld.

Footsteps sounding like elephant feet broke through Michaela's thoughts and she smiled as she saw Travis and Bentley bound out the door.

"Hey!" the teens called in unison.

Vince held out his hand and they each shook like men. They got a kick out of that and Vince was determined to treat them as men. Travis and Bentley, sixteen and seventeen respectively, were the oldest teens who had been caught up in the drug melee that Ricky Cartillo had been running. The boys had successfully gone through a drug rehab program and now stayed with the Lansings while they helped renovate Michaela's house. Vince and Michaela had recently filled out applications to be foster parents, and with the help of Benjamin Walker had been able to supervise the boys. So far it had been a success. They treated Natalie like a little sister and were very interested in construction.

Vince and Michaela had been together forever and their relationship had become complacent, with neither one willing to make changes. But when Michaela disappeared and almost died, Vince's eyes and heart opened up tenfold. He knew that being with Michaela was a priority in his life and he never knew how much he loved her until almost losing her. He wasn't planning on letting that happen again. Knowing that he wanted to spend the rest of his life with Michaela made his heart stutter, but he was going to do this right. First, he'd get this house finished and then he'd talk to Michaela about opening a karate dojo in the Catskills. He found that he liked building and had talked to a few people about opening a construction business around the area.

The boys could help him, making them a nice tight family. He hoped that Natalie would be included in that family, but something told him things were about to change. He had grown to love Natalie so much in a very short period of time. Vince rubbed his hands over his face. All these thoughts of love—he'd better get to the dojo to do some ass-kicking. He didn't want to get wimpy.

Michaela wrapped her hand in his dark curly hair and kissed his cheek. "Where are you, Vince?"

Vince smiled and pulled her into a bear hug. Call him wimpy anytime; he was one damn lucky man.

Leaving Natalie with the Lansings and the boys, Vince drove Michaela back along the half-mile drive to the house. The front door had been replaced and the exterior redone in a natural brown wood siding. The windows were double hung and the porch was painted white. Michaela let out the long breath she hadn't realized she was holding and smiled.

"It's beautiful, Vince! How did you get so much done in such a short time?" she asked.

"Travis and Bentley did a lot of the demolition, but then the locals heard about what I was doing and about ten well-built guys showed up and we had the siding done within a week," Vince said, trying to be nonchalant, while loving Michaela's ecstatic response.

She literally bounced out of the car, which was a normal occurrence for her since she had come back through the hole in the wall. Michaela was like a ball of endless energy, constantly ricocheting from one task to another. Her enthusiasm in karate class had doubled and even the young kids had to really push to keep up with her. Vince tried not to think about why she was changed and chose to be thankful that it was positive. So far there wasn't anything abnormal about Michaela's return, except for the streak of white in her hair and her golden eyes.

"We haven't had a lot of time to do all that much with the

inside, but it's been cleaned up so that you can make some decisions," Vince added.

"Nothing was thrown away, right?" Michaela asked.

"Of course not. All the artifacts, furniture, and books are still here, waiting for you to dive right in."

Holding Vince's hand, Michaela stepped through the front door. "Okay, this is good," she said, squeezing Vince's hand and then letting go. So many memories and emotions flashing through her mind overwhelmed her. All the weapons still hung on the walls and she couldn't wait to swing them around in the backyard. She touched a sword and her mind was thrown into a battle from the second century. Her body rocked from the violence and turmoil of men falling around her and pushing to get to their enemy's leader. Shaking, she removed her hand and laughed. Vince watched her, his face full of concern.

"That's something I didn't know about," she said.

"Are you up for this? We don't have to stay. I can finish the interior and box everything up. This way you can go through it at your own pace."

"It's all good, Vince. I've changed in so many ways that I figured nothing else could surprise me. But I think I'll avoid the back room for a while. Tell me what ideas you have," Michaela said, forcing a smile on her face.

Remembering their future together, Vince pulled out his design plans.

Chapter 4 - Eire

As they cantered along the sandy shore, Maecha heard Goll mac
Morna, a brother of the Fianna, shout out commands to the men
who were doing their best to perform them. Where someone
might detect chaos, Maecha could see the structured planning
that Goll had set in motion. Maecha smiled when she saw Goll
standing on top of a flat rock. His thick, bare arms were crossed
over his barrel of a chest. As he barked his orders, his hair swung
side to side and Maecha's brow rose at the new spike that hung
from his long, red braid. Fortunately, his leather tunic was thick
enough to protect his skin from the three-sided, ragged blade. A
black patch covered his left eye that he had lost in battle when
Maecha was but a babe. Maecha jumped off of Finn and handed
the reins to Kelan, who guided both their horses to the boats.

"I see you have changed the weaponry in your hair,"
Maecha teased.

"And I see a beautiful young woman where weeks ago
there was just a mere girl."

Maecha blushed. He held out his wide hand. She accepted
it and leaped onto the rock.

Goll smiled and changed the subject. "I like to keep my
enemies wondering where my next attack will come from."

Maecha didn't doubt it as she glanced at the battle-axe
that hung from his side.

"You did well last night," Goll said.

"It would have been better if my brother had been
captured." Frustration filled her heart. "I'm still trying to

understand how Cairpre could do what he did. His madness runs to his soul." She kicked at the rock she stood on.

Goll laughed. Inwardly she chastised herself. Kicking at a rock was a child's act. She was nineteen summers and sworn leader of the elite Fianna! That was something no other female had ever been allowed to do. Wishing there was something she could hit she clenched her fists and gave Goll a stern look.

Still smiling, Goll crossed his arms and said, "Go on."

She unclenched her hands and said, "First, Cairpre denounces the Mother Goddess and our matriarchal lineage. My mother was chosen to rule Eire and she chose my father to rule with her. My father is still our leader, because the people love him, as he keeps to the matriarchal way of life and is preparing me to continue the line. Then Cairpre steals a helmet from my father's armory that symbolizes his strength and power over the king of Alba, and he wears it in desecration of my father's status. I know that he thinks it's unfair that he cannot rule. Even if we weren't ruled by a matriarchal lineage, he would never be accepted as king with that wretched limp of his. He sat on top of that hill, as only a coward would do, and watched the Picti destroy the Fianna and all they stood for. The Battle of Gabhra will forever be remembered as cowards fighting the brave."

Goll's eyes darkened at the mention of all the friends he lost especially their leader, Fionn mac Cumhail.

"I'm sorry, Goll. That was selfish of me to bring that up," she said, placing her hand on his arm.

"All that you say is true and I only wish that it weren't so. For now we must look toward the future and bring your father home."

Maecha nodded and felt better for verbally expressing her anger. She peered toward the two boats in the water. It had taken a month to gather the necessary forces and supplies to cross the waters to Alba. The winter cold had arrived and Maecha didn't want weather to stop them from leaving. "Who else do we wait for?"

Goll observed the large number of people working. "Caoilte is loading the weaponry and Osgar is gathering the horses."

"And where is Treasa?" Maecha asked only to hear the haughty laughter of Queen Treasa mac Morna. Maecha watched Treasa swagger toward the boats with her entourage of women warriors trailing behind her. She held her ornate gold helmet under her arm and her long black hair was held back by a band of gold. She dressed in a dark leather tunic and skirt and her long legs were covered to her knees with brown leather boots. The men gaped and didn't hide the fact that they longed for her. She flirted with one or two on her way. Treasa's warriors were dressed in similar fashion and Ciara, her main guard, carried Treasa's shield.

Maecha jumped down from her perch and called, "Treasa!"

A full smile brightened her already glowing face. "Maecha," she said, bowing, and all who followed her did the same.

Maecha still felt uncomfortable with this sign of royalty, but she knew it was important to show leadership and accept her current role as acting queen until her father could be restored to his rightful place as king. Maecha clasped arms with her friend.

"All my warriors are armed and their horses are being taken care of by kind Osgar," Treasa informed Maecha.

"I can see that you are well prepared," Maecha said.

Goll, Kelan, and Caoilte caught up with the women and asked to speak with Maecha.

"It is understood that you will protect Tara with a band of the Fianna, but they need a leader to guide them. I do not believe that the Picti are still among us, but your brother is determined to undermine your leadership and prevent your father from returning," Goll said.

"Finnius can lead them," Maecha replied.

"That is true, but he is an advisor and needs someone to take his advice and lead the men."

"I would stay, my lady," Caoilte said. His face remained stoic as ever, but his eyes betrayed his hopeful thoughts.

Kelan raised an eyebrow, but said, "I believe that Caoilte has proven to be a competent warrior and would protect Eire as well as we could. He will have enough Fianna with him to defend Tara, and word has been sent to the other forths to build up their defenses."

"Caoilte, would you be willing to remain here and defend our home?" Maecha asked.

"With my life," Caoilte said with quiet assurance as he looked her in the eyes. Then overcome by shyness, his gaze dropped and his wispy blond hair fell over his face.

She observed Caoilte. He was tall and thin, but quick. Maecha had been amazed more than once how fast he could release the daggers he hid on his body. She regarded Goll, Kelan, and Caoilte. Caoilte was the same age as Maecha with Kelan two summers older. Goll was the most seasoned among them, but Maecha respected all their skills and opinions. It didn't feel right that they should be separated, and since exiting the Cave of the Warrior where she earned her Fianna status, she had begun to follow her instincts.

"I also believe that you would serve well in this position, but your destiny is not to stay here. I feel you need to be near me." She saw the shattered look on Caoilte's face and added, "I do not mean so I can protect you, for you have already proven your skills as a warrior. The three of you stood with me at the Stone of Destiny and are a part of this journey. I need each one of you to complete our circle."

Caoilte's eyes sparkled at her words and Maecha could see the relief flow through him. Glad that she had handled that properly, Maecha noted movement over Caoilte's head. As she stared, she saw objects flickering farther along the beach close to

20

the cliffs.

Everyone turned to see what had captured Maecha's attention. A flame flickered and its orange-red glow grew brighter as it moved toward them. Instincts taking over, the small band of warriors unsheathed their swords and stood ready. Maecha raised her sword, prepared to attack. But then, from within the glow of the fire, she heard the melodic banging of metal on metal. Behind the flames were blackened men carrying hordes of weaponry and blacksmith tools. As she peered at the flame, she saw a man carrying his own set of weapons. His tunic was black as well as his leggings. His blond hair and face were streaked with shades of coal.

"Put down your weapons!" Maecha yelled. She smiled at Kelan and together they walked toward Lon, the blacksmith.

His flames withdrew to the earth as he knelt.

"Rise, Lon, son of Liomhtha, so that I may see how you have fared from your journey out of the Otherworld."

Lon rose and his brown eyes still bore the flames of his heritage, the flames of the blacksmith.

"I hoped that you would have need of an Otherworldly blacksmith," Lon smiled and his eyes kindled.

"I am glad you have come. You are welcome here," Maecha said.

Lon said, "With your permission, Maecha Ruadh mac Art, I would like to present my gifts to your esteemed warriors before they venture forth on their journey."

"Of course," Maecha said, fingering the ironwood *ton-fa* that lay on her hip. She still remembered the day she met Lon, except he wasn't the handsome blond man that he was now. He had been a monstrous creature who had tried to kill Kelan in order to be freed from his cursed existence in the Otherworld. By removing his head, Maecha had broken the bonds that held him and he had presented both of them with a *ton-fa* made from indestructible ironwood.

21

Lon moved to a very large and formidable man who was blacker than night. The man held an object wrapped in an oiled cloth. With respect, Lon unfolded the cloth. His blacksmith arms strained under the weight of the iron hammer as he lifted it from the cloth.

"Goll mac Morna, please accept this hammer which is made from the ironwood of the Otherworld and whose metal was forged in the deepest depths of the earth. The strength of the metal comes from its owner and the more you use it, the greater the force of the impact."

Goll was moved by this token of acceptance and forgiveness from the goddess. Although he had been forgiven by Fionn mac Cumhail and King Cormac for killing Fionn's father years ago, he had never truly felt accepted. He had meant it when he told Maecha that he would have died for Fionn. Now he would die to protect Maecha if it ever came to that.

Lon held the magnificent weapon toward him and his shoulders heaved under the weight. Goll grabbed it with his left hand and lifted it like it was one of Caoilte's small daggers. The ironwood was grained like the richest oak. It was a dark brown with lines of iron laced through it. At its base was a deep gray metal ball. The length of the handle was as long as Goll's forearm. The hammer was the same gray metal with a spike on the top. Goll swung it left and right and switched it from hand to hand. He faced the rock that he and Maecha stood on earlier. He raised the hammer high over his head and swung down with all his might. A loud crack shattered the air. The rock heaved and fell to pieces. Goll shifted his one eye toward Lon and grinned.

Lon nodded and then turned to Caoilte. "Caoilte mac Ronan. I have heard of the speed and deadly accuracy of your knife throwing. May I present to you a throwing axe made from the steel of the ancient blacksmiths. It will fly as true as your word."

Lon held out a leather belt with four throwing axes. Caoilte pulled out the first axe. Its shiny silver reflected the sun's light. It fit perfectly in his hand and he weighed its balance along his fingertips. It had a blade on each side and a forked blade on the top. Caoilte flipped the axe in his hand. All signs of shyness disappeared from his face as the fierce warrior within him was released. Retracting his hand to his ear, he turned and let the throwing axe fly from his fingers. The axe struck a barrel of grain. The wood cracked and moaned as it split apart. The golden grain spewed forth onto the sand.

Falling back into himself, Caoilte smiled in thanks and then looked at Maecha in apology. Maecha couldn't help but smile and said, "Go fetch your blade, Caoilte."

Caoilte fastened the belt around his waist and ran to get his new weapon.

Maecha heard Treasa laugh.

"And what of my present, Blacksmith? Does not the leader's dear friend deserve a gift from your Otherworldly fire?"

Lon's smile was mischievous and Treasa's eyes twinkled.

Lon bowed deeply to the ground and spoke, "Although I do not think you would ever be in need of protection, to you I give a shield built of the ironwood, but inlayed with Damascus steel. This shield represents your sisterhood and loyalty to Maecha as neither will ever break."

Treasa bloomed with pleasure as she beheld the silver shield. It was large enough to protect her body as well as another's, but was lighter than her current shield. She turned it around to look at the carving on the front. It bore the image of Imbas Skye and the Eyes of the Goddess watching over it.

Maecha was awed by the resemblance to her sword. The blade shimmered with the Celtic snakes as hers did and the ruby on the hand of the hilt sparkled. The blue eye that would destroy her enemies was pale in comparison to hers, but it seemed to have power of its own.

Lon turned back to Maecha. "My lady, I have come with a message from the Lord and Princess of the Otherworld. They have allowed me the privilege to be among you in this time of need. They send you off with their blessings knowing that your land and home will be safe from any sea marauding invaders or those enemies from within. The Mother Goddess believes that those who have sworn to protect you through the Stone of Destiny should be with you."

So her intuition had been right. Maecha faced Goll, Kelan, and Caoilte. They had pledged their loyalty to her when she had proven her right to rule. After Maecha received Imbas Skye, she had gone to the Stone of Destiny, which blesses the next ruler of Tara. She had struck her sword into the stone and was accepted. Circling the round stone were three standing stones. Goll had stood by the Stone of Justice, for he would demand justice for all the wrongs done to the Fianna. By the Stone of Truth, Caoilte swore to uphold his word and be true to his brethren. Already bonded to Maecha beyond their current lifetimes, Kelan had stood by the Stone of Honor knowing that he would encompass all three virtues and honor his vows to Maecha and the Mother Goddess. They were destined to follow Maecha to the end of the prophecy and beyond, just as Maecha had already known.

"Lon, I am thankful for your presence and for your loyalty to the goddess and King Cormac. I will leave you with enough Fianna warriors to protect our lands and to find my brother, Cairpre." She held out her hand for them to join her. "Come, we must go to Finnius for his blessing."

Deep within the forest Cairpre mac Art, son of Cormac mac Art, licked his wounds from last night's battle. When his sister left, he would rule the land. Once again his sister would have called him a coward; he couldn't wait to make her eat those words. He was biding his time and setting up his small schemes that would bring down the kingdom of Art. Then he would begin anew with absolute leadership. He longed for complete rule over Eire and the blasted Fianna who thought they were invincible. He laughed and caught himself. He had proven them only human and not protected by the Faery Folk.

Cairpre had seen the number of warriors Maecha planned to take with her and his only regret would be that he couldn't kill them right away. His men had managed to sneak in right under Maecha's nose and find out their plans. Cairpre was delighted to know that Finnius would be left in charge, but then was surprised by the arrival of the blackened warriors. His anger rose at the man who hugged his sister. Who was this blond god who swore allegiance to matriarchal sovereignty? He had the build of a blacksmith, but he forged fire around him just like the Fire Lord had done. Could he be a god sent to protect Tara?

He scoffed at Queen Treasa and her band of incompetent females. His hands itched to show them true magic and power. Instead, he ran his fingers through his wiry red hair. Cairpre dragged them down his face and winced at the sensitive area of his eyes where his sister's enchanted sword had scorched him when he had attacked her in the Otherworld. His vision was still blurry and he could barely make out colors. He grumbled loudly as he thought about Imbas Skye. That sword would be his; it had to be his. When he held that sword and it succumbed to his will, then the age of sovereignty would be over. He laughed and then scowled when his men stared at him with wariness.

Cairpre noticed the distrust and heard the murmurs of discord among his group. They were afraid that the gods were angry and they would all suffer. He stood and threw his cup into the dying flames of the morning fire. Cairpre smiled when he saw them flinch as he walked among them searching for the most discontent. Once his sister left, he would declare himself king, ban sovereignty under the Mother Goddess, and eliminate any Fianna, including the warrior blacksmith she thought would be able to protect *his* land. He would then spread his warriors across Eire to demand absolute obedience.

In order to do that, he needed more of the power that the

Fire Lord had promised him. He had a taste of it last night when he blasted his sister with a fire ball. Cairpre chuckled when he remembered his sister's shocked face. He would get more power once he told the Fire Lord of the new arrival. Then he would take control of Tara and subdue Finnius. Cairpre felt a twinge of guilt when he thought of betraying Finnius. The druid had always been kind to him. But he was loyal to Cairpre's father and would do what Maecha said, so that made him an enemy.

Chapter 5 - Eire

The Fire Lord marveled at the shape of his hand. It had been centuries since he was in human form. He was still too weak to walk out of the flames where he had been dwelling so long in the darkest depths of the Otherworld, but he had been patient and finally it was paying off. Thoughts of revenge and dreams about that sword kept him alive each time the weak humans failed him. This time, however, he managed to find one that was slightly competent and very close to the woman who now owned Imbas Skye. Yes, Cairpre mac Art had literally fallen into his scheme with his own desire for revenge and lust for power. So the Fire Lord had given him a taste of power and now the boy couldn't get enough. They would see if he fulfilled his end of the bargain. If the brother of Maecha Ruadh mac Art succeeded, then the Fire Lord wouldn't have need of him or anyone ever again.

It burned him, literally, that he had to depend on anyone. Of course he never did until his Tuatha Dé Danaan family thought his pranks had gone too far and tortured him by removing his powers and plunging him into the depths of nothingness. There he had lost his beautiful body and face and could no longer play his tricks on anyone. The Fire Lord couldn't help who he was or had been. Over two centuries ago, he had been born Akir, the son of two Tuatha Dé Danaan gods. His conception was made in the fire of passion, but that was where the passion for him had ended. His parents had loved one another so much they ignored their only son.

In order to get his parents' attention he had played tricks

on them and the servants. One of his abilities was to change his location with a thought. As a child he would move tools from the cook or blacksmith, only to have them show up days after another servant had been punished for it. He was also able to shape shift into other people or hypnotize others to do his bidding. With little concentration he would turn into whoever he wanted to be and act like that person. When he became a teen he walked among the humans and broke the village women's hearts who would lay down for him with one glance. With his wavy disheveled hair, dark and sensuous eyes, aquiline nose and sardonic smile, women would shiver in his presence. They liked that his body was sleek and strong, but not too muscular.

These skills and his manipulating schemes had cost him his god status. His last scheme had involved his two cousins, Sheehan and Reeny. Sheehan was blind and Reeny was prophesied to die at a young age. Reeny's mother had asked all living things that could be dangerous to not harm her son. The gods honored this request and so all that could do her son harm did not. However, there was one living thing that Reeny's mother did not think to ask. It was the mistletoe. The druids taught that mistletoe healed and was a sign of love. It thrived well in winter and thus was an indicator of everlasting life. Having these qualities, Reeny's mother never thought that it would be a threat to her son.

And so time went on and her sons lived safely and in peace. Knowing that no harm could come of it, the gods enjoyed throwing deadly objects at Reeny only to have them deflected. Akir wanted to know how this was possible. He changed into a pestering old woman and questioned his aunt. When she explained, he asked if there were any exceptions. Not thinking of any danger, she told him of the mistletoe. As a trickster god, it was his duty to have fun with this knowledge. Akir gave a dart made of mistletoe to his blind cousin and told him to try and hit his brother. Sheehan hesitated, but Akir assured him that his brother was invincible. Not knowing any better, he threw the dart and killed his brother.

Reeny's mother and everyone in the village went up in arms when they had heard what Akir had done. Distraught over their son's callousness, Akir's parents wouldn't protect him any longer. Gods and humans alike searched for Akir, who was forced to stay in human form and hide on Earth. For months Akir escaped imprisonment until one day he arrived on the hill of Tara and saw a beautiful woman practicing with a magnificent sword. She looked no older than twenty summers, but she handled her sword as well as the war goddess Macha.

Unable to help himself, Akir approached. When he asked her what he could do to have that sword of hers, she told him that the sword of Imbas Skye was made to be held only by a female warrior whom the spirits of the previous owners deemed worthy.

"But I am a god. Surely I should be an exception," Akir had said.

"And I am a warrior and rightful owner of Imbas Skye."

Akir smiled. "You and that sword shall be mine."

"What god are you?"

Not being able to resist, Akir shape shifted into the warrior's very image.

"What evil is this?" the warrior asked.

"What evil is this?" Akir mocked in her exact voice.

Recognition darkened her face.

"You are Akir, traitor to the gods. I know what you did to those poor boys."

Uneasiness crept along Akir's spine. Akir bowed and stepped back. "I will take your sword another time."

The warrior pointed Imbas Skye toward the handsome god.

"Take my sword from me and it is yours. Only then can you share its powers. But I plan to deliver you to the Mother

Goddess."

Akir laughed. He should have disappeared, but he couldn't resist a challenge. Instead he unsheathed his sword, prepared to wipe the smile from the gorgeous woman's face. He hated to kill her, but he had to have that sword.

They parried and struck with equal force. He let her connect and get closer just to make her think that she could. Then he spun to her side and singed her delicate skin with a fire bolt. She yelled in shock and glared at him.

He gave her his sexiest smile, but she didn't fall for it. The warrior was aware that he would not fight fairly, so she summoned the power of the goddess. The blue eye of Imbas Skye opened and saw its mark. As the next fire ball shot toward her, a flash from the eye diverted the flame and it hit the ground.

Akir was impressed and more determined to have this magical sword. He disappeared and then reappeared behind her. He attempted to run a dagger across her throat, but she grabbed his arm and threw him over her shoulder. Akir disappeared, reappearing on her right side. He launched at her. The warrior flipped out of the way. Akir shot continuous flames at her and the blue eye matched fire with ice. The young warrior held onto her sword as the power within it grew. Its deluge of ice overpowered Akir's flames. Akir began to shake and fell back as ice covered him. He was stiff, cold, and shocked. A mere human couldn't be stronger. It must be the sword. He needed that sword. He heated his body and was ready to launch a final attack when all his power left him.

"No," he said, his eyes wide. His parents and the Lord and Princess of the Otherworld, the androgynous form of the Mother Goddess, stood before him. His father, Manannán, stood there fuming like a giant ball of anger. The outrage in his brilliant blue eyes could have scalded Akir. Akir attempted to ask his mother, Aiménd, for protection, but she held up her small hand. Akir cherished his mother more than anyone he had ever known. Her beauty was ethereal. He had a powerful need to imprint her features into his mind. He absorbed her flaxen hair that flowed down her shoulders and past her waist. Reaching out to touch her small pixie face, he felt his heart tear when she stepped away from him. Her pale skin glowed with her goodness and her gown of white and yellow clung to her small frame. She was the light that never glowed within him, but her image would stay with him forever.

Akir tried to explain, but wasn't given a chance. His parents turned their backs to their only son and left him in the hands of the goddess who was not feeling merciful. For days, Akir had been tied to a rock, so that birds would daily feed on his entrails and eyes, and then he had been launched blindly into the deepest depths of the Otherworld where no one ventured to go. His human and god form were gone and he was just a worm, never to see the light of day.

Even though he had not known it then, his betrayal had torn his parents apart. Feeling responsible for their son's behavior, they could no longer revel in their love for one another. Manannán jumped into the depths of the sea and became Manannán mac Lir, God of the Sea, where he was king of all within the waters. Aiménd shed so many tears that she was lost in them and was absorbed by the power of the sun. As such, she became Aiménd, Goddess of the Sky and Light. Over time, the lovers would catch a glimpse of one another, but they could never interact or touch as they once had. Only until their son repented his ways or they changed the course of his actions could they be as one again.

But even in his greatest despair, Akir would never repent. He would play one last trick. He would come back and the sword would be his. Taking over the earth, sky, and sea, he would make everyone pay for deserting him. Then his parents and the Mother Goddess would wish they had been more lenient.

It took two centuries, but over time Akir lured the tiny

Faery Folk toward his lair and stole their spirit. He would hypnotize them into a false sense of security. Once they were close enough, he would inhale their spirit and their powers would live inside him. As he grew stronger, he inched his way up toward the sidhe where the Faery Folk lived and he dined on their spirits and power. He had grown into what could only be described as a blob. He still remained in the deep recesses of the Otherworld, but he was able to sense a little bit of what was happening around him. That was how he lured the good King Cormac's son into his scheme. He had needed a human to help him carry out his plans on earth, while he regained his former glorious self. Cairpre was a fool and had risen to his bait. It didn't hurt that Akir had managed to play mind games on the decrepit sod. Revenge—it was almost time.

He searched his mind and found Cairpre, all snug and cozy in his bed, without a woman once again. How did he stand it? That would be one of the first pleasures he would have once he was human. He only hoped it would be the irresistible young Maecha. Akir let his thoughts seep into Cairpre's dream.

"Cairpre," he whispered.

Cairpre whimpered and stirred. He didn't wake up physically, but he was aware of Akir in his dreamworld.

"Where are you, my Lord?" Cairpre asked, wearing nothing but his breeches. His shock of red hair and white chest stood in stark contrast to the misty ruins that he stood on.

"I am everywhere, Cairpre. You should know that by now."

Akir chuckled as he watched Cairpre lift one bare foot and then another on the jagged rocks.

"Do your feet hurt, my friend?"

Cairpre looked around trying to locate the voice. "The rocks are sharp."

"Then we'll be quick. Tell me what news you have."

Cairpre fidgeted some more, but it wasn't because of the rocks stabbing into his feet.

"Maecha is set to sail on the morrow. She has two boats filled with a few hundred warriors, most of them being the woman warriors of that Queen Treasa."

"Interesting. Who does she leave behind to protect Tara?"

"Uh, she left Finnius in charge. That is until a man came forth. He has the blessing of the Mother Goddess to protect Tara."

The mist thickened. "What man?" Akir asked.

"He came in flames. I think he is a blacksmith. He has blond hair and knew Maecha well."

Flames erupted around Cairpre and he screeched in fear. They stopped as quickly as they came.

"So the blacksmith dares to rise against me. Ah well, he will be a fun diversion. Use your forces and get control of their rath. And Cairpre—do it soon."

"But my Lord, I need more power. I am up against a man who has stronger powers and then there's Finnius."

The flames erupted again, scorching Cairpre's feet. "Do something first to earn your power and it will be yours."

"Yes, my Lord."

"I will be watching you closely now, along with that sister of yours."

Cairpre sat up in his straw-packed bed drenched in sweat. He felt his face, held up his hands in the dark trying to make sure he was actually awake. Then the pain in his feet reached his brain and he cursed. He lifted his leg and felt the bottom of his feet. Blood and skin. It had been real. The Fire Lord had come to him and he knew he had better do what was asked.

Chapter 6 - Eire

Finnius Amergin, Chief Druid and advisor to King Cormac, stood on the high cliffs of Eire, the walls of Tara looming behind him. He let the wind that whirled along the sea whip his long white hair around his face. His hazel eyes stared into the beyond. Finnius had practiced magic long before King Cormac had been born. He had seen queens rule and then perish, but the matriarchal line had always stood as strong as the will of the goddess. He closed his eyes and sniffed. There was a foul scent in the air, yes he knew. And he believed that whatever evil was lurking beyond the sea, above the soaring heights of birds and down so deep even the sidhe didn't feel it, was coming for him; for them all. It would destroy anything and anyone who stepped in its way. He could not allow it to threaten their way of life. Until now, he would have used his magic to defeat the invisible enemy and all would be well once again. However, this enemy had a face, unknown to Finnius at the moment, but for the first time in his very long life, Finnius would not be the one to fight against it.

A girl with tight red curls and haunted pale blue eyes would be the one to pave the way. His daughter. Finnius laughed, but laughter left a bitter taste in his mouth, for he had never met her. She had been lost to him when her mother, Eithne, had been taken. Eithne had never found her way back to him, but his daughter had through her dreams, and for now that was the safest place for her while she trained. Finnius thought of all he needed to teach her. She would have to learn the healing techniques of a *bendrui* and be able to fight like a warrior. The druid would pour all his knowledge, magic, and power into this mysterious girl, and Leann would teach her healing. His daughter would lay the path for the chosen one of the prophecy who would keep their way of life safe forever.

Looping her arm through his, Maecha and Kelan walked down to the great hall to break fast with Finnius. They were all set to leave, but Maecha needed to let Finnius know about Lon and Natalie, although she was sure he already knew. He always seemed to know things before anyone could tell him. When they entered the great hall, she saw Finnius bent close to his *bendrui*, Leann-cháomh. Maecha didn't want to disturb them. She hesitated only a moment before Finnius motioned for them to sit. Conflicting emotions had raced across Leann's face and Maecha had seen that one of them had been adoration or possibly something stronger. Leann had been apprenticed to Finnius when she had shown great healing abilities as a child. He had served as a father figure to her for a long time and Maecha wondered if it had developed into something more.

"Maecha," Finnius said, bringing her out of her personal musings.

She was embarrassed to be caught daydreaming and her face flushed because she had also been staring at the *bendrui*, which was very disrespectful.

Maecha covered her discomfort by hugging Finnius. She noticed how thin he felt under his white robe. She smiled at Leann and sat down next to Kelan. Cold meat and bread were passed to them. Kelan took a large helping, while Maecha could barely think of eating and only took a piece of bread.

"You will not have the energy to fight if you do not eat like a warrior," Finnius said.

"I have too much on my mind to think about eating. I do not want to leave, but I am anxious to return with my father."

35

"And so you will," Finnius said. He pulled on his long white beard as he grappled with some decision.

"The Mother Goddess has sent a mighty warrior to help you lead our people," Maecha said.

"Yes, I know of Lon the blacksmith. That works well with my plan, for there is something else that requires more of my attention."

Maecha shook her head in shock. "What could be more important than saving our people from my deceitful brother?"

They waited. When he still didn't speak, Leann put her hand on his arm. "You must tell them, Finnius," she said in a quiet, but strong voice.

Finnius' hazel eyes squinted as if he was trying to get them into focus, but everyone knew that Finnius could see almost as well as a hawk.

"I have seen an evil presence heading our way. They travel along the seas and settle into our lives, our people, and our customs like a plague. And a plague it is. What comes will change the way of the goddess and bring down our rights of sovereignty. It will demand sovereignty over us."

"That evil is Cairpre," Maecha said.

"No, I hope to bring Cairpre back to our beliefs. He has done evil, but there is good inside of him."

Maecha knew enough to not say anymore. Finnius had been the most surprised and hurt by Cairpre's betrayal. Finnius had taken Cairpre under his wing when the boy was a struggling child. He taught him to love others and never give up. Maecha knew that her brother had always resented the relationship she shared with her father and she had often tried to include her brother in their outings. But more often than not, those peaceful trips would be torn asunder by her father and brother's inabilities to get along. By the time Cairpre was eleven summers, his relationship with their father had been strained to the point of breaking. Maecha felt badly for her father, for he was a calm and gentle man, but his son brought out the worst in him.

So it was Finnius who taught Cairpre the difference between right and wrong and to love the Mother Goddess above all others. Finnius encouraged the other boys to play with the king's son and teach him to fight. It was Finnius who healed Cairpre when he was hurt or ashamed or mad at the world. But no matter how much love Finnius had shown him, Cairpre always had a bitter and angry streak in him. Maecha knew that Finnius would rather die than have that simmering anger take over Cairpre.

"Then what evil do you speak of?"

"I have seen two girls. One is but a babe with hair as black as the night and blue-green eyes. The other is almost a woman whose hair blazes red and a face that is overshadowed by her pale haunted eyes."

Maecha straightened in her chair.

"They are tied to the prophecy that brought you both together. The evil that threatens your world will be the greatest threat to both their lives."

Finnius hesitated. Leann squeezed his hand and he continued. "This older one is my daughter, Niachra—the one 'Mikala' calls Natalie. Eithne is her mother."

"I don't understand. Eithne disappeared a long time ago," Maecha said.

Finnius sighed, but continued. "My dreams had led me to the future where I found 'Mikala.' I had sensed danger in her time and that was the reason why I had to travel through time. It was to protect her and to make sure that she was indeed who I thought she was. Even though 'Mikala' is from the future, her safety was important for your survival. Eithne journeyed with me. We loved one another and she did not want to be left here without me. I agreed, because I knew that I would be gone a long time. She must have been pregnant when she disappeared."

Maecha watched Leann's face crumple before she

managed to remove any trace of emotion from her face. Their feelings, or at least Leann's, had become more.

That explained so much about how Natalie could see into the future and why she was dreaming of Finnius. Maecha reached over to touch Finnius' thin hand. "I dreamt with 'Mikala' last night. She tells me that Natalie, your daughter, is dreaming of a man attempting to harm her." Maecha noticed the sudden tension in Finnius' hand. "She also dreams of you and feels that you are her father. She knows much more than she can possibly handle right now."

He smiled. It was a tired smile, but he said, "Then it appears time I find out more about this young girl and her strengths, for she will be the protector of your child. The child of the prophecy."

Kelan choked on the water he had been drinking and his face actually reddened. Maecha had the feeling that it wasn't the choking that caused the rise in color. They weren't ready to have a child! And what if she carried the child now? How could she travel and fight, risking its life?

"When will we have this child?"

Now it was Finnius who patted her hand. "Be calm, Maecha." He glanced at Kelan and murmured, "Relax your grip on that cup before you crush it."

Unaware of how tense he was, Kelan placed the cup back down on the table and responded, "I was not prepared for your words, is all, Finnius. A child is a great responsibility."

"And you both have the knowledge as you are ready to receive it. All will be well with your daughter. It is after she is born that I worry." Finnius stood and Maecha knew their talk was over. "Now I must concentrate on preparing my daughter. If what you say is true, then already she holds great power. Leann and I will train her in the dreamworld and eventually she will find her way to us. But the bond between you and Kelan must stay true and strong. And you will be blessed with a child who will have the sole responsibility of saving our way of life."

"What are we supposed to do with what you told us? I need you to help keep peace while I am gone. We need to save our way of life from Cairpre right now, not from some force we cannot see or doesn't exist yet."

"And so I will, as much as I can, Maecha, but I also have a responsibility to my daughter, which in turn will help keep the peace of our way of life for years to come. You will know her as I get to know her. Listen to your dreams, follow them, and don't be afraid to flow along wherever they may take you."

He grasped Kelan's shoulders. "You will be tested, Kelan, and you both will falter. Stay true to your heart." He stared into Kelan's eyes and then Maecha's. "Your enemies will be strong, but your love is stronger. For the sake of your people, make sure you keep it that way."

"Nothing will break our bond," Kelan said with positive assurance.

Finnius nodded as if that movement would make it all true. He only said, "May it be so."

At the edge of a grove of sacred oak trees, Leann stood outside the blessed stone circle. Finnius approached her. Her face was calm, but her heart beat faster as she watched him. Behind him were Maecha and Kelan, their heads bowed in respect. Following them were the warriors who had sworn to protect Maecha and bring her father home, along with the blacksmith, Lon, who would stay to protect their lands.

Leann bowed to Finnius as he walked within the circle and then entered after him. Maecha and Kelan entered along with the leaders who would accompany them to Alba. All the warriors circled around the outside with others standing guard in hopes that Cairpre would show up one last time before they left.

Finnius raised his hands and all fell silent. Kelan and Maecha knelt in front of him. Leann stood behind them with her hands on their shoulders while Finnius placed his hands on each of their heads.

He spoke, "Mother Goddess of all that lives around us, protect these warriors on their journey. They travel in your name. They are bound to you in their hearts and their souls and will do your bidding. For now, they venture forth to unite our kingdom once more. May the Mother of us all guide you and bring you and those you love back to us. May they protect all who remain and keep you safe."

Maecha and Kelan spoke together,

"Bless us Mother for all we must do
Bless us Mother for being true
Bless us Mother and we will be strong
Bless us Mother for we belong
To you in heart and soul."

Finnius and Leann blessed the group as a whole.

Maecha said to Kelan, "Are you ready for this adventure?"

"I've been waiting for it all my life," Kelan smiled and gently touched Maecha's cheek.

For an instant she forgot about their journey and let Kelan's love spread through her. Their Awen Crystals sparkled with yellow shafts of light that cloaked them in its glow. They had been given the Awen Crystals when they met the Lord and Princess of the Otherworld who is the faery essence of the Mother Goddess. That was when Kelan and Maecha first found out that their relationship was special and they would be bonded as no man and woman ever had. The Lord and Princess wore the main Awen Crystal that symbolized the balance between male and female, and the unity amongst the earth, sky, and sea.

The middle crystal shone like the mid-afternoon sun and reflected the bright power of the bond between her and Kelan. It wasn't just the physical bond they experienced, but also the spiritual connection of their souls. Kelan wore the same oval crystals and the middle one glowed as hers did. She knew that much would depend on the other two crystals. The crystal on the right was the feminine essence of their union and the one of the left was the male. If one of the crystals turned red, then the other bound by the crystal was in danger. If it radiated green, then the Lord and Princess of the Otherworld and their Faery Folk were in trouble and they were required to aid them immediately. Maecha hoped that her loyalty to the Mother Goddess would not have to take precedence over saving her father. But she would deal with that fate if it ever happened. Maecha shuddered at the thought of the third possible color. If her yellow crystal turned black then her soul mate was either dead or the crystal had been torn from its owner, with death sure to follow. Maecha felt so much of Kelan that she no longer knew where her body ended and his began. They were one and the same and she wanted it to stay that way forever.

Osgar Conchobar grabbed their shoulders, which brought them back to their reality. His light blue eyes were warm with love for both of them. Maecha smiled at her father's faithful friend. "Let us move on! Manannán will not be pleased if we keep him waiting when we are supposed to venture across his sea!"

Maecha Ruadh mac Art's war band consisted of seasoned warriors, as well as young ones desperate to prove their bravery. She watched as they boarded the boats that would take them to Alba. When every last warrior was accounted for, she turned to Lon and his band of metal warriors.

"I expect to come home and find you hammering iron into weapons, Lon," Maecha said.

Lon's deeply tanned face lit up into a smile. "And I look forward to meeting the High King of Eire so that I may tell him how brave his daughter truly is."

They clasped forearms. "I am not brave, my friend. I do what any honorable warrior would do in my place."

"Yes, what you do is honorable, but it also takes bravery. Do not forget that treachery will be all around you. Trust those you know to be completely true, but be wary of all others."

Maecha's Awen Crystal glowed bright yellow and she mindspoke, *"I am coming, Kelan."* She said to Lon, "I must go now. There are those who are restless."

Kelan found them and clasped Lon's forearm and then pulled him into a brotherly embrace. He whispered in Lon's ear, "If you get the chance, hang that traitor's head on a stake for our welcome home."

Lon nodded and stepped back.

Finnius stood before their boat as the acting queen and her champion walked up to him.

Finnius hugged Maecha. "Travel with care, Maecha, and follow the path of your destiny."

Maecha kissed both his cheeks and stepped back. He felt warm to her and she blinked when she saw flames of fire rising around him. The flames had disappeared, so she thought she imagined them. Finnius gently removed her hands. "Be safe," she said and walked onto the boat.

Finnius squeezed Kelan's arms and stared into the young warrior's eyes until Kelan started to squirm. Seeming satisfied with what he found, Finnius let go. "Stay true to your heart and to her."

"I will," Kelan said.

Knowing he had done all he could, Finnius let them go.

Chapter 7 - New York City

Benjamin Walker placed the phone down. He tried not to think of the coincidence of his parents calling him to say his brother was home with the fact that a major New York City drug ring had been destroyed. His mother had whispered all this since his brother, Nate, didn't want Ben to know.

Once again Nate was passing the blame and refusing to take responsibility for ruining his own life. Ben guessed he should be thankful for what Nate did. Nate's disappearance kept Ben on the straight and narrow. Of course this wasn't the first time Nate had shown up at their parents' house acting all innocent. Last time he was touring Europe to inspire the artist that he knew was in him. Ben sighed. Nate had mentioned something about a big drug bust and how he didn't want to be involved. He wanted, no, desperately needed Ben's protection in exchange for information. It was just another tip that he would have to follow and another rift that would separate him and his parents if Nate had any involvement with Ricky Cartillo. Man, could his world be any more messed up? He wanted a real chance with Shannon and if she found out his brother might be connected to the man who killed her father, Ben didn't think she would stick around.

Ben was supposed to meet Shannon for dinner in one hour and he still hadn't showered. He quickly washed and dressed in beige slacks and a blue Polo shirt that intensified his bright blue eyes. It had been a few months since Frank Goodale had been killed and New York City's biggest drug ring had been destroyed. Everyone involved in that crime had gotten off easy. Captain Barry Newman, who had betrayed his brothers, was dead. Detective Malowski had been severely injured and, although he was out of the hospital, still faced charges of murder, fraud, and drug trafficking. Ricky Cartillo, the leader of this whole criminal operation, had managed to escape the United States and was probably hiding in his homeland of Colombia. Ben would have liked to have made Cartillo pay for all the lives he ruined, but sometimes it was best to walk away.

Ben was only twenty-six and already he had lost two partners. Maybe being a New York City police officer wasn't in his long range plan. For the first time in a long time, he had something to live for. He saw Shannon sitting at a window seat in the restaurant. Her sexy red hair hung in tendrils around her small face, and he noticed she was looking around observing as she always did. She did love to analyze, he thought as he leaned over to kiss the top of her head.

"Huh? Ben! I didn't see you!" Shannon exclaimed, smiling up at him.

Ben took a chance and placed a deeper kiss on her lips. Her blue eyes grew wide with surprise and then settled into slits as she surveyed him across the table.

"What was that for?" she asked wanting to lighten the intense shot her gut had just taken.

Yeah, something real special to live for, Ben thought and then said, "Oh, I just wanted to get your attention."

"Well, you have that now."

"Good," Ben said and he clasped his hand over hers. "How's Natalie?"

"She's wonderful. She, Vince and Michaela are up in the Catskills working on the house with Travis and Bentley."

"Oh, so you have a completely free evening," Ben said.

"Yes, I do. It's been hard trying to fit a ten-year-old girl, who has seen more than most would want in a lifetime, into our lives. But it's working. She's brilliant and sees so much more than someone would give her credit for."

"Is she still having hallucinations or dreams?" Ben asked.

"Let's get some food and I'll fill you in," Shannon said.

Most of Shannon's plate was covered with shrimp fried rice, lo mein and spring rolls. Ben heaped on ribs, General Tso's chicken, beef on a stick and any other dish that included meat. He was a meat lover and had a big appetite. He skipped over the soup, figuring it was a waste of energy and added some egg rolls and fried dumplings.

"Wow," was all Shannon could say.

"Yeah, I like to eat," Ben said. "I figure I burn off twice the amount when I'm at work."

"Well, you still have a week off so watch out." Shannon noted the dark cloud that moved past Ben's eyes. She knew they all had their demons to work out and Ben had more than his fair share. "Have you heard anything about Detective Malowski?"

"He's recovering, but not talking. They'll get it out of him once he's faced with a life sentence. Ricky Cartillo is probably hiding somewhere in Colombia where we can't get to him. Plus his right hand man, Boris Althar, is still at large. We did manage to link him to Frank's death. Your sister was able to give us a very detailed description of him, but so far nothing has come up. A huge guy like that with facial burn scars can't hide out for long." Ben felt the sting of losing another partner. It didn't matter that he barely knew Frank Goodale and that he had been deeply involved in something before Ben came along. He respected him and Frank's deceased partner, Jack Sommers, who was Shannon and Michaela's father. They were men of honor and it seemed as though that relentless honor was what had gotten them both killed. Ben knew that he was held by that code and would have done the same thing. As he looked at Shannon, he hoped it wouldn't come down to that.

He and Shannon had been thrown together by an odd set

of circumstances. Her sister, Michaela, had questioned their father's death. Jack Sommers, a veteran police officer, had been killed in the line of duty at a drug raid. Michaela had asked questions, and the wrong people had found out and tried to kill her. Ben wondered just how much Frank had really known and wished Frank would have opened up to him. He may have been alive today. But it was hard to find people to trust when your partner is killed and the police captain had something to do with it.

"Have they hired a new police captain at the precinct?" Shannon asked.

Ben ignored the tingle up his arms when it seemed that Shannon had read his mind. "Not yet. They are considering bringing someone in from the outside, because they don't know how deep the corruption went. The commissioner put someone in charge for now. I'll find out more when I go back next week."

"Are you ready to go back?"

"I don't really have a choice," Ben stated.

"Yes, you do," Shannon said.

Ben's eyes flared. "Listen, I don't need you to interfere and say that I'm not competent enough to do my job. Don't analyze me, Shannon. I've had enough of that already."

Shannon leaned back. "I wasn't planning on doing any analyzing, Ben. I was just stating the fact that if you aren't ready to take on your job, then you could probably get more time. You lost a partner who in time would have been a close friend. It doesn't get much tougher than that. You are entitled to take a break," she finished.

Ben exhaled in frustration. "I know. I know. I just need to get back into my routine or establish one. I'm afraid to get close now. I can't lose another partner. I don't know what it will do to me."

"Is that all?" Shannon asked.

Ben smiled despite the fact that she was analyzing. He liked the idea that someone cared enough to want to know what was wrong. Sure his parents had cared, but his brother caused so much havoc in their lives, they just hadn't had any more energy left when it came to showing Ben much love.

"Just family problems," Ben replied.

"Oh, I know all about that," Shannon said, smiling.

"Your family is fantastic, Shannon. Mine is just messed up and I really don't want to talk about it."

Happy that he had at least mentioned a family, Shannon let it go.

"Michaela and Vince invited us up to the Catskills this weekend. Michaela was going to play with all the toys that were left there," Shannon said, trying to get his mind onto something fun.

Ben took a bite of chicken and said, "I'm amazed that she can go back into that place after all that happened."

"Most people wouldn't be able to, but my sister refuses to let anything or anyone rule her life. She feels a strong connection to the place and to the land. I think she might even open a dojo around there."

Ben's eyes lit up. "Really? Would they live there all-year round?"

Shannon's face fell at the thought, but she said, "I'm not sure yet. She hasn't really talked to Vince about it yet."

Ben took her hand and kissed it. "That would be hard for you if they left."

Unwanted tears splashed her cheeks and Shannon swiped at them. "You'd think they were moving around the world and I don't even know if it's for real."

"Doesn't matter, Shannon. You and Michaela are the closest siblings I have ever met. Even not living together would be hard for the two of you." Ben wiped his mouth on his napkin and stood. "Let's go up for the weekend. I could use some fresh air and you need to spend time with your sister. You're getting all mopey on me."

47

"Am not," Shannon said punching his shoulder.

Ben wrapped his arm around her waist and gave her a quick kiss. "Prove it."

"Let's go to my empty apartment," Shannon said, smiling like a she-devil.

"Don't have to ask me twice."

As Vince, Travis, and Bentley repaired some broken roof shingles, Michaela and Natalie sat in the loft that held hundreds of books. The bookcases ran from floor to ceiling and a ladder with clawed feet on the bottom could be used to travel the main wall.

"Where do we start?" Natalie asked holding a feather duster and rag. The books were layered in dust and as excited as they both were to just dig in and start reading the many books on ancient Ireland, the books needed some loving care.

"I'll start on the right wall and you start on the left. You can flip any interesting books down so that we can read them later," Michaela replied.

Natalie peered up at the top shelf, which was nine feet high, and heaved a big sigh. "Okay."

They didn't get far until they both were sitting on the floor, dust forgotten and words being relished.

"Michaela?"

Natalie's voice brought her out of her book fog. "What is it?" she asked, crawling over to the girl who had gone paler than she normally was.

Not saying a word, Natalie held the book out. Michaela took it and briefly read the title, <u>The Annals of Irish History</u>. Then she peered at the picture Natalie pointed to. Not even getting to the words, Michaela's mouth fell open as she gawked at the picture of the young woman. She stood among a forest of oak trees with a basket of what appeared to be herbs in it. In her other hand was an elaborate sword that, from her confident hold, told the viewer that she knew how to use it. Her long orange red hair curled around her face and her brilliant blue eyes sparkled with happiness and contentment. Michaela glanced down at the caption and read out loud. "Niachra, Healer and Protector, was thought to have lived in the latter half of the third century in Celtic Ireland. She was the chief healer at the end of Cormac mac Art's reign and was protector of his granddaughter, Eibhlin (ay-LEEN), meaning light."

"Look at her necklace," Natalie said.

Michaela did. "It's beautiful. Does it mean something to you?"

Natalie took the book back and stared at the necklace, tracing it with her finger. Three blue stones were vertically inset on a silver circle with three interlocking circles weaving through it. "I've dreamt of it before. The blue of the stone reminds me of the blue light that often surrounds me in my dreams. I have to find the necklace. I think it's in the house."

"This is a version of a Celtic triskele. It can stand for the three realms of the land, sea and sky. The god Manannán is often symbolized by this, but also the goddess Brigid," Michaela explained.

"Wow. Remember how I dreamt about the old man and you said to research Brigid and the color blue?" Natalie said.

"Yes, I do. It appears you are on the right track. Maybe we can find a book on Brigid."

Natalie shook her head. "I have to find it. It's mine."

"We'll look for it together."

Natalie nodded and climbed off the loft.

Michaela didn't know why, but the certainty that Natalie spoke with scared her. Michaela treated Natalie as her daughter and she had grown very protective of her. It felt like she was losing her already and Michaela wasn't ready to let her go. But she also knew that they all were being drawn toward some specific destiny that they really didn't have any control over. Watching Natalie climb down the ladder she vowed that no matter what, she would keep this child safe. So much depended on it.

About two hours later they were sick of looking for the necklace that may or may not be in the house. They had started in the front room peering in drawers, looking for secret compartments in the walls, and then did the same thing in the rest of the house.

"Michaela, where are you two?" Vince called. "We're hungry!"

Michaela groaned and shook her head at Natalie. "Never get involved with a man who can't cook for himself!"

Natalie giggled. She knew that Michaela loved catering to Vince who always did everything for her in return. She followed Michaela down the hall.

"There are my two favorite girls," Vince said giving Natalie a kiss on the forehead and then swinging Michaela into a low dip and laying a big kiss on her. Max decided to do some licking at the same time and Michaela squealed, pulling herself back up.

"Thanks, Max!" she said wiping her face on the sleeve of her arm.

"What were you two doing?" Vince asked.

Natalie piped in as she followed him into the small kitchen. She plopped onto a bar stool next to Travis and Bentley and said, "We were looking for a necklace that I think is hidden in the house, but we can't find it."

Travis grabbed a cheese doodle from a bowl on the counter and as he crunched it said, "I was always told that if you can't find something, just sleep on it."

Vince and Michaela exchanged bemused looks, and Michaela mouthed that she told him so. Vince just shrugged.

Natalie, who had a slight crush on the tall, scruffy blond, took his advice with a serious face. "I think I'll do that." She quietly ate her lunch, thinking of the blue gems.

Chapter 8 - Eire

Maecha waved as her land, her home, her Eire, grew smaller until it blended in with the water. Once settled, Maecha stood at the fore of the boat and watched the water part and flow around them. She was glad they were finally taking action, but she was impatient to get to Alba. Not knowing what to expect made her edgy. Fear of what would happen without her at home and what she would find when she reached her father all but suffocated her.

"Ouch," Kelan said as he wrapped his arms around her waist. "Release those emotions, my lady."

All Maecha felt from Kelan was warmth and love. Guilt was added to her repertoire of emotions. She was always battering his mind with worry. "This sense of unknowing is plaguing my mind! I want to get there, fight some barbaric Picti, and sail back home."

Kelan's deep laugh vibrated along her neck. "You'll get your chance, but how about taking what comes your way first? Take this time to pay attention to me," he said.

Maecha faced him, her red hair wild around her face. "Are you sorry that you have taken on such a burden by bonding with me?" she asked half seriously.

Kelan's black hair was pulled back in a braid inlaid with leather strappings. He wore a sleeveless brown leather tunic and the well-formed muscles on his arms flexed as he gave her another squeeze. He tapped his forehead against hers so that all she could see were his green eyes boring into her gray ones.

"Maecha, will I forever have to reassure you of my desire to be with you, my devotion to you, and my acceptance of our bond? I knew what the Mother Goddess was asking of me when she placed these symbols on my arms."

As Kelan held out his forearms, Maecha saw two sets of brilliant otherworldly eyes staring back at her. It was amazing to think about Kelan's final quest in the Cave of the Warrior. She should not doubt his love and connection to her as he had had to deal with the pain of holding a cauldron of boiling water against his forearms, while he pledged his life and loyalty to the Mother Goddess and vowed to protect and love Maecha. It had been a marriage ritual, except Maecha hadn't been there. Someday they would perform that union together, but their hearts and souls were already united and their paths would always remain joined.

Kelan continued, "I pledged my love and loyalty to you then and I'll do it now, with all the emotional turmoil that flows from you to me. I like feeling close to you and knowing where you are, how you feel, and what you need."

Maecha's gaze shifted to the tattooed snake eating its tail that circled her left bicep. That symbolized her vow to rule after her father. She felt the burden and the pride of it daily, so she knew what Kelan had taken on when he pledged himself to her.

Kelan lifted her pointy chin and kissed her. Maecha relaxed and leaned into him and let him banish any doubt from her mind and replace it with his loving thoughts. There wasn't any room for doubt and she would try not to let it seep in. There was too much at stake.

The next morning Maecha awoke to a blue mist covering the surface of the boat. She felt for Kelan.

"I am here," he said and pulled her close to him.

"What is it? It feels like a second skin," Maecha said.

"I do not know, but it has covered us since daybreak. We

52

have stopped in the hope that it will disappear with the rising sun."

Maecha heard a splash in the water and felt her way to the edge. "Over here, Maecha," Caoilte said as he held out his hand and grabbed her. "There's something swimming in the water." She leaned over hoping to get a better view.

Kelan stepped toward her. "Maecha, move away from the edge." He unsheathed his sword. "Now!"

A sucker-lined tentacle flicked its tip over the edge of the boat and lunged for Maecha. On pure instinct, Maecha ducked under the tentacle and Caoilte sliced its flesh with one of his daggers. Maecha removed Imbas Skye and sliced the tip. The tentacle reared back into the water, and the mist receded unveiling the beast. The Kraken was so enormous it could have been an island in the sea. Before she could back away, another tentacle wrapped around her waist.

"Kelan!" she yelled. Caoilte sliced and tried to pull her back, but the monster lifted her into the air. Maecha held onto Imbas Skye, but the Kraken shook her so hard, she couldn't stab it.

"Kill the blasted beast!" Kelan yelled. Kelan watched the blue-green Kraken rise up above the surface. Its milk-white eye ignored him. Archers shot slews of arrows into the beast's thick body. Kelan grabbed a rope that was attached to the boat's mast. He leaned out over the rail and sliced off one of the Kraken's arms. The Kraken roared and lifted Maecha further away from the boat. Kelan still held the rope and leaned over to follow the beast's trail. Caoilte stood on the prow and launched his daggers at the beast. He hit his mark, but the Kraken didn't flinch.

The Kraken lifted another tentacle that was the width of five men. It slapped the deck, wiping out five men with a flick. Goll bellowed at the beast and swung his iron axe through an arm. Green slime drenched him and the Kraken backed away. It disappeared into the depths of the water taking Maecha with it.

"Maecha!" Kelan yelled, preparing to jump in after her,

even though he was deathly afraid of the water.

"Kelan!" Osgar called. "Get down!"

Goll and Caoilte grabbed Kelan and released him when he whirled around to attack. He scowled at the two men who dared to pull him back. Then he focused on Osgar when he stepped in front of him.

"I failed her," he said, his body tense with adrenaline.

"You didn't fail her. With any luck it is the will of the gods. The Kraken is a creature of the sea god, Manannán, so we must hope that he has sent for her."

"And if you are wrong?"

"I do not know. The sea god is fickle and often seeks adventures for the sake of something to do. I can only hope that this is so."

Kelan's anger flowed through him as he thought about how often the gods toyed with them. Then he remembered what gifts they had also granted and said, "I cannot feel her."

"Your other emotions are too strong. Relax and you will sense her."

Kelan moved away from everyone and with a hesitant step walked back to the edge to wait for her. He closed his eyes and touched his Awen Crystal. Reaching into their bond, he searched for the woman who gave him hope of love.

The Fire Lord sat cross-legged in his fiery lair. He had a dozen tasty faeries that morn and his body had developed much quicker than he had anticipated. They must have been some powerful spirits, he mused. The trickster god moved his arms in front of his face and admired his long perfectly shaped fingers. He curled his fingers and opened his palm. Flames erupted in his hand and he smiled at the scene unfolding in front of him. "What would my father want with the lovely Maecha?" he asked aloud as he watched her descend into the watery depths. He would wait and find out, but while he did, why not have a little fun with her long-haired lover? The Fire Lord laughed in glee as he entered Kelan's mind.

On the deck of the boat, Kelan tried to calm his nerves so that he could locate Maecha. Every time he pictured her, his own fear of the water overcame him. He was launched back to his twelfth summer when he was a gifted, but inexperienced, fighter. His father was a king of his tribe and paid allegiance to King Cormac's realm. They lived in relatively peaceful times, with only the occasional raids from neighboring tribes and even fewer attacks from the Picti. But on that fateful morning, the raid turned into a slaughter.

Kelan had been annoyed to be sent to help his mother and sister who were washing clothes in the lake. The blare of a horn first alerted Kelan to the attack. Then the appearance of ten warriors launched Kelan into action. He had yelled for his sister to run back to the safety of their *rath*. He found out later that she never made it. Kelan managed to take four of the warriors down who did not think that a slightly built youth would have the skills to defeat them. The others didn't make that same mistake and, while two attacked his mother in the water, the others were able to wound Kelan. As he fell back into the water, all he could see was his mother floundering, blood gushing from her multiple wounds. By the time Kelan grabbed his mother she was floating, lifeless. He held her and let the water carry them downstream out of harm's way. When he awoke, he was in Tara, home of King Cormac, and was one of the few survivors. His mother, father, and sister were all slaughtered; Kelan would be raised by the high king.

Water splashed over the boat onto Kelan's face, bringing him back to reality. He glanced over the edge, and this time it was Maecha's deathly white face that peered up at him in accusation. Her pale lips asked him why he hadn't saved her. Kelan shook his head in denial. Maecha was not dead. His Awen Crystal was yellow, if just a little paler than usual, but it told him that she was alive. He pictured her oval face with the pointy chin he loved to nip. He breathed in the scent of honeysuckle that emanated from her long red locks. Her eyes, the color of storm clouds, stared into his. He breathed a sigh of relief and waited.

The Fire Lord closed his hand and the image disappeared. What had gone wrong? How could the useless warrior thwart his attempt to take over his mind? He had allowed the images of his mother to overtake him, but not Maecha's death. That crystal around his neck seemed to hold great power. They were stronger when they were together. The Fire Lord laughed. He needed to separate Kelan and Maecha. He just wasn't sure how he would do it, but Maecha would lose her soul mate and she would be his. Needing to find out more about this delectable and mysterious woman, he found her at the bottom of the sea.

Maecha couldn't believe her eyes. One moment she was being flung to her death by a monstrous sea creature and the next she was swept up by a lovely man riding a brilliant white horse. He had kissed her fully on the mouth and after that she could breathe on her own—underwater. She was dazzled by the creatures that swam amiably around her, watching her as closely as she watched them. Then they arrived at an underwater kingdom that Maecha knew could only belong to the god of the sea, Manannán mac Lir. She peered at her rescuer and when he smiled and shrugged his shoulders, she knew she was right.

Manannán's horse halted and Manannán easily swung off with Maecha in his arms. Maecha squirmed, but he only smiled down at her again and led her into a sparkling room. He gently placed her on her feet and Maecha had to gather her balance, because the floor wasn't quite solid. It shifted like sand on the beach.

"Easy now, my precious lady. I do not want you to injure

yourself in my realm after you were able to escape tragedy with the cranky Kraken," Manannán spoke.

"Are you the sea god?" Maecha asked.

"Yes, I am Manannán mac Lir, god of the ever-enchanting sea. You must have heard many stories of me and my handsome looks," he said, raising a dark eyebrow and smirking.

Maecha relaxed with his easy manner and took the time to study him more closely. His long dark hair flowed over a blue cloak that shimmered with the colors of the sea. His eyes were a vibrant blue and thick eyebrows towered over them with tattooed dots above. His thin mustache and flowing beard elongated his face and when he smiled, his eyes lit up like the sun glinting off the sea water. He was handsome and, from what she remembered of her childhood stories, was also compassionate to humans.

"Yes, I have heard of you and I must say that seeing you in person is much more impressive than listening to all of your adventures."

"Well, I can be too much to handle," he laughed.

"And do you know who I am?" Maecha asked.

"Of course I do. You are Maecha Ruadh mac Art, daughter of the High King of Tara, Cormac mac Art and his lovely wife, Deirdre of the Sun, who died before her time. You are on your way to rescue that father of yours. He always seems to get himself in trouble. I've helped him a few times, but those stories are for another day."

"But how do you know about me, Manannán mac Lir?" Maecha asked.

"Please call me mac Lir. Oh, I know everything about anyone who dares to travel across my waters. Of course when I saw you coming, I felt I needed to offer a little advice on the path you were taking. I do apologize that my little friend was not gentler. He was supposed to offer you a calmer ride down to me," he said a little sheepishly.

Forgetting that she was addressing a god, Maecha spoke,

"A little friend? That horrible monster is your friend? It almost killed me and did kill a few of my men. Everyone is probably worried to death about me, because you wanted to offer advice! Couldn't you have just paid a visit yourself?"

"Now, now. Let's not get too testy and upset over this. Your warrior mate would know that you are fine if he would relax his mind."

"And how do you know that?" Maecha said, with her voice not quite as loud.

"If you would quiet your mind, you would be able to hear him calling for you. He's annoying me, but you will hear him if you listen."

Maecha turned away from the sea god and shut her eyes. Her Awen Crystals grew warm as she wrapped them in her hand. She could hear Kelan calling her name, searching for a sign that she was all right. She pictured him in her mind peering over the side of the boat waiting for her. Worry was etched along his brow.

"Kelan," she spoke in her mind. *"I am well. Manannán mac Lir wanted to meet me. I am in his home under the sea. I will ask him to bring me back to you. Just wait."*

She felt Kelan relax and brought her attention back to mac Lir. "I want to go back to my boat. I have too much at stake to stay here with you any longer. I must be on my way to Alba to save my father."

"All in good time."

"Now," Maecha said in a flat tone.

Mac Lir's eyes darkened and Maecha flinched. Perhaps she had sounded a little too demanding.

"You will be brought back to your boat, Maecha, but first you will listen to me."

Mac Lir motioned to a sea green chair and Maecha sat down in it. She almost fell off when the chair moved with the current. She wiggled her way deeper into it and waited. Mac Lir sat on a chair next to her and smiled like a grandfather.

"My child, you are not ready to face the forces that await you in Alba or at home," mac Lir began.

Maecha stood. "I am nineteen summers—a child no more! I have traveled far and faced many challenges and forces in order to become the leader of the Fianna. I now wield the powerful Imbas Skye that has been handed down to generations of worthy female warriors. I am a leader of warriors and kings who follow me to save my father! Me!"

"Sit down," mac Lir spoke, waving his hand. Maecha did, much easier this time. "I know all you have done. I have seen it and I am impressed. But you are not done training, although I'm glad to find that your confidence is improving. Your actions, not your words, will help you accomplish your mission. You have been gifted with powers you do not even realize you possess."

Maecha thought about what he said. "It's true that some of my powers have been surprising me either in battle or when I'm reacting to Kelan's bond to me. But I have managed them and no one has been harmed who hasn't deserved it."

"Ahh, and there is the dilemma."

"What dilemma?"

"How do you know whether you use your power toward your destiny or because it feels good to you? You have the power to take down entire tribes."

Maecha started, "I do not!"

Mac Lir's face was taut as if speaking from memory. "Yes, you do. It may not seem like you are abusing your powers at first and you may not mean to do it, but eventually if you do not understand all your powers, they can start to control you."

Maecha shifted and her sea chair swayed beneath her. She whispered, "Did that happen to you?"

"No." Mac Lir hesitated and Maecha could see that he was debating how much he should tell her.

"If what you need to say affects this prophecy, then I must know. I would think that the more I know, the more value I could place on my powers. I cannot win by launching blindly into battle."

Mac Lir nodded. "I agree. However, there is still much that you and Kelan must learn on your own."

The sea god turned his chair so that it faced a wall of shimmering sea. Maecha's chair shifted so that she was facing the same way. Mac Lir waved his fingers toward the water and an image of a beautiful young man appeared.

"This is my son, Akir. He was a powerful god, but he was also a trickster and found great joy in playing pranks on others. Watch."

Maecha laughed at some of his harmless antics, but began to see how his actions changed. They became malignant. She gasped when she saw his cousin die.

"What happened to him?" she asked not able to take her eyes from Akir's satisfied face.

Mac Lir sighed like an old man. "He escaped for awhile." He didn't say any more, but turned to the sea screen once again.

Maecha watched in horror as Akir fought with an incredibly strong and beautiful woman who held Imbas Skye.

She grimaced at Akir's punishment, although she knew it was justified. She saw mac Lir and a gorgeous goddess next to him walk away.

"That is my wife, Aiménd, now the sky goddess. His actions were his own, but we could have guided him better, loved him more. Because our love for one another was so strong, we did not honor our love for our son. When he was taken away we lost more than our son, we lost each other. Our souls divided and we could not be together. I drifted down to the sea where I have reigned for two centuries and Aiménd floated to the sky where she has looked down upon the world from a distance. Our interactions with humans are very rare and it is only when the consequences of a human's actions are so integral to our way of life that we are able to intervene."

Maecha reached forward and held his hand. Mac Lir squeezed it and forced a smile. "You are generous and compassionate, Maecha Ruadh, and those qualities will sustain you when you need to make important decisions. But you are not ready to venture forth to Alba."

"With all due respect, Man . . . ,"

"Call me mac Lir," he reminded her.

"My father's life is at stake. I do not know the Picti's plans and if I delay too long, they might kill him. All of Eire will fall to my brother's deceitful hands and we will be doomed."

Mac Lir twirled his fingers toward the sea once again and an image appeared. A vibrant and tall, yet powerfully built girl stood on the cusp of the sea. Her black hair whipped in the wind. Her world, her people, stood behind her in fear. In front of them rolled a black cloud with people in it. The apparition inched its way toward their home. She lifted her hands and with considerable strain, her land and her people drifted away into a mist and the black cloud dissipated into nothing.

Maecha felt goose bumps travel along her arms. Her heart ached with love and fear for this young woman who literally held the world in her hands. Maecha had recoiled from the black cloud, but this girl stood her ground and did what was necessary for the good of all.

"She is yours," mac Lir said. He placed his hands on her shoulders.

Maecha nodded. She had felt the strong bond between them.

"She is the prophecy; my and Kelan's child."

"Yes, but it is not that easy." He moved in front of her and squatted down taking her hands in his. "I failed my son and I have a chance to help you. I do not wish to fail again. My son has grown stronger and plans to take revenge on me, his mother, and everyone who was responsible for removing his powers."

"What does that have to do with me?" Maecha asked.

"He desires your sword. As the holder of Imbas Skye, he will find you. He will try to trick you, Kelan, and any who rise to your cause. I do not know how long you have, but he gets stronger daily."

"Why can't you and the goddess destroy him again?"

Mac Lir sighed. "We cannot find him. Akir has hidden himself somewhere in the Otherworld unbeknownst to us. He knows the sidhe as well as the Faery Folk and has lived there for two hundred years! They have searched, but he destroys them and takes their power. I can only find him when he is in his true form and by then he may be too strong. Maecha, he wants to destroy you so he can claim your sword. Only then can he possess its power. If he does, not only will he seek revenge for all on earth, but the evil that your daughter is meant to destroy will ravage our lands and our way of life until there is nothing left."

Maecha was shocked into silence. The thought that she had an enemy who had been imprisoned for over two hundred years that she didn't even know overwhelmed her.

"What do you want me to do?"

"You need to hone all your skills—mental and physical."

Maecha waited.

"There's only one place you can do this—the Isle of Imbas Skye."

"You want me to train with Scathach?"

"Yes, you and your warriors. Scathach will train your mind. There are many gifts that were bestowed on you when you were in the Otherworld. You drank from the Well of Knowledge and you have yet to even touch the magic that exists within you now. You have the knowledge of foresight if you'd learn to use it. There's so much more you need to know. You are a formidable fighter with that sword, but I think you can benefit from training with the best, and you can do this on the Isle of Imbas Skye."

"Well, the best would be my mother, or so the stories say."

"You will be able to train with her in your dreamworld as

well as the other spirits that have been blessed by the sword."

Maecha's eyes grew wide. "Train with my mother?" She couldn't imagine the experience, but longed for any type of contact. Maecha had only been a small child when her mother died giving birth to Cairpre. Images of Maecha riding on a horse with her mother laughing and chattering behind her floated through her mind. Her mother was so beautiful and happy, yet strong and determined. Her people loved and cherished her and would have died for her if necessary. She was a true queen and Maecha missed her terribly.

"Then it is decided." Mac Lir stood and held out his hand. "Come, we must go. Your champion grows restless."

Maecha took his hand and he swept her outside his liquid castle. They mounted the horse that the sea god had ridden earlier.

Maecha held on as the horse called Enbarr flew straight from the sea's bottom. They broke the surface spraying water all over the deck and Kelan. He jumped back and his eyebrows shot up at the magnificent man holding Maecha. The sea god lowered Maecha to the deck. Kelan pulled her to him trying not to appear desperate to get her in his arms. He held her close and breathed in the briny scent of her hair that was drier than he was.

Kelan glared at the sea god and mac Lir bowed. "Take care of her, Kelan mac Nessa. She holds the key to your future."

Manannán blew Maecha a kiss and backed away from the boats. He whipped his hands through the air and forced the boats forward along the northern winds.

The sea god gazed toward the brilliant blue sky and saw his lovely Aiménd riding the rays of the sun. She bowed her golden head and reached toward her husband in remembrance of the love they once had and hoped to have again one day. He reached toward her, but they never touched. Mac Lir turned away to watch the boats fly across the water. Maecha's success would affect more than she knew. He flicked the reins on Enbarr's back and sank down to his lonely domain.

The Fire Lord's body erupted in flames at his father's interference. "How dare he assume that he can control what happens to me any longer?" he screamed at no one. Petrified Faery Folk shivered at his anger and some cried when the souls of their brethren were consumed by him. He shook at the shackles of his prison, anxious to be out in the world to exact his revenge. "You will be the first to feel the wrath of my power, Father. You will be the first."

But then he thought about what his father had told Maecha. If she was indeed the carrier of the child who would save the world, then perhaps if it were his child, then it could be used to control their world. The Fire Lord chuckled and then broke out in hysterical laughter. Wouldn't that be a kick in the face of all the gods—Akir the father of the child who destroys their world. Well, it sure would be fun trying as he thought of Maecha and that beautiful warrior body of hers. Yes, he would make that a bonus part of his plan.

Chapter 9 - Isle of Imbas Skye

Kelan held onto Maecha until the boat settled on the water. The wind had carried them across the sea faster than they could imagine.

"Kelan, I would speak to you before the others ask what Manannán told me."

She put space between them and smiled in a coy manner.

"I know most of what he told you, Maecha. The images are racing through your mind so quick and strong, I feel like I was there."

"Yes, I know, but there was one part that I have managed to avoid going over."

Kelan crossed his arms over his broad chest, his bare arms tanned by hours practicing in the sun. "Go on."

"He showed me our daughter."

"Did he now?"

"I think it would be best if I just showed you. Hold your crystal."

Kelan's eyebrows furrowed together. She knew he was impatient. "Please, Kelan."

"Very well." He touched the crystal and stared at Maecha.

"Close your eyes," she said with a nervous smile.

Kelan did and his world forever changed. He held a baby with black curls crowning her head and eyes that changed from sapphire to emerald. Then she was a toddler running through the fields. She jumped over a hill and raced back on a brilliant stallion brandishing a sword like it was an extension of her own body. Next she stood on the cliffs of Eire, her hair reaching her knees, hands raised to the sky, as she moved her world to a safer realm. Kelan felt love, fear, and pride as an unbreakable bond formed.

Maecha released her crystal and Kelan drew in a deep breath. He tried to keep the image of her in his mind, but it drifted away like a boat on the waves.

Maecha's face changed when she saw the joy in his. "Oh, Kelan! Wasn't it wonderful? I had the chance to hold her and I felt so proud seeing what she would become. It's amazing to have a glimpse of something or someone before it's even happened."

Kelan's face became serious. "What's wrong?" she asked placing her hands on his forearms. He wrapped her into his arms and lifted her up, level to his face.

"You must be very careful in battle, Maecha. You could be carrying the child as we speak. You could be protecting more than yourself."

Maecha wrapped her long legs around his trim waist. She took his strong jaw into her hands and kissed him hard on the lips. "It is nice that you worry for me, my love, and I will be extra careful."

"Come now, cannot ye save that for the evening?" Goll called behind them.

Kelan spun around and placed Maecha back on her feet.

With mischief in her eyes, she said, "I am sorry if our affections make you uncomfortable, Goll."

Goll flicked his hand at them. "I just need to find my land legs and a willing woman and it won't bother me at all," he replied.

The Isle of Imbas Skye was clearly in sight, and Osgar, Goll, Caoilte, and Treasa waited for an explanation as to why they had passed Alba.

"According to mac Lir—what? That's what he told me to call him," she said after everyone gave her shocked looks.

66

"Anyway, we, or rather I, have another enemy to contend with. His name is Akir, the Fire Lord, and he was the son of the sea god and the sky goddess, Aiménd. For two hundred years, he has lived in the Otherworld plotting his revenge against those who trapped him there. We must be on our guard, because he wants Imbas Skye. He believes that he is unstoppable with it and will destroy all who get in his way."

"And why are we here and not in Alba?" Goll asked.

"Mac Lir wished for us to come to Scathach's realm to train with her so we will be ready to fight the Fire Lord."

At Osgar's grumble, Maecha said, "I'm sure we will not be here for long. We must try to make it to Alba before the winter passes."

"One second on that blasted isle will be too much," Osgar said and stomped away in disgust.

"What's wrong with Osgar?" Maecha asked Goll.

"I believe he knows Scathach."

"Osgar has met Scathach?" Maecha exclaimed. "But that is wonderful! I cannot wait to hear his stories."

"Somehow I do not think these shall be stories he wants to share. I will go speak with him."

They continued to talk about meeting Scathach and were full of anticipation by the time Goll returned with Osgar. The man still had a scowl on his face, but Maecha was not going to interfere.

Maecha looked south toward Alba and then toward the Isle of Imbas Skye that loomed off the northern most part of this rugged land.

When they were alone, Kelan asked, "Why did you not tell the others of our daughter?"

"I wanted it just for us, and who knows how far in the future that was? She was a young woman. We have years before this prophecy comes to fruition and it's better if fewer people know."

"I think that is exactly why the others need to know, so you can be protected."

"That is why I have you. Besides, we don't know if I have a babe in my womb."

Kelan kissed her neck. "Then we must be careful."

Maecha laughed.

"That will be hard. Manannán knows my father, me, and my destiny. He feels strongly that this trip to Scathach is essential to not only saving my father, but to forging a final bond between you and me."

Kelan took one hand, kissed her palm and whispered, "In the name of the goddess, I will let you use my body as you deem necessary."

They sailed quietly throughout the night keeping the shores of Alba on their right. As Aiménd sent the glorious sun out to greet them, Maecha rose to view her surroundings. The sea was calm, and the air smelled salty, but fresh. Some of the tension left Maecha's body.

Osgar met her as soon as he saw she was awake. "Take a look at this," he said leading her starboard. A shimmering fog hid the isle while on the port side the sky was as clear as the eye could see. They steered the boat to sail toward the fog. As the others joined them at the fore, the fog separated like a curtain. A band of tall female Amazons stood like a wall along the shore— each an exact replica of the other—round shield in their left hand, tall spear planted in the ground and held by their right. Their long hair flowed down their backs in braids. Their skin tones ranged from snowy pale to black as the deep sea.

As their boat touched the sandy shore, Maecha called out, "I am Maecha Ruadh mac Art, daughter of Deirdre of the Sun and King Cormac mac Art of Eire. I am holder of Imbas Skye and I seek the knowledge of the Goddess Scathach."

The warriors parted like the fog and a majestic woman

stepped forth flanked by two well-built warriors. Scathach towered over them. Her golden leather tunic was tied tight to the waist and ended mid-thigh. Her bronzed arms and legs rivaled Kelan's, but still held the curves of a very feminine woman. A long broadsword hung from her back; its pommel and hilt alone looked as though they weighed more than five swords. Maecha's awestruck gaze settled on a face tanned from daily training in the sun and surrounded with long hair braided with gold beads.

Scathach, Goddess of the Isle of Imbas Skye, stepped to the edge and raised her hand in greeting. Her voice carried over the sea. "Welcome, Maecha, daughter of Deirdre. Come forth in peace."

Maecha bowed and stepped off the boat, followed by her champion and the other leaders. They circled around a rocky path that led to the cliffs lining the shores of Skye. Behind Scathach, Maecha caught a glimpse of the palace that loomed beyond the gates.

Maecha felt like a child—nervous with anticipation to meet such a powerful warrior goddess, and filled with fear of saying or doing the wrong thing. But she needn't have worried. Scathach clasped forearms with Maecha and touched the streak of white that flowed through Maecha's red hair.

"You have been touched by the all-powerful goddess. May her blessings always be upon you as you fulfill your destiny." She pulled Maecha into a hug. "Now introduce me to your friends."

"This is my champion and soul mate, Kelan mac Nessa, as well as a brethren of the Fianna."

Scathach smiled at the handsome man and, as they clasped forearms of equal sizes, she noted the eyes of the goddess on his arms.

"You are more than a champion, Kelan, for you are the key to Maecha's destiny and together the two of you will bring peace to all."

Kelan bowed. "Thank you, Goddess. I would be honored

to train with you."

"You will have that chance," she said and turned to the beautiful woman standing next to Maecha.

"May I present Treasa mac Morna, Queen of Roscommon in the County of Connaught," Maecha said.

Treasa was a tall and graceful woman, and she held her ground even as she had to bend her head back to stare into Scathach's eyes. Then she bowed and said, "It is with great humility that I present myself to you."

Scathach laughed as Treasa straightened. She had a twinkle in her eye as well.

"I doubt you have ever been humble in your life, Treasa mac Morna."

"I do try."

Scathach laughed again. "I will enjoy your company. Welcome."

Next Caoilte, unable to hide his nervousness, stepped forward with Goll. He barely came to Scathach's shoulders and when he raised his pale blue eyes to hers, there was strength trying to break through.

"Scathach, this is Caoilte mac Ronan and Goll mac Morna. Caoilte is a master of knife throwing."

"Well, Caoilte, we will test you on that later. You are welcome in my home." Caoilte bowed and stepped back.

Scathach turned toward Goll mac Morna. "And what are your intentions, Goll mac Morna?"

Goll bowed and was slightly rankled by the fact that his loyalty would forever be tested. Goll mac Morna had become Goll of the One Eye during the battle where he had killed Fionn mac Cumhail's father. At that time, their families had been feuding over who would be the leader of the Fianna. Fionn's father had died honorably in the battle, but since then Goll's reputation and intentions had always been questioned. Even after Goll had vowed his loyalty to Fionn and proved it many times, people were still suspicious of him. He was prepared to prove it again. "I am pledged in loyalty to Maecha Ruadh and look to her as the leader of the Fianna. She is the acting queen of Tara and I will give my life for her."

Scathach saw the conviction as he peered at her with his one eye.

"I see and I believe you. You have paid your debt and your loyalty to Maecha and King Cormac will be well rewarded."

"My only reward will be to have the king safely returned to Eire."

"Then may the Mother Goddess deliver you the strength and courage when it is needed most."

Goll stepped aside and Osgar strolled up to Scathach. He was slightly taller than she and before Maecha could present him to the goddess, Scathach swung her sword toward Osgar's head. It stopped just before touching skin. They glared at one another.

"I tried to come back," Osgar whispered.

"Only when you were old and feeble," Scathach replied.

Osgar sputtered, "I am not old and feeble, woman!"

Scathach's body seemed to grow larger. "Do not address me in that manner," she warned.

Kelan and Maecha gawked at each other, but no one dared to reach for their swords.

"And what would you have me do? Break my oath to King Cormac? I am a man of my word and I said I would come back when I could."

"It's too late," Scathach answered.

"It's never too late for a goddess."

"That may be true, but you failed me and I have been waiting to repay you." She whipped her sword back toward her shoulder.

Osgar did not attempt to move. Everyone stood frozen, unable to go against the goddess' anger.

"Halt!" a young woman's voice, similar to Scathach's,

71

called out.

It was enough to stop Scathach, but she didn't lower her sword.

"I told you to stay inside!" she yelled, her gaze still locked on Osgar.

The woman who stormed toward them was the glowing image of her mother, but her light blue eyes were a dead giveaway as to who her father was. She faced Scathach and said, "Mother. You would have me stay inside so that you could kill my father?"

"Mother? Father?" Osgar said, looking from the girl who had his eyes and back to Scathach.

"It would have been a quick death," Scathach said, resheathing her weapon.

Everyone around them recovered from the shock of Osgar's impending death to gape at the young woman who resembled both of them.

She moved past her mother and bowed to Osgar. "I do apologize for my mother's rash behavior and I do beg your forgiveness." She stood and smiled tentatively at Osgar. "I am Uatach, daughter of Scathach and you. I look forward to getting to know you while you are here with us."

Mixed emotions played over Osgar's face, but he bowed to Uatach.

Osgar's gaze switched to Scathach and anger filled him again. "Why did you not tell me? I had a right to know."

"What good would it have done? You would not stay and her place is here with me. You never would have seen her."

Osgar shook his head in disbelief. "I would have made the effort, which was more than you have ever done!"

"Enough," Scathach said. "We will not discuss this any longer in front of guests. There is much to be done to prepare Maecha and Kelan, and you will be needed. We will speak of this later."

Uatach opened her mouth to speak, but shut it when Scathach rounded on her. "You have overstepped your boundaries quite enough this morning. I would suggest that you quit while you are still able."

She dismissed Osgar with a cold shoulder and addressed Maecha with a sincere smile. "Drink the nectar of the gods and be welcome in my home." She lifted a large horn filled with mead. Maecha bowed and drank from it. She passed it to Kelan, who did the same. Once all were welcomed and blessed, Scathach said, "I will give you the day to settle your warriors. Come evening we will celebrate. Then you can tell me how much Manannán has told you."

Chapter 10 - Eire

In the great hall of Tara, Lon, son of Liomhtha, assembled with his men and the other warriors who were charged with the heavy responsibility of securing the land and Tara until the high king returned. Finnius stood in silence next to the blacksmith, but he paid close attention to the orders that were administered. Messengers were sent again to the surrounding counties to warn them of the dangers and that the gates of Tara were open to all who needed its protection. Since late morning, local families from the villages were arriving with their precious cattle or sheep and what few possessions they were able to carry. Lon's captain of arms, Murtagh O'Dobhailen, had ordered the formation of tents and provisions for the long winter ahead.

"There be a line far as the eye can see, m'lord," Murtagh said, rubbing his sausage fingers through his thick black beard.

Lon looked up at the mountain of a man and said, "News of danger travels fast and we are most likely to get attacked when women and children are being brought to safety."

"We haf men set on the walls watching fer signs of the enemy and I sent men on horseback to protect those who still travel t'ward us," Murtagh said.

"Very well, Murtagh. Let's also send scouts out to watch for any raids or signs of returning Picti. We cannot be sure that they all have completely left this land. Tonight we will have a change of guard every two hours and any caught sleeping will feel the wrath of hot iron. We have a mission and I have a personal debt to pay." Lon sat down at the large oak table. He rubbed his eyes and stared into the blazing fire that had been started to take the chill out of the room. No debt could be larger than repaying someone who saved your life, Lon thought. Yes, he remembered his debt. He had once thought to join the elite Fianna and so had entered the Cave of the Warrior to do so. He was a simple blacksmith, but had trained relentlessly with any willing warrior. He had been quite successful during the initiation challenges. First, he had stood in a hole up to his neck and deflected nine spears thrown from nine different warriors. If one had managed to nick him, he would have lost. Then, he had evaded warriors in the woods without messing his braided hair or being injured. That had been easy enough. Finally, he had crawled under a low stick and jumped over another without touching them and removed a thorn from his foot while he ran at full speed. It had been easy.

Perhaps he had grown too confident when he ventured through the Otherworld. So when a monster approached him and he was presented with a riddle, he wasn't afraid. He had even felt like laughing when he knew he had answered the riddle correctly. But, alas, it wasn't exactly correct or so the monster had said and Lon had been changed into a giant with one eye, four arms, and one leg. Before the monster left, he transformed into a well-dressed man and roared with laughter. He had told Lon that the only way he would ever be able to leave the Otherworld was to attack and kill another who passed this way.

Lon had waited years upon years. He spent his time perfecting his trade, using the precious ironwood found only in the Otherworld to create his weapons. Some weapons were made for basic use, but as he made them, he knew that the two *ton-fas* he created would have special owners.

His chance for escape had come when the warrior, Kelan, showed up on his journey to become a member of the elite Fianna. Lon had viciously attacked him. He had not been prepared for the likes of Maecha, however. Never had a woman been able to accept the challenge of becoming a member of the all-male Fianna band of warriors. She fought him with a determination and strength he had never seen in a woman. When he saw that blazing sword aim for his head, he had been glad it would finally be over. But he didn't die. Lon had become himself again, because of Maecha Ruadh mac Art. Then he had presented them with the *ton-fas* of the Otherworld as gratitude. They had been made for them. But that wasn't enough. Lon wasn't sure if keeping her kingdom safe would even be enough for saving his life. But he would do what the Mother Goddess had chosen him to do. He would not fail the high king or his daughter.

Cairpre stood hidden in the woods and watched the long line of people trying to reach Tara before dark. His band of warriors was spread behind him while others stood guard at their makeshift camp. Cairpre longed to build a warm fire and sit in his hall listening to a bard praise him in song. He shouldn't be out here chilled to the bone and waiting for dusk in order to attack his home!

Cairpre paced back and forth muttering to himself. "I should be the rightful ruler of Tara. My mother was a weak woman and a cowardly ruler. She couldn't even give birth to me properly." He stopped and rubbed his deformed leg that often hurt in the cold weather or if he walked on it for too long.

He paced again. "My father has ruled since my birth. Laws have been established, the crops are abundant, and his people are loyal to him." He pointed his finger to the sky and exclaimed, "And not once did he think to take another wife. Why?" His voice rose. "Because she would try to claim sovereignty and ruin everything. That's why. And why do I not rule? Despite the fact that I have always loved my father and tried to show him my abilities, he has always, always doted on that conniving sister of mine! He ignored me when it was clear that my leg would never be normal." He bowed his head to the ground and shook it side to side. Then he glanced back at his men. They weren't hiding the fact that they doubted his abilities to rule.

He didn't care and trudged along the grass, dragging his lame leg behind him. It had grown stiff with the cold and was hard to bend, which only made him angrier. He continued his ranting monologue. "Then when Kelan, the perfect warrior, came to live with us, I was all but forgotten. My father doted on the two of them like they were a match made by the goddess. And I guess he was right. But they have been blessed by a false and weak god. Their day of doom will come."

"My lord!" Cairpre heard a man call from behind the group. He dismounted and ran to Cairpre.

"What is it?" he said.

"A small group of the king's men are scouring through the forest north of here looking for signs of us," he spoke in a hushed voice.

Cairpre pulled his gloves onto his hands and said, "Well, what are we waiting for? Let's kill them."

They mounted their horses and slowly circled around the outer edge of the area where his scout had seen the armed warriors. Cairpre raised his hand when he saw the four well-armed men. His men lurched forward on their horses. Of course he would watch and make sure that no other scouts were in the general area. He heard surprised voices and the clashing of swords. He trotted closer and was just in time to see the head of one of his men roll to the ground. Two more fell before Cairpre signaled for them to retreat. He galloped away in case the king's men decided to give chase. He was sure that the blond warrior would love to get his hands on the king's son.

One moment Cairpre rode in the wind and the next he was vaulted off his horse and spitting dirt out of his mouth. Wicked laughter grated his ears. Cairpre saw part of the Fire Lord's face creased in laughter. His face wasn't fully formed yet. He was a hideous sight and Cairpre tried very hard not to shudder. That would be a sign of weakness and he didn't want to give his lord any other reason to singe his skin.

"Rise," the Fire Lord said.

Cairpre did, wiping most of the dirt from his clothing where he had fallen in front of the Fire Lord's prison. He attempted an awkward bow. "You requested me, my Lord?"

The Fire Lord's laughter was deep. "Requested you? I saved your life just now. Didn't you realize how close those men were to killing you? Your other men are all gone, by the way, and were no match for the king's men. Have I made a mistake in trusting you, Cairpre?" he asked as he bounced a flame in his hand.

Cairpre paled and shook his head. "No, no, of course not. I did not expect us to lose. We outnumbered their scouting party, but they were more skilled. It will not happen again. I swear."

The Fire Lord was silent. Cairpre could see flashes of blue where his eyes would eventually be and he squirmed, because he was sure they were staring right through to his soul.

"No, you will not fail me again. Unfortunately, I need you right now, but that could change at any moment. Your men do not respect you. Do you know why?" Cairpre shook his head. "You do not fight! You only give orders. You must be willing to do the same as your men. They need a leader they respect and fear. Since you do not possess these qualities, you need my help."

Cairpre held his hands out and whined, "But it is to be *my* kingdom. Not anyone else's. You promised *me* the halls of Tara and great power. If *I* had more of that power then *I* would be able to rule!"

"You will have more power when you take over Tara. As for now, what I give you will help in this endeavor and it will obey you and make sure that your men obey you also. This will cost me some of my own power that is needed to restore my body, so you had better not fail."

"What is it?" Cairpre asked, fear and greed warring

inside him.

The Fire Lord pressed his hands together and breathed into them. Smoke billowed from between his fingers. His hands moved apart and a ball of fire grew. When it was larger than both his hands, he threw it to the ground where it burst into flames. The flames grew higher and Cairpre could see the image of a warrior being molded like the steel of a blade.

When the flames died down, a naked and very large man knelt in the dirt. He opened his eyes and stared up at the Fire Lord, his expression blank. Slowly he flexed his fingers and hands and then stood. His body was layered in muscle. His orange hair hissed from the smoldering fires that still burned within him.

He exuded limitless power and Cairpre wondered how he was supposed to control such a creature. The man bowed to the Fire Lord. Then he turned to Cairpre and knelt at his feet. In a deep voice he said, "I am yours to command."

Sweat beaded on Cairpre's brow, but he already could see the advantages of having such a loyal servant. "What is your name?" Cairpre asked.

"Althar."

The Fire Lord spoke to Cairpre. "You know what you have to do. Get rid of the good so that evil can reign. You will make sure that no one comes back from Alba alive. You have set events in motion that cannot be reversed. The king must die in Alba and all those who are loyal to him. Take your minion with you and bring down Eire. Then and only then, will I give you all the power you crave."

Cairpre was thrust back to his camp on his rump. His horse had arrived without him so his men were surprised to see him appear of out nowhere and accompanied by a strange warrior.

Anger filled Cairpre at being treated in such a way. It festered and bubbled inside of him until he could hardly contain it. "Don't just stand there! Get me some mead!" Cairpre barked.

The Fire Lord watched Cairpre through his screen of fire. He flicked anger, frustration, and jealousy toward the dull-witted boy. Akir hooted as he spoke to Cairpre's image, "Yes, let's feed the fire, my friend. Let's spark those emotions. And when you are absolutely out of control, I will be in complete control of you."

With the flag of Cormac billowing behind him, Cairpre rode into the village that lay on the outskirts of Tara in the county of Laigin. The dirt paths were muddy from recent cold rain and snow showers. The simple village farmers stood in the entrance of their thatched houses. Poorly dressed children held onto their mother's stained skirts and the few men who remained were either elderly or not quite old enough to be wielding a weapon. With makeshift swords and sticks, they stepped forward.

Cairpre spied down the row of houses. He narrowed his eyes to bring them into focus, but a haze still surrounded his vision. He remained on his horse, so the villagers would not be reminded of his limp. It didn't matter that it was a birth defect, his mother's weakness had caused it. When he was granted full power by the Fire Lord, then he would regain his vision and he would walk like a healthy man. He scowled and focused on the mediocre peasants who stared up at him with hopeful eyes. With or without violence, he would have control over these people.

"Villagers!" he began. "I urge you to join me in the fight to unite our lands. As we speak, a foreign force has invaded the hill of Tara and would take charge of us in my father's absence. As the male and rightful heir of Tara, I urge you to gather what arms and worthy men you have and join me to take back our land."

An older man, stooped with age and hard labor, spoke, "This land is ruled by the Mother Goddess. Your sister is the rightful heir and she has set off to Alba to save your father. We are farmers and will stay here to protect our women and children."

Cairpre scowled. "You insolent sod. I am the rightful ruler of Eire. I do not need a woman to allow me to join her on the throne. I'll do it on my own. The days of matriarchal sovereignty are over. You must trust your lives to me and the all powerful Fire Lord. He is a god worth worshipping!" Cairpre watched as some of the villagers dared to turn away from him.

The farmer spoke again. "You and your warriors should be fighting to bring the king home. From what I hear, the great lady herself placed special warriors in Tara to protect us."

Anger rushed through Cairpre's body. "The Fire Lord has more power than your earth mother and he has given me his blessing to rule our land! Listen to me carefully. All who resist me will fall! Either come now or suffer my wrath!"

The old man bowed his head and turned away from Cairpre. Althar raised his sword and removed the man's head. The others screamed in horror and fear as the fragile body crumpled to the ground. Reality of the enemy set in as the villagers attempted to run.

"Kill all who will not yield and burn down their homes."

Cairpre's men hooted and laughed as they finally had supremacy over someone. The fact that they were old or defenseless didn't bother them. They ravaged the land and its owners.

Althar stood in his saddle and, with a sick grin on his face, slung fireballs from his hands. Flames erupted from their homes and burned to the ground.

When his father's people, many that he had known, were dead, Cairpre could only stare at Althar. Blood spattered the creature's face as well as his sword. He wiped his sword on his trousers and Cairpre breathed in relief when he sheathed it. This creature was one step away from complete chaos and Cairpre only hoped he wouldn't turn on him.

His men walked among the dead looking for whatever

pitiful reward could be found among these poor, worthless farmers. For the first time in weeks they appeared satisfied, and satisfied men were controllable men. Cairpre felt hope, and his ambition to rule Tara helped him overlook the numerous flaws in the creature that the Fire Lord had sent to him.

The scouts returned to Tara with the same tale over and over again. In the counties of Laigin and Mide villages were burned and men, women, and children executed where they stood. There were only so many warriors who could venture out to take down Cairpre's men and still leave enough to protect Tara.

Lon sat at the large wooden table in the main hall and looked at the men who had come with him out of loyalty. He was in a worse situation than when he served his sentence as a hideous monster in the Otherworld. At least innocent people hadn't been dying then.

"Could there still be Picts in this land? I cannot believe that Maecha's brother has the ability or leadership to command all these warriors," Lon said.

Murtagh replied, "Maecha was sure of her brother's betrayal and warn'd us o' this. I say t'is he who be plundering this land. But the destruction is occurring over different areas at the same time."

"They are supported by the Fire Lord."

Finnius ambled into the hall. His face was pale and he looked unwell. The men bowed and Finnius bade them to rise.

"Who is this Fire Lord?" Lon asked.

Finnius settled himself in a large chair. He placed his chin on his hands and shut his eyes. When he opened them, he began his story.

"I dream traveled with Maecha last night. She has met with the sea god and he spoke of him."

"How fares Maecha and the others?" Lon asked.

Finnius held up his hand. "She is well. They are at the Isle of Imbas Skye."

"With Scathach?" Lon asked.

"Yes. There is more here than we first imagined. The Fire Lord is the offspring of the Tuatha Dé Danaan gods Manannán and Aiménd. He is a trickster god and was banned to the depths of the Otherworld for ruthless treatment of humans and gods alike. His powers are returning, and it is only a matter of time before he ventures forth on earth again. Until he does, he controls the minds of men to do his bidding. I believe that he has done this with Cairpre. He has used Cairpre's own desire for power to convince him to join the Fire Lord's ranks. Cairpre has only minor powers from this god, so he still can be defeated. But the Fire Lord has provided Cairpre with a warrior who is ruthless and powerful. This creature has no conscience and does exactly what his master tells him. Of course Cairpre thinks that he controls this minion, but the Fire Lord appears to know all that is happening and has enough power to control events from his hidden lair."

"What does this Fire Lord want of Tara?" Lon asked.

"It is not Tara he wants, but Maecha."

Lon held his clenched fists at his side. "Why?"

"She is the holder of Imbas Skye and the Fire Lord believes that with this sword he will rule the sky, earth, and sea. His need for revenge is so great, he will take anything that will give him the advantage."

Lon stood and paced in front of Finnius. While he paced he flipped a well-balanced knife in his hand. "So this god has tricked Cairpre into thinking that he will rule Tara and have limitless power if he does whatever he is told?"

Finnius stretched out in the chair and watched the tension coil in Lon's neck. "It would seem so, but do not underestimate Cairpre or dismiss his actions. He has been bitter and vengeful since he was old enough to realize that his body was flawed and he would never rule Tara. He does not accept the law of the Mother Goddess and would seek the downfall of her way of life even without the Fire Lord's influence."

Knowing what Lon was already thinking, Murtagh spoke, "Ye cannot expect to speak rationally w' these men, m'lord. They have killed in a ruthless and unforgivin' manner and must be dealt with like the dogs they are."

Lon's eyes flashed with flame. He launched the blade he had been holding and everyone watched it sink into the wooden column by Murtagh's head. Murtagh didn't flinch. "I do not expect to speak with them at all, Murtagh. I have had enough of this bullying and browbeating of innocent people who have faith in their leaders. I will do what must be done to ensure that Tara is still standing for the king."

"What would you suggest?" Finnius asked, satisfied with Lon's reaction.

"We will fight, but first we must get the villagers within the walls by nightfall. I will not have the king come back to hear that his people were completely destroyed."

"That be well and true," Murtagh said, "But all these people must be placed somewhere and fed."

"I will not turn away anyone who wishes protection, Murtagh. I will do as I believe Maecha or the king would do. We will sleep on the dirt floor if necessary. Double the guard and gather whatever carts we have to move the villagers inside. We only have until nightfall. The fires are getting closer and whether it is Cairpre or this Fire Lord, we will settle this."

By the time the winter sun lowered her weary eyes, every last living villager in the surrounding areas of Tara was safe within the walls. Chaos loomed wherever people struggled to find a place to lay their beaten bodies. Children who had lost their parents cried in fear. The injured were tended to while others attempted to serve food.

Lon stepped up on a platform in the open arena where the

majority of the people were housed. Glowing fire light flickered off his silver chain mail. His blond hair hung loose around his shoulders, but his face was as hard as a seasoned warrior. People were scattered all around to get a better view of the man who would keep them safe.

Finnius stood next to Lon in a regal purple robe. His white hair stood stark against the night. He lifted his hands and bellowed, "Silence!"

All went silent. "People of Tara! Hear what I say! Our king has been taken! His daughter sails across the sea to bring him back to us! It is time for you to show your allegiance and protect your own. Maecha has appointed Lon, son of Liomhtha, to protect you. I vow that he will give all that he has for you, but you must do what he asks."

Lon nodded to Finnius and his eyes blazed with anger and determination as he took in the bedraggled condition of the people of Tara. He knew his fiery eyes would cause fear, but he also hoped they would force them to listen.

"I am a blacksmith by trade, a warrior by choice. I come to you in Maecha Ruadh mac Art's name. She, as well as the Mother Goddess, appointed me and my men to help your warriors defend your land and maintain ownership of Tara until King Cormac's return."

"A fine thing for you to be hiding behind these walls, but my husband died defending us out there!" a woman yelled as she crumbled in tears next to her children.

Lon held up his hands again and waited for silence.

"I ventured into the Land of the Otherworld to become a warrior of the Fianna. I was taken captive, cursed by an evil presence, and stayed a hideous creature until the king's daughter set me free. By Maecha's hand I have become a member of the Fianna. As a warrior who owes his life and allegiance to your sovereign, I will sacrifice my life for your protection. My heart grieves for your losses, and I promise you that whoever has done this will pay. Know that you are safe within these walls."

A burly man with long hair and beard stepped forward. "My Lord. I have seen the enemy and it breaks by heart and tests my loyalty to see one of our own destroy with such abandonment."

Lon's eyes blazed even though he already knew who was behind the attacks. It was necessary for one of their own to name their enemy. "Who did you see attack your people?"

The man straightened his shoulders and said, "It is Cairpre mac Art, son of the high king."

The crowds of people spoke at once and Lon heard the desperation in their voices.

Lon raised his hands for silence.

The man continued. "But he does not act as we would. He holds power. There is a giant with him who makes fire with his hands!"

"I thank you for your allegiance. Cairpre is not worthy of his name and he will pay, as will all those who follow in his stead. Now, be at peace with one another. Any who would raise a sword in defense of your way of life and your homes, come with me."

He jumped down from the platform and was followed by every able man.

Chapter 11 - Eire

Finnius Amergin held a powerful position. He was a trusted advisor, maintained the oral history of his people, and held the magic of the land. For others who wanted that magic and power, they would need to conquer the druid. For when a druid died, his power was taken into the person who killed him.

With troubled thoughts, Finnius and Leann walked away from the clamor of people and headed toward the sacred realm of oaks. They continued until the trees grew closer and the ground was a soft bed of leaves, not yet touched by winter frost. Within the recesses of this enchanted place, they stepped into the sacred oaks where magic always lived.

As Leann placed a stone bowl on the ground and burned sage, acorn, and juniper, Finnius sang the sacred song that would protect them within the realms of their dreams.

"Reigning, reigning over me,
I am protected by this tree.
Reigning, reigning over me,
I take comfort within thee."

He would dream travel to learn about this evil that tormented him and share what he found with Maecha. Oh, he knew about the Fire Lord and the immediate danger that the god presented to all of them. But he was a minor distraction compared to what was coming. Finnius also wanted to find out more about Niachra with the flaming curls and distant eyes. With their pathways blessed, Finnius sat and lay his back against the sturdy oak. It added strength and kept him centered for his journey.

"May the Goddess go with you," Leann spoke as she beat the rhythm of dreams on her drum.

Finnius allowed the methodical sounds to soothe and calm him. Beginning with his mind, he relaxed his body. By the time his toes were one with the earth, he was soaring. As his animal spirit, the hawk, Finnius flew above the trees and soared over the cliffs and emerald green land of his home. He let the wind tilt his wings as he floated along the currents, allowing his mind to soar up and around him. He sailed past the adventures of other dreamers, letting them absorb their visions in peace.

His sharp eyes caught the slash of blue and black before his mind touched that of a foreign presence and goodness of the girl. He angled down and screeched as he flew past the battle. He noted the long black robe that covered the face and hands of this presence and he felt heat when he flew too close. The girl struggled to control the powerful energy that surged toward her. Finnius felt her power, and he knew that much of it was untapped. She did not hold the knowledge to bring forth any more. Screeching again, he dove toward the mage's hood and sunk his talons in the cloth and pulled back. The mage's concentration was broken and a blue flash of light singed his robe against his shoulder.

Finnius faltered when he saw that it was a man. Not just any man, Finnius had to remind himself, but someone who would threaten their ways with his own powerful magic. Finnius noted the symbol of a cross that the man bore around his neck. Its meaning was unknown to him, but the consequences of its victory would be daunting and a threat to their order. Not giving himself time to think, Finnius flew to save his daughter.

A sense of righteousness surged through the mage's eyes as red flames shot from them and knocked the girl back. She fell and hit her head against the ground. The light that surrounded her dimmed.

This time Finnius was distracted by a feeling of love and concern. He only managed to move a little as the flames shot through the sky and singed his wing. He faltered and tried to stay afloat with the use of one wing. As he fell toward the ground a large eagle swept up under him and flew away from the relentless rays.

"Finnius! Finnius! Wake up!" Leann said as she awoke from entering Finnius' dreamworld. She shook him as hard as she could. She had barely made it in time to catch him. Their circle had been strong, but somehow the man in the robe had broken it. Leann only hoped that his daughter was not hurt. She had courage and an untapped power that Leann had not known since Finnius. A stab of jealousy ripped through her heart and she tried very hard to staunch the flow of pain. What he and Eithne had was in the past and, although she probably would never be able to replace that woman, it was her desire, her need, to share Finnius' love.

Finnius still lay unconscious. Leann knelt down at the top of his head. She placed her hands on either side of Finnius' temple and breathed. Her hands pulsed with the energy of the land and the heat traveled into Finnius' mind. She felt an evil presence around his mind loosen. His eyes opened.

"Finnius." Her eyes clouded with tears. "Can you speak?"

"They are coming," he whispered. "The unthinkable has happened. More will come and she must be strong enough; we must be strong enough to fight them."

Leann could hear the fear and love in Finnius' voice. "She has your power," Leann said.

Finnius peered at the woman who had cared for him for many years and had shared so much with him, but never his bed.

"And because of that power she will be thrust into a time, a battle that no one should ever have to face."

89

"She is blessed with this power and if called upon is honor bound to use it for the safety of all. That is the druid's code."

"I know, but it is different when it is your own in danger and she knows not what she fights for," he said.

"We will do what is needed to make sure she is ready and able to protect herself."

With Leann's help, Finnius struggled to his feet and leaned his forehead against the wise oak. He felt the power of the earth seep into him. The oak strengthened his fortitude. Stroking the tree in thanks, he said, "Come. We shall do what we can to keep our land safe, but she comes from afar. We must teach her our ways."

Leann stood where she was, her chestnut brown hair disheveled by her flight and her worry over Finnius. Her deep brown eyes once again filled with tears and this time she did not bother to hide them.

"You almost died," she said.

Finnius stared at his *bendrui* and healer. He moved his left shoulder and only felt a slight twinge of pain. "I thank you for what you have done for me and I am sorry that I have once again caused you pain. I seem to do that quite often."

The younger woman wiped her eyes, not angry at their betrayal. "You do not cause me pain. I bring it upon myself. I could not have watched you fall."

Finnius cupped her elegant face in his hands. Her tears glistened in his palms. "I have given my heart to another who has long since been taken from me. But alas, my heart has not been returned. You have brought me so much joy in my life, but I do not know that I can give you the love that you search for."

Leann tried to push his hands away, but he would not allow her. "Look at me," he said. "I will give you what I can, but you must not expect more."

When she said nothing, he kissed her.

Leann let her shoulders fall and she leaned into him. She clasped his wrists and held on as her world flew upside down. There was power in that kiss and she would take what he would give, if only for a short time.

He released her and took her hand. "Let us go. We must see what Lon needs and prepare for the coming of the prophecy. I will pass what I know to Maecha."

Chapter 12 - Catskills

Natalie crawled into the bed with Michaela and Vince. Her body hurt with the exertion of her dreams and she was pretty sure she had a burn on her shoulder.

Michaela stirred and wrapped her arm around the small girl's waist. "What is it, sweetie?" she asked.

"Bad dreams," Natalie whispered.

"I got you," Michaela said and pulled the blanket tighter around them.

Michaela's hand felt cool on Natalie's shoulder and soon the throbbing pain was barely there. She fell asleep.

"She is a child, Finnius. How can you expect her to be pulled from her world and take on such responsibility?" Maecha asks as they sit under a large willow tree whose gnarled branches reach down toward them like a loving grandmother.

"First, she is a young woman according to our time and her experiences and visions are that of a much older woman. She is drawn to us and it may be that she can only survive in our world," Finnius says.

Michaela steps into their line of vision. "What do you mean? Must Natalie leave our time?"

"Ah 'Mikala,' you look well," Finnius says as he holds out his arms. Michaela hugs the old man and then her soul sister. "Sit and I shall explain. Tonight, Niachra fought an enemy whose skills and powers are unlike any I have ever seen."

"I know, right now she is in my bed," Michaela says.

"Is she well?"

"She suffered a burn, but by my holding her she was soothed and able to sleep. I won't stay long so that I can help her stay in a dreamless sleep. She needs it. I also saw what she dreamt."

"Good, so you know what we face. We all have work to do. 'Mikala,' you must keep Niachra healthy and train her physically. Maecha, continue your quest to bring your father home and join us in the dreamworld for Niachra's training. It can only be beneficial as you get to know her."

Maecha stands and bows. "I will do what I must and right now I am destined to train with Scathach. We will be on our way as soon as possible. Good night, 'Mikala.'" Maecha fades away.

"Goodnight, Sister," Michaela says. "Natalie is very concerned about a necklace that she feels is hers. We saw a picture in a book of a woman who resembles her very much."

Finnius rubs his beard. "Yes, the necklace. I will make sure she gets it. Keep her with you at all times. Expect anything and protect her with your life. All of ours may depend on it."

It was ten o'clock in the morning before a sleepy-eyed Natalie walked out of Michaela's bedroom and into the kitchen.

"Hey there, pumpkin," Vince said, pulling her up onto his lap. Vince liked that Natalie was small enough to cuddle with and didn't seem to mind the attention.

Michaela opened the rear sliding door and the cold air drifted into the warm house. "Good morning," Michaela said to everyone as she kissed Vince on the lips and rubbed Natalie's head. "How are you feeling, Natalie?"

"Tired," Natalie moaned, not wanting to open her eyes.

"You had a rough night, but we have a lot to get done today and we are going to start with some fun exercising," Michaela said. She ignored Vince's raised eyebrows and the boys' snickers. After a brief hesitation, she added, "That means the two of you. While we are up here, we're going to continue your

93

martial arts and start Natalie's training."

Natalie popped her head up off Vince's shoulder. "I'm going to learn how to fight?"

"You are going to learn how to avoid bad situations and to defend yourself when you are left with no other options," Vince explained.

Natalie pumped her arm. "Yeah, I'm going to learn how to fight. You two had better watch out!"

"Oh, yeah?" Travis said. "Let's get her now before she becomes as good as Bruce Lee!"

Bentley hopped off the bar stool where he had been leaning over the island and took off after Natalie. She squealed in delight and Travis followed threatening to tickle her until she wet her pants.

"Wow, I didn't think it would have such an uplifting effect," Michaela said, sitting next to Vince and steeping her green tea.

"She likes anything that will force their attention on her," Vince said. "Plus, I think it's a great idea. It's too bad this place doesn't have a big room for a dojo. I was thinking that since we are going to renovate the place, we will be spending more time here."

Michaela nodded and sipped her tea. She added more honey. "I agree. This will be a nice place to visit on weekends and for vacation. We can teach the kids how to ski and there are so many trails to hike in the summer."

Vince took a slug of his black coffee and said, "I was thinking that it could be more of a permanent place to stay, like maybe all-year round and we could travel to the city once a month for testing. Robin and Carl have been helping with the dojo and perhaps they would like to take it on full-time." Vince raised his hand before Michaela could discount all his reasoning. He shifted toward her and grabbed her hands. "We could open a dojo. There isn't one in the area. It could be in town or we could add a separate building here behind the house. Then the kids could get a taste of the outdoors. We could have a summer camp for city kids who have gotten into trouble or need rehab, and they can come to our school as a retreat. They'll connect with nature and learn martial arts."

"Vince," Michaela began, but he was on a roll.

All the turmoil, mixed emotions, guilt, and love he felt for Michaela had built up to this moment. He felt like if he didn't get everything out on the table now, he never would. They had been together for so long, they took one another for granted. He wouldn't do that again.

"I was also thinking how much I enjoy renovating the house and I'd like to try my hand at building the dojo and maybe starting a business on the side. Of course I would help you with the school, but it would be something I could grow, something to call my own, and Travis and Bentley could be my apprentices. They both have already said that they'd like to get their GED's and maybe try architecture or construction. It could work."

Michaela couldn't help but smile. Vince started to speak again and this time she held up her hand and took hold of his. "Please, let me say something." She took a deep breath and watched the sun peek its eyes through the trees to kiss their clasped hands. *That's as good a sign as I could ask for*, Michaela thought to herself. "We have been together for what seems like forever. When I was stuck in Maecha's dreamworld, I didn't know if I would ever see you again. Then I did when you allowed yourself to be open to possibilities. It kept me alive and I love you for that. Now you are sharing your vision with me. I have to say that I was already thinking about how we could open a karate school here. I love this place, the woods, the silence, and the serenity. But what I love even more is how you took a dream and transformed it into something that we can grow with and will make a difference. It keeps my father's legacy of helping children alive. And I love you even more for that."

95

Vince kissed her and attempted to stand.

She pulled him down. "Hang on, I'm not finished. I watched you talk about designing the dojo and opening a construction business and you looked alive like I haven't seen you in a long time. So I'm all for it and I'm excited about the possibilities. We just need to be careful with Natalie. She's special and I'm not sure where her destiny is going to take us. So keep that mind open, Okay?"

This time Vince pulled her into his arms and kissed her. It all felt so right and for once Michaela just enjoyed the moment.

Chapter 13 - Isle of Imbas Skye

The guests followed Scathach and Uatach in a grand procession toward towering wooden walls that were six men high. Guards with bows and arrows patrolled along the tops and others were seen walking around the outer walls. The Isle of Imbas Skye had been hidden from mortals for centuries and only expected visitors were allowed to pass beyond the veil of fog. It had never been necessary to guard the walls in such a fashion.

Scathach smiled at Maecha's surprise and thought of her mother, Deirdre, who had been Scathach's greatest warrior. "Yes, much has changed since your mother left. Even though the traitorous Conan Maol was killed by your mother for breaking into our sanctuary and trying to steal our treasures, his death tainted our isle. Others, made confident by Conan's attempt, have ventured forth believing they can enter our world. I do fear that the veil of protection we have depended on for so many years has thinned. Now we must stand guard and train our warriors to be faster and stronger than our enemies."

Maecha took a deep breath as the large doorway opened and they stepped into the fortress of Skye. It was more than she had ever dreamed of. Her curiosity got the better of her and she ventured forth into the large arena. The ground was hardened dirt. The chill of winter did not touch them beyond the enchanted walls and for that she was grateful. In different corners of the arena women were wrestling, sword fighting, practicing archery, and martial arts. The walls along the outer edge were covered with every size and shape of shield beyond Maecha's imagination. They ranged from iron to wood, some with combinations of both. Next to those were spears and long sticks with curved blades on the end of them. Swords of all varieties, as well as daggers and knives, covered another wall. Flails, maces, and axes adorned the other side and Maecha circled taking it all in.

"Come, you are keeping a goddess waiting," Kelan whispered in her ear.

"My mother trained here, Kelan. Her spirit is even stronger in this place. I know if I drew Imbas Skye she would be right here with me."

Kelan squeezed her shoulder.

"I am overwhelmed," she said with tears glistening in her eyes.

Kelan said, "I know. It has been a long and rough start to our journey and you are tired. But first we must ensure the comfort of your warriors and pay our respects."

Maecha went to answer him, but her eyes glazed over and the image of Finnius encompassed her vision. Scenes passed through her mind faster than she could grasp of people from Tara being beaten and killed by her brother. A giant of a man wielded power ten times stronger than her brother's.

The images dissipated and Maecha found herself leaning against Kelan.

"Where did you go?" he asked concerned for her.

Maecha blinked her eyes to bring him back into focus. "It was Finnius. I was barraged by images of our people." Fear filled her. "They are being destroyed by my brother and I cannot help them."

"It is in Lon's hand, Maecha. You can only do so much. Finnius is showing you what is happening, but you cannot let it hinder what you need to do here."

By the evening, everyone was ready to enjoy Scathach's hospitality. Maecha had fallen into a deep sleep and woke up revived. She wore a sleeveless brown tunic with a short brown and orange skirt. Her hair flowed in long tendrils down her back. Kelan's ebony hair was pulled back in his customary braid that accentuated his forehead and showed off his brilliant green eyes. He wore a sleeveless tunic and the light material molded to his skin. The air in the Isle of Imbas Skye was forever warm, so many of the Amazons dressed in as little as possible. It was in stark contrast to the chill wind that howled outside Scathach's domain. Maecha thought that the small patches of clothing worn by the Amazons were as much for the weather as for the celebration of their very fit bodies. Their group assembled around a bonfire that lit up the night. The heat was expansive, so they had made a very large circle around it.

Treasa entered on the arms of Goll and Caoilte. Caoilte's face was bright red, so Maecha could only imagine how Treasa had teased him. The exquisite queen wore a deep green dress that shimmered in the firelight. Her wavy black hair was loose and framed her sculptured face.

On the other side of the fire, Osgar leaned against a tree, his face still set in a scowl. When Maecha tried to get him to join her, he only grunted about not being wanted. The sounds of a drum echoed across the air. The beat grew faster and more drums accompanied it. The Amazonian warriors chanted with the rhythm. Just when the beat seemed faster than Maecha's own heart, the chanting stopped. A woman jumped into the circle and began to spin and flip to the breakneck beat. She was such a blur that it took the guests a few minutes to realize that she was swinging and spinning swords in each hand. Sparks flew into the sky as she clashed the swords, and everyone held their breath when the warrior threw the swords into the air and caught them on a roll. With a final swipe, she stopped, breathing like she had just been on a pleasant stroll. The crowd applauded. Next, two other women somersaulted into the circle and swung long sticks at one another. They were scantily clad in loincloths and leather brassieres with gems sparkling at the tips. Their bodies were well toned and they moved faster than anyone Maecha had ever seen. Their sticks connected inches from their bodies and they danced together in the art of war. When they finished, many of Maecha's men were on their feet cheering. It would be a long night for many of them, she was sure.

Finally, the drums beat for the arrival of Scathach. Scathach wore a blue headdress that was so tall it seemed to disappear into the night sky. Her tanned and toned body moved with a grace and fluidity that Maecha could only admire. The drum beat in a slow intoxicating rhythm and then the melodious sound of a lute combined to pull the goddess completely under its spell. Scathach's top and skirt only covered the essentials and gold bangles moved in unison with her body. Her arms and feet joined with the music in this primeval mating dance that spoke of her power and domination of her own body. As she spun around the fire to dance in front of her guests, Scathach seared Osgar with a look of desire that made the man's eyes flame with undeniable lust. Scathach laughed and began to move quicker as the beat increased. Someone threw two fire sticks to Scathach, which she caught and kept spinning at a dizzying speed. As fast as the music had sped up, it slowed and Scathach ended her dance as she tossed her fire sticks into the flames.

Two women removed her headdress. With her guests applauding their approval, Scathach kissed Maecha and everyone else on both cheeks. Then she walked over to Osgar and kissed him on his lips. The man was so lost in lust he didn't object or remember that she had wanted to remove his head. She took his hand and led him over to the others, demanding that their night be spent in peace.

Five women carried trays with goblets of nectar and mead. Maecha, Kelan, and their group were all handed a drink. Scathach raised hers.

"We thank the sea god, Manannán mac Lir, for sending

you forth to us and to the Mother Goddess for her wisdom and guidance. May she protect you on your journey as you fulfill your destiny."

Everyone drank, and the fruit of the gods warmed their hearts and spirits. The music began again and both Amazons and guests joined in the festivities.

Scathach sat down with the others to eat and talk.

"You remind me of your mother, Maecha," Scathach said.

Maecha smiled. "I am glad of that. I only wish that I remembered her more. I have only heard some stories of her, but it is not the same as knowing her."

"True, but it is with stories that we keep our history and loved ones alive. What stories do you know?"

"I know of when she trained here with you and fought the invader, Conan Maol. That was when she was bestowed the sword, Imbas Skye."

"Yes. Your mother was a formidable warrior. She had proven herself over and over again that she could rule Tara, and so it was only right that she be the holder of the most powerful sword known to humans."

"And I know that she chose my father to rule with her after she saw him compete in a tournament."

Scathach laughed as did Osgar. "Is that what your father told you?"

"Well, yes. Is that not so?" Maecha asked, feeling a little self-conscious.

"There certainly is more to that story," Scathach said.

"If you'd allow me," Osgar said, gesturing with his hand. "You are a wonderful storyteller."

Osgar stood and bowed. Osgar didn't look any less menacing without his full leather armor. His brown tunic and breeches were simple, but they could not hide the very healthy man that wore them. He may have been the same age as Maecha's father, but he, and her father for that matter, was still a warrior to be reckoned with. Osgar's biceps swelled as he took a swig of mead. His light blue eyes twinkled as he transformed himself from a formidable warrior to an eloquent bard.

"After Deirdre of the Sun finished her training with Scathach, she traveled back home to take her rightful place as Queen of Tara. As is custom, she decided she wanted a man who would keep her warm at night and help her rule the land. Word traveled that the queen was in search of a king. Men arrived in droves, because they had heard not only of how beautiful Deirdre of the Sun was, with her golden hair and dark brown eyes, but also that she was the holder of Imbas Skye. She had proven to be one of the best warriors ever trained on Scathach's Isle. Those words had come from Scathach's own luscious lips and it is well known that she does not give praise easily."

Osgar's gaze fell on the formidable queen and, for a moment, both their minds were swept back to their time together. Scathach broke the enchantment with a swipe of her hand and said, "Continue."

Osgar inclined his head and turned his attention back to his audience, seemingly not only captivated by his story, but also by the drama happening right in front of them. "In order to give the men a chance to prove their worth, Queen Deirdre held a contest to find out which warrior would be her king and lover. There were four challenges that had to be met. The first was to mount the royal chariot without frightening its steed and ride it forth against other chariots and beat them all. Once the warrior had accomplished this, then he would drive that same chariot through two sacred flagstones that, if he were the rightful ruler, would mysteriously open before him. Next, he would don a special mantel that is only kept by the Druid of Tara. That unique mantle would have to fit him perfectly and it would be up to the Chief Druid to announce if it did. Finally, if the man was fortunate enough to pass these first three tests, then he would touch the 'Lia Fail,' the Stone of Destiny. If the stone screamed its approval of the king, then he would be accepted. Over the years some have made it to this point only to be disappointed when they were not accepted. It is ultimately up to the stone to decide, for it is the mark of the Mother Goddess and she chooses all who will rule."

Osgar paused and drank. He saw the eager faces and expectant looks of his audience and he enjoyed prolonging the story to build the anticipation.

"Well, get on with it, man!" Goll said.

Murmurs of consent resounded around him.

Osgar laughed and Scathach smiled up at him. He was reminded of the first time she lay warm and willing in his arms. Perhaps it was the other way around. But that memory was for another day. He addressed his audience. "The day of the challenge arrived and it was a day to remember. It was in the height of the summer solstice when the air was warm and the days lasted forever. Hundreds of challengers entered the contest. There were peddlers selling their wares and entertainers of all types lining the streets, showing off their talents. On the fields surrounding Tara, the chariot event began. More than half of the men failed. The steeds were large wild creatures that were raised by the goddess Epona, and they did not tolerate humans. Eight men won the challenge. They were able to drive the chariot and beat the other charioteers who attacked them. Cormac mac Art, son of Conn of the Hundred Battles, was one of them.

"Cormac's mother was Achtan, daughter of a mighty druid. When Cormac was born, his grandfather placed five protective bonds on him against slaying, drowning, fire, sorcery, and wolves. For twenty years, Cormac was fostered by a group of druids. When it was time for him to leave he was given his father's sword, golden thumb ring and assembly garment. They all fit and thus he was deemed the rightful king. Of what kingdom was yet to be decided.

"On that fateful day, all eight men were presented to

Deirdre and she watched them very carefully. Most were arrogant and very sure of their ability to succeed, plus they were many years older than the queen. When her eyes met Cormac's, it has been said that a flash sparked between them marking true love. That may have been what happened, but it wasn't enough to only have the queen's approval. So the challenge continued. Four men split the sacred flagstones and moved on.

"Then it was time for our Chief Druid, Finnius Amergin, who still lives strong among us, to place the sacred mantle on each man. On the first man it hung loosely and he was released. The second could barely place it on his shoulders. On the last two, one of whom was Cormac, the mantle fit perfectly. The decision now lay between Cormac and a man named Naoise. Naoise was dreadfully in love with the queen and believed that they were destined to be together. He made an agreement with a black druid who would ensure that the Stone of Destiny would scream its approval when Naoise touched it. And when the time came the stone did scream its approval, but Deirdre asked that Cormac also be given the chance. When the stone also screamed for him, there were rumors of black magic, which had indeed occurred."

"What did they do?" Maecha asked.

"They did the only thing they could do. The men would fight to the death. Deirdre was distraught and knew that Naoise had somehow placed a spell on the stone, but she couldn't prove it. Her heart had already been given to your father and she feared for his safety. She would not interfere, for if a man could not defend himself in a single combat fight, then he was not worthy to rule next to the queen.

"They waited until the next morning. Cormac strolled onto the field in his leather armor, his red hair braided on either side of his face as he still wears it today. He searched for the queen and their eyes met and held until everyone knew the love that was between them. He bowed and walked toward Naoise.

Naoise had also seen the exchange between the queen and his enemy. His plan was to destroy this man who stood between him and his ambition. They were an equal match. They fought for two days with only short periods to sustain themselves with food and to release their bodily fluids. When darkness hinted its arrival on the second day, Naoise again used black magic to try and win. He knew that Cormac was the better man, but was too proud to relent. When they clashed their swords for the final bout that night, Naoise blew a magic powder into Cormac's face that rendered him temporarily blind. The crowd yelled for vengeance, but Deirdre let them continue. Cormac fell back and rubbed at his eyes, but that only made it worse. He became silent and knelt in prayer to the Mother Goddess. When he stood, some say that it was the Eyes of the Goddess that led the way. He no longer went toward his opponent, but waited for Naoise to come to him. Each time the man did, Cormac's sword would be there to retaliate. Cormac's blows to Naoise were filled with power and accuracy. Finally, when Naoise was exhausted from his attacks, Cormac moved in and dealt the killing blow. Naoise fell from the wound to his heart. He looked up at Deirdre, pledged his love to her, and died."

Scathach stood, took Osgar's hand, and held his gaze. She said, "Deirdre ran onto the field and wrapped her arms around Cormac's neck and kissed him full on the mouth. The crowds roared with approval, for the queen had found her match and the Mother Goddess blessed their union with her assistance. They lived in love and happiness. You tell a bewitching story and I thank you. I will say good night to you all as we begin training in the early morn." She nodded at Osgar and left with her retinue of warriors following behind her.

After listening to Osgar's story of her parents, Maecha wasn't able to settle down. She and Kelan walked along the camps set up by the Fianna and Treasa's warband.

"What I don't understand is why the Mother Goddess would take my mother from us when she was needed so much. She was too strong to die in childbirth," Maecha mused.

"It is not for us to answer, but I think you would be a different person had your mother lived."

Maecha thought that over. "You are right, but I would have learned her style of fighting, would have had her brave spirit, and probably wouldn't be here."

"Then perhaps we may not have trained together."

"We only trained together because your family died."

Kelan was silent.

"I'm sorry. I didn't mean to bring it up."

Kelan paused and drew her into his arms. "I would have wanted all of you in my life—my family, your mother, and especially you. But I am glad that it is you."

Maecha wrapped her arms around his neck. Kelan lifted her up and carried her back to their hut.

After loving one another, she and Kelan settled down on a firm bed of hay covered with thick blankets. Maecha thought of what Scathach had said about her mother. She felt above her head where she had laid Imbas Skye and looked forward to seeing her mother, if only in spirit. What Kelan had said was true. She was happy they were together, but it amazed her how that loss could still hurt so many years later. There was so much she would have shared with her mother, especially now. She would tell her how she felt about Kelan and her mother would be able to guide her. And what about having a child? If her mother had trouble, then would she? Her mother would provide comfort and help her be strong. Perhaps her brother would have had a mother to love him and none of this would have started.

"Go to sleep, Maecha," Kelan said, pulling her closer.

Maecha closed her eyes and fell asleep wishing for her mother's love.

In the arena at night, Maecha pulls the sleeping Imbas Skye from its sheath. The eye opens and its light flows up the blade until the area around her glows in a blue light. From the tip of the blade flow the spirits of the warriors who have held the blade before Maecha. They are the past while Maecha is the present, but all are the power within the blade that will protect the future. Maecha searches for her mother, but does not see her. She lowers the sword and the light falls on a warrior much like Maecha, but taller. She walks into the circle of light, her blond hair full and flowing, a band of gold encircles her forehead. Maecha gasps and tears pool in her eyes.

"Mother," she says.

"Daughter. I have waited a long time," Deirdre of the Sun says as she raises her sword.

Maecha smiles and wipes the tears from her eyes. They move slowly, each assessing the other. Maecha's fighting stance is low as she faces her mother. Approving, Deirdre taps Maecha's sword to the left and then flicks it effortlessly to the right. Back and forth they spar and as their speed increases, the other spirits of Imbas Skye form a circle around them. Their power soars into Maecha's arm and she moves with the flow and grace of a well-seasoned warrior. But she is still young and rushes forward thinking that she is fast enough. Her mother hits her arm with the side of the sword, winning the sparring match.

"You have become strong and think like a warrior, but you must be faster and use the knowledge that is within you. I will be there for you, but you must be ready, for the time is coming," Deirdre said as the spirits flow back into Imbas Skye.

"The birth of my daughter?"

As Deirdre fades away, she sends Maecha a vision. "That and more. Watch and listen. I love you, Daughter, and will be back to train with you."

Maecha turns and is confronted by a battle-torn village and strangers desecrating the ways of the Goddess. She pulls Imbas Skye once again and screams into battle. As she fights, a loud voice rains down on her.

"Only one can join all together. Alba must remain whole and only then can Eire be saved. Yours will be the one. Yours and Kelan's, but others will try to stop you. Your bond will be tested and sabotaged again and again. Believe what only you both already know to be true."

"Maecha! Wake up!" Kelan yelled as he shook Maecha. Her screaming had finally shaken him out of the nightmare that he watched from afar. He had been fighting to get to Maecha through the midst of the battle and heard the voice booming down on them. Maecha's scream had broken through the vision and now she lay streaked with sweat and tears. Kelan did his best to soothe her as he tried to calm his own pounding heart.

"Where were you? I couldn't reach you," he said.

"I don't know," she sobbed. "I saw my mother. We were sword fighting and she thought I did well, but still needed more training for this prophecy. When I questioned her, she threw me into that battle and spoke those words to me about ours being the one. It frightened me, Kelan. I'm not as strong as they think me to be, but I cannot fail."

He gripped her hard. Because he knew that whatever lay ahead of them would shape their history and the history of lands around them, he spoke carefully. "We were chosen. Our bond makes us stronger and we grow closer each day we are together. We will be tested. We know that, because so many want what we have; but it is you and I who have it and we will not fail. Together we are more powerful and sometimes we may need to lean on one another, but know that I will always be a part of you. You complete me, Maecha. We complete each other."

Maecha leaned into her closest friend, her lover, and knew he was right. Yet she worried that he always had to remind her. At some point, she would have to stand on her own two feet.

Chapter 14 - Eire

The Fire Lord danced in his towering inferno. He was overjoyed as he watched his minion wreck havoc over Eire. So what if Cairpre thought he was in control? Let him believe he had all the power in the world. He would be dead as soon as he wasn't needed anymore. Akir admired his perfectly formed arms and he touched his face. The skin on his cheekbones and forehead was smooth, but his head was still bald. His tawny hair would grow back. Soon he would be able to walk and seduce that luscious young woman who thought she was satisfied with her champion. With a wave of his hand, he found her. He sighed in lust. Maecha wore his favorite leather armor and was working up a nice sweaty sheen on her full breasts. He waved his other hand and could see Kelan staring at his soul mate like she was the only person in the world.

"Oh yes, Kelan," the Fire Lord said. "It will be so easy for me to take her from you. She needs a real man, and I will satisfy her like you were never able to."

Over the next few days, Cairpre managed to destroy every village surrounding Tara. Anyone who hadn't hidden in Tara and went against him was killed. Others decided that fighting for a ruthless leader was better than not having one at all. It was with a good number of armed men that Cairpre approached the *rath* of Tara to suggest a gentle takeover.

Cairpre was pleased to see the number of men set to fight against him. Surely it showed how much they feared him. Cairpre and Althar separated themselves from the others and ventured closer to the *rath*.

"Finnius!" Cairpre called.

Finnius stepped into an opening in the wall and glared down upon his liege's son. "Think what you do, Cairpre!"

"No concern over my welfare, old friend?"

"I am concerned for your life and your well-being. Let us talk together to find a way to end this madness."

"It is too late for that. I grow tired of standing in the background while my sister gets all the attention and glory. Her time is over and a new order has begun."

"And what order may that be?"

"Why, the order of the Fire Lord, of course. I have been blessed by him and will rule here in his name. He will prevail and all who do not honor him will perish. That especially includes you. He seems to have a keen interest in you."

"The Fire Lord's power has diminished in his imprisonment. He is leading you astray. Give up this farce now, Cairpre, and I may be able to save you from death."

"This…is…no…farce!" Cairpre said, his face red and blotchy. "Show them," he said to Althar and rode back to his men.

Althar sneered at Finnius as he launched a fire ball from his hand. The flames shot over Finnius and landed in a batch of hay within the *rath*. It caught quickly and many of the warriors were distracted by putting it out.

"Attack him!" Lon said. Some of the archers released arrows at Althar. They burnt to ash when they hit him. Cairpre stood beyond their reach and laughed at the spectacle before him.

Althar launched fire ball after fire ball at the fortress. At each impact the warriors grasped the stone walls as it shuddered under the assault. Finnius raised his hands and directed a strong wind toward Althar, extinguishing his flames. Althar growled and prepared to throw more, but the wind became stronger. Clouds billowed overhead and came dangerously close to dumping their fill.

"We'll be back, Finnius!" Cairpre roared. "And the next time, Tara will be mine!"

Lon shot an arrow and it pierced Althar's shoulder. Althar yanked it out. He blew on the tip and fire burst forth. He launched it at Lon who ducked out of the way.

Cairpre stared at Lon. "And you! The Fire Lord is waiting for you. It seems as though you are due for a reunion!"

The group rode off into the woods as unnatural thunder rumbled over the winter sky.

"What did he mean? I do not know this Fire Lord," Lon said.

"There is so much here that we do not know and that bothers me," Finnius said. He searched for Leann. When he saw her, he called, "Come, we must find some answers."

Leann followed Finnius to the hill of the sacred stones. They built a fire within the circle. Upon his request, other druids joined him to form a stronger circle. Finnius needed all their power to conjure the spirits of knowledge. They clasped hands and closed the circle in prayer.

"With this circle we are one,
our strength and power may not be undone.
Bless us, dear mother,
and guide us through the fire,
so that we may search for a way to save our Eire."

The fires flickered high within the circle as they chanted around the flames.

"What do you see?" asked Finnius.

The druid to his left said, "I see eyes of fire."

The next said, "He grows within from the powers without."

Another said, "He cannot surface until all is complete."

"One of the three will defeat him," the last druid said.

111

"What do you see, Leann?" Finnius asked.

Leann shuddered.

"Tell me."

Their eyes met. "I see you imprisoned in fire."

Finnius nodded. He did not offer what he had seen. His mind had touched upon the edges of the others' visions, but only one stood out in his thoughts. He had seen the Fire Lord in their realm, spreading destruction, but he had also seen his daughter fighting another evil to protect the child of the prophecy. It was this evil that he must now contend with and Lon would have to deal with the Fire Lord.

He closed the circle and the other druids left. "Are you well, Leann?" Finnius asked. She had been quiet since the other druids had revealed their visions.

"Yes," she lied.

"Come, you will travel with me today."

Hope lit her eyes. "Are you sure? Who will protect us?"

Finnius laughed. "Do you not have faith in my ability to protect our circle? No one can see us from the outside and we will be cautious in the dreamworld. You will watch for any signs of danger while we are there. I must work with the girl to see how strong her magic is. Then you shall teach her what you know of healing herbs."

"I am not that skilled in herbs."

"I know, but I cannot trust any other. You will teach her all that you know and that will have to be enough."

He removed his heavy cloak and laid it on the ground. Finnius circled it three times quietly asking the Mother Goddess to protect them on their journey. Then he took Leann's hand and pulled her down next to him.

She placed her head on his shoulder and molded her body close to his. She felt his warmth and energy.

Finnius closed his eyes and the image of his Eithne popped in his head. Yes, he knew that she was the master of herbal lore, but she was not there to help their child. She had disappeared years ago and only time would tell if she would or could find her way home.

With these thoughts floating in his head, Finnius said, "Sleep and dream, Leann."

He quieted his mind and focused all his energy on the small girl with the big eyes and bright hair. Leann's body relaxed against his and together they drifted off to their entwined dreamworld. Finnius soared through the sky, taking the form of the hawk. As an eagle, Leann followed him along the currents of the wind, searching for his daughter. Finnius' hawk eyes spotted the flash of red hair in the fields. She was on her hands and knees searching for something in the grass. He screeched to Leann and they floated down toward her. The young girl watched them descend. As they landed, their beaks turned to mouths, their wings to arms, and then they were in their human form.

The girl stared at the man with the long white beard and chanced a sidelong glance at the enchanting woman next to him.

Finnius smiled. Yes, she has her mother's eyes, he thought. "Are you looking for this?" He opened his left hand and held it out to her.

Natalie responded with a gasp and said, "Why, yes I was. I knew it would be around here somewhere. I think it belongs to me." Her big blue eyes looked up at him. "Does it?"

"Yes it does. You may take it."

She did and clasped it around her neck. The silver chain held a large silver triskele. Three blue gems adorned the circle in a vertical line.

"It feels warm," Natalie said, holding the talisman.

"It holds the magic of the three Celtic cauldrons. You are the holder of the cauldrons and we are here to teach you how to use them, but to also learn to control the powers that are growing within you. Do you remember your other dreams in this realm?"

Natalie nodded.

"There is an evil force that will soon threaten our way of life in the world we live in. Do you know who I am?"

"Yes, you are Finnius Morgan. You gave my friend, Michaela, the house to live in. There are some wonderful books there. That's how I knew to look for this necklace. I'm Natalie."

Ahhh, Niachra, Finnius thought. The connection to her mother was strong, but Finnius knew that Eithne was not with their child. It would take time and deep meditation to decide how she could come to him.

"That is correct, Niachra, but in my time during the third century AD I am Finnius Amergin, Chief Druid of Tara. I must prepare you to protect the child of a prophecy that will save our people's way of life. You must know what I know, while you build the magic within you. You will learn the ways of healing from my *bendrui*, Leann."

Natalie didn't correct Finnius' pronunciation of her name. It sounded right when he said it. She looked at Leann with respect. Leann smiled.

"But why have I been chosen for all this? It's so much for me to do and I'm not even eleven."

"That is one of the reasons why you have been chosen— for your youth. It will be some years before you are called to fulfill your duty. You need time to prepare and you have been blessed with gifts beyond your imagining. You are not of your time in the twenty-first century, Niachra. You are of our time and some day I will explain that to you. Here you are known as Niachra and you will protect a child who has not even been born yet. But this child will secure our way of life and she must be protected beyond all costs. It will be up to you to do this. Do you understand what I am asking of you?"

"Yes," Natalie said in an older sounding voice.

Finnius nodded. "Then we shall begin. We will meet in the dreamworld and you will learn all that we know." Finnius motioned toward an oak tree. "Let us sit here and I will teach you

114

of the Three Cauldrons."

Natalie followed him and Leann stayed where she was.

"What about Leann?"

"She will keep guard. As you know there are still dangers in your dreamworld. We do not have much time, so let us begin."

Natalie said cross-legged and leaned back against the oak tree. Her bright red curls framed her freckled face and her pale blue eyes took in all that Finnius said.

"There are Three Cauldrons, which are your life force." He lifted her necklace and Natalie peered down her nose at it. "This top gem represents the Cauldron of Wisdom which resides in your mind or the sky. It is the knowledge that is already in you. This cauldron is born upside down in all people, but can be turned through training and deific inspiration. This will magnify your healing ability."

Finnius pointed to the center gem. "This is the Cauldron of Motion which lives in your chest or the sea. It processes and expresses our emotions and people are born with it on its side. In order for a cauldron to be effective, it must be turned upright so it can be filled with knowledge. The cauldron is shifted through understanding, expression, and openmindedness. It requires powerful emotions to stand it upright and determines whether you will have access to the next cauldron. When you are open to others you will be better able to accept their love and love of yourself.

"The final cauldron is that of Incubation, which is located in your abdomen or the earth. When this cauldron is upright it maintains one's health and basic survival skills. If it turns on its side, you will become ill and it can even cause your death. Your energies will be fully accessed when all the cauldrons are in their upright positions. It will feel like a fire flowing from your abdomen through your chest and into your head, like a quickening. When this happens, you will learn to leave your body behind, for it is your spirit that has the ultimate power. It is not seen, but its power can be felt."

When Finnius stopped, Natalie breathed a sigh of relief. Finnius laughed. "I gave you much to take in."

Natalie hugged her knees. Finnius' heart clenched. It was how her mother had often sat when she listened to Finnius recite their people's oral history.

"It is a lot and I don't understand all of it," she agreed.

Finnius stood and motioned for Natalie to follow. They were in an open field of grass. "Try this. Place your left hand facing skyward in front of your abdomen, then place your right hand over it, but don't touch your palms."

Natalie did what he asked.

"Close your eyes. Now move your hands as if you are holding a round ball and you are molding it. You will feel the heat of the cauldron as it turns upright."

Natalie lifted one eyelid. "Keep your eyes closed and concentrate. Call forth the energy."

Natalie took a deep breath. She focused on her hands in front of her stomach and the imaginary ball. "I don't feel anything."

Finnius placed his hands on her shoulders and matched his breathing to hers. "Feel the energy that is all around us, that is in you. Breathe." She began to feel something warm within her hands. As she moved her hands to mold it, a heat spread through her hands and toward her stomach.

"I feel it!" she exclaimed.

"Now channel that heat throughout your body and push the cauldron upright."

Natalie turned her hands to face her body and moved them up and down. The heat spread from her stomach and reached toward her feet and up to her chest. With the warmth came strength and joy. She felt completely happy and at peace for the first time in her life. Tears sprang up and leaked through her lashes. She opened her eyes and saw Finnius smiling proudly at her.

Embarrassed, she lost her concentration and the heat dissipated in all the areas of her body except for her stomach.

Finnius held out his hand and Natalie took it. "It is a wonderful feeling, is it not?"

"You can do this, also? Do you have a necklace like mine?"

"Yes, I can do it, but I no longer need the necklace. My cauldrons have been upright for so long that they naturally stay that way and I can channel my energy from any point in my body. You will learn this in time. Your power is that great. Now we must part ways. I will be back soon. Practice all you know and keep safe."

Natalie watched as Finnius transformed into a hawk and Leann into an eagle and they flew away. As they faded Natalie became aware of something watching her, but she didn't feel the fear that had ravaged her body when the evil man tried to hurt her. Acting calm, Natalie peeked over her shoulder toward the wooded forest. The colors were so brilliant in her dreams. It was like another reality and she longed to explore it. For now she stayed as she was and waited. Movement. She waited a little longer and she could finally see a gold pair of eyes about waist high staring out at her. Placing her hand palm up in front of her, Natalie slowly eased her way closer. More movement. A white wolf edged out of the cover of the trees and stared. Natalie gasped, not from fear, but from the sheer beauty of her. Oh yes, she was more than sure that this was a female wolf—a feeling of warmth and comfort flooded over her. Natalie tried to move closer, but the wolf pricked her ears and peered around.

"It's all right. I won't harm you," Natalie whispered, but it was too late. Whatever had spooked the wolf was coming closer. Natalie heard a voice in her head telling her to leave and she listened, hoping she would get to see the wolf again.

Chapter 15 - Isle of Imbas Skye

Maecha watched the young girl train with Finnius. He was right about her having a great deal of power. Maecha had been brought here, while she floated within her own dreams, to see the child who would protect her babe. The thought threatened to break her concentration, so Maecha had watched and learned some techniques that might unleash her own powers. As the hawk and eagle flew away into the darkening sky, Maecha stirred awake into her world.

Kelan was already dressed. Maecha stretched and sat up. "How long have you been awake?" she asked.

"Not long. I thought about waking you, but you seemed to be in a very deep sleep."

"I was. I dream traveled with Finnius and Leann. They are training Niachra, the girl who will protect the daughter that will be born to us. It's all very odd to think about. I lose track of the present thinking so much about what the future will hold."

"Keeping that future in your mind will motivate you to act smart and train hard."

They broke fast with bread and watered wine and walked to the arena as they had done every morning. Maecha stretched her stiff body. The air was slightly cooler than in the castle, but that was fine since they would be sweating shortly.

Maecha jumped around and twisted her upper body. "Are you ready?" Maecha asked behind him.

"Just waiting for you," he answered.

"You aren't going to warm up your muscles? They could cramp."

"I do not need to warm up my muscles. They are already warm from last night," he said tugging her into his arms.

"Kelan! The guards are watching."

"Good for them," he said kissing her.

Maecha pushed him away. "We have much to go over and I want to train with my mother."

"It's not like she's going anywhere," he said keeping her close.

Maecha gave in and enjoyed his embrace. Then she peered up at him and smiled. "I want to practice a kata—the first one."

Kelan rolled his eyes in feigned exasperation and dropped his arms. "All right, let us practice."

They were positioned next to each other at arms length in a horse stance. In unison they took three deep breaths and Maecha called out each move.

"Block your opponent's arm and punch. Step toward the left and punch. Block an attack to your groin and punch three times. Look to your left, step and block. Look the other way, step and chop. Look again, step and chop to one side of the neck and then the other. Move into a fighting stance. Kick your opponent and poke his eyes. Turn to face behind you, block a blow coming toward your head, and chop across the enemy's body like a sword."

"I'd rather be using my sword," Kelan commented.

"Concentrate, Kelan. Side kick. Come back to a horse stance and breathe."

"Now as long as my opponent attacks me in exactly that manner, I will be able to protect myself," Kelan remarked.

Scrunching her face in determination, Maecha said, "Attack me any way you wish."

"Maecha, it's time to train with your mother."

"Attack me!"

Kelan swung his arm like a club toward her head. Maecha blocked it with her arm and then chopped Kelan in the neck. Grabbing behind his neck, she kneed him in the stomach and threw him to the ground. Turning over to his back, Kelan smiled.

"Those are bits of the kata that if practiced over and over again, become a part of you. It's just like practicing with your sword or *ton-fa* until it becomes an extension of your hand."

She held out her hand and he placed his in hers. He let her pull him up.

"I just prefer to have a weapon in my hand. Used in combination with my sword, it does have some effective defenses. And if it makes you a better fighter, then I am willing to practice."

"Scathach wants us both to become natural with this. We can't leave until that happens."

"I promise to practice this as much as my other training, but you must trust in the fact that I was the one who taught you how to wield a sword properly. I do know how to fight."

Slightly ashamed at her nagging, she said, "You are right, of course. I need to learn so much before I can get to my father. It makes me edgy."

"We'll get there, Maecha, but now you must meet your mother."

They left the arena and Maecha settled in a cross-legged position against a large tree. Kelan planned to keep watch while Maecha visited the dreamworld. He trusted the guards, but he was trained to watch his own back.

As she settled her body and mind, Maecha thought of the image of her mother that she had seen the other night. She let her thoughts and fears flow away like the wind.

Deirdre stands on a cliff. She swings her sword with grace and deadly accuracy. Deirdre peers down at her daughter and

120

motions for her to come closer. Maecha steps forward and is on the cliff, teetering on its edge.

"Careful. What you wish for happens immediately in your dreams."

Maecha watches her mother. She is exquisite in a way that Maecha could never match. Her blond hair is tamed into a braid so that her doe-like eyes and full lips are even more pronounced. The leather tunic and skirt that she wears are similar to the one that had been given to Maecha when she received Imbas Skye. Maecha wishes to have her mother back in her world, but she doesn't put a voice to that wish.

"Let us begin. The sword is an extension of you. She senses the opponent as you do. You have called her before. As your bond grows, she will anticipate and fight with you. The spirits that reign within her will guide you." Deirdre draws her sword. "Raise your sword."

Maecha unsheathes Imbas Skye and holds it in front of her.

Deirdre lifts her arms toward the shimmering sky. Her blade reflects the otherworldly glow.

"Warrior Spirits of Imbas Skye,
Come forth and unite.
Your powers will raise us high,
And help us in this fight."

The silver snakes on the blade of Imbas Skye gleam and slither to its tip. They hiss and reveal their fangs, and from their mouths come forth the spirits of the other female warriors who had once wielded the sword.

Maecha had felt the spirits before as they swirled around her in battle, but she had never seen them solidify as they did now. Five warriors stand at attention in front of Maecha wearing golden armor: breastplates, helmets, guards on their forearms and shins.

"Fight!" her mother yells.

Without hesitation, a woman who makes the Amazons appear petite steps in front of Maecha. Her hair is shorn from her

121

head and her eyes are heavy lidded. Her shoulders are slumped forward, like her body is too heavy to hold upright. She unsheaths her sword and holds it toward Maecha. Maecha touches the warrior's blade with her own. The spirit warrior nods and swings her sword low toward Maecha's left side. Maecha blocks the attack. They exchange blows circling around the dream field.

"Change attackers!" Deirdre calls.

The next spirit warrior matches Maecha in height, but her arms are large like Scathach's. Her hair is black and braided with intricate beads so that she sounds like a bell chime when she moves. She challenges Maecha with a sweeping blow of her battle axe. Maecha blocks upward with her ton-fa, but the impact forces her to the ground. She loops Imbas Skye toward the warrior's legs, so that she must retreat.

"Change!"

The next one releases a long fighting stick and twirls it above her head. The warrior moves with silent speed like a weightless wrath. Maecha doesn't catch the stick until it whips across her cheek. She groans and falls to the ground. The stick comes within inches of her face. Maecha rolls out of the way and slices the stick in half with a swipe of her blade.

"Change!"

The fourth attacker is tiny compared to the others. She has elf-like ears, and glitter sparkles around her as she glides toward Maecha. Maecha doesn't know what to expect, since a weapon is not revealed. With a yell, the warrior flies straight in the air and crashes down on Maecha with an elbow to her shoulder. Maecha's arm crumbles. The warrior jumps again, but this time misses when Maecha flips out of the way. She is tiny, but her impact is like a falling oak tree. Maecha sheaths Imbas Skye and attacks with her ton-fa. Holding the perpendicular handle, she spins the back end toward the warrior and hits her hand. Glitter spills from it like blood. Maecha continues to strike whenever the warrior jumps at her.

"Change attackers and switch your sword arm!"

"I am not as strong on this side," Maecha protests.

"That is the object of this exercise. You must be able to defend yourself and attack using both arms and sides of your body. Now switch arms."

The last spirit warrior encompasses all the physical traits of the others, and her sword is wide and long. She is well-built, but her face rivals the beauty of a goddess. Jewels hang from her ears and neck and her hair is tied back with gold bands. She holds the sword without effort and waits. Maecha recognizes that this is the warrior that Akir had fought. Maecha strikes. The warrior matches the swing and Imbas Skye crashes into Maecha's chest. The spirit warrior waits.

"Focus, Maecha!" Deirdre yells.

The other spirits gather to watch. Maecha takes a deep breath and calls upon the power of the eye. The blue eye opens and senses the spirit warrior. A blue glow flows from it and settles around Maecha, imbuing her with its strength, power, and clarity.

She moves into a fighting stance, sword in left hand and swinging her ton-fa in her still numb right hand. Maecha raises her ton-fa in front of her head and blocks the warrior's downward blow. Maecha strikes toward the warrior's side, but it is blocked.

Maecha flips her ton-fa in toward the warrior's head and it's deflected. Her sword soars over and in. The warrior changes her stance to block it. Faster and faster Maecha swings her sword and ton-fa toward different targets. The last strike goes through the warrior spirit and she disappears.

The blue eye closes and its power leaves her body. Maecha is drained physically and emotionally. The other warriors turn to mist and drift into the sanctuary of the sword.

"You have done well, my daughter," Deirdre says and then spins her head as if she hears something.

"What is it?"

Deirdre holds up her hand.

"Cormac," Deirdre says.

"What of him? Is he hurt?"

Deirdre touches her daughter's face and in the realm of the dreamworld, she can feel her mother's gentle touch. She smells of honeysuckle and spring mornings.

"I will watch over him until you are ready. I must go and make sure he remains well." She smiles and disappears.

Maecha opened her eyes in the same position against the oak tree. She let the breeze play through her hair and the feel of the earth centered her once again. It seemed that she was spending as much time in her dreamworld as she was in her current reality and it often left her fatigued and disoriented.

Kelan knelt down next to her. He touched her face much like her mother had, but it produced desire in Maecha instead of longing. She cupped his hand and kissed his palm.

"Did you see any of it?" she asked.

"I could sense a great deal of fighting, but it was like watching it through a fog. I think that I would have to be asleep to enter the dream completely. I did have the feeling that something was wrong before your mother left you."

"It's my father. I was fighting the warrior spirits of Imbas Skye. I defeated my final opponent. Then mother called my father's name and told me she would look after him until I was able to get to him. Then she disappeared. Something terrible must have happened. Otherwise I do not think my mother would have left. I wish that I knew how long we would be here."

"You are due to train with Scathach now, so perhaps she will enlighten you," Kelan offered.

They walked into the arena to find Scathach.

Scathach posed like a statue in the arena's center. She held her sword to her nose. Faster than a cobra, she struck to her right, lunging deep. Her body flowed up into the air like an eagle spreading its wings. Her sword, an eagle's talons, struck the

124

ground, capturing its prey. Her legs whipped out, snapping the air like a sea serpent's tail.

Entranced by her grace and power, Kelan and Maecha did not dare to interrupt the goddess.

Taking a slow cleansing breath, Scathach pivoted in a controlled motion maneuvering her sword left and right in a circle. She stepped forward in a deep fighting stance maintaining her fluid arm movements. Quicker than a scorpion, Scathach flicked her sword inches from Maecha's face.

Scathach smiled and said, "You were wise not to move, Maecha." Sheathing her sword, Scathach accepted a cloth from Uatach and continued, "Are you here for your lesson?"

"Yes, but," Maecha hesitated.

Scathach raised a brow and asked, "What is it, Maecha?"

"I trained with my mother and the spirits of Imbas Skye today."

"Well, that is a fine sign of your improved skill, but you do not look pleased by it. Why is that?"

"At the end my mother became concerned about my father. She said she would look after him until I arrived. I'm worried that we will not make it in time."

"I see," Scathach said as she wiped the cloth over her face. "And what is the question that you are burning to ask?"

"I need to know when we shall be able to leave here and venture forth to Alba. I fear for my father's life."

"Ahh. So it is the fear of the unknown that plagues your mind. Sit." She motioned for Maecha to join her as she sat on a wooden platform in the far corner of the arena. "You may as well join us, Kelan, since you are so well connected with Maecha. I feel that your bond will only strengthen her abilities."

"My abilities?" Maecha asked.

"What do you remember from your last challenge in the Cave of the Warrior, when you competed for a place amongst the Fianna?" Scathach asked her.

125

Maecha thought. "My strongest memory is fighting Cairpre on the Bridge of Swords, and then I really cannot remember much until I met the Mother Goddess and came out of the cave. I do know that I was badly wounded."

"You were mortally wounded and were allowed to drink from the healing waters of the Well of Knowledge. You would not have lived without it or the blessing of the Mother Goddess. So with that blessing and healing comes the power of knowledge. You have all the knowledge of the worlds within you. You have the knowledge of past queens, past lives, past histories. Along with that knowledge is foresight, which is the ability to see what may come." Scathach paused to let all she said sink in.

Maecha's eyes gleamed. "How do I access this knowledge?"

"That is our lesson today. But remember—knowing the future does not mean you can change it. For some, it becomes an unwanted burden."

"Does this mean that I might know more about my father without being there?"

"Yes, but sometimes knowing makes your journey harder, Maecha."

"And how does Kelan play into this?"

"It takes some energy to access this knowledge and foresight. Kelan can add his energy to yours and, as your bond grows, you can share this knowledge through your minds."

Excitement sparked through Maecha and she was ready to embrace this new source of power.

"Your energy flows through you, from the top of your head through the bottom of your feet. The earth restores it and grounds you. Knowledge does not come lightly, so use this ability for good and only when absolutely needed."

"I understand," Maecha said, although she didn't really quite understand why Scathach would be so serious about such a wonderful gift. However, she did remember Manannán's warning.

Scathach continued. "Place your middle finger against your third eye, which is between your eyes and just above your eyebrows. When you place it there, bring an intention or need into your mind. Knowledge will come quicker for it is already in you. Foresight may take a bit longer as the energy must stretch into the unknown. I must also warn you that as you become more sensitive, your intuition of others will grow when you are near them or touch them."

Maecha closed her eyes and placed her right middle finger against her forehead. She took a deep cleansing breath, and pictured her father alive and strong as he was the last time she saw him.

After a few minutes, Maecha opened her eyes and said, "I didn't see anything."

Kelan took her left hand and clasped it in his. Closing his eyes, he connected his mind with Maecha's. Her father's image popped into his head and they waited. Tendrils of fog swirled around this image until it disappeared. Then just as Maecha was about to open her eyes, she saw him. He stood on the top of a cliff with Picti guards surrounding him. His face wasn't clear, but Maecha felt that he was searching and waiting for his daughter. She felt the sense of urgency and his need for her. Then he was gone.

Maecha's eyes shot open. "He needs me."

"Of course he does," Scathach began and raised her hand when Maecha would talk over her. "But we do not know when in the future that image will be, and you cannot force the present to catch up too quickly to the future. You are not ready, so do not ask to leave."

"But what if I know something will happen to him and I can't do anything to stop it?"

"Then it is the will of the Mother Goddess."

"What is the use of this gift if the goddess will always have her way?"

"Be careful of how you speak of the mother of us all! Your gifts are granted through her to help in your life journey. Do remember that they are gifts, which can be taken away."

Kelan interrupted Maecha as he felt her anger rising. "Scathach is right, Maecha. We cannot rush our time here. Let us do what is needed, for it is clear that these skills will help us."

Maecha turned on him and spat out, "So now you take her side? We are supposed to be in this together!"

"We are, but that does not mean that we shall always agree. Let us go eat," Kelan offered. "It will revitalize you and then we can discuss more of what we saw."

Maecha stood and said, "I do not want to eat or discuss anything. I want to act." With those words Maecha stormed off.

Kelan bowed to Scathach and said, "I apologize for her impetuousness. She is either too unsure of herself or ready to act without thinking things through."

Scathach smiled remembering another student exactly like that. "She will learn, as you will learn not to splay yourself on her sword."

She lay back on the rocky beds and covered her eyes. She felt Kelan searching for her, but she let her mind drift above the clouds to escape her despair. When she heard strange music, she let herself fall into the dream of Michaela Sommers, the warrior from the twenty-first century.

Maecha believed that through druid magic, 'Mikala' had traveled from a time Maecha never could have dreamed of. She was a warrior and had been stuck in Maecha's dreamworld. Maecha soon realized that this warrior was there to teach Maecha fighting skills using her hands and feet and an effective weapon called a *ton-fa*. It was mainly due to 'Mikala' that Maecha was prepared enough to venture into the Cave of the Warrior to complete the three challenges needed to become the leader of the Fianna.

By doing this, Kelan and Maecha's bond was complete and 'Mikala' could no longer stay in Maecha's head. Through a ritual older than the world, 'Mikala' was extracted from Maecha's mind and entered third century Celtic Eire—Maecha's time. The soul sisters' victory and joy at seeing one another in the flesh was cut short by Cairpre's treachery. The ritual was performed in a stone circle, which was a sacred area where violence was strictly forbidden. Cairpre proved his unworthiness and cowardice by attacking Maecha in the circle and fatally wounding 'Mikala' in the process. But once again he had sent another to do his deed. 'Mikala' would have died if not for the healing marrow of the green serpent tooth that Kelan had taken during his challenge in the Otherworld. It would save one worthy and eat one unworthy from the inside out. 'Mikala' had lived, but her eyes had turned golden and her hair had the same white streak that Maecha now had. She was only beginning to realize other changes within herself.

"I think I have drifted off into your dreamworld," Maecha says.

"What ails you that you have come searching for me?" Michaela asks.

"I argued with Scathach today."

Michaela fixes her golden eyes on her ancient friend and asks, "The mighty goddess?"

"Yes, and I feel as though I have lost her respect. My father is in trouble. I need to leave, but she does not feel that I am ready. Besides that, Kelan, who is supposed to be on my side in all we do, went against me. I know I am not the best warrior, but I need to be there to save my father! I do not know what she is waiting for. I am strong. I can use my sword and ton-fa well. I have been training hard with my mother, but still I am not ready."

Michaela sits back in her chair and thinks. "When I was preparing for my black belt, I was in great shape. I ran, hit my heavy bag, and biked. I knew all my self-defenses, and my katas. I thought I knew everything. When I approached my teacher, I told him I was ready. He said I was not. He continued to train me. A year went by. Again, I told him I was ready. Again, he said I was not. Then we began to train for a tournament, which was a requirement to get my black belt. I worked on my sparring, my speed, and timing. I needed to anticipate my opponent, know when and where he would strike, sometimes even before he did. As we sparred over and over and over again, something changed. It wasn't physical anymore. I felt a confidence in myself and in my art. My body had been ready, but my mind and my spirit weren't. I began to see the attacks in my mind before they occurred in reality and my body was able to respond to what I perceived. Sometimes you have to stop thinking and just react. And possibly the hardest part of all is to trust your teacher. Once that happens, what you learn becomes instinctual; it's a part of you. During the weeks leading up to my black belt, I went through challenge after challenge. I was exhausted, but I overcame them. When it was time for my test, I already knew that I had passed."

Tears run down Maecha's face. Michaela grabs her hand.

"Do you understand?"

Maecha nods.

"You will know when you are ready. You will stop feeling this insecurity, this self-doubt. Be patient. This is something you cannot rush. Open your heart and mind, body and soul to your training, and you will find your way. Then Scathach will see that you are ready."

"You are right, but I do not have a year to wait," Maecha says.

"Try and push it and it will take longer. You will know when you are ready. Use Kelan's strength and your connection with him. You are together for a reason. Do not take it for granted. Be strong, my friend."

'Mikala' hugs her soul sister and Maecha drifts away.

Osgar and Goll were practicing in the arena when Maecha arrived after a much needed rest. Caoilte nodded at her and went back to his target shooting. Goll and Osgar continued their sparring match. Goll swung his axe with ease at Osgar, but the older warrior managed to evade the attacks and launch his own each time.

"You overcommit, Goll!" Osgar told him.

"You just know me too well and can anticipate my moves," Goll challenged.

Osgar called to Maecha, "Come here!"

Maecha shook her head. "I would like to train on my own for a bit."

"Like hell! Get over here so I can show this one-eyed lout that he overcommits when he fights."

Knowing he wouldn't back down, Maecha walked over. She unsheathed her sword and stood facing Goll with a scowl on her face.

Goll snarled. "I cannot fight her when she's full of pity for herself."

"I am not full of pity!" Maecha retorted.

"Then wipe the sour look off your face and act like you mean to attack me with some zeal. Otherwise I might hurt you."

Goll flipped his axe in his hand like he hadn't a care in the world. Maecha was infuriated by his attitude. She whipped Imbas Skye around and hit his behind with the flat end of the sword.

Goll pretended to be shocked. "Oh, so that is how it's going to be, eh, little lady? We'll see what your lover thinks of me skinning your bottom."

Maecha lunged toward Goll, her sword coming very close to his eye patch. Goll stepped to the side and swung his axe toward her head. Maecha ducked out of the way and clobbered Goll on his back. With a miffed look he attacked again making a figure eight with his weapon. Maecha stepped back just out of reach and Goll followed with the same movement. Then he switched and brought the axe straight in toward her waist with all his strength. Maecha moved to the outside of his arm and walloped him on the head with her *ton-fa*. He fell on his face.

"Goll, are you all right?" Maecha said kneeling down next to him.

"Of course, I'm all right, but you didn't have to hit me so hard. That's why I fell."

Osgar laughed. "That was part of the reason, my friend. You put so much of your momentum into your swings that all your weight is on that front leg—hence you are off balance. Just a little advice between friends," Osgar finished and tugged on his beard, like the advice really wasn't a source of their arguing just minutes ago.

Goll grumbled. "I've been fighting longer than this girl has been alive."

"And I've been fighting twice as long and I can still learn something. We all can."

Maecha laughed.

"Maecha!" Her laughter stopped.

"Yes, Kelan?"

"Are you speaking with me now?"

Maecha contemplated and then said, "Yes, I do believe I am. I came for our afternoon training. As Osgar just said, we all have something that we can learn and I have learned patience. I am sorry if I was unkind to you earlier."

"You should be saying that to Scathach, but I acknowledge and accept your apology."

They held each other's gazes and their Awen Crystals glowed.

"Tame those things will you?" Goll said blinking his eye.

Kelan slapped him on the back, pushing Goll forward.

"I saw you get your head clobbered, so some light would do you good," Kelan laughed.

Maecha turned her head to hide the laugh that wanted to escape.

"Everyone's a jester," Goll grumbled with a grin on his face.

Chapter 16 - Eire

The Fire Lord fell back against the wall of fire in his prison. He needed to break this bond between Maecha and Kelan, and he thought the little tiff they had over challenging Scathach would give him an edge. He felt a slight weakening in their bond when Maecha had been angry, and he was able to tap into their connection. But then, just as quickly, it was gone. What had happened? Such joy had filled him when he had sensed discord between the two lovers. He thought Maecha brave and very stupid to speak that way to a goddess. She was lucky to walk away. It only proved that Scathach was weak. That was why they needed guards on their tower. Akir would have removed her head for challenging him in such a manner. But that was the chance that he had been waiting for. If their bond could be weakened by anger, then he might have been able to control one of their minds to do his bidding. But now that they made up once again, their bond was that much stronger. Akir thought of the Awen Crystals that glowed around their necks. That was a major source of their power. He snapped his fingers and was pleased that he was able to.

That was it! All he needed to do was get the Lord and Princess' Awen Crystal and he would have the power to control those two lovers. But he could not do that until his body was fully formed. Then a thought formed in his mind, and he was amazed at his own brilliance. What if he killed Kelan and took his Awen Crystal? Then he could have that power and Maecha. Then when he was done with her, he'd just kill her and take her sword. He slapped his knee and guffawed. A diversion would occur at the Isle of Imbas Skye, but the real goal would be Kelan.

Seething with impatience and the desire to be out of the dungeon, the Fire Lord entered Cairpre's mind, radiating pain all around him.

"Why have you not defeated them?" The Fire Lord hissed in Cairpre's dreams.

"I have tried, but their leader is strong. They are all but imprisoned in Tara."

"Any man can be strong until you find his weakness, his fear. I do not want them imprisoned in Tara. I want them out of Tara and you in control of it!"

Fire raged up around Cairpre and he recoiled from its licking flames.

The Fire Lord laughed. "It is good you fear me, Cairpre. You need to take over Tara. Block off the druid and I will take care of Lon. It is time he knew me again."

Flames roared up around Cairpre and chased him out of his nightmare. Sweat covered his body. He felt his arms. There were raised welts on both of them. Burns. He shuddered as he remembered his dream. What did the Fire Lord mean to block off the druid? How could he defeat Finnius?

Chills ran down Cairpre's spine as he thought of Finnius dead. Was it even possible to kill the druid? He was only a man after all, but he was a powerful one and had always been there for Cairpre. Finnius was the one person who knew how Cormac's betrayal had hurt Cairpre. Of course the druid never chose sides; he just sympathized with Cairpre and tried to help him fit in. But the king's son never had. He learned long ago that it was a weakness to show fear. It was much better to let the anger and pain bubble up inside and fester, so that it would all explode at the necessary time.

134

Cairpre remembered when it happened after he had had enough of the taunts and jeering. He had lost all sense of calm and had erupted like a volcano when he attacked a boy much bigger than him. Again, it was Finnius who separated them and Finnius who had attempted to teach him to act with love and not vengeance. Well, where had that gotten him? Right back where he started.

It was his time to rule. He didn't need a woman to *allow* him to rule. He would do it on his own. Of course he had the Fire Lord's support, but he was a god worth worshipping and every mortal needed a god to back him up. The Fire Lord had the power and Cairpre was blessed by him. Cairpre couldn't wait to see his father's face when or if he came home. He knew that the Fire Lord wanted his father dead, but Cairpre wanted him to live long enough to see the power his son had gained. His father would know he was wrong allowing his sister to take over. Then, Cairpre would have Imbas Skye. He hadn't told the Fire Lord of his plan to let Maecha come home so he could get the sword. The god didn't have to know everything. If Maecha was killed over in Alba, then Cairpre would lose his chance. So they would come home, but he would be prepared to kill them both. The decision was made. If the downfall of Finnius was a part of the master plan, then he would do what was needed.

All thoughts of sleep gone, Cairpre erupted from his tent, with dawn barely in sight. His hair was a mass of pandemonium. He half ran and limped in front of every tent, hammering his sword on his shield.

"Get up all of you!" he ranted.

By the time his men scrambled to get their clothes and equipment on, Cairpre's eyes were bulging out of his head with anticipation.

They stood at attention in front of him. "You have all done well and victory is now within our reach. It is time to take what is ours. Once we have invaded the *rath*, we must imprison

135

the druid, Finnius."

"Finnius?" one man questioned. "But he is the king's chief advisor and possesses magic. He will curse us all if we go against him." Others murmured in agreement.

"Silence! Do you question your leader? The Fire Lord has commanded this and once we do it, we shall not be challenged."

"What about the blacksmith?" another man asked.

"The Fire Lord will take care of him," Cairpre said.

"I will take care of Lon," Althar said pushing through the ranks.

Cairpre attempted to lengthen his body to intimidate the Fire Lord's minion, but he only managed to reach his chest. Still he clenched his teeth and said, "The Fire Lord will take care of Lon."

Althar pushed Cairpre out of the way. "Ha! He told you what you would do. He will work through me to take down their leader. Then you can have your precious Tara. I have no use for this life. I will move forward and destroy all of the Fire Lord's enemies."

Cairpre watched in horrid fascination as Althar's smooth skin began to shimmer and his eyes sparked.

Althar jumped astride his horse and said, "Let us begin. I grow tired of this place."

Cairpre scrambled onto his horse and announced, "Mount your horses and let us ride to Tara!"

Looking forward to destruction, the men mounted their horses and followed their leader, although they weren't quite sure which one it was.

Ahead of Cairpre, Althar approached the gates of Tara. "Lon of Liomhtha!" he bellowed, but his voice was not his. It was the voice of the Fire Lord who was using Althar's body to venture forth from his wretched lair.

Layers of snow had fallen the night before and ice formed on the soldiers' cloaks as they tried to stay warm. Lon was stationed on the highest rampart. His tired face, bedraggled with stubble, heated at the voice calling him. Somewhere deep in the recesses of his mind, that voice touched on a memory and it was not a good one. As the voice continued to call for him, sweat fell freely from his body and his palms were too wet to wield his sword. He stood, but Murtagh pulled him down.

"Ye look ill," Murtagh said.

"I must go to him," Lon said. He heard the voice again and couldn't understand why it pulled him so, but an image of the Otherworld came to him. Trying to staunch the fear that had collapsed his heart, he stood.

Murtagh blocked his way. "Are ye mad? 'Tis what they want you to do."

As Lon pushed harder, Murtagh called, "Finnius!"

Finnius took in Lon's ghostly pallor and asked, "What ails you?"

"It's him," Lon said. "It's the one who imprisoned me in the Otherworld. I must go or else he will destroy all of you." Flames flickered in Lon's eyes and they stared unfocused on the two men attempting to restrain him.

Finnius touched Lon's arm, which grew warmer. "He no longer has a hold on you. Maecha severed that bond."

"I know, but he grows stronger and more impatient by the day. If I go, he will spare the villagers."

"That is a lie," Finnius said. "He will spare no one, only those who will swear to follow him. Tell him you will not come."

Lon struggled with his fear, imagining Maecha's face and remembering his promise to her. He grabbed his bow and lit an arrow from a torch. With deadly speed, Lon opened fire on the man whose voice was tearing apart his mind.

"Leave here, demon! I will not serve the likes of you ever again. I have been freed!"

Althar absorbed the flaming arrow into his body, which then erupted into a volcano of fire. Shafts of fire continued to hit the stone walls.

"The walls are crumbling," Murtagh yelled. "Jump!"

Those at the bottom of the walls scrambled out of the way of the falling debris. They hurried into the inner arena where the rest of the villagers sat in fear.

Cairpre arrived in time to see Althar's body erupting in flames. He was too shocked to move, but reacted when he saw the walls falling.

"Attack!" Cairpre called to his men.

Back in his human form, Althar jumped over the crumbled wall and shot all who fought him. Cairpre and the rest of the men followed in pursuit.

"What have I done?" Lon cried.

"You did what Maecha would have done. Now fight!" Finnius said.

"Goddess of War, protect us!" Lon yelled and charged at Althar. His sword erupted into a flame. Althar grabbed the blade and bent it in half. Then he grabbed Lon's neck and lifted him off the ground. Both bodies were engulfed in flames. Murtagh fought to get to Lon, but the heat was too intense.

"Fight!" Murtagh yelled to his friend.

Althar and Lon were no longer visible through the firestorm. Then as the Fire Lord's laughter tormented his victim, Althar and Lon disappeared.

"Nay, it cannot be," Murtagh said and ran to where Lon had been moments ago. Three men surrounded him with their swords raised.

Murtagh prepared to fight until his death, but Finnius yelled, "Stop!"

Murtagh listened and saw that Finnius was also surrounded by Cairpre's men. Cairpre angled his horse toward Finnius.

"Finally, you make a wise decision, Druid."

"You dare to betray your family," Finnius began.

138

Cairpre slapped his face.

"Silence! Yes, I dare betray you, my father, and your cursed goddess. She is no more! The Fire Lord shall rule the Otherworld and I shall rule Tara as the rightful heir should."

Finnius spit out the blood pooling in his mouth. "Your character is as marred as your physical features, Cairpre. No one will follow you. The crops will fail, the water will run dry, death and disease will torment your rule, and the people will despise you. That is the will of the goddess."

Fear flickered for an instant on his face, but then Cairpre laughed with a cynical and bitter sound. "That goddess has no place here."

"Your father will come back and you will rue the day you ever thought to defy him."

"If we are lucky, my father and that damned sister of mine are dead already. There are others who follow my lord and have seen to it," Cairpre said, knowing this to be untrue, but he needed to feel a sense of superiority over the druid.

Finnius stared at him in disbelief.

"I've had enough of you, old man. Bring him to the underground prison. The Fire Lord has a special treat for him."

Two of Cairpre's men grabbed Finnius and dragged him to an underground dungeon. The air was damp and smelled of dirt and waste. One of the guards grabbed a torch that led them deeper into the cold underground.

"Throw him in there," Cairpre said pointing to a small area that was carved out of the stone.

They tossed Finnius in and he hit the back wall. The ceiling was so low he had to sit on the stone floor and the walls closed in on him like a shell.

"Think about what you do, Cairpre," Finnius said, his face stoic.

Cairpre ignored him and called forth a flame that flickered on his palm. He spoke an incantation that made

Finnius' skin chill. Bars of flame rose from the ground and sealed Finnius in.

Finnius closed his eyes and prayed to the Mother Goddess to protect the villagers, who were now under Cairpre's tainted rule.

Leann watched them from the shadows, her face ashen with fear for Finnius. She could do nothing for Finnius right now, but she would find a way. She crept out of the dungeon through a secret tunnel only known to the druids and prepared for battle.

Cairpre stood on the crumbled stone rallying the disenchanted villagers to follow his leadership.

Cairpre raised his sword. "People of Tara! I am Cairpre mac Art, heir to the throne of Tara! Your High King, Cormac mac Art, is dead! He has been killed while in captivity in Alba! As the rightful heir, I now decree myself as High King of Tara!"

Voices of dissent could be heard rumbling along the crowd like thunder.

Cairpre swiped his sword through the air and silence ensued. "Let it be known that all who defy me will be punished most severely. Your precious, and now useless, druid is secured in a dungeon for his defiance. Since we do not have a large number of prisons to hold dissenters, anyone else who chooses to test me will be killed, as well as his or her family. This is a new day, a new kingdom, and I promise those who follow me all the riches and power you could ever desire. Now return to your homes and enjoy the prosperity of a new age."

No one moved. Cairpre's guards prodded them like cattle and yelled at them to move. Finally, some did and rummaged to get their few possessions and return to their bedraggled and, in most cases, destroyed homes.

"Bring him closer," the Fire Lord insisted. He wanted to grab the prisoner, but could not step out of his flaming cage. The Fire

Lord felt like a baby bird stuck in its mother's nest. Not quite ready to fly, it needed more worms to get stronger. Akir needed more spirits.

Althar carried the unconscious Lon closer to the Fire Lord. He dumped his limp body onto the dirt.

"And the druid?"

"Captured."

"They both must be bound. For only then will the protection over Tara be broken."

"What will happen?" Althar asked.

The Fire Lord's eyes glinted fire at Althar. "I will come forth."

He stared long and hard at Lon. Finally, Lon awakened.

"Welcome back," the Fire Lord said.

Lon shoved his body back from the heat and the fearful being that lurked in front of him. He ran into Althar who picked up him with one hand.

"Acknowledge the Fire Lord," Althar hissed.

Lon just stared.

"You don't remember me?" the Fire Lord asked.

Lon kept silent.

The Fire Lord blasted Lon with a searing flame. He fell to the ground. "You thought you were rid of me when the king's daughter saved you, but you never were. You are bound to me and will do my bidding."

Lon shut his eyes and pictured all the men and women who had depended on him; all the children whose lives may have been lost because of his inability to defend them. He would not forsake their memory. He opened his eyes. "No, I will not."

Raging heat flew at him and Lon was thrown against the far stone wall. The Fire Lord used his power and lifted him higher until he hung mid-air. Flaming shackles latched him onto the wall. The Fire Lord shot flames at the ground in front of Lon and reddish orange bars grew from the dirt and connected to the stone ceiling above them. They encircled Lon so that he was engulfed in a glaring red hot prison.

The Fire Lord laughed. "No one defies me." He turned to Althar. "Invade Tir-nan-og and bring me Tannackta who is the keeper of the passageway to their sacred land. Once I have his spirit, I will be strong enough to steal the Awen Crystal. Then I will have the power to take my revenge. I will have it all."

"What about the rest of them?" Althar asked.

"I do not care. They will all die eventually for betraying me. Kill the Faery Folk if you wish. I will fill the Otherworld with my own creations."

Althar bowed and left to do the Fire Lord's will.

Chapter 17 - Isle of Imbas Skye

Maecha and her warriors trained on the Isle of Imbas Skye throughout the long cold winter. Her and Kelan's martial arts' skills had become fluid and in tune with one another. Their hands and feet were weapons that few could beat. Maecha's sword fighting rivaled her mother's and she was soon defending herself admirably against multiple attackers. The hardest obstacle had been training her mind to accept the powers that she had gained from the Well of Knowledge. Scathach had taught her to read people's auras, which resonated around their bodies. There were good and bad auras, but most people had a combination of both. So Maecha learned to trust her instincts, and then only had to touch a person to learn about their recent acts or feelings about someone. It often left her weak with headaches. Scathach said that her body would eventually adjust, but once again time was needed and there was so little of it.

Outside Scathach's domain, the wind was brutal and the snow drifted to one's waist. But inside Scathach's world, the weather was perfect for training. Every day Maecha would venture out in her heaviest leather and fur to brave the cold weather looking for a sign that winter was ending. She knew that travel before Beltane was impossible and accepted the fact that she needed to put her heart and soul into her training or else she would never be ready.

One morning when the snow was melting, Maecha stepped out of her training haven and was surprised to see Osgar staring out at the water.

"What brings you out in the cold, Osgar?" Maecha asked moving closer to him for warmth.

He put his arm around her and gave her a fatherly hug.

"I was thinking that we would be leaving soon."

"Will you miss your daughter?" Maecha asked.

"Aye, that I will. I would not have been able to see her much, so I'm sure she was right in keeping us apart. But I long for her childhood that I missed."

"Can you come back and see her again?"

"That will be up to Scathach."

"Love is confusing, is it not?" Maecha asked leaning her head on his shoulder.

"It is, but in my position the good of the many must always take priority. You are lucky to have Kelan as your soul mate and your champion, but don't let the two become entwined. Then you may love or fight for the wrong reasons."

"Do you love her?"

"If you mean Uatach, then yes I can say that I have a father's love for his daughter. If you mean the other, then I must say that I do. But it is not meant to be, so I do not dwell on it. She believes that I wanted to leave her. Maybe I did for a time, but she should understand my allegiance to your father. I would have come back to her. I have never loved another, only her. I daresay she never forgave me for not coming back. How was I to know it was a cursed test? Damn the woman for not being straightforward. If you love someone and you want them to stay, just tell them! Don't chase them out of your life and then blame them for doing exactly what you told them to do in the first place!"

"Well, I think she loves you and would want you to stay."

"Perhaps in time she will welcome me back. Let us go in. It is not that warm yet."

Uatach greeted them just inside the gate. She still smiled shyly at her father, but her affection had clearly grown. Maecha couldn't wait to hug her father again. There was so much she wanted to tell him, especially that she loved him. Training with her mother had made her feel like she had her parents back again.

"My mother requests your presence in the arena."

Maecha noted Uatach's excited gleam in her eyes when she said it, so that piqued her interest.

"Let us go and see what Scathach has in mind today," Maecha said.

Goll, Caoilte, and Treasa were dressed in hard leather tunics with guards on their arms and shins. They each held a sword and Treasa held the shield that Lon had made for her.

"Ah, so you have decided to honor us with your presence," Scathach said as she swung her own sword in the air.

"What is the urgency?" Osgar asked.

Kelan slipped in behind them and stood next to Maecha.

Scathach grinned. "Today, we will work with energy flow."

As excited as Maecha was to learn another form of what was called her 'abilities,' she felt overwhelmed by all that she had learned. Her skills were many and she feared there wouldn't be time to master any of them. She wondered how this use of energy would drain her body.

"It's like intense physical training. Eventually your body catches up. You are merely training your mind," Kelan mindspoke to her.

"Easy for you to say. You aren't the exhausted one," Maecha replied.

"Remember who holds you up when you falter," Kelan said and joined the circle that Scathach had made.

Scathach addressed them. "You both gathered energy when you entered the Cave of the Warrior and were blessed by the Lord and Princess of the Otherworld. Plus, the bond that you share through your Awen Crystals helps you access that energy. It can almost bounce from one to the other, which can be a powerful weapon against this Fire Lord.

"The reason the rest of you are here is to act as their targets and learn how to defend against these attacks. However, they'll come in whatever form the goddess gifted you with."

"That's just great," Goll grumbled.

Osgar joined the others and waited for the attack.

"As I taught you to access knowledge through the third eye, you access this energy through your center." Scathach held her hands in front of their chests. She continued to speak as she slowly moved her hands in a circle. "Moving your hands will generate the energy and then that energy will transfer itself to your palms. That is where your attacks will come from. Do you feel heat?"

They both nodded. "Good. Now take your hand and continue the circular motion as I did."

Maecha and Kelan each did as Scathach said, "As the heat builds, you will feel the need to move your hands away from your body. When you feel this, cup your hands close to one another, but don't connect them. Imagine you are forming a ball of energy."

Maecha realized she was doing the same thing that Finnius had shown Niachra in the dreamworld. She felt the power within her hands building to the point that she needed to release it.

Sensing that, Scathach said, "Now face your palm toward your opponent and focus the energy at them."

Not waiting another moment, Maecha raised her hand and a cold blast of wind and ice erupted from her palm. With lightning fast reflexes, Treasa lifted her shield and the ice ball shattered to the ground.

"Well, how do you bloody expect us to guard against that without a shield?" Goll asked.

"Let me show you," Osgar offered.

He faced Maecha and held his sword up in front of him.

Ice pellets shot from Maecha's hand in quick succession, but Osgar easily deflected them with his sword.

"That was impressive," the usually quiet Caoilte said. "May I try?"

"Be my guest, boy," Osgar said.

Taking out his longer knives, Caoilte stood ready with each casually at his side.

"Put up your guard, Caoilte," Maecha said. "This will hurt."

"Trust me, my lady," Caoilte said.

Shrugging, Maecha lifted her palms and was amazed at how easily the energy flew out of her. She was equally amazed at the speed and competency of Caoilte as he wielded the knives against her weapon.

Satisfied, Scathach moved her attention to Kelan who didn't look happy.

"Release your energy, Kelan," Scathach said.

Kelan stared at his palms and then shrugged at Scathach. "There's nothing there."

"There's nothing between your ears is the problem. Your soul mate just pummeled us with ice chips! Show us what you got," Goll taunted.

Ignoring Goll's remarks, Kelan spoke to Scathach, "The energy feels weak."

"Weak. Knock him on his arse, Maecha. That'll help him feel his energy," Goll said.

"Leave the lad alone, Goll, before we have you spar with Maecha again and she takes out your other eye with an ice chip," Osgar said.

Goll sneered at Osgar. "I'm only fooling with him."

"Be that as it may, he needs to focus."

Goll muttered something about everything losing their sense of humor unless it's toward him and sat down.

Unease and a hint of fear ran through Maecha's mind as

she connected with Kelan's. She could see the sweat building at his brow. Not needing to touch him, Maecha reached a little further and saw the source of Kelan's doubt.

"Your energy is water?" Maecha mindspoke to him.

"I do believe it is," Kelan answered.

"Perhaps your greatest fear will be your strongest weapon," Maecha offered.

"Stop with the mind talk," Scathach said. "What ails you, Kelan?"

Kelan faced the goddess and said, "I cannot use this weapon."

"Why not?"

"It's water."

"Water could be a powerful weapon. Let's see what you can do."

Upon hearing that his energy weapon was water, his friends fell silent. They knew his fear and how hard it was for him to even enter lakes to bathe. Usually Kelan stayed in the shallowest part when he absolutely had to go in.

"Let's see it," Scathach repeated.

"It's not strong enough," Kelan said through clenched teeth. He was willing to be the brunt of his friends' jokes, but he didn't like Scathach's intense attention on him.

"Sca . . . ," Maecha started.

"Stay out of it," Scathach said.

Scathach squared her body in front of Kelan and, staring him down, said, "This is the only weapon left between you and the Fire Lord, who is going to rip Maecha's heart out. Are you going to quit?"

"This won't be my only weapon," Kelan replied.

"It is right now," she warned and shoved him back.

Kelan stepped back and stood still again.

Yelling, Scathach ran at him and hit him back further. Again and again she knocked him until he was against the wall.

Maecha closed her eyes and held her Awen Crystal in her palms. She added her energy to Kelan's like he had done for her in earlier lessons.

Kelan could barely see Scathach. Visions of his mother floating in the water assaulted his mind, his heart, and his soul. He could almost feel the water rising up over him and he choked, sure that he was drowning. Gasping he realized too late that Scathach had grabbed a rather large stick and was going to pummel him with it, if he didn't make some kind of effort. Raising his hands he channeled as much of his energy toward her and a stream of water flowed from his palms.

Scathach stopped within an inch of his skull and Kelan let out a big sigh. Then the world erupted around him and Kelan was thrown into another wall by a fierce gust of wind. Shaking off the knock to his head, Kelan and the others stared around them, weapons ready and minds wary.

Kelan started to ask what the hell was going on when he was lifted off the ground in another whoosh of wind, twirled in the air, and thrown across the arena.

"Kelan!" Maecha yelled. She ran to him and held up Imbas Skye wondering when and where the next attack was going to occur.

"It's the Fire Lord," Scathach called. "He appears to have an interest in your champion."

"How do we stop him?" Goll yelled. The wind was so loud it was close to impossible to hear anyone.

Akir laughed as he swayed his arms right and left, up and down like a winter's snowy dance. He blew at Kelan forcing the wind to become stronger, taking the man's breath away. Kelan was whipped up into the air once again and as Akir had him in his hold, he battered his mind with thoughts of deep, black, murky water. "Nothing can save you, Kelan," he spoke to the warrior's mind. "You are drowning and will soon join your mother. Feel the air leaving your body, your chest contracting as it fights for breath that is no longer there. You feel lightheaded, your vision is dimming; soon you will be gone."

Maecha placed her hands on him as he dropped to the ground. "He's drowning," she said out loud and then mindspoke to him. *"Kelan, you are not in water. You are not drowning. Open your eyes and see me. Now!"*

Maecha hit Kelan on the chest for that was the only thing she knew to do at that point. She grabbed his face in her hands and could feel the pain that he was going through. She gasped but held on, mindspeaking to him, calling him back to her.

Through his foggy brain, Kelan felt a light seeping toward him, and he tried with all his might to swim toward him. Evil beings clawed at him, but he kicked them away, knowing that the light would save him. Then he heard Maecha calling to him. Kelan gulped in air and held Maecha's gaze like it was a rope pulling him from torrid waters.

He reached up and held the hands that were cupping his face. Maecha whispered, "You are here with us, not in water."

Kelan nodded as Goll and Caoilte helped him to sit up.

Scathach knelt in front of Kelan. "Are you well now?"

Nodding again, Kelan placed his head in his hands. "I almost let him defeat me."

Scathach squeezed Kelan's shoulder and said, "But he didn't and the fact that you had this power bothers him. I'm proud of you for trying. If you hadn't tried, then you would have let yourself down. The biggest obstacle one can overcome is the fear that is so strong, it stops your heart. Even the most seasoned warrior breaks out in a sweat after he has been severely injured in a battle and has to fight again." The great goddess looked around the arena. "The Fire Lord is near. He entered your mind and used your fear, your doubts against you. He is gaining in power and has yet another weapon against all of you."

"Aye, but he got through to me. I have shown weakness," Kelan replied.

"Oh, bullocks. We all have weaknesses and fears. We wouldn't be human if we didn't," Osgar said. "It's what we do despite them. Now you know how this enemy fights and we build a shield against him. We don't let him in."

Osgar felt Scathach's gaze on him. When he returned the gaze, he caught a glimpse of the goddess who had once found love in her heart for him. It vanished as soon as she realized he saw her watching him. Osgar shook his head and heaved a big sigh of regret, not knowing how he could prove himself or his love once again.

Chapter 18 - Eire

"Finnius?" Leann snuck up along the wall of his prison, careful not to alert the guards. She had tried to release him, but even their combined magic could not break through the fiery bars. No one had bothered to feed the druid, so Leann brought dried meat and bread small enough to fit through the bars and not get scorched.

Finnius crawled like a caged animal. "I must finish training Niachra," he said.

Not questioning his need, Leann said, "Then that is what we shall do. Make your own circle and I will make mine. I will meet you in the dreamworld by the oak tree. She must be waiting for you and we cannot let her down. Her quest is too important."

"But if someone comes while we are in the midst of this, they could kill you."

Leann smiled for it had taken this long for him to show stronger feelings toward her. Oh, how she wished there had been more, but a stolen kiss and a soft embrace had given her hope and joy. And now it might be too late to see where their love could have taken them.

"I am not afraid," she said. "Let us begin. She needs us."

"So be it," Finnius said.

They formed their circles and settled on the cold ground to let the silence bring them together. They soared in the land of dreams, crisscrossing one another's paths. Time and place stopped, if only for a moment, and they both treasured their flight together. Finnius found his daughter sitting under the oak tree. He swerved his wings downward and transformed back to human form. Leann followed and did the same. They glanced at each other for they could sense the building power emanating from Niachra's body. Her eyes were closed and her hands were palm up on each knee. A blue ball hovered over each hand.

They stepped closer and Natalie opened her eyes, a serene look on her face.

"Hello, are you both all right?" she asked.

Finnius knelt down and held out his hand. Natalie placed a sphere in it and he felt her power even more. "Why do you ask?"

Her eyes clouded with tears. "I felt your struggle, but I couldn't do anything." The spheres disappeared.

"We are well, Niachra. And even if something happens to us, you must continue to strengthen and hone your skills. You cannot let your emotions overrule your ability to use your magic."

Natalie wiped the tears streaming down her face. "I know. It's just hard now that I have people who care about me. It was easier when no one loved me."

Finnius squeezed her shoulder. "It may be easier, but it's not better. When you love another, then you have something worth fighting for. Remember, you are fighting for those you love and those you have yet to love." She nodded and he released her.

He pulled her to her feet. "We may not have a great deal of time, so I must teach you the other two cauldrons as quickly as possible."

"All right," she said.

A movement to their left caused both Finnius and Leann to raise their hands to attack. They relaxed when they saw Maecha walk toward them. She wore a simple pair of breeches and a matching brown tunic. The tattooed snake slithered along her bicep forever chasing its tail.

Maecha smiled at Natalie and knelt down in front of her.

"Greetings, Niachra. I wanted to have the chance to join you in your training," Maecha said.

Finnius knew better than to think that training with his daughter was the only reason why she was here.

Maecha glided over to the druid and touched his cheek. "How do you fare, Finnius?"

Finnius clasped her hand and said, "I fare well." He lowered his voice. "Do not fear for me, Maecha. I will do what is needed here and you shall see me in your dreams, if not in your world."

Tears pooled at Maecha's eyes. She knew what he said was true, but it was hard to know something bad was happening and not be able to do anything to prevent it. "May I join you for your training?"

Finnius nodded. "Of course. Niachra is still learning to access her powers, so perhaps you can assist with your own while Leann protects our circle."

Maecha positioned herself by the oak tree and raised her hands to the dreamy sky and then brought her palms together to assist Natalie.

Finnius brought Natalie's attention back to him as she stood in awe of Maecha. "Since your emotions are running so high this morning, it is the perfect opportunity to learn the Cauldron of Motion that resides in your chest. This cauldron plays with your emotions, so you must learn to control them in the midst of an attack. I want you to hold your hands toward one another with your fingertips pointing to the sky."

Natalie planted her feet firmly on the ground and let its energy travel through her, as she positioned her hands.

"Now breathe in and lift your hands upward, bring them out and back to the beginning position, and then exhale."

Each time Natalie breathed in she felt the energy in her chest rise and when she breathed out, she felt it come together between her hands. She also felt Maecha's energy surround her and it gave her confidence. Each time she did this, the power was greater, but she also felt an overwhelming sense of emotion that wanted to spill over. She knew that the emotion was the cauldron and as long as she kept control of the energy, her cauldron would remain upright. When she finished breathing, her hands were farther apart, because the power between them had grown.

She opened her eyes at Finnius' request.

"Now concentrate, Niachra, and do not lose control of your energy."

Without warning, he zapped her with his own energy. Shocked, Natalie could feel her emotions reaching the brim. She took a deep breath and when Finnius tried it again, her right hand whipped out and redirected the attack. He sent two attacks simultaneously and Natalie felt pain in her leg. Her energy wavered.

"Breathe. Put your emotions aside. Remember what you are fighting for," Maecha said close behind her.

Natalie remembered the girl in her vision she had last night. Straight black hair, alabaster skin, and enchanting eyes. Beauty and strength combined with the power of her heritage. She needed someone to protect her, so she could grow into the amazing woman the prophecy said she would be. She would save them all. That was worth fighting for.

Finnius could sense the change. He slowly launched one, then two balls of energy at Natalie, and she absorbed them into her own or deflected them back at him. They came at her faster and faster until it was hard to see who was attacking and who was deflecting. Finnius lifted his hands and the assault stopped. Leann caught Natalie as she slumped to the ground in exhaustion.

Leann placed the girl's head on her lap and touched her temples. Moments later, Natalie opened her eyes and looked up at Leann.

"Thank you," she whispered.

"You are most welcome," Leann said.

Natalie sat up and Finnius joined them on the soft grass. "You did well, my child. The last cauldron will give you the knowledge to sustain your energy and how to revive it. We must go now, but will be back tomorrow." He gazed at Maecha. "Lon has been taken. We will try to hold on as long as we can, but the Fire Lord grows stronger. He has something planned that will release him from his prison, so beware."

Maecha began to fade. "I shall. We soon travel to Alba."

"Be safe," he said and waving to Natalie, he and Leann disappeared.

Natalie watched them leave and before she was drawn away from her dreams, she ventured toward the thick woods where she had felt the eyes staring at her. After staying still for a few moments, she caught sight of the golden glow. Natalie tiptoed closer and the wolf, lowered on its front paws, waited.

Natalie held her hands out and spoke, "Do not fear me. I am your friend."

The wolf took a couple steps and then stopped. Its ears pricked up in alarm and then jumped back into the woods. Natalie heard the noise and turned to listen. In the distance, she heard horns blowing. High above the trees, she saw the symbol that she knew from her own world—the sign of the cross.

Finnius struggled to sit up in his cell. Leann could see the pain and weariness in his face.

"I will bring you restorative herbs," she said to him.

They stood as close as possible to the flaming bars. Finnius held up his hands and closed his eyes. The area around them reverberated with his magic. Leann felt his arms enclose around her in an intimate embrace. She savored the moment, even though she knew this reckless use of magic would weaken him even more. He released her and tried to smile.

"I will be back soon."

Cairpre sat regally in his father's chair, *his* chair he chided himself. He observed the room like it was for the first time. It was a vast hall that could hold one hundred warriors at various tables with enough room for dancers and villagers to join in a celebration. The columns rose high in the four corners and banisters ran along the outskirts of the hall. This was his. He was the king, but he didn't feel like it. A king would have his druid by his side to advise him. Finnius should have been next to him, but instead he had imprisoned the one person who had ever believed in him. Why had he done that? Cairpre pressed his palms against his head and leaned against his knees. He rocked back and forth attempting to block out the doubt that assuaged his mind. It was the Fire Lord. Yes, that was why. Finnius was a danger to the one he called lord now and Cairpre would do whatever he said. Regaining his composure, Cairpre placed his hands on his lap and took a deep breath. He surveyed his surroundings once again and now he felt like a king; a man in control of his destiny. In a few days there would be a celebration that would require the tribe leaders (whoever was still alive) from the surrounding areas to acknowledge him as their overlord and king. They would pledge their loyalty to him or they would die. One of his warriors interrupted his thoughts and Cairpre scowled at him.

"Well, what is it?" he asked.

"The man named Murtagh and his men are removing the rubble so that new walls can be erected. Most of the villagers have gone and the situation is under control."

"Fine, that's just fine," Cairpre replied.

The rather pale man did not leave. Cairpre noted that sweat had beaded along his forehead.

"Spit it out, man. What ails you?"

The man stammered. "Uh, well, some of the men have

noted a bad omen at the bottom of the hill of Tara."

Cairpre's skin grew cold. "What kind of bad omen?"

"Ravens, my lord. Thousands of them have come together and they are waiting," the man's voice drowned into a whisper.

Cairpre couldn't help himself. "Waiting for what?" he asked.

"Death."

Cairpre sprung up and kicked the air in front of him. "Get out and make sure the prisoners are doing what they are told or else kill them!" He stormed out the door and hobbled around to the back side of the *rath*. Ravens—too many for the eyes to count—covered the ground, all the way to the woods. It looked like death had risen from the ground to claim the living.

Cairpre raced as fast as possible to the stables and mounted his horse, not waiting for the stable lad to assist him. He galloped toward the birds and raced his horse right through the center of them. The birds cawed and pecked at him, but flew into the sky briefly before they settled back down. Two ravens remained with him flying on either side of his head. Cairpre slapped at them, but they would not disappear. He ignored them and continued to ride full speed toward the woods.

"Finnius was always so kind to you," a voice by his ear said.

"But times have changed and you must change with them," a different voice on the other side spoke.

Cairpre yanked on his horse's reins. The two ravens settled on each of his shoulders. Wide-eyed, Cairpre could only listen to their words.

"Your father will kill you when he finds out what you have done to his oldest friend. You have insulted the Mother Goddess and she will not forgive this outrage."

"Nonsense, the Mother Goddess is no more. Think about what the future holds for you. Listen to the Fire Lord and you will have your power."

"Goodness."

"Power."

Those words echoed in Cairpre's head as the birds flew away.

Cairpre let his horse amble without direction. Sliding off its back, he stumbled into the woods. He held onto the trees to keep him upright, finally settling on a fallen trunk. He dropped his head and pulled at his hair. How he longed for simpler times. There were so many decisions to make and too many people to try and appease. Demands were thrown at him every day. He just needed some solace and quiet time. That was all.

At first Cairpre thought that a warm breeze had somehow found its way through the trees, but then he remembered the cold winter air. The heat swirled around his head, then his shoulder and when he felt something like an embrace, his body stiffened. He was used to the torching burn of the Fire Lord, so did not think that he was present. Pain was a feeling he could understand and accept. This warmth petrified him.

He lifted his head and peered behind him. Nothing.

"Who goes there?" he growled.

The embrace disappeared and he was sorry for yelling. But warmth had never gotten him anything. Cairpre thought of Finnius and admitted that all the old man had ever shown him was warmth and love. But what good would that do him now? He had already betrayed Finnius. Surely the druid would never forgive him. Plus, he was sworn to Cairpre's father, not to him. Cairpre scrunched his face in thought and tapped his temple. Perhaps if he made Finnius swear allegiance to him, then the people would follow him. He didn't want or need warmth. He needed power and, along with Finnius' support, he would have it.

Cairpre rode back toward Tara right through the ravens. He saw the man who had first told him of them.

"Get your best archers and have them kill as many ravens

159

as they have arrows. We will have raven stew tonight!" Cairpre said and rode toward his prisoners. This wall would be built in two days. He would be prepared for any adversity and he would succeed.

Tannackta, one of the Faery Folk of Tir-nan-og, was the Keeper of the Passageway and Protector of the Doorway to this sacred land. Anyone wishing to speak to the Lord and Princess of the Otherworld would have to get through Tannackta. He was tall for a faery, reaching about waist high on a human, but his powers and his strength were formidable.

Althar found him standing erect in front of the doorway, just as the Fire Lord said he would. Althar barely stifled a laugh at the comical creature he meant to capture. He had to give him credit though, standing there holding a spear that was twice his body length, with his conical hat that sported red stones around the rim.

It was in the wee hours of the morning when the changing of the guards took place. This was when Tannackta would be alone for a short amount of time. Althar approached the faery and bowed.

Tannackta squinted in suspicion and spoke, "What brings you to the doorway of Tir-nan-og?"

Althar lifted his head and said, "I seek you, little man."

Tannackta raised his spear. Before he could sound the alarm, Althar blasted him with a beam of fire. Tannackta fell to the ground and didn't move.

Althar shook him and hoped he didn't kill the small creature. He lifted him with ease and rushed to bring him to his lord before the other guards returned. Althar entered his master's lair and dropped Tannackta at the base of Akir's fiery prison.

The upper part of Akir's body was now human, but the top of his head was still engulfed in flames. Akir smiled with excitement when he saw the keeper.

"Bring him closer," Akir whispered.

Althar lifted Tannackta so that he was eye level with Akir. Akir reached forward and took the little man's face in his hands. Tannackta woke from the searing heat on his cheeks. Akir smiled at the look of fear in the faery's eyes.

"Welcome to my domain, Tannackta. You do me great honor by visiting me here. Not many faeries do, since they know they will never leave."

Tannackta tried to shove free, but could not.

"You shall donate your spirit for the good of the Fire Lord. With your spirit, I will be human again and able to make a visit to the Lord and Princess. It has been so long. Of course, they will think that I am you."

Tannackta grabbed at the Fire Lord's arms, but it scorched his skin. Steam rose from his burnt cheeks. The Fire Lord opened the faery's mouth and breathed in. The faery struggled, but sparkling glimmers of his spirit began to escape from his body. As the Fire Lord consumed them, his own features became more defined. By the time Tannackta lay dead on the ground, Akir was standing on his two feet once again and flames no longer flew from his body. It had taken centuries of suffering, but the Fire Lord was finally whole.

He stepped out of the fire and held out his arms toward Lon, who had watched the entire scene from his own prison. Akir brushed his sandy brown hair out of his face and looked down at his perfect body. Althar handed him the clothes he had requested. Akir slowly donned his black tunic and breeches, along with a black cloak that billowed around his narrow frame. He touched his clothes, his face, and his hair with reverence.

"Give me wine," Akir said to Althar.

Althar handed his master a large horn and, after inhaling the rich scent, Akir drank deeply, not caring that wine dribbled down his chin.

"Ah, that is delectable," Akir said savoring the last few

drops in his mouth. "Gather me the best food possible."

With a satisfied smile, Akir stepped closer so that Lon had a clear view of him. "What do you think, my friend? Now do you recognize me?"

Lon nodded in surrender and said, "It is you."

Akir let out a hearty laugh. "Yes, it is me! I am free once again. What happened in the Otherworld was nothing personal, I hope you know. You were just in the wrong place at my right time."

"But why? You said you were a creature of the Otherworld and had been there for centuries, waiting for someone to take your place. Why would you pretend to be something you were not? All those warriors who had died because they couldn't answer your blasted riddles—it was a waste!"

"A waste? Not to me. I was quite entertained. Parts of it were true. I had hidden in the Otherworld after my cousin died. It was the one place where the gods couldn't seem to find me. I was there so long that I became bored. What better way to entertain myself than to put another's life on the line. But, like I said, don't take it personally."

"I do take it personally and I will see that you pay for it once and for all!" Lon said.

Akir's lip twitched and he grew serious. "Not in your lifetime, my boy. You will die here and I will get my revenge."

He swirled his cloak with a flourish and ignored Lon's onslaught of verbal threats.

Althar returned with sweet meats, fruit, and cheese. Akir took bites of each, murmuring approval with each morsel. He said to Althar, "You may do what you want down here. I will make a quick visit to Tir-nan-og and then I have some other visiting to do."

Althar bowed. "Yes, my Lord."

Akir closed his eyes and took in a deep breath. He spread his arms wide and, when he exhaled, his body began to change.

162

His form shrunk, his hair grew longer, until he was the exact replica of Tannackta. Ignoring Lon's shocked gasp, he transported himself back to the Doorway to Tir-nan-og. He picked up his spear and turned to a guard who was just entering the realm.

"You there!" he said in Tannackta's voice. "I must see to the Lord and Princess. Stand guard."

The faery guard bowed and stood at attention.

Akir stifled a giggle of anticipation. He hoped that having Tannackta's spirit in him would be enough magic to open the door. Turning the knob, he felt a vibration. The door opened and he stepped inside. Akir knew that this was the time of day when Tannackta removed the Awen Crystal from the Lord and Princess to lock it in their crystal safe for the night. All the Faery Folk would settle down for sleep.

As he walked across the crystal bridge, he saw the flying fish soaring out of their watery home. He was tempted to blast them when they came too close, but that would give him away. There was only one goal to this visit—to get the Awen Crystal. Taking it would render the Lord and Princess virtually powerless to do anything against him. Then he could venture up to earth and do what he had been dreaming about for two hundred years.

The Lord and Princess appeared as he stepped up toward the throne that was as white and shiny as the rest of the surroundings. Because he also held Tannackta's memories, he knew the ritual that needed to be performed. He bowed and paid homage to the Lord and Princess, an androgynous being that respected both the male and female essence of all living beings. They existed in respectful balance and harmony. Akir could not wait to break that harmony to pieces.

"Peace of all is upon you," Akir heard himself say in the faery's nasally voice.

"And upon you," the Lord and Princess said as they simultaneously lifted the Awen Crystal from their necks.

Akir had to avert his eyes for fear that his greed and desire for the object would show through. His heart beat wildly and he wanted to snag it and run. But he had to continue his farce long enough to get out of the Otherworld. He would be long gone before they even realized what happened.

Before taking the Awen Crystal, Akir touched his forehead, chest and stomach, and then held out both his hands. The crystal was placed in his palms. He stepped back to pretend that he was going to place it in the crystal safe, when the princess' voice stopped him.

Akir saw them staring at him with their hand outstretched. A flaming ruby flashed at him. For a second, he couldn't reach Tannackta's memory and didn't know what to do. The Lord and Princess eyed him warily, until he leaned forward, took their hand and kissed the ring. Then he stepped back and watched them exit the throne room into their inner sanctum.

Akir threw off the conical hat and placed the crystal around his neck. The power emanating from it staggered him at first, but then he absorbed it all. He felt and knew everything at once. The best part was that his connection to the lovely Maecha was even stronger. He would destroy their relationship. By the time he got to Maecha Ruadh, she would be ready for him. The rear chamber opened and a group of Fian, the Otherworldly warriors ran in after him.

"Halt!" he heard one yell as he bent sideways to avoid a sword aimed toward his neck. As Akir ran, he transformed back into his original form and blasted the door open. Laughing, fire surged from his hands engulfing them in flames. He transported himself out into the world.

Chapter 19 - Catskills

"Hi, you two!" Michaela called as Shannon and Ben arrived at their place. Shannon swung her car door open and ran to Michaela. They hugged one another for a long time and then Shannon stepped back to check out her sister.

"You look great! Have you been running?"

"We've been running, hiking, and doing some self-defense training." Michaela hugged Ben when he stepped closer and gave him a kiss on the cheek. "How are you, Ben?"

"I'm doing better now that Shannon dragged me away."

Michaela could see dark circles under his eyes and he looked thinner. She made a mental note to take a walk with Shannon later and see what was happening in New York. She was so busy that all the crazy attacks and her father's death seemed like another lifetime. Michaela almost didn't want to know what was going on. But it affected her sister and there still was a small fear that the psycho Boris or Ricky Cartillo, for that matter, would show up unannounced. She hoped that Shannon would be happy for her, knew she would, and couldn't wait to tell her about their plans.

"Let's go wake up Natalie. She'll be so excited to see you," Michaela said, opening the front door for them.

Vince came around the corner and picked up Shannon to give her a big smack on the lips. "How's my second favorite redhead?"

"I used to be your favorite," Shannon jokingly complained. "But I don't blame you. She's all our favorites."

Ben and Vince shook hands and went to the kitchen when Vince offered him a drink. "Where are the boys?" Ben asked.

"Running around in the woods, being teenagers," Vince said.

Last night Natalie had woken up drenched in sweat like she had run a marathon. For the last week she had been spending what time she wasn't reading or practicing her self-defense deep in sleep. Michaela didn't know how the girl could sleep so much, but when she told Michaela that she was training with Finnius, she understood. The only problem was that all this training was starting to wear her down and, if that wasn't enough, Natalie was seeing visions of this wolf and a cottage by the cliffs during the daytime hours.

"She's been working hard and has been tired," Michaela explained to Shannon. "I'll need to catch you up on some stuff though. She's changing."

Shannon had known that this time would be coming, but so soon? She didn't want to think about losing Natalie. Kneeling on the floor next to Natalie's bed, Shannon whispered, "Hey sleepyhead. The sun's shining and it's time to get up."

Natalie opened her eyes and smiled tiredly at Shannon. She let out a big yawn and said, "Hi, Shannon."

"What are you doing sleeping in the middle of the day?" Shannon asked.

"I was training with Finnius. We have so much to do and he's not feeling well. Something bad happened and he needs to hurry up and train me. It's hard work."

"I can see that. Your pj's are wet. I'll help you get dressed." As Shannon stood, she noticed a necklace around Natalie's neck that she had never seen before. Shannon leaned over and, lifting it from Natalie's chest, asked, "What's this?"

"This is the necklace that I'd found in a book. I can show you the picture. Michaela and I searched all over the house, because I knew it was mine. But we couldn't find it. Then Travis

166

said to sleep on it and I did. In my dream Finnius gave me the necklace. He used to have one, but now he's so strong he doesn't need it." Natalie changed her clothes and didn't take a breath. "He said it was mine and would help me to access my powers. When I woke up it was around my neck."

"It sounds like you have been very busy. You must be hungry. I brought some bagels and *White Castle* hamburgers," Shannon said knowing that would get Natalie revved up.

Natalie asked Michaela, "Are the boys here?"

Laughing, Michaela said, "No, so you'd better hurry and get your share."

"Thanks, Shannon!" Natalie said, hugged her, and ran out of her room.

Shannon sat on the bed. "It would have been easier if you had given me updates in smaller dosages. This is a lot to take in."

"There's a lot more. Let's eat and then go for a walk," Michaela said.

Shannon and Michaela started off on a path that was wet from the melting snow and headed downhill toward the sounds of water.

The trail ended and Shannon gasped at the scene in front of her. Far below, the water flowed at a rapid pace and rocks jutted out at different depths.

"This is the Catskill Creek," Michaela explained. "I guess it's a hot spot for teens to come and hang out in the summer and do some cliff diving."

Shannon peered over the edge and shook her head. "I don't think I'll be doing that, but it does remind me of the places where we went white water rafting with Dad."

"There's a stretch of 17 miles where people do just that. Maybe we'll try it at some point, but right now this water is very cold." Michaela sat near the edge and her sister sidled up next to her. "So do you want me to fill you in on everything or do you have questions brimming over in your head first?"

"First, I want to know about you and Vince. How are the two of you doing? Did you talk to him about opening a dojo?"

"No," Michaela laughed. "I didn't talk to him about it, he talked to me!"

Michaela explained how Vince wanted to start his own business, have a separate dojo on their land, and bring kids up from the city during the summer. "We have become so much closer and realize that we want to spend our lives together."

Shannon was so excited. "Do you think he's going to ask you to marry him?"

Michaela shrugged. "I don't know. I would be fine with how things are. We have already pledged our love to one another, but I can't help thinking about a small reception at the inn with all our friends celebrating with us. We'll see."

"I am incredibly happy for both of you. I wasn't sure if you were going to make it. You both drifted apart even after spending most of your lives together. Sometimes it takes a kick in the butt or, I don't know, time traveling to another century to realize how much you love each other," Shannon joked.

"Yeah, it's amazing how that can change things," Michaela said.

Shannon's face turned serious. "How is Natalie handling all that has been thrust upon her? She's still trying to get over the physical and emotional abuse she suffered from Ricky Cartillo."

"She's handling it amazingly well, but I do notice that she's on her own quite a bit. She's either reading the history books about ancient Ireland or she's sitting in the woods and staring out into space. When I ask her what she's looking at, she'll start like she didn't know I was there, and say that she's watching both the past and the future."

"She can see what is happening during Maecha's time?" Shannon asked, trying to get it straight in her head.

"It appears that way, but then she keeps talking about this white wolf who feels very maternal toward her. I dream traveled with her, but the wolf ran away as soon as it saw me. I don't think it trusts me."

"And what about this cottage by the cliffs. Where does she think that is?"

Michaela hesitated knowing this would just bring on a barrage of more questions. "We think it's from Ireland in the twenty-first century and that Natalie needs to find the person that lives there."

Unexpected tears formed in Shannon's eyes. "Hey, what's this about?" Michaela said wrapping her arms around her sister.

Shannon wiped her eyes and said, "I don't want to lose her. We have all bonded so quickly and it seems like she's not going to have a choice and leave us. Also, I don't know what I'm supposed to be doing. I feel so useless. You and Vince are starting a wonderful life and, even though you won't be that far away from me, it still seems like you are in another country."

"Why don't you move up here with us?" Michaela suggested. "There are more than enough rooms in our house and Vince could eventually build you your own house on all this land Finnius gave me."

Shannon smiled and said, "I've thought about it, but I have a flourishing business and I really want to see where Ben and I are heading. We've been spending a lot of time together, and he's still working on trying to find Cartillo and that horrible man who attacked you. I'm worried about him. He's so disenchanted about the police force with all the corruption they unveiled. He just wants to do the right thing."

The mention of Ricky Cartillo's name sent chills up and down Michaela's spine. She and her sister, as well as Natalie, were all very lucky to be alive and it was Ricky who had started it all, by leading a major drug cartel in Manhattan and using kids and local businesses to transport the drugs. The people who could tell the police where Ricky was hiding were either dead or in hiding themselves. It was frustrating and a little scary knowing that he was still out there.

"I think you are doing what you are meant to do and are best at. You're helping Natalie deal with everything that happened to her as a child and you are supporting Ben."

"I know, but it's so boring. You're traveling in your dreamworlds and training an ancient warrior, starting a new business, and renovating a beautiful mansion. My life sounds very drab next to yours," Shannon complained.

Michaela stood and helped her sister up. "Sis, I would give a lot to have plain boring. We all depend on you tremendously. You are the backup support staff that keeps the networks running smoothly. Without you, we don't have squat."

They started to walk back to the house. Shannon made a face and said, "Great now I'm a server."

"No, you are a saver. You save people's lives and I can't think of anything more important than that."

Chapter 20 - Isle of Imbas Skye

The early signs of spring had caught up to the Isle of Imbas Skye and, after a winter of training both mind and body, Maecha and Kelan, as well as their companions, were feeling antsy.

"It is time for you to show me that you are ready to leave," Scathach said in the main arena.

"And how shall I do that?" Maecha asked.

"You will do what you have been dying to do since you came here. You will fight me. But first let's see what you can do against your companions."

Maecha donned the leather tunic that Goll handed her and unsheathed Imbas Skye and her *ton-fa*. This was the moment she had been training months for. Instead of worrying about the outcome, she breathed in, asked her mother for her blessing, and pointed her sword toward her brethren.

"Begin," Scathach said as she stepped away.

Osgar asked, "Shall I join in the games?"

Scathach rubbed his arm in an unnaturally friendly gesture. Osgar didn't mention it in hopes that she would continue. "No, let us enjoy for now."

Maecha's opponents immediately circled her. She knew that this was the worst possible scenario and so swung at Treasa, forcing them all to be in front. Treasa made a half-hearted attempt to slice through Maecha's middle.

Scathach yelled, "If you are going to attack then by the light of the goddess, please do so! How will she be able to save her life and others if you don't attack her like you mean it?"

Treasa's next swing held some force, but Maecha blocked it with her *ton-fa* and, sliding in, elbowed Treasa in the chest. Her tunic provided protection, but Treasa still fell back from the impact. Maecha swung around in time to connect swords with Goll and then spun her *ton-fa* out toward Caoilte, knocking him onto his back.

The fight continued with Maecha defending more attacks than she gave. Caoilte and Treasa attacked at the same time and as Maecha defended one strike with her sword, the other hit her hand with the flat end. Wincing in pain, Maecha dropped her sword and flipped the back of her *ton-fa* at Caoilte's wrist. He stepped out of the way and Maecha fell. Treasa dove toward Maecha to pin her to the ground, but Maecha turned in time to flip Treasa over her head.

Maecha jumped to her feet and blocked Goll's punch with her arm and jammed the head of her *ton-fa* into his gut forcing him to bend forward in pain. Grabbing the hand that punched her, she twisted it over toward Goll's head shoving him to the ground. Winded and tired, she was about to get hit in the head by Caoilte, when Kelan jumped in and blocked it.

Scathach unsheathed her sword and strode toward Kelan. "This is Maecha's fight. You'll get your chance."

"It was instinctual. I am here to protect her," Kelan said.

"You may not always be here to do that, Kelan. There will come a time when she will have to fight her own battles. She must be able to stand on her own and we are making sure that she can do that. Back away. Come, Maecha, it is time for you to fight me."

Kelan studied Maecha. Her nose bled and she couldn't catch her breath, but she radiated excitement. He felt foolish and didn't know what had made him react in such a manner. They had fought together often enough, and he had trained her for so long that he should have had more confidence in her abilities.

"*I need to do this,*" Maecha mindspoke to him.

"Forgive my intrusion. I do not know what got into me," he responded and moved out of the way.

Maecha wanted to talk to Kelan more, because his tone sounded strange to her, but it would have to wait.

Goll handed Imbas Skye to her. "It is within you."

"Thank you, Goll," she said.

Maecha studied Scathach as she stepped into her fighting stance. Scathach held her sword horizontally, which left her belly exposed. Maecha knew that the goddess had the speed to deflect any strike she made, but perhaps changing her targets would distract Scathach.

Keeping her eyes on Scathach's shoulders, Maecha easily deflected the first strike toward her head. As her sword bounced off the blade, Maecha pivoted to the right and flicked her wrist. Scathach blocked the attack to her waist and raised an eyebrow.

The fight continued. They took turns striking and defending. Instead of tiring like she had with the others, a sense of calm came over Maecha, and she was able to anticipate Scathach's next moves. Even with the sword, she flowed through the movements of the katas 'Mikala' had taught her and, when she was too close for a sword strike, she would defend with the punches and kicks of the *cada'me* martial arts style. Maecha smiled, and her body relaxed with the knowledge that can only come from constant and relentless practice.

She knew that in order to be released from the isle, she would need to take Scathach down to the ground. The goddess hadn't shown any sign of weakness, but Maecha noticed that she tended to keep her front leg extended out when attacking. Maecha waited. Scathach struck out with powerful blows and each time Maecha slid just out of reach. With each assault, Scathach stretched her leg further and further, trying to make up the distance. Finally, Scathach overextended and Maecha saw her chance. She stepped out to the side, letting Scathach's sword flow past her. Blocking Scathach's arm, Maecha grabbed it, struck her in the elbow, and then followed it with a palm strike to the face. Scathach's head flew back and, with her momentum, Maecha swept Scathach's front foot out forward, while shoving her upper body down to the ground. The warrior goddess hit the dirt like a fallen tree.

Maecha didn't know whether to yell in happiness or run for her life. The goddess' hearty laugh kept her still. Scathach held up her hand and Maecha clasped it, pulling the mighty woman onto her feet.

Scathach grabbed Maecha behind the neck and pulled her into an embrace. "You have done well."

Maecha nodded not trusting herself to speak at the moment. She felt Kelan's pride and it made her own soar.

"Come, let us talk," Scathach said and they all followed her into the castle.

"Please, sit down," Scathach said as she sat at the head of a large wooden table. Drinks were poured for all. Scathach raised her horn and saluted Maecha. "These past few months have been hard for all of you. I cannot remember the last time this arena has been filled with such talented warriors." She focused on Maecha. "I have taught you all that I can. It is time for you to move toward your destiny. If you like, four of my Amazons will travel with you," Scathach said.

"Five," Uatach announced as she entered the room. "I wish to see Alba and these Picti, as well as hone my skills."

Scathach looked at her daughter and then at Osgar. Anger flashed in her eyes. He shrugged his shoulders and she could see that he was just as surprised by this announcement as she was.

"We will discuss this after," Scathach said.

"No!" Uatach responded, surprising both her parents yet again. Uatach was always the quiet one who did as she was told and did it well. "I have only begun to know my father and I want to be with him. I do not know how long it will be until I see him

174

again."

Osgar stood next to his daughter. "There will be a great deal of fighting and very little time to get to know each other."

"Warriors get to know one another through their fighting. There is a special camaraderie that is developed. I can fight by your side," she said, but then her face fell. "Unless you do not want me."

Osgar looked at the mother of his beloved daughter. Scathach's face softened, so he continued. "I do want you to be with me and I would be proud to have you fight by my side. You have taught me a thing or two, I must say. If your mother agrees, then I will take you with me and bring you back when the King of Eire is restored."

They both looked at Scathach with high hopes. She couldn't say no, but fear tugged at her heart. She would keep a close eye on her daughter, and her time with Osgar only proved what she had known nineteen summers ago—he was a good man and she loved him.

She smiled, "You may go."

Uatach squealed, which was an uncommon sound from her mouth, or any Amazon's, and flew across the room to hug her mother. The extreme display of emotion shocked Scathach, but she wrapped her arms around her daughter.

She pulled back and, as she started to speak to this talented group of warriors, a battle horn blew.

"It would seem that you shall test your skills sooner than you thought. Prepare for battle," Scathach said and left to kill the enemy who dared to desecrate her sacred ground.

The warning had come from the cliffs by the sea, and the Amazons on guard were already killing many with arrows. Immediately, Maecha could tell that these were not ordinary invaders. They ran with an otherworldly speed and it was only when the arrows pierced their hearts that they went down.

"The Fire Lord," Maecha said.

"He must be strong enough to have escaped his prison," Kelan said.

Goll ran up to them and said, "Treasa and her women are riding to the right of Skye and will take out the enemy from that side. I will take some warriors and go to the left while the Amazons attack from the walls."

"They must not get into Skye. Their evil will taint this sanctuary and will leave us susceptible to more invasions." Her bronze shield was decorated with interlocking spirals with metal spikes protruding from them. Scathach unsheathed her sword and hundreds of Amazons dressed for war responded to her battle cry.

Osgar followed with Scathach and she turned on him. "Fight with Maecha."

"She is well protected. I prefer to fight with you," Osgar said, his voice calm and determined. Scathach looked up onto the wall and could see Uatach spewing arrows from her bow like lightning bolts.

"Very well, but keep an eye on Uatach." Scathach broke into a trot and yelled for the guard to open the gate. The Amazons attacked with the ferocity of a mother defending her cubs.

Maecha and Kelan rode Finn and Octar toward a large group of warriors. They stayed close to one another and, even though the enemy was large and highly trained, they managed to kill many in a short period of time.

Suddenly, one of the creatures yelled, "There he is!" A swarm of larger warriors ran toward Kelan.

Octar lifted his legs to trample some that were crowding in front of them and Kelan turned his horse to get closer to Maecha.

"Why are they running toward you?" she called out to him.

"The Fire Lord seems to have taken an interest in me," he

yelled. A large warrior rode toward Kelan and swung a battle axe at his head. An arrow from the wall pierced the enemy's shoulder, but he didn't falter. Kelan whipped his flail against the enemy's head without any effect. Quickly blocking a downward sword strike with his *ton-fa*, Kelan retaliated with a swipe of his sword. The warrior bellowed, but didn't go down.

"Move back, Kelan!" Maecha yelled and she blasted the stubborn enemy with the blue eye of her sword. He stared down at his missing middle and fell over.

"What was that thing?" Kelan asked moving next to her again.

"I don't know, but you seem to be the fighter of the day. Everyone wants to attack you."

"That may be true, but right now I think Caoilte is struggling."

Maecha turned to see Caoilte fighting two men with his short sword. Treasa was fighting her way toward him, but she was going to be too late. Kelan jumped over the enemy, trampling a few in his way, and pounded the man on the head with his flail. He didn't know what hit him and didn't get back up.

"Thank ye, Kelan," Caoilte said. Kelan pulled him up onto the back of his stallion when he felt a pain in his arm.

"Maecha." He spun around and galloped back to where he had left her. Maecha was now on the ground holding her sword tightly while the eye blasted everyone in its path. Maecha was concentrating so hard on keeping the sword in her hand, that she hadn't noticed the man getting ready to jump her from behind.

"Halt," Caoilte said, as he grabbed two daggers and flung them with superb speed and power. Arching back from the pain in his neck, the man fell on Maecha. She staggered forward, but not before Kelan jumped down in front of her, while Caoilte took the reins. He blocked the next attack while she regained her footing, but then felt a shaft of pain in his middle.

"Kelan!" Maecha yelled and pulled him back away from

the throng of warriors.

Suddenly, the sky burst open and the winds blew against them. Scathach screamed like a banshee and struck her sword into the ground. The more they fought, the more enemies appeared. She did not know from where they came, but she knew that the Fire Lord was behind it. So it was time to give him a taste of his own medicine. The ground reverberated with her power and opened up, sucking in all who fought against her. The screams were loud and many begged for mercy before utter silence filled the land.

Scathach peered around hoping that the injuries were few.

"Kelan, are you all right?" she asked as Kelan held his side and kept his sword raised, making sure that no one else was going to attack them.

"I think I am," he said and then removed his hand from his waist. Blood flowed freely and, it was only when he pulled up his tunic, that they realized how bad it was. Kelan lifted his head to Maecha and said, "Get the marrow." Then he fell.

They carried Kelan's limp body back to their hut. Maecha dumped his bag of belongings, looking for the small pouch that contained the tooth of the green serpent that Kelan had killed during his third challenge in the Cave of the Warrior. He had succeeded and also managed to knock out one of its teeth. The marrow was said to have healing powers, and they would quickly find out how well it worked.

Kelan was pale, and his breathing shallow. Maecha handed the tooth to Osgar, because her hands were shaking too badly to extract the marrow. Uatach held Kelan's head and whispered, "Drink, Kelan. This will help you accept the powers of the marrow."

Maecha looked at Osgar who only nodded. Through his talks with Uatach, he had learned that she possessed great healing skills, but even she would not be able to do much for this wound. Osgar took a knife and gouged marrow out from the center of the tooth. He placed it on Kelan's open wound. The skin around the injury bubbled, oozed, and then it began to close. Within minutes, the skin looked as healthy as the rest of him.

Kelan took a deep breath and then settled into a peaceful sleep. Maecha lay down next to him and sent him all her energy. Exhausted, they slept until the next morning.

The boats were loaded with supplies and the horses had been settled for the one day sail to Alba.

"I will miss you, Scathach," Maecha told her. It was hard to say goodbye after all they had been through. This woman had taught her so much; had given so much.

Scathach waved her hand as if trying to ward off the emotions. "I will be near at hand since my daughter will be with you," she said.

"I know and I vow to care for her as I would a sister."

They clasped arms and Scathach pulled her into a hug.

Kelan strode up to them still tired from his injury, but completely healed. Preparing to hug him, Maecha felt it before she saw the color change on Kelan's Awen Crystal. The crystal on the right, symbolizing the male force residing among the earth, sky, and sea, resonated with a pulsing green light.

"No," Maecha whispered and scooped up her own crystal. Her female essence was clear, while the middle crystal glowed bright with the strength of their bond. Maecha lifted her tearful eyes to Kelan. The look on his face told her that he was just as surprised and unhappy about this change in their journey.

"What has happened?" Scathach asked.

Not taking her eyes from Kelan, Maecha said, "Kelan." She hesitated, fear filling her. "Kelan has been called to the Otherworld by the Lord and Princess."

"And what is the purpose? The Mother Goddess knows how important your mission is."

When Maecha didn't answer, Kelan said, "Whoever is

179

called to the Otherworld is honor bound to assist them immediately. They must be in grave danger."

"But we are stronger together and you've been wounded," Maecha said, forgetting about everyone else.

Kelan grabbed her shoulders. "That we are, Maecha. But what we have will not be weakened by distance or time. We will still know how we fare through our minds and through our crystals. I am well enough to travel."

Kelan looked over her shoulder at Goll, Caoilte, Treasa, and Osgar. They all nodded their silent pledge to protect Maecha with their lives. Kelan didn't need the acknowledgment, because he knew that all of them would have done it anyway. It did make him feel better about having to leave her though. This would be the test that Finnius had warned him about and he would not let any of them down.

Kelan lifted Maecha's chin with his finger. "Be brave. You will bring your father home, and I will be there to share that special time with you. For now you must trust in our love and in yourself."

He kissed her softly on her lips. Maecha wrapped her arms around his neck and hugged him.

Maecha was the first to pull away. She touched his stubbly cheek and smiled. "May the Mother Goddess go with you and protect you on this honorable journey. I will be there if ever you need me. I do love you."

"And I you." He stepped away and addressed Scathach. "Goddess, I ask permission to travel through your portal to Tir-nan-og."

Scathach bowed her head in acquiescence. "Follow me."

Kelan walked toward the standing stones that stood on the cusp of the sea. The early spring wind whipped at his cloak. Spray from the sea gave his black hair a bluish sheen. He clasped his companions' hands and moved within the circle of the stones. A singular stone stood in the center and Kelan walked clockwise around it. Each time he came within view of Maecha, he memorized her face. On the third and final turn, he smiled and disappeared.

Sitting on a large rock, Akir watched the vision of Kelan disappearing through the portal. Who knew that they had healing marrow! This pair surprised him more than he ever dreamed. He was enjoying the challenge, but it was about time he got rid of that interference. Maecha's devastated face pleased him. "I will be along to comfort you, Maecha. Fear not." He bit into a luscious grape. "I know that you are sad, but it was necessary to remove your lover, so that my plans could continue. Together your powers are impenetrable. We shall see how you fare being apart."

He closed his hands and the flame that held Maecha's image vanished. *Of course,* Akir thought as he hopped off the rock, *it will be heartbreaking to Maecha when Kelan is killed in the Otherworld, but that cannot be helped.*

It was a brilliant spring day. The sky was unusually clear and the air was filled with the scent of flowers as they unfolded their petals to the world. It had been two hundred years and seven days since Akir was able to smell anything besides dirt. Well, he really couldn't even smell the dirt since he hadn't had a nose, but his whole being had been immersed in the earth's soil for so long, he had quite forgotten the wonders of the world.

Akir stood on the cliffs of Eire. He strolled until he found a village girl in the prime of her womanhood. She was all too willing to welcome him, although she didn't even begin to satiate him. Only Maecha would, but first he would seek revenge. The gentle rays of the sun warmed his cheeks like a mother's caress. Akir laughed, because it was too late for forgiveness and second chances. He stared into the sun until he could see his mother's forlorn face. Akir knew that she hadn't had much choice when faced with what he had done, but that knowledge didn't soften her ultimate betrayal of her son. With the power of the Awen Crystal, Akir transformed into a solar flame and shot up through the air toward his mother's home.

Aiménd of the Sky and Light stood proud and brilliant on her throne. Her flaxen hair flowed unbound down her back. In her right hand, she held a golden scepter with a sun beam on top. She placed the scepter on her throne. Her golden eyes were hard to gaze into, but Akir did not look away as he grew to his normal size and the flames died out. He smiled with the satisfaction of catching a flicker of fear and regret in his mother's eyes.

"Hello, Mother," he said with a mocking bow.

He noted that Aiménd had regained her composure before speaking. "Akir. It is good of you to visit me upon your escape from exile. Do you come to ask my forgiveness?"

Akir tamped down the flames erupting in his eyes and kept his voice calm. He stared at his carefully trimmed nails. "I was actually thinking that you might ask for my forgiveness."

Aiménd stepped down from her dais to meet her son's gaze.

"It was not I who destroyed countless lives in the name of boredom."

"Perhaps not, but what you did was the ultimate betrayal to your own flesh and blood." He turned away from her and waved his hand through the air. "Really, Mother, why did you and Father even bother to have a child when it was obvious you didn't have time or love for one?"

Aiménd gracefully walked toward him, her white dress shimmering like the sun shining on water. She said, "It was important to continue our line. Besides many children thrive being raised by the community. It was my mistake, however, not to realize how needy you were."

Akir whipped his head around. "Needy? Is that what I was? I think not! I was a child whose only wish was some love and attention from his parents. And when I didn't get any from

182

you, I found ways to force you to notice me."

"But what you did could not build love. It hurt us in so many ways."

Akir laughed. "Well, now you know how I felt for all those years."

His mother reached for him and he saw pity in her eyes. He pulled away. "Do not pity me, Mother, but rather fear me."

Akir lifted the Awen Crystal from inside his shirt and smirked at his mother's shocked face.

"What have you done?"

"What I have been waiting centuries to do—exact revenge."

Aiménd reached toward her scepter, but Akir shoved it out of her reach with a wave of his hand.

"What, no more motherly concern? You have made me what I am and so I will return the favor."

Aiménd's sunny face darkened. "I've had enough favors from you for all these years. I have been without your father for what feels like forever. We get quick glimpses of one another, but can never touch or speak. That was how distraught we were over sending you away. We punished ourselves for not doing more for you."

"How very noble, but at least you had a body and a rather cozy place to live." Akir scrutinized his mother's palace, thinking that when all was destroyed, he would take this place for himself. Flames rose from his hands as he addressed his mother. "I had to grovel and fight for my measly existence! But not anymore! I will rule all and you will regret the day you gave birth to me!"

Quick as lightning, Aiménd grabbed her scepter and shot a bolt at Akir. He was ready and deflected it with ease. It shattered a marble column that crashed to the ground. A fire bolt erupted from Akir's hand and hit his mother square in the chest. She flew back and connected with a wall, then fell to the ground. She didn't get up.

Akir looked down at her. She opened her eyes and watched him. Nothing remained of her maternal affection. Akir only saw hatred in her eyes. That was what he wanted—the connection to be severed forevermore.

"I'm going to pay Father a visit. I'll tell him you are feeling a little under the weather." Akir spun around with a flourish, his cloak swinging behind him. Then he was gone.

Chapter 21 - Alba

Maecha sailed from the Isle of Imbas Skye soon after Kelan traveled through the portal. They reached the shores of Alba at the first sight of dawn the next day. In the distance jagged mountains of rock extended toward the sky. The land of the Picti was surrounded on two sides by the sea and the boats stopped in the Firth of Forth where cliffs of rock towered on either side. Maecha ordered everyone to be prepared for battle. She covered her cloth tunic with a hardened leather vest and wore the trousers that allowed her legs to move freely. Next, she donned her *ton-fa*. Her short dagger lay in its sheath on her left side. She placed the scabbard which cradled Imbas Skye across her back and, pulling it out, raised it to the sky.

"We step on foreign land in the name of the the all-powerful Mother Goddess. We strive to protect our land and will take back our king. May the goddess spare our lives and bless our venture. But if we die today, we die as warriors and shall see each other again in the Otherworld."

Maecha, Osgar with Uatach standing next to him, Treasa, Goll, and Caoilte walked on the rocky path that led to the top of the cliff. As they approached, the landing above them filled with Picti warriors. Their bodies were intricately decorated with blue tattoos and their wild hair was bleached yellow. They carried spears, shields, and swords; some held bows and arrows. They raised their voice in a cacophony of sounds that ranged from screeching to howling. They stopped and the group separated. A large man stepped forward, a tattoo of a V-shaped crescent on his forehead. He wore a deerskin vest and trousers of bright plaid. On his arms were circular lines of blue dye. His hair hung long down his back.

He raised his hands. Another man came into view and Maecha recognized the vision she had in Skye.

"Father!" Maecha yelled as she moved toward him.

Osgar held her back, whispering that it was not the leader's place to go running to her father.

Maecha could barely control her temper. His red hair wasn't braided, but hung limply around his haggard face. His stance was stooped, and his right arm was cradled to his chest in a sling. Numerous lines wove their path along his face. His once twinkling blue eyes squinted like she was a hallucination. What had they done to him? She swore they would pay for hurting the man she held so dear to her heart.

In that moment, Maecha's memory of her immortal father, astride a magnificent horse, was shattered. Her body tensed for action, Maecha addressed the king. "I am Maecha Ruadh mac Art, daughter of High King Cormac mac Art of Eire."

Cruithne spoke in a voice that carried over the waters. "I am King Cruithne of Alba. You are welcome here, Maecha Ruadh mac Art, as is your band of warriors, so long as they do not raise their arms." He gestured toward the line of archers and continued. "As you can see we are well protected and any wrong move on your part would not be wise."

Osgar grumbled what he would like to do, and Maecha raised her hand to silence him, determination flowing through her veins.

"We are the ones who have been aggrieved. You have taken a high king from his land against his will and, from the looks of my father, have not treated him well. I am willing to discuss the terms for his release, but there will be retribution if I am not satisfied."

Cruithne laughed. "You are all that I expected. Alas,

everything will be explained in due time. As I said, you are all welcome, and I invite you to come and bid greetings to your father. Then I shall introduce you to my sons and tell you the reason why you are here."

Maecha was taken back by his sudden change in demeanor. What did he mean that she was all he had expected? Had he planned to get her here all this time? Was it a trap? Not knowing what else to do, Maecha climbed the stone steps to her father. She was closely followed by her entourage of guardians.

"Maecha," he said hugging her with his one good arm.

"Father, I thought you would be dead. I didn't know what to expect."

"I am proud of you for venturing this far. All will be well." He released her and looked around him.

He saw Osgar and tried to speak, but coughed instead. Osgar grabbed his arm to steady him.

"Ah, my faithful friend. Thank you for keeping watch over my daughter."

Osgar said, "Your daughter has made our journey easy. She is a fierce warrior and a strong leader of the Fianna."

"The Fianna?"

"Aye, she and Kelan entered the Cave of the Warrior and succeeded in their challenges."

His little girl was a woman now and deserved the respect of a warrior. Cormac nodded in acceptance and looked around him.

"But where is the lad? You two haven't been separated for years," Cormac asked Maecha.

Maecha held back the tears that wanted to rush forth. She would not cry over this! She would prove her ability to lead under any circumstances and make her father proud. "Kelan was called to assist the Lord and Princess of the Otherworld, Father. We will see him when we get back to Eire."

Cormac's face scrunched in thought. "I know he will

187

succeed as you will. A finer set of warriors has yet to be found."

Cormac turned to Queen Treasa. "My dear girl, you are looking remarkable in your war gear!"

Treasa smiled and said, "I try to look my best when going into battle, my king."

"Ha, ha," he coughed and continued, "And so you do. And who do we have here?"

Osgar placed an arm around his daughter. "This is Uatach, my daughter with Scathach."

Cormac raised his eyebrows and looked at the pair. Deciding they looked very happy to be together, he put out his hand to Uatach. "It is a pleasure to meet my niece."

Uatach smiled in response and took his hand.

Goll mac Morna and Caoilte stood back from this main group. Cormac acknowledged Caoilte first as he bowed to the king. "It is no small task for you to venture forth across the sea to protect my daughter."

"But."

"Ah, do not deny what I see to be true. You have pledged your loyalty to her and to me, beyond all that I could have ever asked of you. I appreciate it, and your faithfulness will be well rewarded." He tapped the young man's cheek and turned to Goll.

"My king," Goll began.

Cormac held up his hand and Goll paused. He gazed at all the warriors who had traveled across the sea to bring him home, but who also pledged their loyalty and acceptance of his daughter as the next in line. They believed in the power of the goddess and the right of matriarchal sovereignty. These were the warriors who would see to her safety when he was no longer able to.

"You humble me," he spoke so that all could hear. "When your future is uncertain, when your families may be unguarded, you venture forth in the name of the Mother Goddess and Maecha. You have followed her here, which tells me that she is a true leader who has found her path. Many of you were with me when we were attacked and I captured. I see that some of you still have not healed from your physical injuries, but also suffer from deeper injuries to the heart, due to loss of loved ones and fellow warriors. But still you came. And you came, passing on leadership that you may have once deemed to be yours."

He and Goll stared at one another. Cormac could see the hurt and pain that Goll had endured, not only from his recent battle. At that moment, Cormac knew Goll would die for his daughter and that moved a place deep inside him.

Addressing Goll, he said, "I do not know the story behind Maecha leading the Fianna, but I know that you must have had a strong role in making that happen. For this, I honor you. I know you have given up much in your life and that you would have given your life for your friend. I grieve for him, as you must allow yourself to do. But I thank you for guiding my daughter to me."

Cormac grasped Goll's forearm and pulled him into a hug. "There is much that we have to speak of." Cormac turned toward his daughter and was caught in a gut wrenching cough. Maecha wrapped her arm around her father.

"What have they done to you?"

Cormac wheezed and attempted to stand tall. He staggered and Osgar's hand steadied him. "My arm was wounded in the battle at home, and I did not fare so well on the journey across the sea. I fear I have an illness of my blood, but I am much heartened now that you are here. All will be well."

He walked with his daughter and his oldest friend on either side of him. Cormac tried to move like a healthy man, but his chest burned and his muscles ached. He needed to get Maecha back home and placed as the heir of Eire. That would be the motivation to keep him going.

Cruithne led Maecha and her father over a stone bridge that crossed deep ditches that served as protection for their tribe. The king's hill fort stood on a raised plateau. All around the settlement were large *brochs* that appeared to be piles of stone until you entered one of them and saw the different areas for cooking, sitting, and eating. Maecha noted how they were allowed to walk on their own accord, but the guards were close by. Three young men stood as they came forward. Cruithne gently clasped her elbow to lead her toward them. Maecha unwillingly felt a warm feeling toward this man. His aura was golden, which exuded goodness. It didn't excuse how he had treated her father, but she knew that he was a strong king who cared about his people.

"Allow me to introduce my sons to you, Maecha," Cruithne said.

He clasped Fidach around the back of his neck and pulled him closer.

"This is my oldest son, Fidach. He is next in line to my throne, and needs a strong woman to continue our matriarchal line."

Maecha brows furrowed at the inappropriate comment, but she ignored it. Instead she studied him and his energy. He held an aura of passion and kindness. Maecha was soothed and excited at the same time just being in his presence.

Cruithne slapped his son's back with a little too much force that moved him closer to Maecha. Fidach was slightly taller than her. His hair was not shocked yellow by the sun and standing on end like the others, but was blond and just touched his shoulders. His face was handsome with its chiseled edges and his azure eyes were friendly.

"Welcome," Fidach said.

Maecha clasped his arm and a sense of joy spread up hers. His comfort and concern for her was surprising. These people had taken her father and treated him ill, but yet this man seemed kind like his father. She didn't understand it. She thought that maybe she was misreading them. Cruithne continued his introductions, so Maecha focused on the next son.

"This is Ce," Cruithne said. "He is one of our strongest warriors on foot and horseback."

When Ce greeted Maecha, she felt the strength of a warrior, but also anger toward their group. He was a large warrior, equaling Kelan, and Maecha found herself wondering who would win in a battle between the two. At least his feelings were more in line with what she expected.

The last son stepped forward. He was smaller than his brothers, and it was obvious by his body language that he did not want to be there. His father pushed him forward.

"This is my youngest son, Circenn. He is but sixteen summers and is still finding his way as it would be," Cruithne said.

Circenn reminded Maecha of a vulture. His beady eyes looked into hers with menace. His long neck made his head crane toward hers and his back was slightly curved forward. His aura oozed black and evil. He clasped her forearm and she felt his underlying strength. A burning sensation traveled up her arm followed by violent aggression. The evil in it wrenched at her insides. She pulled her hand away and, slipping backwards, grasped at her midsection. Treasa caught her arm to steady her.

"Are you unwell?" Treasa whispered in her ear.

"I am well," she whispered back. "I only felt a sense of evil in this one."

"Then we will watch him." Treasa shot Circenn a menacing look and motioned for two more of her warriors to guard each side of Maecha.

Ignoring the exchange, Cruithne said, "Come, you must be hungry." Again, he took Maecha by the elbow and led her to a table.

They were treated as guests and ate well. After they had their fill, Cruithne raised his drinking horn and all were silent.

"I have a story to tell, which will explain why you are here."

191

Maecha and the others settled down in front of a blazing fire. She was glad that they would finally hear the cause of her father's kidnapping.

Cruithne began, "There is a village along the western sea that is under my protection. Two harvests have passed since, but many women, children, and older men were fishing to stock enough food to make it through the winter. The highlands are brutal during the winter months and, as you know, preparations are essential. It was a clear day, and the wind whipped off the sea and snapped at their heads. But still they worked hard. My wife and only daughter were among them. My wife had always helped with the labor, as well as the festivities of our people and enjoyed being among them. She was the matriarch and her lineage would rule through our daughter, Muiren.

"They heard a horn blow and were taken aback, since the sound came from the sea. A vessel appeared and warriors jumped onto our land with a death vengeance. They screamed and sliced, destroyed and desecrated. Adults and children were hacked to pieces, mutilated and left to die in their own excrement." Cruithne turned away gasping to maintain control. He grabbed his forehead and squeezed. One of his sons touched his shoulder, but he shook him off. All were silent now, knowing that the king's story was for their benefit as well as their guests. It was important never to forget what your enemy can take away from you when you let your guard down.

"It was your men, warriors from your Eire, who killed them. You may ask, 'How does he know this if everyone was dead?' I will tell you. My wife, my lovely Brogna, managed to get away with a deep sword wound. She rode her horse as hard as she could back to our dwelling, and then fell into my arms. I immediately organized an attack, but it was too late. The vessel was already gone." Cruithne grabbed Cormac by his tunic and yanked him up. Maecha stood, hand on her sword. Fidach and his brothers did the same. They each contemplated the other as the king continued. He spat. "Even my daughter, my precious Muiren, was dead. Dead!" He shoved Cormac away and, although he could barely manage it, he stood there waiting to hear the rest. "I begged my wife to tell me who did this, so I could take my vengeance. All she could do was hand me this."

He pulled a brooch out of his tunic and held it out in the palm of his hand. Cormac stared in the Picti king's pain stricken eyes and thought of his own children. He thought of Deirdre and how even losing her through childbirth was horrific; he couldn't even begin to understand this man's pain. Cormac switched his gaze to the brooch and his fingers, working on their own accord, picked it up. It was the brooch of Tara, made of sterling silver, with interlocking knots that encircled the green stone in the center. Cormac had given it to Cairpre as a present upon becoming a warrior, but Cairpre had claimed he had lost it. It was not possible! Cairpre could not have gathered a force of men, no less a vessel, to carry him across the sea to kill people for no reason. The Picts and the Irish had been raiding each other's lands for years, but only for a few cows and pieces of silver, never to the extent that Cruithne had just spoken.

Cormac started to speak, but the Picti king was not done.

"I buried my family, friends, too many to count. We had to wait until the land thawed to take our revenge, and I ended up losing another child, my eldest son."

Cormac moved forward and put his hand on Cruithne's shoulder and held up the brooch. He spoke softly so that only a few could hear. "This is my brooch." He felt the man's body tense and only squeezed his shoulder harder. "I gave it to my son, Cairpre, as a gift for becoming a warrior. I gave it to him, because I was proud and he had worked hard to gain the respect of the other warriors and, because since his birth, he was blemished with a limp that caused him much hardship. My heart bleeds for you, but I must tell you that I have never, ever sent a fleet of my men here, and I would never in my life allow them to kill innocent people. When we face fellow warriors, then it is only right that the bravest and stronger fighter wins. There is honor in that. But I beseech you to believe me that I would not strike down your loved ones in this manner."

He looked down at the brooch and tears stung his eyes. "I also want to tell you that my son would never do this, but I cannot. I only know that he would not have the man power or the means to travel here. But alas, long ago he turned from our Mother Goddess and the ways of sovereignty, and I cannot say what that has done to his soul or what he has found to replace her."

Cruithne was taken aback by the man's admission to owning the brooch and his denial of the attack. The sympathy displayed in Cormac's eyes surprised Cruithne, but he deserved to be treated as he had. Cruithne had to remember that he was a hostage to them, brought for a specific purpose. Cruithne's eyes shifted to Maecha. "Now you know of the loss of our matriarchal line through the death of my wife and daughter. Although my sons would rule with power, my eldest son is in need of a woman who is both warrior and nurturer. A woman who will bear his children and fight to the death to defend them."

Maecha felt a chill run down her arms and she noted her father's confusion.

"I cannot prove whether you were personally responsible for the death of my loved ones, Cormac. But by your own admission, this brooch belongs to your son and it was found on our land in the midst of the desecration."

Osgar Conchobar stepped forward and spoke to Cormac. "By your leave, my king, may I speak?"

Noting Cruithne's acquiescence, Cormac nodded. Osgar motioned for Cormac to sit and he did, not able to stand any longer.

Osgar lifted his wide shoulders up and back to his full six feet. His silver hair glistened in the morning sun. Eyes the color of a clear sky captured even his enemies' attention. He spoke with the voice of a bard. "We were in the midst of our Beltane celebration. Women and children were enjoying the festivities; young lovers were enjoying each other. The food was abundant, the sky clear, and the weather warm. I remembered the first blast from the horn and was astonished to see a wave of blue upon the horizon. Even on a day of peace I had my sword close by, and so I grabbed it, wondering what the aberration was that would dare invade our sacred day. As the wave flowed closer, I saw Picts covered in blue woad, their bare bodies shimmering in the sunlight. Hair bleached yellow struck out in all directions like the sun. One man stepped forward. I remember him well. Broad of shoulder, thick arms." Osgar's regarded Cruithne's arms. "Much like your own. He wore one of the most fascinating helmets I had ever seen. On top were the tusks of a boar, its tail flowing down his back. All I could see of this warrior were his black eyes and angry mouth. When King Cormac asked him to leave and not enter our sacred ground, he spat, raised his sword and ran at him. Our warriors defended our loved ones and our land, and many died on both sides. Many women and children were cut down trying to get away. The fighting continued, for the enemy was skilled and hungry. The man in the helmet was a mighty adversary. A brave and powerful warrior, but he tired and the king took advantage of this, removing his head from his body. All those left alive scattered and we let them leave, because enough senseless blood had been shed."

Ce rushed forward, shoved Osgar out of the way, and placed a dagger at Cormac's throat. "You all lie!" he screamed. "Let me kill him, Father! For Fíb! We must have vengeance, and then we can take their land and kill as they did to us."

Cormac laughed. "You already have. Your men attacked me and my Fianna while we were on a hunting expedition. You slew my champion and dear friend, Fionn mac Cumhail, and killed more than half of my elite fighting group, the Fianna. It was almost as if you knew how they fought and what we would be doing."

Ce retorted by pushing the dagger deeper. Blood trickled down Cormac's throat.

"Enough," Cruithne yelled. "There will no killing today. I have brought him here to ensure that we are not attacked again and to negotiate a union and truce. Although in truth, it was your daughter that was supposed to be taken." Ignoring Cormac's attempt to interrupt, he said, "But it seems to me that there is more going on than either one of us realizes. Release him, Ce."

Ce did and Cormac wiped the blood from his throat.

"This is my demand for your release—the union between your daughter, Maecha, and my son, Fidach. Then you and your warriors will be free to return home. We will no longer have need for bloodshed for our lines will be united."

The cheer from the Picti was deafening. Maecha's anger at her father's treatment was replaced by shock. Her face paled. For the first time she was glad that Kelan was not here with them. He would have torn the king's tongue from his mouth for making such a request.

"I can appreciate your need to continue your matriarchal line, but I cannot fill that role, for I am bound to another and am next in line to rule Eire," Maecha said over the roaring approval.

Cruithne looked around for the man. He did not see anyone step forth. "And where is this man?"

"He was called to protect the Lord and Princess of the Otherworld. He is honor bound to protect them. The Awen Crystal that I wear around my neck is our connection to the Otherworld and each other. He was summoned in this manner. The glow of our crystals represents our connection and love."

Cruithne didn't know what to think about this story. He turned to Cormac. "Have you given your daughter to this man she speaks of?"

"Under the rights of matriarchy, it is the Goddess's choice

as well as Maecha's. They have had a special bond for most of their lives, and their union has been blessed by the Mother Goddess."

Cruithne had come too far and would not let anyone thwart his plans to continue a strong line of warriors. Since she was touched by the Goddess, her line would be even more valuable.

Cruithne blew out a breath. "It may be that you and the man you speak of have a relationship, but he is not here to speak for you. Thus you and my son will join together." Cruithne motioned to his guards and they grabbed Cormac. Osgar unsheathed his sword, but the guards already had a dagger to Cormac's throat.

Maecha withdrew Imbas Skye and raised it toward the men who held her father. A blue ray shot from the eye and the man dropped his dagger. Both sides unsheathed their swords.

"By the light of the Mother Goddess, halt!" called Fidach.

Everyone turned to the son pledged to Maecha. He looked as confused and angry as she did. It was obvious to her that he had not known of his father's plan.

"We have shed enough blood on both sides to last many lifetimes. There must not be anymore." He turned to his father. "Father, I understand what you feel you need to do, but you cannot expect us to join, in any manner, if you continue to treat them as our enemy. A union that will strengthen our matriarchal line must be done in love, not with anger and threats. They must be here as our guests so that a decision can be made."

Pride showed in the king's eyes. He said, "Put your weapons away! You speak true, my son, and I am shamed that you were able to see what I could not. I am too filled with anger and the need for revenge to think clearly." He turned to Cormac and helped him stand. "You and your people are our guests, but I strongly advise you to consider this union as a form of retribution for the grievances that have been done to my people."

"What of my people?" Cormac said. "What retribution are you prepared to pay?"

"Peace to begin with. Look at them! They would make fine children for us to enjoy!"

Maecha's face reddened in embarrassment and rage. She wasn't sure which one was the stronger emotion. She was glad that Fidach at least felt the same.

Queen Treasa stepped up to Cormac and bowed. "With your permission, King Cormac, may I make a suggestion?" She stood and batted her luminous green eyes at the other king.

Cormac spoke to Cruithne, "May I present to you, Queen Treasa of Roscommon."

Treasa bowed and the king took her hand and kissed it.

"It is a pleasure, my queen. What have you to say?" Cruithne asked, all traces of anger and hatred gone from his face, as he admired her beauty and grace.

She stepped between the two kings and linked her arms with theirs. "Since we are here as guests," she said smiling demurely up at Cruithne. "Perhaps we should give the young man and Maecha some time to get to know one another. Then they can decide if they wish to be united. As your son so beautifully said, a union of love is a stronger bond than a forced one. You want children born of love, not obligation." Treasa winked at Maecha.

Cormac and Cruithne eyed one other and nodded. Treasa moved away and said, "If you both agree, then we can give Fidach and Maecha a sennight to get to know one another and make a decision. That will also give you both time to learn more about the attacks on one another's lands, to see if there isn't another enemy working to destroy any alliance you may make."

Maecha could feel her father's eyes on her. She closed her own, hoping to get some connection to Kelan. She couldn't even sense him. It was like a black void filled part of her body, threatening to suffocate her heart. If she didn't agree to these

198

terms, then it was very possible they would fight. That certainly was a good choice in her way of thinking. But if she was seen as giving Fidach a chance to get to know her and it didn't work out, then they could come to a peaceful understanding. Maecha opened her eyes and peered at her father. He definitely could not survive a battle. She nodded her agreement.

"I accept this plan. We are bound by honor to wait a sennight. No decisions will be made and they will be chaperoned at all times." Cormac stared at Fidach, and said, "Is that clear?"

Fidach gave him a slight bow.

Then Cormac said to Cruithne, "I believe that there is something we are overlooking concerning these attacks, and would like to discuss them further with you."

Cruithne nodded. "Then it is set. You two will spend as much time together as possible to get to know one another. It grows late, so let us rest for tomorrow promises to be an eventful day," Cruithne said.

Cormac and his retinue were allowed to venture to their *brochs* on their own. There was no way they could escape anyway, and they needed to get some sleep.

Circenn watched the group leave. He had hoped that the king would die from the poisoned weapon he personally injured him with. His hand had itched to grab his sword and kill them all. But there would be time. Once his brother started wooing the woman, he would be able to get closer. He had decided to ignore Cairpre's message to let the king and his daughter live so they could travel to Eire. Circenn wanted the glory and when he showed the Fire Lord how worthy he was, then he would be granted the power that Cairpre craved so much and their precious Eire.

At Cormac's request, Osgar informed the leaders that they were to convene in Cormac's *broch*. Warriors, druids, and bards usually lived in these dwellings. About thirty feet in diameter, there were three to four levels with small cells for sleeping and storage. The first floor was meant for a gathering area with stone slabs set in a circle for sitting. Cormac and Osgar sat on these slabs and waited for the others. His body was racked by coughing and his face was flushed.

"What can I get you, my friend?" Osgar asked.

"Some wine is all that stops this wretched cough," Cormac said.

As Osgar handed him a mug full of wine, he said, "My daughter is said to be something of a healer among the Amazons. Perhaps she can concoct a potion for you."

Just as he finished those words, Uatach entered. She bowed to the king and her father. She stepped toward Cormac and handed him a small goblet. "Drink this. It will settle the illness in your chest."

Osgar smiled and laughed. "You see? She was already thinking of a cure. Thank you, Uatach."

Uatach smiled and sat near her father. Everyone else arrived.

Cormac drank the tonic and said between coughs, "Explain, Treasa."

Treasa stood with a hand on her hip. "Agreeing with the king is the only way to get us out of this place without a great deal of bloodshed. Although he appears to be respectful toward your rank, he is very bitter and is looking for a solution to save his lineage. That doesn't mean that Maecha is the answer, I assure you. However, by agreeing to his terms, you are showing your sympathy to his cause. Then at the end of the sennight, when neither of these youngsters are anywhere near being in love, the king will have to let you go. He's already warming up to you by wanting to discuss the attacks further."

There was silence while everyone thought about Treasa's logic.

"What if young Fidach actually falls for Maecha and wants her as his own?" Goll asked.

"Maecha will have to make sure that she gives him no reason to like her," Treasa said.

"What do you expect me to do?" Maecha asked.

"Offer little information about yourself to him. Be friendly enough so that the king knows you are trying, but don't offer any reasons for him to love you," Treasa offered. "I think it could work."

Everyone agreed and Maecha did also, but her gut was telling her that something wasn't right. She would follow the plan for now. Guilt wracked her as she tried in vain to contact Kelan. He had to understand the need for this ploy once she told him. Maybe it was a blessing in disguise that she couldn't contact him. Feeling a cramp in her gut, Maecha reached for some wine.

Treasa trapped her hand and studied her. "What ails you, Maecha?"

Maecha replied in jest, "Besides the fact that I need to pretend I am interested in another man?"

"Yes," Treasa said.

"My stomach is all," Maecha answered and sipped her wine.

Chapter 22 - Eire

The Fire Lord smacked his lips after tasting the chunks of meat that had been forbidden to him for so long. Hot juice tickled his tongue, and he licked his fingers once he had devoured the boar he had killed. His appetite had been insatiable, since his body was restored, and he savored every morsel he could get his hands on. He watched the scene unfold in front of him and actually giggled. "I already feel your bond weakening, my fine, delectable Maecha. You will find yourself enchanted with the Picti warrior and I will make sure that the chaperone disappears. Then it will be you and I who will conceive the child of prophecy." Akir had managed to block Kelan and Maecha's connection using the main Awen Crystal. It was turning out to be quite useful. Next, he would work on Cruithne to make sure that he encouraged his son's quaint union, although he didn't think he would have to work too hard in that area.

Akir stood and stretched his lithe body. It felt so good to be whole again. He removed his cloak and walked closer to the edge of the cliff where he had been enjoying his visual entertainment. The sun had barely showed its face since Akir had visited his mother. Dark, angry clouds hovered low over the cliffs. It was just as well. She probably couldn't handle what he planned to do to her beloved. Perhaps he should have just killed her, but seeing the hatred in her eyes was enough satisfaction for now. She would die anyway after he destroyed his father. "Yes, Mother," he growled. "It sure has been hard for you and I will not give you the pleasure of being with your love."

Akir's body shifted. It elongated and his skin smoothed. He fell into the water as a predatory shark searching for its special prey. Letting the flow of the ocean currents pull him deeper into the water, Akir arrived at his father's domain. Swarms of life swam around. Akir shot toward the bottom of the sea turning into a slippery eel.

He entered Manannán's realm and transferred back into the powerful god who now had the means to destroy his father. That knowledge brought a crooked grin to his face.

"Are you that happy to see me?" Manannán asked from across the sea foam blue floor.

Akir zoomed in on his father and his smile disappeared.

Manannán laughed. "Well, I guess not."

"Greetings, Father. I am extremely pleased to see you, but not for the reason you may think."

With a casual air, Akir strode closer to his father, displaying feigned interest in the clear walls that brought the beauty and strangeness of the deep ocean right into the sea god's living space.

"Oh, I know the only reason you would be here."

Manannán stepped out from behind the half wall. His blue cloak shifted like the current. Cobalt eyes bored into his son's—the friendly demeanor gone. He held the trident of the sea, his ownership to power.

Out of habit, Akir shifted with nervous tension. He shook his head realizing that even after two hundred years, he still feared his father. Akir stretched his body to its full height, which still left him a head shorter, but that didn't matter. He touched the Awen Crystal and watched his father's eyes dart to it.

Slightly annoyed that his father hadn't showed any fear like his mother had, Akir accessed its power. "Mother sends her regards."

Manannán's face darkened. "Be careful, Akir."

"Your time is over. You must pay for all the misdeeds you

203

have done to me."

Manannán laughed, but it sounded bitter. "You are such a confused young man. You still do not take any responsibility for your actions." He raised his hand in exasperation. "You could kill a man right in front of me and then deny it."

"I have nothing to be responsible for!"

"Do you deny killing your cousin?"

"I did not kill my cousin."

"Maybe not directly by your own hand, but it was through your manipulation that it occurred."

"I am not responsible for how people act. I am the product of my parent's negligence," Akir said in a haughty tone.

The air around Manannán bubbled with his fury. "I will hear no more of your excuses. You are a man now and are responsible for your actions. And what do you do the moment you are able, you escape from your exile and cause destruction. Have you learned nothing?"

Akir's eyes flared and his brows furrowed together. His sand colored hair erupted into reddish, blue flames, while his hands transformed into blue blades of fire. Further angered by his father's nonchalant reaction to his power, Akir jumped through the air and swung his fiery blades toward his father's head. Manannán shifted out of its path like a change in the currents.

The son of the sea god growled and struck toward Manannán's feet, but he wasn't there. Akir stood and found his father simply watching him like he was a new species in his vast ocean world.

Anger, frustration, and blood curdling rage filled Akir, until he was like a volcano erupting after two hundred years of dormancy. He bellowed and fire spewed from his mouth. Just as it was about to burn him to ashes, Manannán lifted his trident. Water flowed like a broken dam toward the flames and it was snuffed out as quickly as it started. Akir gagged on the sudden ingestion of water and shut his mouth. He was knocked back from the torrent.

A large wave lifted Akir and he was thrust from the sea god's domain. The waves spit him out like a dead fish and dropped him on the rocky cliffs. Akir coughed, forcing air back into his lungs. Once he knew he could breathe, he grabbed at his throat making sure he still had the crystal. It was intact and so he laughed. Akir sat on the ground.

"Fool! You should have taken it while you had the chance. Once I get my sword, I'll come back and you'll be powerless to stop me!"

Angry at his defeat, he shot flames at the seagulls that flew around him. Their screeching halted as their ashes were carried away in the wind. Akir went in search of some people to fry since the birds weren't very satisfying. Then he would concentrate on making sure that weak man, Cairpre, would not mess up his plans to get the sword. He would need his full power to destroy his parents. Nothing else mattered more.

Manannán watched his son from the back of Enbarr. He knew his child was forever lost to him. His banishment had only embittered him more. Now it was time for the gods to finish him all together. Manannán gazed up at the sky. The sun was hidden behind thickened clouds.

"Aiménd," Manannán whispered.

She remained hidden from him, walking in what he knew was a mother's pain and guilt for thinking she hadn't done enough for her child. The first drops of rain hit Manannán in the face. He felt his love's pain, her tears, and shared her loneliness. Overcome by his own despair, the sea god sank down into his watery realm to figure out a way to stop his son before many more lives were killed.

Kelan appeared in the woods outside the hut where he and

Maecha had begun their journey in the Otherworld. He gave his head a chance to settle after the mind-boggling travel through the portal. The land was silent except for the trickle of the water rolling over rocks into the river that ran along this realm.

Touching his Awen Crystal, Kelan closed his eyes and searched for his soul—for Maecha. She was his soul—or at least a major part of it. It was impossible to know where his ended and hers began—their lives, hearts, and spirits had become so entwined.

Suddenly, he saw Maecha sailing across the water toward her destiny, toward her father. Kelan felt pride and love knowing that she would succeed. It made him feel better for having to leave her.

He hadn't been away from Maecha for more than a day since he was fifteen summers, and he had finally decided to stay with her family for good. He had lived with Cormac and his family since he was twelve. Kelan remembered the despair and anger he felt when he had awakened at King Cormac's *rath* and not at his home or the Otherworld. He should have died with his family. They told him that some warriors found him in the reeds at the edge of the river. He had been injured, but Kelan would have preferred to have been left to die. And he would have died long after if it hadn't been for Maecha.

Every day she brought food to him and either fed him directly or stayed there until he ate every last bite. Kelan chuckled. Maecha had been a scrawny thing at ten summers. Her long locks overcrowded her small face. But behind the tiny body and face was a smart and determined girl who would not stop bugging him until he was well.

At first it had only been food that she gave him, but then she started talking to him, telling him about how she was going to be a great warrior. She often skipped out on her lessons to watch the warriors train. Luckily, she caught on quickly, so no one was the wiser. But the heir to the sovereign of Tara had to be a strong fighter, a fair and equal leader, as well as learned in all the aspects of ruling a kingdom.

She had appealed to the warrior in him and they had developed a mutual friendship. Maecha would come in after her training to show him the bruises she acquired during fighting. She would also bring her sword, which was way too big for her, and demonstrate what she learned. Half the time, she would come close to slicing through the torches on the wall or stabbing her own leg.

Kelan had become irritated by the incompetency that she showed and couldn't believe that the great warriors of Tara would allow such horrid instruction to occur with the king's daughter. Thinking that Maecha didn't know, Kelan began to strengthen his muscles and gain the flexibility and strength he used to have. He was a young warrior, but had started when he was only six and had proven to be very adept at it.

Maecha had forgotten a sword in his room, which he had eventually learned was on purpose. Kelan honed his skills until he was quicker and more accurate than before. He had vowed that no one would ever take him or someone he loved by surprise again. On the day that Kelan liked to call 'coming home' Maecha had run into his bedroom very excited.

"Kelan!" she had exclaimed. "You will never guess what weapon I have learned to use!"

Kelan had been sitting up in bed and feigned slight interest. Maecha had hefted an axe whose handle was longer than her torso. Her skinny body, toned from all her training, almost buckled under its weight.

"Simeon said that this would be the appropriate weapon for me in battle."

She struggled to place it on her shoulder and had tried not to grimace at the weight. She had asked if he agreed.

Kelan's mouth had opened and then he had swung the blanket off his legs and flew out of bed. "No! I do not agree!

What kind of warrior does Tara train anyhow?"

Maecha's eyes had widened in innocent surprise. "What do you mean?"

"What do I . . . ?" Kelan had begun to say and then approached her. "Swing the axe at me."

"Oh no, I could not."

"Maecha, I am well." He had pounded on his chest to prove it. "I'm healthy as a horse."

"But it would not be fair. You have not trained for months."

Kelan had picked up the sword he had been training with. "Let me worry about that. Now swing the axe."

Maecha had shrugged and heaved the axe off her shoulder toward Kelan. She had been too far away to do any damage and the weight of the axe forced her body forward. Kelan had swiped the axe away from his body with the side of the blade and Maecha fell to the ground.

Kelan had immediately knelt down next to her to ask if she was all right.

Maecha had laughed and had thrown her arms around him. "You're back. I'm so glad."

Kelan remembered the wicked gleam in her eyes. "Did you plan this?"

"Me? Of course not, but I did think it would be helpful to have someone closer to my age to train with."

Kelan had eyed her warily, but realized that it was the first time since…well, in a while that he felt like smiling.

"Well then," Kelan had said, pulling her up. "I think it is time someone really taught you how to wield that sword."

Kelan shook the memories from his mind. Thinking of the time he had last been away from Maecha would have to wait.

Chapter 23 - Eire

In the soft grass under the oak tree, Finnius sat facing Natalie. His face was thinner and pale, but he trained her relentlessly during the short time they had left together. Today was the culmination of all their training and the third Cauldron of Wisdom was upright. Natalie had mastered them all in less time than the strongest druid ever had. He had taught her all he knew, and now it was up to her to transform it into her own power and magic.

Natalie watched Finnius like a hawk, which was appropriate, taking in every nuance and movement that he made. She felt him fighting to stay with her in the dreamworld. She wanted him to stay forever, but dared not tell him. When she asked if she could transport herself to him in the 'real' world, he told her it wasn't time.

"Concentrate," she heard him say and opened her eyes. He had his hands up with his palms facing her. She lifted her hands and placed them to his palms. She felt the warmth build until their hands were sweaty. Then they slowly moved their hands away from each other and she could see the brilliant blue light emanating between them. They moved their hands further back until a person could have fit between them. Natalie chanced a look at Finnius and he held her gaze. She smiled at him and was treated with a rare smile. Her energy never wavered and she felt a shift. More of it was coming her way.

"What are you doing?" she asked Finnius.

He kept smiling and she felt his power, his energy

channeling into her. She couldn't do anything about it.

"Finnius, no. You need your magic, your strength."

She tried to pull away, but he wouldn't let her.

Tears filled her eyes. His sparkled. "You have great power and you have the tools you need for now. Never use it for your own gain or for the evil in others. I am proud of you, Daughter."

With a burst of energy, she fell backwards. When she straightened, he was already fading.

"Father!" she called, but he was gone. The eagle circled as if waiting, but it too disappeared. Natalie began to cry, but stopped when she heard his voice in her head.

"Do not cry, child, for we will see one another again. Follow the wolf and she will bring you to me."

Through tear-streaked eyes, Natalie searched for the wolf she had grown used to watching them. Each time Finnius was around her, the wolf had become braver. She found it sitting on the grass a little farther from the woods, but still close enough where it could escape if needed. Its familiar and comforting eyes watched her. She stood and embraced her power, embraced her destiny—if only to see her father again and to tell him how much she loved him. She walked toward the wolf and it waited.

Cairpre sent out envoys to the other four forths. They were to convene at Tara for the Beltane celebration. Weeks, then months had gone by without a word and it was during the first signs of spring that Cairpre feared they might not come at all. The whole purpose of this gathering was to declare supremacy over everyone. How could he do that when no one was there?

The sound of boots on the stone floor caught his attention and he turned, prepared to take his anger out on the poor soul who dared to interrupt him.

"What is it?" he asked the man named Cedric.

Cedric, a powerfully built warrior, couldn't face Cairpre. "My lo—uh, my king."

"Yes, what do you want?" Cairpre spat.

"We have word from the villagers and the farmers. Due to the heavy losses that they incurred over the winter, they cannot afford to send any of their livestock for the Beltane celebration."

Cairpre's ragged eyes darkened. "Go on."

"Uh, they also say that the land is dead. Any seeds they saved over the winter have gone bad, and milk has soured."

The man licked his lips and looked around the room for someone to save him.

Cairpre stood, flinging his chair behind him. "Out with it or I'll remove your tongue!"

"There is a rumor that pestilence is spreading across the land. At least a score of children and old folks have died. People say," he hesitated, took a deep breath, and got it over with. "People say that because your kingship is not accepted by the Mother Goddess, she is punishing us."

There was nothing to throw and it wouldn't be worth killing his man to make him feel better. He slammed both his hands on the table. "The cursed Mother Goddess does not control the land. These people who refuse to take care of their livestock or the land are the ones in control of it. Curse them all!"

"What would you like me to do? Shall I burn their houses again?"

Cairpre stared at the man. "No, do nothing. Just leave."

With a quick bow he was out the door.

What was he to do? The surrounding forths didn't recognize him as king and his own people disrespected him. What would his father do? "Ah," he said, disgusted that he would even think of his father at a time like this. But then he realized that his father had never had to deal with resistance and disrespect. Everyone loved him, the crops and livestock were abundant, the rivers flowed, and people did as they were supposed to do. King Cormac was a beloved king. He bestowed fair law upon the land so that justice and peace had prevailed.

Once again, Cairpre set out toward his trusted woods, away from the glares and whispers of those around him. Even his own men spoke poorly of him when they thought he wasn't listening. Without Althar or any major display of power, he was back where he had started. Damn the Fire Lord and damn his family. He wanted power and respect for himself, but it never came.

He jumped off his horse and yelled up into the trees. Birds flew out of their nests and he sneered. At least something feared him.

"Why must people fear you?"

Cairpre whirled around at the voice.

"Who are you and why do you bother me?"

"It would seem that you are in need of someone to talk to, my son."

"Your son? I am no one's son."

A vision in white floated toward him. She hovered just above the ground and Cairpre was struck by her ethereal beauty.

She smiled. "You are my son, Cairpre. You came from my womb. Now I ask again why you must always rule through fear and let anger taint your decisions?"

"I am not angry!"

"Oh no? Then answer my question."

"Because that is the only way people will respect you— I mean me. People don't respect me like they respected Father, because I have this cursed limp and now my eyes are damaged. Do you see my ruined eyes? It was your daughter who did this to me, and I will have my revenge on her and anyone else who ever disrespected me."

"As I recall, *you* attacked your sister. Our land is ruled by the Mother Goddess, Cairpre. You do not have the respect of your people because you do not respect their beliefs. You rule for power when you must rule for your people."

Cairpre eyed his mother as she floated closer and laughed. He must be finally losing his mind. Anger filled him. "Like my father? He ruled for his people and now he's probably dead. Did the people try to help him? No. I'd rather have the power. Now go away, I need my solitude."

Deirdre bowed her head and started to disappear. "I love you, my son, and I regret each moment that I am not with you or our family."

Cairpre's eyes stung. "You are just saying that. You would have scoffed at me just like everyone else did!"

Deirdre reached out her hand and Cairpre felt a light brush along his cheek. He swiped it away and was surprised to feel tears running down his face. It angered him all over again. He searched for the woman who had abandoned him, but she was gone.

"Fire Lord!" Cairpre screamed flailing his hands toward the canopy of trees.

Akir appeared, sitting on a bough of a tree, eating a bright red apple. Cairpre stared at the perfectly groomed young man.

"Fire Lord?" he asked in hesitation.

"Yes, you did call, didn't you? I know I look quite dashing. I am free from my confines so now I may roam the earth, sky, and sea as I please."

Somehow having the Fire Lord contained in the depths of the Otherworld had made Cairpre's pact with the god seem less real. Now he was face to face with him in his own realm and it unnerved him.

"Well? What do you want? I'm a busy man. I have gods to punish."

Cairpre recovered. "I need more power. My people will not listen and no one will pledge their fealty to me. I must show them that I am a powerful ruler."

Akir laughed and Cairpre felt his face redden.

"All you think about is power and how much more you

213

can get. What will happen when I give you more power, more magic, and the people still resist?"

"That won't happen. They will have to listen to me."

"Fine, have it your way. Kill them for all I care."

"I don't want to kill them, but I must have control if my father and sister come back. With Maecha's sword, I will break this matriarchal sovereignty and all of Tara will be mine." Cairpre cringed at his own confession. He hadn't meant to tell the Fire Lord his true intentions.

Akir lifted a brow and rubbed his chin. He had underestimated this man. So, he wanted the sword, did he? Akir would let him think he would get it.

"You want Imbas Skye, do you? Well, I do know that your father and sister still live. Apparently, the young warrior you said would be effective in carrying out their deaths has not quite succeeded. If they make it back here, then you may try to take the sword from your sister, but you have to be the one to mortally wound her. Do you think you can do that?"

Cairpre still cursed himself for letting the god know of his plans, but when he seemed quite willing to help, ambition and greed gleamed in Cairpre's eyes. With that sword, the villagers would have to respect him.

"I can do that."

"Have a taste of some more power, but do not fail me if your family comes home. I want every one of them killed."

Akir waved his hands in front of his face and Cairpre felt a slow burn flow through his veins. As it traveled through him, a part of his soul disappeared. His eyes glazed over.

"Use your power wisely, Cairpre. It will flow from you easily now."

Cairpre bowed and spoke softly, his eyes never leaving the Fire Lord's. "What do you wish me to do with the druid?"

"Yes, the druid. He is of no use to me anymore. I am free

and apparently he has diminished his power beyond redemption. I personally won't gain anything from killing him myself. Do whatever you wish with him."

Chapter 24 - Alba

Fidach waited by his father. Maecha found her own father sitting quietly with Osgar. She knelt down and kissed his forehead.

"How are you feeling this morning, Father?"

"I am well." His tired gaze told her something different. She glanced at Osgar.

He only nodded and said, "Do what you have to do. I will watch over your father."

Cormac grumbled. "I do not need someone to watch over me, Osgar. Be careful or I will smite you where you sit."

"I am sure you can, my friend. I meant no disrespect."

Cormac let it go and addressed his daughter. "You are a beautiful young woman. Be careful of how easily that can influence a man. Goll will be your chaperone today."

Maecha nodded to Goll as he approached. She was nervous, but having Goll with her alleviated the anxiety building within her. She had always felt comfortable around men since she had spent most of her childhood learning to fight with them. But she had only been very close to Kelan and, even though her relationship with Fidach would not go beyond getting to know one another (or at least pretending to), she was unsure of herself.

For her father's sake, she pasted a smile on her face and walked over to them.

"Good morning, King Cruithne. Fidach."

Fidach swept into a low bow and greeted her.

"By your leave, Father, I plan to take Maecha on a tour of our *rath*. On horseback, if that would please you, Maecha."

"I would enjoy a good ride. It's been a while since I have been able to do so."

"I took the liberty of having your horse groomed and ready for you."

Maecha smiled in delight and hugged her horse, Finn, when it was led over to her. "That was very kind of you, Fidach. Thank you."

It was a clear day, which was a rare treat in Alba. All four seasons could be experienced in the expanse of one day. The air was crisp and Maecha tightened her cloak around her shoulders. They rode out of the *rath* at a gentle clip. Maecha savored the peacefulness and waved to people who stopped to let them go by. Soon the makeshift path out of Fidach's home turned into rocky paths. Maecha matched Fidach's increasing pace.

They raced along the moors and Fidach stopped when he neared the sea. Maecha followed suit and he helped her from her horse. Goll took Finn's reins and tethered the horses to a nearby tree to let them graze.

"I will sit here for a bit," Goll told her. He glared at Fidach. "Do not make me get up."

Fidach bowed in understanding and led Maecha toward a hill fort that had seen better days. The beams within it wore the scars of fire. No one was around and when they walked closer to the water, Maecha could see why. On the backside of the hill, where the dwelling once stood, were numerous graves. They were marked by simple crosses.

"This is where my mother and sister were when the boat came to destroy them." He pointed to a barren field. "They were working there in the fields at summer's end, picking the harvest for the coming winter. The warriors who came from the sea were ruthless."

Maecha put her hand on Fidach's arm and he placed his hand over it, leading her away from the graves toward the water.

"When we arrived, bodies floated in the water, broken

where they were cut down. If it weren't for the few dead enemies scattered here and there, we would have thought that the gods had struck them down. That is a hard burden to bear. It is difficult to carry on."

"But that is what you must do. Your line must continue and I understand that. I also understand the pain of losing someone before their time. My mother died giving birth to my brother. I barely have memories of her, but have been blessed with her presence in my dreams."

"Aye, my mother has come to me, but she is not peaceful. She worries about our line. I want her to find peace."

Fidach unrolled a blanket on the sand and took out a sack of dried meat and bread. He poured wine into two goblets and gave one to Maecha. "To friendship."

Maecha smiled. "Shouldn't it be to uniting us since that is what your father wants?"

"As I said, I will not marry only for the sake of a strong line. I know that it is necessary, but a strong line also must come from powerful love."

"You do not strike me as someone who would be so enchanted with love."

"Ah, but I am. If you could have seen my parents together, then you would never settle for anything less than absolute love."

"I was only three when my mother died, but I remember their love. How my father still talks of her tells me so much about their relationship. She was a beautiful woman. She's an even more beautiful spirit. I wished I could have grown up with her. My life would have been very different."

"Yes, it would have. You wouldn't be here, trying to pretend that you want to get to know me."

Maecha's eyes widened. "Oh, but I do want to get to know you. I just—"

"Don't want to marry me."

"I am pledged to Kelan and our union goes must deeper

218

than the physical. Our spirits are united. We are held by the rights of the Goddess to fulfill a prophecy that I am only just beginning to learn about. He is a part of me that I could not live without. And I love him."

Fidach smiled. "Now that is love. I think I could grow to love such an intense and passionate woman."

Maecha laughed at his description. "I have been known to be both at one time or another."

Fidach leaned closer and touched her cheek. "I am sure you have."

"You forget the rules, Fidach," Maecha said, pulling away from his touch.

"What if I want to change the rules? How do you know if Kelan is the right one for you? I assume that he is your first love."

Maecha blushed not sure how to handle the personal inquiries. Of course she knew that Kelan was the right one. How could there be another if the Mother Goddess had already blessed them? No other man could know her thoughts as Kelan did. But that was also because of the Awen Crystal.

"I see I have raised some doubts in your mind," he said taking her hand and kissing her palm.

"I do not have any doubts about my love for Kelan or his for me. We have known one another for many years. He is a wonderful man and warrior."

"He is barely a man, whereas I am more seasoned."

"He is twenty and one summers and a member of the Fianna." Maecha pulled her hand away and stood. "I would like to go back now."

"Is something wrong, Maecha?" Goll asked, appearing at her side, his hand on the hilt of his sword.

Maecha had forgotten that Goll was with them and she blushed at the thought of him hearing their conversation. "I only wish to return to see how my father fares."

They rode back in silence.

When they reached the stable, Fidach said, "I enjoyed our ride today, Maecha, and look forward to spending the evening with you. I hope I did not make you uncomfortable."

Maecha nodded, not trusting her voice. When Fidach left, Goll touched her arm. He searched her face and could see her distress. "If he offended you in any way, I'll remove his head."

Maecha smiled at her companion's ferocity. "I am fine."

"We can find another way."

Maecha sighed. "There is no other way."

As the sky darkened to welcome the night, Akir sat high on a rampart enjoying the vision. "Oh, sweet Maecha, how hard it is to stay in love when your loved one is gone. I shall make it even harder," Akir whispered. Before he cleared the vision hovering in his hands, he blew a kiss to a very unaware Maecha. The kiss would awaken a longing for Fidach that would not easily be extinguished.

Akir jumped up and spun around quite happy with the way all his plans were unwinding. He spotted a fair damsel walking by herself. Quite dangerous for a young lady, he mused. Straightening his tunic and cloak, Akir flew down to land in front of her. She was taken by surprise and, as fear shone in her deep blue eyes, Akir smiled.

"Let me escort you, my lady, for it is dangerous to be out alone at this time of night."

The young lady curtsied and thanked him as she wrapped her hand around his offered arm. She walked in silence as Akir whistled a happy tune. Yes, all would be well in the world once again and, after he enjoyed this lovely young thing, he would pop in on Maecha in person to speed events along.

Later that evening, Fidach visited with Osgar, who was pleased about his interest in the Isle of Imbas Skye. Any chance to talk of Scathach made the time away from her easier. When Maecha joined them, Fidach greeted Maecha with a warm smile.

"Where is your father?" he asked.

"He is not feeling well," Maecha said.

"Did he take the tonic I gave him?" Uatach asked joining her father.

"Yes, but he needs more."

"I will get it for him now."

"Then come join us for the dancing and festivities," Osgar said. He turned to Maecha and asked, "Are you well?"

Maecha realized she had been staring at Fidach in an absentminded manner and stepped back. "Uh, yes. Why do you ask?"

"Your cheeks are quite red. I hope you are not with fever."

"No, I was training. I think I will get some wine."

"I will accompany you," Fidach said, taking her arm and smiling down at her.

Maecha smiled back, feeling quite giddy.

Osgar noted the exchange and said, "Very well, I shall be here if you need me, Maecha. I am your chaperone tonight."

"Yes, thank you, Osgar," she said, without taking her eyes from Fidach.

Lively music started the festivities. Food and drink were abundant and people began to dance. Fidach took a sip of his mead and staggered. Osgar caught him. "What's ails you?"

Fidach shook his head and laughed. "I'm quite fine." He took Maecha's hand and asked. "Would you like to dance?"

Osgar was about to object, when Fidach pulled her along behind him and swung her into his arms. The Picti dance was primitive and wild. The dancers formed a circle around the large bonfire and spun to the music. Then each partner separated and joined another in a fast spin before continuing on to the next partner.

The music changed to one full of yearning and passion. A handsome musician joined the dancers while he accompanied the tune on his pipe. He circled around Maecha and then Fidach. Maecha watched the man smile seductively at her. Suddenly, the man disappeared and Maecha felt herself being pulled and spun all around the fire, losing track of who she was dancing with. She decided to stop fighting it and enjoy herself. On her next spin she found herself in Fidach's arms on the far side of the fire. He pulled her tight against his body and his black eyes flickered like the flames that rose behind him. His normally loving aura felt tainted, but Maecha didn't feel in control of her intuition and ignored it.

Fidach smiled at her and he looked dangerous and provocative, much more so than he did that morning.

"You seem different," she said as he held her tighter.

"I am different. I feel more alive when I am with you. Do you feel it, Maecha?"

She tried to pull away, but he wouldn't let her.

"Kelan."

"You don't want that barbarian. You want me," he said and kissed her.

Shock and an unexplained pleasure raced through her. Although she knew she should, she couldn't pull away. As the enchanting music continued, they were launched onto a sandy beach by the water. Fidach kissed Maecha with reckless abandon and begged her for more. Maecha wanted more, but something nudged at the back of her mind. She shouldn't be doing this, but couldn't remember why. She heard the music again and the doubts dissipated. Yes, she wanted this. Not knowing how she came to be where she was, she reached for Fidach, but his features were no longer that of the Picti heir. A seductively handsome man with sandy brown hair and fiery eyes gleamed at her.

"Who are you?" Maecha asked. He looked familiar and her mind knew she was in danger, but her body wouldn't react.

"I am everything you have ever wanted," Akir whispered to her.

Suddenly, the man was torn away from Maecha. They were back in front of the fire where they had been dancing. Goll and Caoilte grabbed Maecha as she fell to the ground. Osgar struck Fidach across his jaw and he dropped. He removed his sword and put it to Fidach's neck.

"Halt!" Cruithne yelled.

Osgar kept his eyes and sword on Fidach.

"What has happened?" Cruithne looked across the fire at Maecha's stricken face.

"Your son was kissing Maecha. Does his word have no honor?"

Fidach seemed to finally notice that there was a sword at his throat. He pushed it aside and Osgar let him stand. He noticed Maecha's distress and, as the fog in his mind cleared, he asked, "What did I do?"

His father clouted him on the head. "When we give our word, then that word is sacred! You swore not to touch Maecha and then you violate her for all to see!"

Fidach focused on Maecha, confusion clouding his eyes. Then a slight memory of what he had done came to him. "I am sorry, Father. I do not know what came over me." He knelt down next to Maecha. "I am sorry, my lady. I would never do anything to distress you. I will not bother you again this evening." He left the group.

Maecha wanted to answer, but all she could see and feel was the man touching her on the beach. May the goddess help her, but she wanted to be there again.

"Start the music!" Cruithne called.

"Let us go see the king," Osgar said and Cruithne went with him to apologize for his son's barbaric actions.

As everyone went back to their reveries, Akir handed the pipe back to the musician he had put to sleep only minutes ago. Kissing Maecha had been scrumptious. Oh, how he looked forward to doing it again. It wasn't fair to let Fidach have all the fun now was it. Unfortunately, the poor man didn't remember anything about it. But Akir did and she would be his. He disappeared to bide his time for the next step.

Maecha removed herself from the crowd, embarrassed by her untamed behavior. Treasa followed her into the *broch* at the request of Osgar. He felt she needed a female companion at this time.

"Drink this," Treasa said, handing Maecha some light wine.

Maecha sipped it, but it soured her stomach. "What is happening to me?"

"Can you tell me more about it?" Treasa asked sitting next to her friend.

"I felt like my body wasn't my own. I knew I shouldn't be doing it, but I didn't feel in control. Fidach felt different too and then suddenly we were on a beach and he wasn't Fidach anymore."

"What do you mean he wasn't Fidach? Who was he?"

"I don't know, but he was lovely and full of passion. He wanted to love me and may the goddess help me, Treasa, but I wanted to love him. How could I do that to Kelan?"

Treasa thought it over for a moment. She observed her friend and watched as Maecha placed the goblet next to her barely touched.

"Did you eat tonight?" Treasa asked her.

"No, my insides feel all knotted up and I have not had a good appetite. I fear all this turmoil over pretending to like Fidach is affecting me."

"Hmmm."

"What do you mean, hmmm?"

"Nothing, but you should try to eat light and more often. Perhaps that will help. But going back to the other matter, I feel

224

that we may be dealing with the Fire Lord once again. He did get into Kelan's mind. Maybe he is now able to get into yours. You have a strong bond with Kelan, but isn't it interesting that he's suddenly gone and you are feeling this way. There are more ways to fight than just with a sword, Maecha. You must beware."

Maecha agreed, but she thought that she had never faced a harder adversary and hoped that she could defend herself against the next attack.

It was hard for Maecha to fall asleep that night. Visions and images would float through her mind and, just as one was going to stay with her, she would jolt awake. It was in the early morning dawn when a vision hit her like a blacksmith's hammer.

Betrayal. Treachery. Death. Two faces familiar yet different souls. Good. Evil. Forest. Brothers.

Chapter 25 - Alba

"Circenn," a voice whispered next to his ear as he tossed in his bed.

Circenn opened his eyes, but only saw the pitch black of the night. "Yes," he whispered back.

"It is time to fulfill your duty to me."

"Fire Lord?"

"Yes, it is me. Bring the woman, Maecha, to the borders of your fellow tribe. I must have her sword."

"I will not fail you."

"See that you do not," the Fire Lord said and he was gone.

Wide awake, Circenn devised a plan that would get Maecha away from the others, especially his brother.

Fidach avoided Maecha during the first part of the next day. Maecha knew that he was embarrassed over his actions from the previous night but, if it was the Fire Lord's actions and not his, then he should know about it. Concerned for him, she sought him out.

She found him with his horses. "Fidach. May I have a word with you?"

"As you wish," he said, continuing to brush his stallion.

"Are you going to ignore me for the rest of our time together? We do need to make an effort at getting to know one another."

"I realize that. I'm afraid I am still confused about my actions last night."

"Confused?" Maecha asked. She knew that Fidach hadn't

been in control of his actions, but a part of her had hoped he enjoyed what he remembered.

Fidach realized the implication and sputtered, "That's not what I meant."

Maecha put her hand on the one that brushed the horse. She could feel his aura. It was a color blue like a clear summer day with the light of the sun warming it. Maecha closed her eyes so she could memorize the feeling. It could come in handy if Fidach attempted to kiss her again. Then she would know if he was in control. Opening her eyes, she asked, "What did you mean?"

He dropped the brush and took her hand. "You are beautiful and I enjoyed your company very much yesterday. But when I asked you to dance, I felt like I was watching us dance and not participating. It was like I was outside my body and someone else was being me."

"What else?"

He tried to look at her, but desire overwhelmed him. He let go of her hand and retrieved his brush. Better to have his hands on the horse, than on a king's daughter.

Maecha touched his arm. "Did you think you were by the water with me?"

Fidach's hand stilled. This time he did look at her. "Yes, we were on the sand and I wanted much more than I had a right to. But then I wasn't anywhere. We never left the dance floor. How can that be?"

Maecha tensed at his words. So he had been there for part of the time. She just didn't understand how the Fire Lord could take over a person's body.

"Is something wrong?" Fidach asked.

Maecha smiled. "I believe that an ex-god named the Fire Lord is toying with us. Somehow during this whole kidnapping of my father, he has become my enemy. He wants my sword, because he believes he can rule our world if he owns it. I think that he might be trying to get it by pretending to be you. We must be more careful when we are together."

Fidach laughed and touched her face. "I can't blame this god or whatever he is for wanting to be near you, and I'm jealous that he seems to have enjoyed himself more than me."

"Really, Fidach," Maecha exclaimed. "This is very serious. If he takes my sword, he can kill me and destroy all our lives."

"Understood. I will try to fight him as best I can, but I really don't know what to do."

"I don't either, but we must find a way. I know that your eyes and your whole demeanor were suddenly different last night, so I will watch for any changes. What do you have planned for today's activities?"

"We have planned a hunt for this afternoon and would like all of you to attend. Circenn has asked for a big gathering, so we shall need some bountiful meat."

"Is he always so pensive?"

"He has been for some months now. Of course he wasn't quite the same after my mother and sister died. He was very close to our sister. I think she made him feel special."

Maecha thought of Cairpre and felt a stab of guilt for not paying more attention to her brother. But her duties and caretaking of Kelan had taken priority. Maybe if she hadn't been so occupied, she would have seen all of this coming. Then she thought about the evil feeling she had about Circenn when she first met him. Maybe it was pain that she had felt. She would try to get to know him more. In that instant the images from her dream vision came back to her. Her heart leapt in her chest as she thought that Fidach was in danger. Would Circenn hurt his brother and why would he? Before her own brother's betrayal, she would never have thought it possible, but she knew better now. Maecha vowed to stay close to Fidach today and keep an even closer eye on his brother.

An hour later, a large hunting party prepared to set off

into the woods.

"Are you sure you don't want to come?" Osgar asked Uatach.

"Yes, I would like to gather more herbs and make some ointments for the king. He is improving, but not as much as I would like. I feel that something inside him is broken."

"I do not like you being here without us."

Caoilte overheard. "I would be more than happy to stay with your daughter, Osgar."

"Are you comfortable with this, Uatach?"

Uatach replied, "That would be suitable, Father."

Cormac wanted to ride with the group, although he couldn't pull a bow. Full, dark clouds threatened rain. They rode across the rolling fields until they reached the entrance to the forest, and then separated into smaller groups. Maecha rode with Treasa, Goll and Fidach.

Maecha had been relieved that Circenn would go with the other group, until he said, "Will you usurp Maecha's company yet again, Brother, or may I join you?"

Surprised by his easy manner, Fidach replied, "That is the purpose of my getting to know our lovely queen, but you may join us."

"No!" Maecha started and then recovered herself. "What I mean is that my father needs a guide and with both of you here he may get lost with the others."

Fidach smiled at her. "Ce can go with them," he started to say, but then changed his mind when he saw Maecha's fallen face. "But perhaps it would do some good for you to get to know Circenn more. I will accompany your father and we shall meet after the hunt."

"Thank you, Fidach. That is very kind of you," Maecha said, relieved that she had kept the brothers separated for now. Later she would have the opportunity to go back into her vision and find out more. They traveled deeper into the heart of Alba. The trees were still sparse from the beginnings of spring and they made their way easily. Circenn appeared to be very relaxed so Maecha wanted to have a conversation with him.

Before she could, Circenn reacted. "Did you hear that?" Circenn asked, looking toward his right.

"I hear nothing," Goll said.

"I heard the breaking of branches over that way. It could be the boar that has been irritating the farmers by killing their livestock."

Goll harrumphed thinking the lad was hearing ghosts, but said nothing.

"Perhaps you and Queen Treasa could branch off to the left and Maecha and I can scare it your way," Circenn suggested.

"Perhaps we should call the others," Maecha said.

"Let's try this first. I've traveled in these woods all my life. We won't get lost."

Circenn gave Maecha a rare smile and she didn't want to let him down.

"I do not like this," Goll said.

"We'll be fine, Goll. We won't go too far from one another and I'll call you if need be."

Maecha rode close to Circenn. A large branch broke in front of them and Circenn stopped her by placing his hand on her arm. Circenn's whole body resonated with a black glow that made her skin crawl. She wanted to believe that this boy was hurting from grief, but Maecha felt that she was riding toward danger. She knew that Fidach wasn't anywhere near them, but this didn't seem to have anything to do with that.

"Circenn, I'm turning back."

Before Circenn responded, Maecha heard a scream. It sounded like Treasa. Maecha saw Ce riding toward her. "Ce, is Treasa hurt?" A hard object hit her on the head. She fell forward.

"What are you doing, Circenn? Are you mad?" When

Circenn didn't answer, Ce brought his horse closer to Maecha and tried to lift her. The pain sliced through his middle. Shocked, he stared down at the protruding tip of the sword and knew the enemy behind him. He steered his horse and faced his baby brother. "Why?" he gasped.

Circenn's face twisted into an evil grimace. "Power, Brother. Power that won't fail like your strength just did. It will be mine. The Fire Lord will make it so."

Blood trickled out of Ce's mouth when he tried to answer. He slumped forward in his saddle. Circenn redirected the horse back toward the other party and slapped its rear. It took off.

Holding Maecha on her horse, Circenn trotted to the cave that the Fire Lord had shown him in his dream. He saw a fire glowing within the cave.

"Leave her there and go back. You know what to do," the Fire Lord said with his face in shadows.

"But they will not believe that we were attacked. I am not wounded."

A flash caught Circenn in the arm and he bled profusely. Shocked, he stared at the slash in his arm and then ran back the way he'd come.

He found the others fighting the men he had hired to attack them. He yelled in pain. "They took Maecha!"

"Where!?" Goll yelled.

Circenn pointed back the way he had come.

"Treasa!" Goll called.

Treasa finally caught up with him after killing two of their attackers.

"Maecha has been taken."

They rode hard down the path that Circenn had indicated, but couldn't find any evidence of Maecha.

"Maecha!" Treasa yelled.

Nothing.

Maecha opened her eyes to find someone removing her from her horse. It wasn't just someone. He was the most beautiful man she had ever seen and she remembered him from the beach. Where Kelan had a rugged, warrior look, this man was refined and elegant. His hair fell over his eyes as he steadied her. He held onto her arms and she felt trapped by the intensity of his gaze. Her head came to his chin and she marveled at the cleft in it.

"Are you all right, my lady?" he asked, his voice melodious and intoxicating.

Maecha shook her head.

"No?"

She gazed at him again and found she couldn't speak.

He brushed his lips across hers and Maecha felt her whole body slacken by the sheer sensuality of it. She knew she was in the arms of the same strange man, but she couldn't remember why it was a bad place to be.

"Yes, I am fine. I'm just a little shaken. I was hit on the head." She looked around her and saw that she was in an unfamiliar place. "Where am I? Where is Circenn?"

"Circenn? I do not know of whom you speak. I found you and brought you here. Please sit and drink. It will make you feel better."

"Did I see you the other night playing music?"

"Yes, I am a musician by trade."

"Your music was enchanting."

Maecha took the cup from him and instinctively reached out for Kelan.

Akir felt the Awen Crystal around his neck become warm. He touched it and a black mist covered Maecha's connection. She frowned. She had not been able to sense him since he had left and she felt vulnerable being so alone.

"Is anything amiss?" he asked, with amusement showing in his eyes.

"No, but I must find the others."

"In time, Maecha, in time."

She looked at him in alarm. "How do you know my name?"

"From the dance, of course. Who wouldn't know the lovely daughter of King Cormac? Plus, you did seem to be enjoying yourself with Fidach. He is a fine man."

Maecha blushed. "I…that was a mistake."

"It was with him."

"What do you mean?" Maecha asked feeling uncomfortable with his lingering gaze. She wished her head would clear. This man was dangerous and she needed to find Goll and Treasa.

He laughed, his face full of amusement now. "I know so much about you and that sword of yours."

Maecha felt for her sword and noted the man's greedy eyes upon it.

Maecha's blood ran cold. "Who are you?"

"I am Akir."

Akir. The name brought up a memory in the back of her mind, but she couldn't quite grasp it. Taking a deep breath, her vision cleared and she not only felt a negative energy pulsating off this man, but he was the danger that she had noted when following Circenn.

Akir smiled and with that glint of mischief in his eyes, Maecha remembered. Akir, the Fire Lord. He was the man on the beach. Her face reddened. "I need to find my friends," Maecha said. She walked toward the entrance of the cave, but a wall of fire blocked her way. "Let me go."

"I am sorry, but I cannot do that. You have something I want, well two things really," he said, raking her body with his eyes. Suddenly, he was directly behind her and yet she never saw him move. He touched her shoulders and she jumped away.

"Don't touch me."

"You wanted me to touch you before," Akir teased.

"I did not!"

Akir played with her hair. "Oh, but you did. You remember last night on the sandy beach? You wanted me more than that bullish warrior of yours. What you need is a refined man, Maecha. I could make you want me to touch you. I could make you do anything, but it is much more exciting if you decide to do it on your own."

"You created that vision of Fidach and me. It wasn't real." Maecha slapped his hand away. "Step away!"

"I love it when you get angry. I have been looking forward to having that angry pout of yours directed at me."

"What are you talking about?"

"I have been watching you for quite some time now. I see the games you play with your lover, Kelan, and now the handsome Fidach. Which one will you choose?"

He was toying with her, Maecha decided and she had enough of it. She stepped back and withdrew Imbas Skye.

"I demand that you let me go."

Akir's eyes flashed red as he took in the sword.

Maecha was afraid and her arms felt like jelly, but she stood her ground.

"Ah! The magical sword of the Isle of Imbas Skye. Do you know how long I have waited to behold it once again?" Akir asked. He licked his lips as if he was waiting to kiss a lover.

"Two hundred years and it'll be two hundred more if I can help it."

Violent hunger raged through Akir as he unsheathed his sword. The sword Akir held was shorter than hers, more like a broadsword. Its blade was very wide. Akir waved his left hand and they were in an open field with swirls of mists surrounding them.

They assessed one another. "Only one who fairly *or unfairly* takes the sword from you can be its rightful owner," Akir said. "It is my time to own the sword and the witch who destroyed my powers. I will own it and then I will own you." He smiled and struck.

Maecha was thrown off by the speed of his strikes and the pain that pierced her arm. At the next flash of light, Maecha deflected it. Then Akir attacked with his sword. They parried back and forth, blades of light becoming a blur as they matched one another.

Akir's eyes glowed in delight. "You fight as well as the warrior before you, maybe even better."

Maecha ignored his comment, not wanting to break her concentration. Akir shoved her back and held his hand up. "It is nothing personal, but I have a world to destroy."

The fire ball grew; red, orange, and yellow flames competing for space. Maecha yelled to the spirits of Imbas Skye, and they did not let her down. A wall of warriors surrounded Maecha and shielded her from the intensity of Akir's fury. Maecha could feel the heat of the flames but, as long as she held her sword and focused, it couldn't touch her. Try as he might, he could not break through. He used all his power and thus the mist dissipated.

Maecha heard Goll and Treasa calling for her.

Akir cursed. "This is not over, Maecha Ruadh. I will have that sword and then I will destroy you."

Akir disappeared. They ran to Maecha who dropped onto her knees. Goll bandaged her arm and lifted her onto her horse.

"Let's get you back to camp so Uatach can have a look at your arm."

Fidach had already arrived back at the *rath* and had rushed his brother to their healers. But they were too late; Ce was dead.

Uatach and Caoilte had just come back from gathering herbs and ran to them as they saw Maecha slumped over her horse.

"Follow me." Uatach hurried inside her *broch*. Sweat

rolled down Maecha's face and her cheeks were flushed.

"Was it a poisoned sword?" Uatach asked.

"No," Maecha moaned. "Fire." Maecha leaned over the side of her pallet and vomited onto the ground. Treasa gently wiped her face.

"There, there, Maecha. All will be well." Treasa vowed to double the guard around her friend for there was more to protect than the others knew.

Uatach removed the bandage around the wound and inhaled sharply. It had festered and angry red lines ran along her arm.

"I thought it would have been Fidach," Maecha cried. "Ce? Is he alive?"

Treasa looked across at Goll who shook his head. She bowed her head toward Maecha not wanting to add to her distress.

"Tell me," she said with clenched teeth.

"He is dead."

"Oh, Goddess. I thought it was Fidach. How could I have been wrong?"

"Drink this," Uatach urged. "It will heal the fire that burns inside you."

Maecha did as she was told and slipped into the comfort of her dreams.

"What ails your mind, Maecha?" Scathach stands along her shores reaching out to the high king's daughter.

"What good are these powers if they do not provide the answers needed to save someone? I thought Fidach was in danger, but it was his other brother. I couldn't save him. I didn't know."

"And you think you can know everything?"

"I thought this gift would help others!"

"What if they don't want your help?"

"How could Ce not have wanted my help? He's gone. Dead!"

Scathach raises her hands to the shapeless sky and sparks of light glitter around her. "Just because they are gone from this world does not mean that they are dead. As hard as it is to let others go, they have to follow their soul's journey, and it is not up to us to hold them back. You do not control the Universe, young one. Until you understand this, you will never feel the full strength of who you are."

Tears fall down Maecha's cheeks. "I understand." Her shoulders shake. "I understand."

One moment Maecha's connection was like a dark fog and then suddenly she was there and so was the pain. Kelan's Awen Crystal scorched his skin and it blazed red. Maecha was in danger and he was stuck in the Otherworld trying to enter Tir-nan-og. What was he to do? The only thing he could at this point. His mind reached for hers, soothing her as he would have done if he'd been there. Another thought crossed his mind. It would never have happened if he'd been there. What had Goll and the others been doing when this happened? The injury was severe and Kelan cursed the fact that he had the healing marrow.

He felt Maecha's torment as clearly as if he'd been right next to her. "Hold on, Maecha. Hold on."

Akir screamed and howled like a toddler having a tantrum after he didn't get his way. How dare she get away when his plan had been going perfectly! Out of control flames shot from his hands and seared anything in its path. Standing on the cliffs overlooking the torrid sea, Akir screamed, "Manannán! Aiménd!"

His father's image appeared in the sea mist. "Which one of your plans have been thwarted?" mac Lir asked like a parent used to seeing his child's tantrums.

"Rahhhh!" Akir bellowed and shot flames at his father. The mist dissipated and then his father's image appeared again.

"Didn't think I'd appear in person with that rage

happening, did you?" mac Lir asked.

"Come closer, you coward," Akir spat.

"Ha, ha. You are the coward who skulks around in other's minds and uses people to get what he wants. Give it up now, Akir, while you still have a chance of keeping your body and soul."

Akir peered up over his father's head and saw his mother riding a ray of sunshine. She had been silent, letting his father try to talk sense into him. Seeing her son look her way, she held out her hands in earnest, wishing he would stop this madness.

"You will die," Akir sneered and shafts of fiery blades raged toward his mother.

"NO!" Manannán yelled and lifted waves to protect his wife. He barely succeeded and Akir dropped his hands to his sides.

"And still you choose her over me," Akir said.

"You don't give me much choice," the sea god said.

Akir screamed in frustration and disappeared into thin air.

Manannán raised his eyes to take in the beauty of his lovely Aiménd and said, "What do we do, my love? It is the same as two hundred years ago, but he is stronger and angrier."

Aiménd sent shafts of sunlight to touch her husband's face and, as his tension lessened, she softly spoke, "He chose his path a long time ago, just as we chose ours. Now we must see it through and protect those that we can. Although it breaks my heart, he is not the son of my womb."

The god of the sea gasped that he had felt his wife's love and could hear her. Clearly they were on the right path. "So it shall be," Manannán said and then slipped down into his vast sea.

Clouds enveloped Aiménd as she went back to her castle in the sky to wait until she was called to take a stand. For now it was up to the humans.

Chapter 26 - Eire

Cairpre entered the dank surroundings underneath Tara. He observed Finnius sitting in solitude behind the bars of fire that his power had created. A smile of satisfaction lit his face. Finnius opened his eyes and observed the young man he had taken into his heart.

"It would seem that I underestimated you, Cairpre," Finnius said.

"That is because you have grown old and careless."

"Perhaps, but it does not take much to know that there still is goodness in someone. I had thought that perhaps you still possessed some."

Cairpre thought of his mother and her desire to see some kindness and mercy in him, too. A part of him wanted to please her and to also please the man who had loved him unconditionally. He pushed those weak thoughts aside. "I cannot say that I do. I have finally been rewarded for all my hard work, and the best is yet to come when my dear sister returns."

Finnius leaned closer. Cairpre shifted back.

"She will return and shall possess something that you do not."

"And what is that, old man?"

"Goodness, love, and the respect of her people."

"My people respect me!"

"Respect and fear are two different emotions. Where respect will gain you loyalty and prosperity, fear will only fester until there is nothing left to lose. Then they will revolt and you will lose everything that you think your power has given you."

Cairpre shot Finnius with a spark of fire. Finnius flinched, but otherwise didn't move. "Do not provoke me, old man. The Fire Lord is done with you. I am the only one keeping you alive."

"And even that you cannot do well."

Cairpre shot the druid again and this time Finnius flew back into the wall. "What's wrong? You can't fight back? You are worthless."

"Cairpre, wait," Finnius said, but he walked away. "Cairpre, you will die if I don't help you!"

Cairpre turned and scowled. "No, Finnius. You will die, but I will live forever."

As soon as Cairpre left, Leann snuck over to Finnius. She peered into the cell. "You are hurt!" she said, fear filling her eyes.

"It is nothing." He raised his eyes to meet Leann's and all he saw was love. They should have enjoyed each other all these years. Now it was too late. No matter. It was done. "You must get me away from here. Cairpre must not destroy any more of my magic or else I will never be restored."

"But how? I have tried and do not have the power to break this prison," Leann said.

"Cairpre will do it for us."

"Then what will we do, where will we go?"

"You will take me to my cavern and leave me there. I will rest until my daughter comes."

Leann gaped at him. "What do you suppose I do while you are waiting?"

Finnius attempted to grin. "Wait with me?"

Her face lit up in surprise and longing. "You want me to stay with you?"

Finnius held her gaze and nodded.

"Who will care for your daughter?"

Finnius rubbed his arms despite the sweat that ran down

his face from the heat of his prison. "Have you noticed the wolf in Niachra's dreamworld? She stands among the tree line."

At the mention that the wolf was female, Leann felt a cold chill run up her spine. "I have, but what of it?"

"It is Eithne. For some reason she has remained in her animal spirit state and I cannot communicate with her. It seems that Natalie has formed a relationship with her. I feared that she had died in the twenty-first century, and even though she lives I do not know how to contact her. I only know that she will care for our daughter."

"I am glad for you. It will bring peace to your mind while we are away. I will prepare and come back for you."

"Where we go, nothing is needed. Tell Cairpre that he has mortally wounded me and I have requested his presence."

Cairpre watched as the stone wall of the *rath* was rebuilt. He refused to think of Finnius in any other way than as a means to an end. A path to more power. The memories of the old man in his youth (for even then Finnius was old) flashed through his mind. Cairpre swatted them away, but they were relentless. The differences in the length of his legs had been apparent at birth. It was only the people's love for his mother that had kept him from being left for the wolves. When he was a crawling infant, his deformity hadn't mattered, but as he matured, the pain that his uneven legs caused him and his irregular gait were more than a child should have to bear. He would often hide in the woods, away from the teasing that even the son of the queen would not be exempt from. That was where Finnius would find him, alone and dejected. Finnius didn't offer comfort, but a solution. It wasn't perfect, but it had warmed Cairpre's cooling heart that someone would attempt to help him.

Finnius had attached a piece of wood to the bottom of Cairpre's shoe. It had been shaped to match his shoe, but the difference in the heel was still apparent. Cairpre practiced walking on it and was happy that the pain in his hips disappeared. He began to meet Finnius in the oak groves, and Finnius would tell him of the ancient lore that had brought the Mother Goddess to their land. Cairpre would have been content to stay in the woods forever with the kind druid, but once he was old enough to hold a sword, he was required to learn to fight with one.

Cairpre turned at the sound of someone calling his name, thankful for the break from that dreadful memory. Leann ran up to him, tears threatening to overflow.

"Cairpre! Finnius is ill. You have hurt him, fatally, I fear. You must let me tend to him. He will not last the day if you do not do something."

He watched the woman for a sign of deceit. She was clearly distraught, but he would not be swayed.

"Finnius cannot die," he said and turned his back to her.

With an unforeseen strength, Leann grabbed his arm and swung him around. She elevated her height to match his and her eyes bore into his soul.

"Is this how you treat the man who loved you uncondi-tionally? He has always, always believed in you and you show him no kindness?"

Cairpre hesitated, his commitment to the Fire Lord sparring with his love of the old druid.

Leann scoffed at him. "Even with your basic intelligence, you should know that you will get nothing from a dead man."

A hand flew up and struck Leann across the cheek. She stumbled back stupefied. Cairpre stared at his hand, disbelieving that it was his own actions that would hurt Leann. It was Leann who would wrap his wounds and treat him with kind words.

Her eyes hardened. "You turn from the Mother Goddess and she will not have mercy." She walked away.

"Leann! Wait!" He ran after her, ignoring the disgusted looks from his men. She didn't stop until she was back with

Finnius.

"I did not mean to strike you," Cairpre said.

Anger soared through Finnius, but he had to continue his ploy. Cairpre would get what was coming to him.

"Are you sorry or have you realized what you could lose?"

Cairpre remained silent.

"That's what I thought. Take down these bars so that I can help him. Now!"

He looked in the cell at Finnius' lifeless body and waved his hand. The bars dropped. With his last bit of strength, Finnius flew into the air and flung Cairpre into the wall. Cairpre fell to the ground unconscious. They ran down a narrow passageway that exited at the back of the *rath*. Leann grabbed one of the fastest stallions and mounted it, with Finnius riding behind her, limp from using so much of his remaining power.

They rode up into the hills to the secret place Finnius had long ago shown Leann, the place where he came to restore his health and energy. Only this time it would be up to another to do that for him. His daughter would have to find him and Leann to bring them back.

Leann abandoned the horse and helped Finnius walk up the rocky path that led to the cave's opening. The late afternoon sun illuminated the interior and Finnius knelt down into the cave.

Leann helped Finnius settle into a comfortable position against the stone wall. She could not see beyond where the sun lit their way, but knew that the cave wove deep into the mountain. Blankets were folded neatly on the opposite wall. Leann covered Finnius who began to shiver.

Hearing men yell, she peered out the entrance of the cave. Finnius grabbed her hand. An arrow flew past her head.

"Stay, Leann. Close the cave and we will be gone."

She concentrated on the magic that would remove any signs of the cave's opening to the naked eye. Weaving thread upon thread of concealment, Leann began to sweat from the exertion. Leann opened her eyes and could still see the world in front of her.

"I don't have enough power. Can you help me at all?" she asked peering down at him.

Finnius shook uncontrollably and sweat ran freely down his face. He could be dying. She couldn't tend to him and close the cave at the same time.

Leann leaned over and kissed Finnius' forehead, his eyes, his cheeks, his lips. "I have waited so long for you and I will always love you, Finnius. I cherish all the moments and love you have given me. This is my gift to you."

"No," he moaned, but couldn't move to stop her. Finnius knew that her magic wasn't enough to hide both of them.

Leann stood and smiled down at him. She removed her triskele charm that Finnius had given her at her initiation ceremony and placed it in his hand.

"May the Mother Goddess protect you," she said and left the cave. With a wave of her hand, she chanted the incantation that would enclose the cave until another opened it. An arrow pierced her shoulder and she fell back against the rocks. She saw Cairpre on his horse, anger and the pain of betrayal distorting his face.

Leann raised her hands to the sky and called to the Mother Goddess to protect her love. Storm clouds rolled overhead and the waves crashed against the cliffs. As Leann clapped her hands together, the cave disappeared.

"NO!" Cairpre yelled. In uncontrolled anger, he zapped Leann until her life was extinguished.

Above them a hawk and eagle flew across the sky, chasing one another in play. The eagle screeched as its wings grew heavier. The hawk circled to the ground and the eagle followed. As they touched, Finnius' spirit reached out to catch Leann's falling one.

"You came for me," she whispered.

"Of course," Finnius said.

"I must leave you now."

"I am always with you in the spirit world, Leann."

"Your daughter is beautiful. I only wish—"

Her spirit form became lighter.

"I know. Leann. I know."

"I loved you, Finnius. I always will."

"You humble me with your love."

Finnius allowed the tears to fall as her spirit drifted along through its circle of life. Her body fell to the ground and died for love.

Cairpre shook to the core of his being. He rode down the cliffs as if in a trance. None of his men spoke to him, but he could feel their contempt burn into his back. He had let his anger get the best of him and had destroyed two symbols of the goddess that the people, not even *his* people, trusted to keep them safe. He glanced up at the sky, fearing that at any moment the Mother Goddess would strike him down, or the Fire Lord would burn him to ashes.

He gathered his men in the great hall and decided to play the hand that was dealt him. He stood at his father's throne, wishing that he didn't feel like a child trying to play king. "We have won a great victory today!" he began. "Followers of the Mother Goddess have been destroyed and she does not care. Why?" He dared any to answer. None did. "Because she holds no power over us! The goddess is dead and a new kingdom shall begin. My kingdom! All of you shall be rewarded for your loyalty and your patience.

"But our quest is not complete. For as we speak, our enemy returns. My sister is on her way here, planning to force the ways of the goddess back upon us. She will take you all as prisoner and make you suffer! Do you want that?!"

No one answered.

"I asked if you want that!"

They grumbled their answer.

"Then now is the time to prepare for their arrival. We must commit to start a new Tara under my rule."

"What if the king comes back?" one man asked.

"We will kill him," Cairpre said with mild irritation.

"I shan't kill the king," another man said.

The air sizzled with heat as the man was incinerated by Cairpre's flame.

The other men stepped away from the dead man's ashes. "Does anyone else dare to oppose me?"

They were all silent.

"Very well. Then prepare to welcome my family home."

Chapter 27 - Catskills

The shrill scream broke the night's silence and Michaela vaulted from her bed, racing to Natalie's room in seconds. She scanned the area for signs of danger, fearing that her past enemies had found her once again.

"Natalie! Wake up!" Michaela said touching the small girl's shoulder. Once again she was soaked.

"What's up?" Vince said entering the room, all signs of sleep gone.

"She's soaking wet and is in the midst of a damn nasty nightmare," Michaela said. She picked up Natalie and, sitting on the bed, held her close and rocked her. "It's all right. Come back to me, sweety. Come back to Michaela. Vince get her some new pj's, will you?"

Vince grabbed a pink frilly top and bottom and placed them on the bed. "Let me know if you need help," he said. "I'm going to check on the guys."

"Mi...Michaela?" Natalie hiccupped.

"I'm here, honey. Just take it easy. Can you tell me what happened?"

"The other night Finnius gave me all his power so I could help that girl I need to protect, and now he tried to escape and Leann helped him, but she's...she's dead, Michaela! That horrible man killed her!"

What was this child talking about? Michaela tried to avoid the sickening thought that Finnius Morgan was dead. "All right, why don't you calm down? Change your clothes and I'll get a washcloth to clean your face. I'll be right back, okay?"

Natalie nodded and slipped off her lap.

"Is she all right?" Vince asked.

"I don't know. It was hard to understand her." Michaela noticed that Vince started a fire in the living room.

"The house was feeling cold and I thought she would be chilly after sweating so much. The boys slept through it all."

Michaela kissed him. "You're perfect. I'll bring her in here."

After Michaela cleaned Natalie up, they came into the living room. Vince was on the couch closest to the fire and said, "Come here, Peanut."

Natalie flew into his arms. "Why don't you tell me and Michaela what's going on?"

Michaela sat next to them and rubbed Natalie's bare feet.

"You know that I've always had visions of future events. That's how I knew about Michaela and found Shannon. It was always during this time period." She waited for both adults to nod and then she continued, "Well, since I have been training in the dreamworld with Finnius and Leann, I've noticed that my visions have focused on ancient Ireland. Sometimes I'll dream it or sometimes I'll slip away from here and feel like I'm there."

Michaela felt Vince stiffen after Natalie mentioned the dreamworld. He had no choice but to believe that it was possible to visit in dreams, since that was how he had communicated with Michaela. However, it still was a major stretch for his imagination to accept.

"Go on, Natalie," Michaela said, putting her other hand on Vince's leg in reassurance.

"Finnius had been locked up in the fire prison, but he's still been able to train me. Maecha's brother wanted to kill him, but Leann and Finnius managed to escape. The last time I saw Finnius he told me that he would be going away, and it would be up to me to find him when I came to that ancient Ireland."

Now it was Michaela's turn to flinch. She knew that this was what would eventually happen, but hearing Natalie speak about it in such an accepting way upset her.

"Where is Finnius now?" Vince asked.

"He's in some hidden cave. Leann was supposed to go with him, but she gave her life to save him. She's dead, Michaela. I was just getting to know her and now she's dead!"

Not being able to help herself anymore, Natalie burst out in tears and Vince held her.

"I'm so sorry, Natalie. I bet her spirit is free like an eagle—that's how you said she visited you right? As an eagle? So whenever you see an eagle flying around here, which is rare, you'll know that Leann is saying hello to you. And I know for sure that you'll see her in your dreamworld. She's no further away than she was before, just different."

Natalie nodded and Michaela hoped that it made her feel better. To be so young and see so much death was overwhelming.

"There's something else," Natalie said, daintily wiping her nose on a tissue that Michaela handed her. I've been seeing a white wolf at the end of each training session."

"That's great. Wolves are protectors and if it's white, it has pure intentions. Perhaps it's your animal guide," Michaela suggested.

A wry smile lifted Natalie's lips. "It definitely is a guide. Finnius told Leann about it just before she died. It seems that the wolf is my mother."

Michaela didn't know what she had expected to hear, but that was not it. "Your mother? But I thought she died?"

"I guess not. Finnius hasn't been able to talk to the wolf, but he told me to trust it. I think it will lead me to her. I just don't know where or when that is."

Vince gently lifted Natalie off his lap onto Michaela's. "That's a lot to digest," he said, running his hand through his thick and wavy, dark hair. "I'm getting some coffee."

"Can I have hot chocolate, please?" Natalie said, giving Vince a smile she knew he couldn't resist.

"Why not, I don't think any of us will be going back to sleep tonight."

Chapter 28 - Alba

"Walk with me, Maecha," Fidach said.

Maecha brushed Finn. Her left arm was still wrapped with a bandage since the wound had not healed completely. Maecha gave Finn a quick kiss and took Fidach's offered arm. They walked along the cliffs, and Maecha let the wind whip her foul mood away.

"Shouldn't we have a chaperone?" Maecha asked.

Fidach paused and searched Maecha's face. Then he smiled. "You are safe with me, Maecha."

Over the last few days, they had grown closer as friends and found that they enjoyed each other's company.

"You miss Kelan," Fidach began.

"Yes, I do."

"When you were injured, you said that you felt connected to him again."

"Yes, after the Fire Lord failed, I felt like a fog had been lifted from me. When I reached for Kelan, I could feel him and knew he was all right. He stayed with me for as long as he could."

"And your wound?"

"It is fine for now. I am able to move around and still have a good arm. I think the Fire Lord is hindering my connection to Kelan. He will stop at nothing to get this sword. I am sorry that it ended in your brother's life."

Maecha hadn't wanted to express her suspicions about Circenn since Fidach had already lost two brothers. Losing another through betrayal would be too much to bear. Instead she said, "Sometimes these images are more confusing than helpful. I wish they would have made a difference."

Fidach bowed his head and said, "I know you would have done anything to prevent it. Who knows it may have been me who would have been killed. Have you felt Kelan since the injury?" Fidach said sitting closer to her than he should have.

Maecha was still recovering and didn't have the energy to move away. "No, I have not, but I felt his fear. He has lost so much in his life."

"What happened?"

"His father served my father as a warrior and king of his own tuath. One day they were raided much like your family was. Kelan watched his mother get attacked. She was washing clothes in the water. He was brave and fought well, but he was only twelve. His mother died in his arms, and later he found out that his father and sister were also killed."

"What did he do?"

"He came to live with us. I quickly latched on to him. It took him a while to break out of his despondency, but I managed to convince him. He was the one who really taught me how to wield a sword. We did everything together, and so I think it's only natural that we grew to love each other more than friends."

Fidach nodded. "And this prophecy?"

"Kelan and I entered the Cave of the Warrior together as our challenge to become members of the Fianna. In the Otherworld, the Lord and Princess bound us together with this Awen Crystal."

Maecha removed the crystal from under her tunic and held it up to Fidach. She sighed at its pale color. "As we completed each challenge, we became more aware of one another, physically and spiritually. After the final challenge, we could sense each other's moods, dream within one another's dreams, speak through our minds, and fight as if we were one person."

"Why did you agree to get to know me? Why not just tell my father all you have told me?"

"I wanted to build trust. There has been too much bloodshed between our people and we need an alliance, but not the one that your father is suggesting."

"I agree. Do you feel that you can trust me?"

"I believe you are a good man, Fidach."

Maecha flushed under the heat of his gaze. How could she even be thinking about this man when Kelan was possibly fighting for his life? She put her hands up against his chest as he moved in toward her. "Fidach, we shouldn't."

"Oh, yes we should." He kissed her. Maecha's lips burned with his passion. With all her will power she tried to pull away, but their lips lingered together. It was the heat of her Awen Crystal that brought her back to her senses. She pushed Fidach away. Flames flickered in his eyes and that same foggy feeling that she had the other night lifted from her mind. Fidach shielded his eyes from the powerful light of the crystal and, when he lowered his arm, his eyes were back to normal.

"We are being controlled by the Fire Lord."

It took a moment for Fidach to realize where he was, and to take note of the fact that Maecha was standing and breathing very heavily.

"Did we?"

"Yes, we did and it cannot happen again. We are not destined to be together, Fidach. I am sorry."

"You are right. If I am to love you, then I want it to be of my own volition. We will speak to my father together, and I will tell him that we are not suitable for one another."

"What about your matriarchal line?"

"We will find a way. That is no longer your problem."

"It is, if your father does not let us leave."

Fidach sighed. "He will let you go if I say so."

"Oh thank you, Fidach. Kelan will be so relieved,"

Maecha said. She wrapped her arms around him and kissed him square on the mouth. Not one for missing an opportunity, Fidach held her and enjoyed the contact himself.

A sinister laugh sounded around them and, at that exact moment, the Fire Lord opened the connection between Kelan and Maecha. Kelan had been resting by the river trying to remember the path that would take him to the Lord and Princess. He couldn't understand why they would make it so difficult to find them if he was needed so much. Why must everything be a test?

But that thought was shattered by the image of his Maecha cooing in the arms of a Picti warrior. That she was kissing him willingly was quite obvious. They were locked together like old lovers. Fury raged through Kelan and he blasted that anger to Maecha. When he finally could feel some sort of calm in his mind, he paused. Anger was the chief emotion that coursed through his veins. He refused to let the loss and hurt from Maecha's betrayal touch his heart.

Kelan stood and raised his sword to the unearthly sky. "Goddess, I call you! Help me find you so that I can lend you my aid!" An enormous oak split in two. Through the opening, Kelan could see the water of Tir-nan-og. He entered, putting Maecha out of his mind.

The heat from her crystal burned like steel from a blacksmith's forge. She felt Kelan's wrath and pulled back from Fidach.

"What's wrong?" he asked, holding on to her arms.

All Maecha could remember was how she felt when Kelan had been entranced by Gaia from the Isle of the Blessed. It was Maecha's pain and anger at his betrayal that had shocked him out of that trance. Now Maecha was on the receiving end, even though her actions were innocent.

Maecha pushed away from Fidach and ran toward the *rath*.

"Wait, Maecha!" Fidach yelled, following her.

She found her father by the central fire. It broke her heart as she watched him struggle to stand. She rushed to him and tried to wrap herself up in his strength, like she did when she was a little girl. Whenever she was hurt, he would sit her on his lap. She would curl up in a little ball, and his arms would make her feel warm and safe once again. He would whisper that all would be well and his voice would woo her to sleep. But he couldn't put her on his lap anymore, and he could only lift one arm to place around her trembling shoulders. He did comfort her with his voice, and she felt that powerful tug of love wrench at her soul.

"What is it, Daughter?" he asked.

The others had gathered around, but kept a respectful distance.

Maecha stepped back and they both felt the gap. "It's Kelan. He saw me…he saw me kissing Fidach, but it was only out of happiness and friendship. What I mean is that we realized the Fire Lord is controlling our minds to take my sword. Once Fidach understood how much I loved Kelan, he said he would explain everything to his father. I was so overjoyed, I kissed him. That was when I felt Kelan again. He was so hurt and angry. And now I cannot connect with him to explain!" Uncontrollable tears ran down her face.

"What has happened?" Cruithne asked, hearing the clamor.

"Let us sit and have some wine, while Maecha and I explain all to you," Fidach said.

Everyone complied. Maecha sat next to Fidach, so they could string their stories together. Osgar stood next to his daughter who appeared to be restless.

"What ails you, Uatach?" Osgar asked.

Uatach's face turned red, which was something that Osgar had never seen on an Amazon. "It is nothing, Father. I only feel on edge."

"Do you think we are going to be attacked?" Osgar asked placing his hand on his sword.

"No." Uatach bit her lip. "I would like to stand here and think for a moment, if that suits you."

Not knowing what else to do, Osgar sat to hear what Maecha and Fidach had to say.

Treasa linked her arm through Cormac's in a loving manner that Maecha appreciated. Cruithne sat with a grumpy Circenn, while Goll and Caoilte stood behind Cormac.

Fidach began. "Maecha and I have spent many hours together this week and I thank everyone, especially my father, for giving us the opportunity to find out on our own if we are right for one another." He smiled at Maecha. "I just told Maecha that I would be honored to be her husband."

Cruithne cheered, but Fidach put up his hand to silence him. Uatach took a step back, her face flushed with heat.

"While I would be honored, it is very important to me that the woman I share my life and my bed with be not only suitable, but in love with me. My parents shared a passionate love that withstood all life could throw at them, except death. And even in death, their love overshadows everything else in my father's life. I too desire that and so does Maecha. And while we could grow to love each other, we wouldn't have that kind of love."

Maecha spoke, "Fidach understands that I feel that way about Kelan." Maecha held her Awen Crystal and mindspoke words to Kelan, but she felt nothing.

Cruithne paced, not sure what to do about the situation. He had said that it was up to them to decide, but he had been quite sure they would choose each other. He looked at Cormac with questioning eyes.

Cormac shrugged. "It is their decision and I support it. I could not have imagined living with someone I was not passionate for. That is why I have never taken another wife. My

Deirdre is irreplaceable."

Cruithne nodded. "I understand what you say." He turned to Fidach. "But that still leaves us with the need to find you a strong wife."

Uatach lifted her long legs over the fallen tree trunk that served as a seat for everyone. She stood in front of Cruithne and shifted her eyes to Fidach. Everyone shifted with nervous tension when she didn't speak. Osgar stood to take his daughter's hand, thinking that she must be ill. Quiet Uatach would not place herself in the center of attention unless she was delirious or else had something very important to say.

She raised her hand to stop her father from interfering. Taking a deep breath, she said, "I will take Fidach as my husband."

Fidach's mouth fell open in surprise, but then his eyes took in the strong, breathtaking woman who had just offered herself to him. In that instant, Uatach revealed her goddess stature. Reaching her full height, her skin blazed with the brightness of the sun. As she held her hands out to him, Fidach was dazzled by her beauty and felt a connection to her that he had never felt with another person.

Recovering from his shock, Osgar rushed in between his daughter and Fidach. He took hold of Uatach's arms and shook her a little. "What is the meaning of this, Uatach? You don't even know him."

Uatach didn't take her eyes from Fidach. "But I know his heart and it is good." She took her father's face in her hands and said, "We belong together."

Osgar yanked on his beard, not knowing what to do. Maecha remained silent. The golden aura that surrounded the two of them was overpowering. How had she not seen it before? But then she remembered that Uatach had made every possible excuse to not be around her and Fidach. Had Uatach known all along and waited to see what they would do? Not knowing any of the answers, except that this union was right in so many ways, Maecha gently pulled Osgar away.

Chapter 29 - Alba

Ignoring the dead silence, Fidach moved around Osgar and held out his hand. There were many gasps as Uatach clasped his hand and stood next to him. "I present Uatach, daughter of Scathach of the Isle of Imbas Skye and Osgar Conchobar, King of Leinster."

Cruithne sputtered. Fidach laughed. "What, no quick words from you, Father? Then I assume you approve."

Cruithne laughed. "Of course I approve. How could I not? Uatach, are you sure you wish this union?"

"Yes," Uatach said.

"And Osgar, do you approve?"

Osgar was still dumbfounded. "I do if my daughter wishes it, but there is one other who must approve of this union."

A bolt of lightning rent the sky. At the sound of thunder a figure appeared in the midst of the crowd. Everyone shied away from Scathach. The other Amazons who had accompanied Uatach bowed to their queen as she marched toward the platform. She glared at Fidach.

"You dare to take my daughter from me without my permission?" Scathach towered over him.

Fidach turned pale and stammered, "I am sorry, Goddess. She asked me."

"You thought that her mortal father held the power to give her away?"

Osgar flinched, but held his head high as she shifted her glare to him.

"She loves him," Maecha heard Osgar say.

"How can she love someone she barely knows?"

"We did," Osgar said in a quiet voice.

Scathach bristled at the reminder. "Her destiny is to be a warrior, not to suckle children!"

Maecha felt warm. Something, a thought or vision, was just beyond her grasp. She stared at Uatach and saw her own mother standing next to her. Deirdre smiled, nodded, and disappeared. Maecha stepped between Uatach and Fidach. She smiled at both of them.

"Give me your hands."

They did. Osgar shushed Scathach and pointed behind her.

Maecha held their hands and closed her eyes. Happiness and love enveloped her. Babies were indeed abundant and Amazons protected the land alongside the Picti. One child stood out from the rest. A boy with golden hair. He was strong, skilled, intelligent, and part of the prophecy. Maecha turned in her mind's eye and saw her daughter. Her heart exploded with love at the dark-haired beauty. These children would grow up together. As adults, they clasped hands and the prophecy was born. She opened her teary eyes.

"I bless you both for you are a part of me and my future."

Maecha bowed to Scathach. "These two have found each other and love. There is no stronger power than that. They are as much a part of this prophecy as I am. It is Uatach's destiny. My mother has already blessed their choice and your blessing will only add more strength to this union."

Scathach said, "So you finally can see." She addressed her daughter. "This is what you want?" Uatach nodded again, her face a brilliant glow. "So be it."

Fidach hugged Uatach and bowed to Scathach. Osgar hugged both of them.

"You are becoming soft, my goddess," Osgar whispered in Scathach's ear.

Scathach scoffed at him and then touched his cheek. "Perhaps."

"Come," Treasa dragged Maecha and Uatach toward their *broch*. "We must prepare Uatach for her marriage bed."

"I know what occurs in a marriage bed," Uatach said.

"Ah, but you do not know all the different forms of pleasure in a marriage bed," Treasa said.

"What kind of pleasure? My mother never spoke of pleasure with a man."

"Oh, I shall have so much enjoyment telling you," Treasa said.

Uatach opened her mouth to question Treasa some more, but saw Fidach watching her. Her cheeks burst into red blooms and she closed her mouth.

On impulse, Fidach took Uatach's other hand and held it. Treasa smiled at Fidach. She brushed her hand along his cheek. "Do not keep her long for she must prepare for her wedding night." Fidach's blush made Treasa laugh. "Let us go, Maecha. Do not tarry, Uatach!" They ran to prepare some surprises.

Scathach was there when they arrived.

Both women stopped laughing and bowed to the goddess.

"Rise," Scathach said. "Where is Uatach?"

"She was speaking with Fidach and is on her way," Maecha said.

"That is good. I am preparing her clothing for the ceremony."

Maecha stepped forward and saw the leather garb on the straw bed. Scathach's fingers lingered on the feathered headdress above it.

"Was this yours?" Maecha asked.

"This was my ceremonial garb for when I became guardian of the Isle of Imbas Skye. I was never joined to Osgar except in the unity of our daughter. Nor did I want to be. Men are a nuisance and are only good for momentary pleasure."

Treasa laughed. "I do agree that having a man does provide a moment's pleasure and sometimes much longer, but I also like having a man in my bed every night. Don't you agree, Maecha?"

Maecha couldn't believe she was having this conversation in front of a warrior goddess, but she said, "I love having Kelan with me and I feel empty without him now, but it's important to be self-sufficient."

"Exactly! And I do not want my daughter to become a commodity for this Fidach."

"Mother!" Uatach said from the doorway. "I am no man's commodity. I have learned from watching Kelan and Maecha that a union can be equally respectful and loving. I feel love for Fidach and I plan to stay here and help him in all aspects of his kingdom."

"I know you love him or else I never would have agreed to this."

Maecha was confused. One moment, Fidach was lusting after her, and the next moment, he and Uatach were in love. A fear spread through her. Was the Fire Lord somehow controlling them? She asked Scathach, "How can Uatach know so quickly that she loves Fidach? They have hardly spoken."

"When an Amazon chooses to take a man for her mate, it is quite often a spontaneous feeling that comes over them. When I met Osgar, I knew that I would mate with him."

"Then why didn't you marry him?"

Treasa poured some mead and nibbled on some hard cheese. She passed a horn to everyone, and they had an impromptu gathering to honor Uatach's ceremony of love.

"Sit, all of you," Scathach demanded.

They sat on the same bed, eager to hear a story from the great warrior who was taken by love.

Scathach drank her fill of mead and then settled across

from the three women, who only had the love of fighting in common and perhaps a good story.

She cleared her throat and began, "I was raised to divinity thousands of years ago."

Maecha interrupted. "You weren't born a goddess?"

"Do you want to hear this story or not?"

Maecha clapped her hands like an inexperienced maid and said, "I am sorry, please continue."

Scathach scowled. "Thank you. My father was the King of Scythia." Scathach held up a warning hand to Maecha. "It does not matter where Scythia is. My mother was a powerful warrior, and she trained me until I rivaled most men in my father's army. I thought they loved one another for our lives were always joyous. But it was through my father's betrayal that my mother was killed. He chose the greed of men over his love for her.

"Filled with anger over her death and frustrated that I could not exact revenge on my father, I begged for assistance from the war goddess, Macha. She appeared to me and made only one demand—that I would never give my heart to a man. I would be made for war and would serve her."

Treasa refilled the goddess' cup and she took a deep gulp. She continued, "I readily agreed and my father was killed, although not by my hand. I spent a few years waging wars in the goddess' name and was satisfied with my life. Then it so happened that a demi-god, who had been scorned by Macha, managed to trap her. He wanted to humiliate her as she had done to him. He planned to shame her in front of her patrons and then kill her.

"I was on a mission for the goddess, but when I heard of this atrocity, I killed the demi-god with my bare hands, so filled with rage was I. To show her gratitude, Macha raised me to goddesshood and named the Isle where we live in my name. There I remained and trained the Amazonian women who resided there, as well as other women who came seeking my aid."

"But what of love?" Uatach asked, forgetting that her mother didn't want questions.

Scathach rolled her eyes at her daughter. She would have her daughter up at the crack of dawn training until she dropped. There was nothing like a good sweat to reverse the effects of a man.

"Over the years some men were allowed to train with me and I admit that I used them for my own pleasure or taught them the ways of women, but never did I give them my heart. At least not until Osgar."

The young women squealed. Scathach stood in disgust. Maecha grabbed her hand. "We are sorry. We won't say another word. You have to finish, Scathach, please."

Scathach returned to her seat. "Osgar Conchobar was marooned on my isle when his boat was tossed from the sea and damaged. Some say it was a curse to have him land there and others believe that Macha tested me. It didn't matter. I trained the warrior with the dark hair and light blue eyes." Scathach smiled and her eyes glinted with mischief. "I even spread my thighs for him."

Everyone giggled.

"It was during this time that Conan Maol invaded our home. Osgar was with me in bed. With only his breeches, he ventured forth to kill the invader, but Deirdre had beaten him to it. Osgar would have died for me and for all my warriors. No man had ever put me before himself. Alas, the seeds of love were planted and, no matter how hard I tried to dig them out, they grew."

Maecha couldn't help herself. "Then why did you let him go? Why not tell him?"

"When his ship was repaired, he told me of his allegiance to his king, but he would be back if that was my desire. Macha had seen into my heart and wanted to kill him to punish me for breaking my vow. I begged her to spare him, and said that I would never let him come back for me."

It was Treasa who couldn't hold back. "Then how is it that he came to the isle without being killed?"

"The gods are tricky. Since neither one of us knew that he was coming, I could not hide the isle. Also, he came for a greater good and not to see me. He would have been killed otherwise, and I would have died knowing that I caused him pain. I have already caused him so much torment; I don't think he will ever forgive me."

Uatach knelt down in front of her mother, shocked that the greatest warrior ever known should be so stricken by love. Then she smiled with the knowledge that her parents loved one another. "Is there nothing you can do?"

"No, child, and he must not know of this," she answered, giving each one of them a warning look. "This knowledge will kill him. Only an act of sacrifice will bring him back to me safely." Scathach stood, slapping her face for its betrayal of her feelings. She pulled her daughter to her feet and said, "Come, let us prepare you for the next journey in your life."

Chapter 30 - Alba

Uatach strode out into the afternoon light. The sun highlighted the large feathered headdress adorning her head. Her hair, braided with sparkling beads, trailed down her back. A leather halter lifted her breasts to bless the sky. Bands of gold were intricately sewn along the bodice and the waist fit snugly around her firm body. As she walked, her leather skirt separated along the numerous slits to reveal healthy, long legs. Leather boots were strapped up to her knees and she towered over her attendants. Scathach strolled next to her and Maecha behind her. A trail of Amazons followed in a semi-circle as an honor, but also to protect the future queen of the Picti. Osgar approached Uatach and placed a gentle kiss on each of her cheeks.

"You are beautiful, my daughter," he said. He moved to her right side, and she gratefully clasped her hand around his arm. Her hand shook and Osgar squeezed it. "He will bring you joy and laughter."

Uatach smiled at her father, glad that she had had this chance to get to know him. She glanced over at her mother and thought she saw a twinge of regret. It was gone and Uatach knew that her mother would hide any emotions she felt. The fact that Scathach had treated her father poorly for his own good burned a hole in her heart. She wanted to help them, but didn't know how.

Fidach wore a black sleeveless tunic and breeches tucked into leather boots. Gold arm bracelets depicting wolves were wrapped around his muscular biceps and his hair was streaked away from his face and dyed black. His arms and face were decorated in intricate blue designs.

Maecha scanned the crowds and the trees for any signs of danger. Her senses were heightened and she felt uneasy. Her heart broke as tears fell down Cruithne's cheeks. She understood his feelings of happiness and security of finding a suitable match for his son. Plus, having the blessing of a goddess for this union made the Picti security even stronger. Once word spread, many would think twice about attacking the Picti. She also felt the sadness that hung over the crowd at all the useless death and destruction they had suffered. Many had died for reasons yet unknown. They still did not know who was behind these attacks so everyone was wary of letting their guard down.

Maecha smiled at the joy on Fidach's face and was glad he had found love to fulfill a duty. The place where Ce should have been was left empty in honor of Cruithne's third son. Then her gaze wandered over Circenn, but shifted back to him. Beads of sweat ran down his forehead. His eyes were riveted in fear. Perhaps he also was afraid of being attacked, Maecha thought. Or maybe he was mourning the death of another older brother. Only he and Fidach were left, so much of the family responsibility would fall to him. Maecha hadn't warmed up to this brother, but maybe she needed to give him another chance. She didn't know what had happened in those woods and Circenn had come back wounded, claiming he had been attacked. But her vision had clearly shown betrayal between brothers. Was she trying to find evil where it wasn't or was she in denial? The best solution would be to remain close to him during the celebration and find out who he really was.

Uatach and Fidach never broke their gaze as their hands were placed together. Their parents stood behind each of them. The druid stepped forward carrying a bowl. Fidach murmured words in his language that Uatach couldn't understand, but the tone was clear. He declared his love for her. Then he drew a pattern on Uatach's face with the same blue woad that he had used on his own body. When finished, Fidach took her right hand and lifted it up to the druid, who tied cloths, taken from their garments, connecting both their hands. He spoke to all of the strength of their bond and how no man could break it. When he was about to conclude the ceremony, Scathach stopped him. She stepped up onto the altar. Rising to her goddess stature, she raised her hands over her daughter and Fidach.

"As the sun and moon, earth and sky, I bless this union. Let no one come between them and let the power of the Isle of Imbas Skye forever bless this union and this land." As she spoke thunder and lightning darkened the sky and a tiny bolt shot through her and into the young couple. Both their eyes widened in surprise, but then they beamed at each other.

Uatach said, "Thank you, Mother."

Scathach bowed to her daughter. She looked at Fidach and smiled. He bowed to her and the ceremony ended.

Maecha leaned over to Osgar and asked, "What did she do?"

With tears in his eyes, he said, "She has given them a most powerful blessing. Their union is as strong as the Lord and Princess of the Otherworld. No man or being can ever come between them, and they will always be stronger together. Whereas Uatach is a demi-god, so now is Fidach. It is a great gift that she has given."

Maecha touched his arm. "Do you wish she gave this gift to you?"

Osgar sighed. "I would give anything to end my days in Scathach's arms."

"There is still time, Osgar. Love is powerful."

Osgar smiled. "And you are filled with it, so can see all the endless possibilities in life. Alas, I am happy just being able to see her and share in this moment."

Maecha pulled him to her and kissed him on the cheek.

"Come, the festivities begin and I want to dance."

Maecha grabbed his hand and they spun together. Pipes and drums filled the air with lively music, while dancers jumped and swung one another around in the open field. Endless vats of mead and beer were passed around in celebration. Everyone from the surrounding tuaths had come to see who would stand in ascension with the king's son. They had all lived in fear, since the queen and her daughter had died, wondering when that ill stroke of luck would reach them. For now it had only struck the king and his immediate family. Hopefully, the Mother Goddess would be appeased with their choice and good tidings would ring for all.

Cormac ambled over to Cruithne and, in friendly silence, they watched their people push away their sorrows and bask in a happy moment. All too soon, their minds would return to those they lost.

"What is your plan, my friend?" Cruithne asked Cormac.

"We must leave as soon as we can. Maecha has told me of her dreams of discord and strife in our land. If we wait any longer, we may be too late."

"What can I do for you?"

"Keep Uatach and your home safe. I do not feel right leaving you with danger still lurking, but the longer I stay the worse it will be when I do return home."

"We shall prevail. Scathach will not leave her daughter unattended, and we will always keep our guard up. Although, I do not believe we will ever feel completely safe again."

Cormac watched as Osgar danced with Maecha. He tapped his hand on his leg to the music. "I think I will take a turn with my daughter," he said and moved among the dancers.

As Maecha swung out of Osgar's arms, her father grasped her around her waist and slowed the dance.

"How fares my lovely child?" he asked.

"I am having a better time than I thought I would."

"We shall head back to Eire within the next day or two."

"So soon?"

"It is time. Your dreams tell of danger. I have not dreamt of your mother and that makes me feel uneasy, also. There is nothing more we can do here. Scathach will make sure the Picti are well protected. She will not jeopardize the safety of her daughter."

Maecha nodded. She noticed Circenn standing by himself outside the dancing circle. He stared at her, but it was as if he didn't see her.

"Circenn does not seem right to me," Maecha said.

Her father looked at him and a shiver ran down his neck. "No, he does not."

"Perhaps I will see if I can get him to dance. He must be distraught over his brother's death."

"Aye, that would be nice of you," Cormac said and let her go.

"Circenn?" Maecha said. He didn't answer, so she placed her hand on his arm and her world turned askew.

She saw a figure laughing in a raging flame of fire. His eyes were red torches and they glared at her—no, at Circenn. Her body quaked in fear at this creature. Then it flashed to the forest where they had been attacked. Someone yelled at Circenn. Ce confronted his brother when Maecha was slumped over her horse. It felt odd seeing her limp body and being unaware of what happened around her. She watched Ce move closer and felt the pain as it surged through Ce. A sword tip protruded from the front of his belly. Maecha shifted her eyes and saw the holder of the sword. Evil flourished in the attacker's eyes, deep into his soul. Of course he didn't expect the attack. It was his own brother who had murdered him. Circenn had killed his brother, and then brought Maecha to this Fire Lord. Her vision. It had been right. The betrayal had been between brothers.

She stumbled back into one of the dancers, who grabbed her before she hit the ground. Circenn flashed a menacing smile at her. Maecha started to scream. She couldn't release herself from the pain. Cormac grabbed her.

Pointing to Circenn, she cried, "He...he killed Ce!"

Cormac glared at Circenn who wasn't smiling any longer.

Fidach approached his brother. "Is it true? Did you kill our brother?"

Circenn smiled again and a bolt of fire shot from his hand, and hit Fidach squarely in the chest. His tunic caught on fire and those around him threw him to the ground to stamp it out. Circenn drew his sword and raised it over his head. "Death to the Matriarch! Hail to the Fire Lord!"

He swung his sword down toward Maecha as her father flung himself in front of his daughter.

Cruithne's sword flew down in front of them and stopped Circenn in his tracks. Rage and disbelief struggled across the king's face. Circenn dropped his sword and scurried back from his father, fear finally showing itself.

"Is this true, Circenn? Did you kill your brother, when you knew how much we have already lost as a family and as a tribe?"

Circenn lost control. Like a trapped animal, he glanced around for an escape. Then with a malevolent glare at his father, he spoke, "Yes, it is true. Do you think that I would wait for another woman to take over our land and lead it to ruin? You are nothing but a weak man. The Fire Lord is all-powerful and through him I will rule all the Picti!" His face broke out into a lopsided grin, like one who has been cleansed of all sin through confession.

Cruithne clutched at his heart as this final blow shattered it to tiny pieces. "And your mother? Your sister?"

Circenn's sinister laugh told him all he needed to know. Cruithne shut his eyes and lifted his head to the sky. "What have I done?" He shoved his son to the ground. "Take him away," Cruithne said before he killed his son in cold blood.

An eerie scream escaped from Circenn's mouth as he withdrew a dagger from his breeches. Everyone yelled at once as the dagger flew true toward its mark in the middle of Cruithne's back. Treasa flipped into the air, screaming like a banshee. All traces of the regal queen gone as the warrior within her emerged. She rolled in front of Cruithne and held up her shield. The dagger bounced off the shield and dropped to the ground. In the same moment a bolt of lightning shot out of the clear sky and struck Circenn. He stared down at the burning hole in his chest and fell to his knees. Calling out to the god he thought would save him, Circenn cried, "Protect me, Fire Lord. I have tried to do your bidding."

No one answered and Circenn collapsed to the ground. Holding on to Treasa for support, Cruithne gaped at Scathach, her hand outstretched toward his son. She had done what he knew he never could.

Cruithne nodded to her and knelt down by his son. He touched his face. His skin was warm and becoming warmer. Suddenly, it burst into flames and Cruithne was wrenched back. Where his son had been was now only ashes.

Fidach knelt next to his father and held the shaking man. Cruithne grabbed his last living son by the shoulders and buried his head in his chest. His body shook and convulsed like a man with fever, while sobs of grief escaped from his throat. Fidach never let go, but only held the man who had lost so much in such a short time. Cruithne quieted and took a deep breath. His body stilled and he gave Fidach an enormous hug. He lifted his face and held his son's gaze for a moment. Then he kissed Fidach on each cheek and stood on his own to address his people.

"I do not know the depth of my son's betrayal, but it has cut to the deepest part of my soul. All those, who have had any association with him in this matter, had best come forward."

A group of young warriors attempted to leave, but Goll and Osgar held them at sword point along with a handful of

Treasa's warriors. After a halfhearted attempt to escape, the men were captured and imprisoned to be dealt with later.

Osgar lifted Maecha onto her feet. Her arm had bled through its bandage and she was pale. Treasa assisted Cormac who started coughing once again.

Maecha kissed her father. "You put yourself at risk to save me! I thank you."

"It was the least I could do, when I couldn't even pull my sword out to defend you."

Maecha touched her father's cheek. It was so cold. She took his hands in hers to warm them. "You will be better, Father. We only need to get you home."

The vision caught her like the butt of a sword in the gut. She fell to the ground breathless.

"What is it, Maecha?" her father asked kneeling down beside her.

Maecha clutched her arms tightly around herself and stared at the ground. Her voice sounded far away. "It is Leann and Finnius. Leann is dead. My brother killed her." A sob escaped her lips.

Treasa knelt next to her and held her shuddering body. "What has happened to Finnius?"

Tears fell to the earth. "He is gone. He has used the last of his powers to tell me what has happened. There is a cave where he shall sleep until his daughter is able to release him if she can find him. Eithne is alive and will bring her daughter home."

She said to her father, "What has he done? How could Cairpre do this to them?"

"He may not be in control of his own mind, Maecha. I cannot believe that my son would do this, but we have to expect anything. He may have completely turned away from us and our ways."

Exhausted by her injuries and visions, Maecha couldn't stand. Goll scooped her up into his arms and brought her to her *broch*. Once asleep, they took turns guarding her door, knowing that the Fire Lord would come for her soon, now that Circenn had failed.

The next morning, Goll and Caoilte met Osgar.

"Maecha and the others are gathered in her hut," Osgar said.

Noting Osgar's concerned look, they said nothing and followed him. When they entered the dark interior, they saw Maecha huddled in her father's arm, her face swollen from tears.

When she saw Goll and Caoilte, fresh tears fell.

Goll strode further into the room. The young girl was still within, he thought. He took note of Cormac's condition and knew that their king was nearing the end of his rule. It was time for the daughter to embrace her destiny.

Goll towered over Maecha so that she was forced to look up at him, when he addressed her. "And will you sit there and pine in your father's arms, or will you fulfill the oath that you worked so hard to swear? What is done is done. You can only change what will happen from this moment on."

Maecha straightened, surprised by Goll's cold words. But those were the right words. She squared her shoulders and stood. Goll kept his one eye on her face. Maecha's eyes were lit in anger, but she only said, "I thank you for reminding me of my oath, but make sure you do not overstep your boundaries."

Goll stepped back and bowed, hiding the grin on his face. When he straightened, he addressed her like the queen he knew she would soon be. "I apologize if I have overstepped any boundaries, my lady. Know that I honor your oath above my life and will do your bidding."

"Fair enough." Maecha scanned the room and took in the dejected and worn faces of her companions. She faced her father and a spasm of fear gripped her. "Father?" Cormac peered up at her, pride lighting his weary eyes. "Don't you think it's time we headed for home?"

"Aye, I do."

"Then let us go home."

Disguised as a raven, the Fire Lord sat perched on a tree watching Maecha. Only the red of his eyes would have given him away. *They look all proud of themselves,* he thought. He knew that the closer Maecha got to Tara, the stronger her hold on that sword would be. Of course, Cairpre would be upset that he didn't get the sword, but it wouldn't matter. It was time to take the blasted weapon away from her. He flew away into the thickness of the trees and transformed back into himself. Akir closed his eyes and opened his palms. Fire and energy filled him until his body burned with it. He could see in his mind's eye that Maecha and her entourage were seated around a fire speaking with the Picti king. They were relaxed and unaware of the danger that would soon envelope them.

Maecha sat between her father and Cruithne who had his last remaining son and daughter-in-law next to him. Uatach's gaze was soft, and her face held a look of love as she sat contentedly next to Fidach, who had his arm around her waist. Maecha's heart dropped as she thought of her last connection with Kelan, but then she remembered Goll's words. She would be their leader and not let them down. There would be time to make everything right with Kelan. She would make sure of it. They had gone through too much together to not believe in one another. The others joined them.

Cruithne took her hand. "So you must leave us, eh?"

Maecha smiled. "Yes, it is time we were on our way. I think that we have accomplished more than we had ever dared here, and a lifelong friendship has grown from it. We have allied our tribes and if you ever have need of us, Uatach will be able to send word quickly through her mother."

"I thank you for your generosity in light of our treatment of you," Cruithne said, his face crumbling.

"Cruithne, what you did, I would have done myself. But we have reconciled, so let us leave the past and look to a future filled with hope," Cormac said.

The Picti king smiled. "You are a true friend and will be remembered as a benevolent king."

Without any warning, Maecha felt the uneasy sense of evil, like something slimy running down her neck and spine. She stood and unsheathed her sword.

"Maecha?" her father asked, pushing himself off the ground to stand with her.

Those around her did the same as they had grown to respect her instincts. The ground shook slightly, then with more intensity. Cruithne was about to call for their horses, when the earth ripped open in front of them. Two warriors fell into the abyss. Maecha clambered back and regained her balance. Flames shot ten feet high into the air. The earth closed and, when the flames fell back to the earth, they molded together. A beast of fire, twice the size of their biggest warrior, stared down at Maecha.

Goll shoved Maecha behind him and attacked the beast.

"Goll, no!" Maecha said, but it was too late. The beast launched a spark toward Goll and scorched his thigh.

Caoilte pulled Goll out of the line of fire and flailed the beast with his daggers, but the beast shot them back at him. Treasa jumped in front of Caoilte just in time to protect him with her shield.

Turning its attention to Maecha, the beast spit fire balls at her. She easily deflected them with Imbas Skye. The beast roared. His hand became a flaming torch that singed everything in its path.

Goll rushed in from behind and rammed his axe into the beast's leg, dropping it to one knee. It quickly recuperated and swung a fiery arm forcing him to run for cover.

"Maecha!" Treasa yelled, placing herself in front of Maecha. She held the shield toward the beast, who pummeled it with all his power. The flames hit the shield, but protected the two women behind it. Everyone else had to move out of the way or be roasted alive. Behind the shield, the only heat Maecha and Treasa felt was where the flames hit on either side.

"When he stops," Maecha yelled over the roar. "Protect me as I stand."

"What are you going to do?"

Maecha smiled. "It'll come to me."

Treasa shook her head, but agreed.

The flames stopped and the beast was silent. Maecha knew it waited for her to make the next move. She prayed to Imbas Skye and the blue eye lifted its lid.

"Stand!" Maecha yelled to Treasa. Maecha held her sword toward the beast, and the blue eye blasted it with ice cold fury. The beast reared back, but didn't fall. It struck toward Maecha who rolled out of the way. With the other hand, it shot at Treasa, who hid behind her shield. She was trapped there.

"I can't get to you!" Treasa called.

The beast turned its other hand to Maecha and laughed, hot steam billowing from its mouth. The Fire Lord watched through his vision, and he joined in with the riotous laughter, because victory was finally going to be his. She could not attack and protect herself at the same time. He wished he could join in, but he was using the majority of his power, and he couldn't attack her, while keeping the beast moving.

Black flames shot from the beast's fingertips.

Knowledge came to Maecha in a flash of remembrance. It wasn't her memory, but one of the warriors who dwelled in her sword. The small warrior with the elf-like face appeared next to her. Maecha mimicked the warrior and opened her hand toward the flames. White light flashed from her fingertips and connected

277

with the dark evil. She also remembered Scathach showing her how to channel her energy into one area of her body to give it power. She did the same. The light grew stronger and the beast's flames were pushed back. Suddenly, the glowing light grew brighter and the beast faltered. Imbas Skye bolted the beast with the power of the warriors within it. The beast stumbled back. This gave Treasa the chance she needed to protect Maecha. She aimed her shield toward the beast and a blue flame shot at it. It was enough to distract the beast. Maecha yelled to Uatach. "Shoot it with your bow!"

With precise accuracy, Uatach shot the beast and her arrows turned to ice as they hit their mark. The beast screeched in pain. The flames solidified into patches of ice. The blue eye spewed the beast with her power, while Maecha sliced at its entity with her shards of ice. The beast was overwhelmed and fell back to the ground, frozen like a statue. In rage, Goll pummeled it with his axe shattering it to bits. Any remaining flames smoldered and then hissed as the last ember was extinguished.

The Fire Lord gasped as his hold on the beast dissipated. His fingertips turned to ice and his body shivered with cold. Not being able to hold onto his power, he disappeared.

The blue eye winked closed and Imbas Skye fell silent as the warriors went to rest once more. Maecha stared at the ice frozen to the tips of her fingers. The memories of others and the knowledge that had flooded into her mind, at such an incredible rate, exhausted her. She looked around in stunned amazement. "We won," she said to no one in particular and staggered. Both Goll and Caoilte grabbed her arms before she fell to the ground.

"She's ice cold! Get me some blankets."

Maecha was placed close to the fire and wrapped in multiple blankets. Her own memories intertwined with the memories of the warriors from Imbas Skye, and the powers that had been unleashed by the attack from the beast. Had the Fire Lord known that he would increase Maecha's abilities tenfold, he might have changed his strategies. All the power that Maecha possessed vibrated within her with such clarity, she couldn't control the simplest act. She shook and moaned with the heavy burden her mind and soul now carried. The only thing she could think to do was call out to Kelan to take some of it away, but he was out of reach.

She could hear those around her calling, asking what they could do. They did not know what happened to her, and she couldn't find the voice to explain it. Maecha tucked her head under her arms and rocked back and forth. Just when she thought she would not be able to bear it any longer, she felt loving, warm arms envelope her. She shivered and the arms pulled her closer. Joy and love seeped into her, and her mother's voice carried a lullaby that she would sing when Maecha was a baby. The words and melody soothed her and her mother's love warmed her. Everyone watched as she appeared to cuddle up to something that wasn't there. Her teeth stopped chattering. Then she closed her eyes and drifted off into blissful sleep.

The Fire Lord was back in his lair, and he paced in front of a piping hot fire to warm his hands. They had turned blue from the intense cold. Even the fear of a small part of his body being maimed was enough to make his temper soar. "So you think you can best me, do you, Maecha? You are nothing without that sword. As soon as it is mine, I will show you just how much power you lack!" The Fire Lord yelled into Maecha's dreamworld. He ignored the fact that ice had spewed from her hands and perhaps her power was within her. "You will have nothing, nothing! Already your precious Tara has been taken. Your brother rules and that worthless blacksmith is my prisoner. And if you think your lover can help the Otherworld, then you are sadly mistaken!" He launched image after image of the fall of Tara, of the disease and famine that had stretched across the land, the death of Leann, the downfall of Finnius, and he added the eventual death of Kelan just to push her over the edge, like she had done to him. Then he yelled to Althar, "I need more power! Send me all the spirits of the Faery Folk!"

Maecha screamed and sat up. It was nightfall and she had thrown the blankets off as the Fire Lord's visions burned her from within. Everyone guarded her like a precious baby. Maecha looked around her, willing the images to remove themselves from her mind.

"What is it?" she heard someone ask.

"The Fire Lord. He's done all this. Tara. Lon. Leann. Finnius," she choked back tears. "He is responsible for everything, even the attack on Cruithne's people. The Otherworld is in ruins. Kelan." She shook her head. "No, I would know if he was dead." She lifted her crystal and their bond still held. It was pale, but Kelan was still with her. She pushed herself up into a sitting position. "How much time before dawn?"

"Two hours," Goll said.

"Are we prepared to leave?"

"The boats are packed. We are at your command," Goll said.

Maecha peered down at her hands. They appeared the same, but she felt different, older. The memories, now hers, felt as ancient as the earth, and she would use them to save her home and her people.

Chapter 31 - Eire

Deep in the recesses of the darkest part of the Otherworld, mud began to boil and pop. With each bubble, a dark image appeared and traveled over the mud to the dry land where Althar waited. As each bubble approached him, Althar engulfed it in fire. Hands and feet emerged, followed by the body and head of a black mage. Each one, hooded and dark as a moonless night, gathered together and a chant as ancient as the oaks arose around them.

"Fear the Fire Lord, for he has come.

He will bring your death and doom.

Serve the Fire Lord, for he holds the key,

To give us power and set us free."

The mages stood with heads lowered and hands folded in the sleeves of their black cloaks. Their bent heads barely reached Althar's chest. When the bubbles ceased, so did their chanting. One of the mages in the front of the group asked, "How may we assist the Fire Lord?"

Althar puffed out his chest. "We are to invade the Otherworld to destroy the Faery Folk and the Lord and Princess."

The black mages glided, while Althar marched to the mists that separated them from the Faery Folk. The mages raised their hands and the mist was swept away like a reluctant dust ball. The mages filed into small boats lined along the water with Althar in the front boat. Without rowing, they traveled across the water in darkness. Then the blackness ended and the land of the faeries and the Otherworld appeared before them.

Althar was surprised they hadn't been spotted yet.

"They cannot see you," the same mage said. "We have spun an apparition around us, so they only see water. We will make ourselves known in a moment."

The Faery Folk were even smaller than the mages, yet they carried spears that were as tall as Althar. Some wore cone shaped hats, while others had caps that covered their hair completely. The Faery Folk stood guard along a path that was lined with white and black crystal. Following that path would lead to the Lord and Princess.

"Now," the mage said, and the looks of incredulity on the Faery Folks' faces told them that they were no longer hidden.

With a cry of alarm, the faeries ran to their defenses, but it was useless. The black mages flew through the air and battered the small warriors with black flames of death. Wherever the flames hit, the faeries disintegrated. With each death, a spark shot into the air and, as it disappeared, Althar felt an intense heat rising within him. Then the sound of psychotic laughter reverberated in his head, and he knew that the Fire Lord ingested the spirits of the Faery Folk. He wanted the Fire Lord to thrive, so this motivated Althar, who now destroyed as many Faery Folk as the mages did. He raced along the path killing anyone who stepped in his way, until he came upon a solid crystal door.

Standing in front of the door was a tall, thin man. He wore his blond hair long. His olive-green eyes bore through Althar. In one hand, he held a long handled axe.

"Step aside," Althar said, wanting to get to the Lord and Princess himself.

"I am Each-Lúath, leader of the Fian of the Otherworld. None may get by."

Althar laughed. "You don't have a choice. Your warriors are dead and the Fire Lord has taken back his human form. He is now the leader of your Otherworld."

"Leave this place while you can. You may not enter here,"

Each-Lúath repeated.

Anger filled Althar. He wanted to kill and that was what he was going to do. He lifted his sword high over his head to cut the man in half. Each-Lúath slid under Althar's sword and sliced his side open. Althar screamed in surprised pain. Each-Lúath jumped back and flipped up over Althar's body, and sliced his forehead open. Blood poured into Althar's eyes and he bellowed in rage.

Althar swung his sword blindly and Each-Lúath blocked every swing, retaliating with another cut to Althar's flesh. With a spinning jump he slammed the side of his axe into Althar's knee, crashing him to the ground. Each-Lúath was about to deliver his final blow when a fire ball seared his side. He staggered back in pain, but still faced his enemy. Two black mages approached him. One levitated the Fian warrior, who struggled to catch his breath against the invisible force that held a firm grip on his throat. The other circled around him and said, "They are all dead. And now we shall take over the guard of Tir-nan-og as it should be."

Each-Lúath tried to remove the shackles from his neck. Althar's wounds healed. He howled in delight. He couldn't die.

Each-Lúath dropped his spear as white dots flashed in front of his eyes. He sent a warning to the Lord and Princess that he could no longer protect the doorway. But he had an idea that they already knew this. Another member of the Fian stepped into his dimming line of vision and attacked their enemies. As his rescuer fell to the onslaught of mages, Each-Lúath disappeared.

"Where did he go?" Althar asked.

"It does not matter. Move aside," one of the black mages said.

The black mage struck the door with a pointed flame that shattered it into pieces.

Althar entered a crystal white cave. The walls, the ceiling, and the floor were smooth and glossy white. A bridge in front of him stretched over dark water. It looked like the only other doorway was on the other side, so he ventured forth onto the bridge. Images of the battle that had been won were displayed on the walls. The mages were no longer by the water, and had ventured further into the Otherworld to lay claim to their own findings.

"Who dares to enter my realm?" a loud voice bellowed, bringing Althar back to his purpose.

"A servant of the Fire Lord!" Althar yelled. "The Fire Lord has claimed the rights to the Otherworld!"

"You would dare to invade Tir-nan-og in belief that we would forfeit anything to you?"

"You will forfeit your everlasting life if you do not surrender to the Fire Lord."

Althar heard a crack and jumped to the side, just in time to miss having a sharp crystal pierce his head.

"So that's how you want to play?" Althar asked. He opened his hand and yanked it back to hurl a fire ball toward the door. A wave flew up over the side of the bridge and drenched Althar, extinguishing his fire. He sputtered in shock and humiliation.

He turned to see the black mages watching him. "Well? What are you waiting for? Attack!"

Too numerous to count, the black mages swarmed over the crystal cavern. Red flames shot from their hands and their eyes. The crystals began to melt. Still the Lord and Princess did not show themselves. Crystal shards fell from the ice ceiling, piercing mages as they continued their assault. More faery guardians entered from the front and attacked the mages. Their spears deflected the flames, but only caused more of the cavern to disintegrate.

Behind the crystal wall, the Lord and Princess thought as one. "They have taken the power of the Awen Crystal. We leave it to the One to fight. What lingering power we have, we pass on."

The Princess of the Otherworld lifted her hands and spoke.

"As you are the earth, sea, and sky
Hear our cry.
As you are the earth, sky, and sea
Heed our plea.
As you are the sky, sea, and earth
Listen for all that we are worth.
Take this power and spread it between the two
Who share the earth, sky, and sea.
For they are the chosen ones
Who will fulfill the prophecy."

They took a deep breath and blew into their hands. The power of the Lord and Princess of the Otherworld went forth to find Maecha and Kelan.

Other members of the Fian revealed themselves.

"Lord and Princess. We must remove you from the cavern. The mages have destroyed the outer sanctum and it is no longer stable."

They nodded and, as they lifted a hand, a hidden door revealed itself. "We will be safe in here."

The Fire Lord huddled near his dimming flames, but perked up when he sensed the first of the spirits spinning toward him. Lon watched in horror as the glittering spirits of the Faery Folk were lured to the Fire Lord. As they came closer, the Fire Lord opened his mouth and inhaled. The spirits, powerless to respond, flowed into his body and combined with his own spirit. Flames shot high, scorching the ceiling of the cave. The Fire Lord laughed in cheerful mirth as his body regained its power and added more. A shimmer caught Lon's eye and he stared at the entrance to the cave. Another spirit lingered, the last of its strength holding it there. Lon opened his mouth and inhaled with all his might. If he could have one spirit, maybe he would have some defense against the Fire Lord. Sensing Lon's intention, the spirit let all its strength lead it toward him. Lon breathed deeply and felt the spirit enter his body. Little sparks of energy tingled down his throat, through his middle, and extended toward his legs and arms. This was a strong spirit. Lon told it he would do all he could to make things right. He just needed to wait.

The Fire Lord approached Lon who acted weak and dazed. With a sneer, Akir said, "I have no more need for you, Lon, and your friends are too late."

"Wait, I can help you!" Lon tried to stall him.

Akir assailed Lon with firebolts and vanished.

Kelan ventured down the path that would lead to Tir-nan-og. A shock of fear had run through his veins, when he felt the surge of power that had illuminated his Awen Crystal only moments ago. He knew that a danger far greater than they had yet to face was near, and the Lord and Princess were in grave peril. Knowing this made him feel better that Maecha was far away, even though his heart broke from her betrayal. He searched for her, but her image was a muted shadow. He would worry about that later. As the opening to Tir-nan-og appeared, Kelan unleashed his sword and flail, prepared for anything.

Nothing could have prepared him for the scene that his eyes were forced to witness. Hundreds of Faery Folk lay tattered, beaten, and dead along the shore. Wisps of smoke whispered along the water and fires were still being fought by the few remaining faeries. A tiny faery walked like a drunkard, holding her bleeding head. Sheathing his weapons, Kelan scooped her up into his arms.

"Where are the Lord and Princess?"

Overwhelmed by her own sorrow, the little faery shed tears and pointed to the battered stone door that had protected Tir-nan-og for centuries. Kelan lay the faery down by others who were being treated for injuries. He paddled the small boat that brought all visitors across the shallow water. He took in all the death and the damage, while images of his own family's slaughter threatened to overtake him. They had called him too late. Again, he was too late. Kelan jumped out of the boat and ran to the tall warriors that were huddled together.

"Brothers!" he called.

They turned and eyed Kelan with suspicion. Kelan did not pull out his sword when they pulled out theirs. Instead he looked past them onto the flat stone that held a warrior who bore the symbol of the Fian. Kelan did not doubt that he had fought bravely, and his anger rose once more by the injustice.

"I am Kelan mac Nessa, champion to Maecha Ruadh mac Art, daughter of High King Cormac mac Art. I have been summoned here by the Lord and Princess of the Otherworld through this." He held up the Awen Crystal, so that there would be no challenge to his claim.

A tall, powerfully built man nodded to him and said, "We are the brotherhood of the Fian who protect the Otherworld. Come with me."

They entered a sealed room lined with black crystal. A group of men gathered around a stone table deep in thought and discussion. Kelan noted the tall thin man with long blond hair. He looked prettier than some of the maidens Kelan used to chase in his carefree years. The man looked up at the interruption and his green eyes held nothing pretty whatsoever. They held anger and passion so deep, it sparked Kelan's desire to rid the Otherworld of whatever beast had swarmed through it.

The man who had brought Kelan in whispered something to the green-eyed man.

"Kelan mac Nessa, we are honored that you have come to assist us. I am Each-Lúath, Leader of the Fian of the Otherworld." Each-Lúath held out his arm and Kelan grasped it.

"I did not come in time," Kelan said.

"It appears that the Fire Lord has used our Awen Crystal

in more ways than one," a voice spoke.

"You did not summon me here?" Kelan asked confusion warring with oncoming anger at having to leave Maecha.

"Come and sit," Each-Lúath said.

The men moved, so that Kelan could see the Lord of the Otherworld sitting on a crystal throne. Kelan kneeled in front of him.

"Rise, Kelan mac Nessa. You do us proud by honoring your commitment to the Otherworld. We know what it cost you to leave Maecha."

Kelan's green eyes filled with regret. "It appears that you did need me, but I fear that I have come too late. There has already been so much death."

The Princess of the Otherworld came forth. She rose and held her hand out to him. "Sit with me, Kelan." He did. "There will always be unwanted death in any war. The Faery Folk fought well. We were surprised by the power of the Fire Lord. We did not think he would ever be able to free himself from the bonds that have held him for so long."

"How did he get into Tir-nan-og?"

"He dwells in one of the sidhe caverns that may have long ago been abandoned. He was held at bay by the balance of the sky, earth, and sea. But he has caused an imbalance, and he was able to take advantage of the disturbance."

"We were attacked in Alba by men who had sworn allegiance to the Fire Lord. Perhaps his powers grow as others support him," Kelan offered.

"That may be true, but there was one druid who kept the Fire Lord's powers from strengthening, and I fear that something has happened to him." She looked at Kelan with sadness.

"What druid?" Kelan asked.

"Finnius Amergin."

"Finnius? What does he have to do with any of this?" Kelan asked worried even more about his homeland. Knowing that he had to fulfill his duty here and not sure where Maecha was warred inside him. Never had his obligations bore down on him so much. All Kelan wanted was to have Maecha safe.

"Finnius is possibly the most powerful druid who has ever lived on earth. He found the ability to time travel, so that he could help Maecha and you fulfill your prophecy. All the steps you and Maecha have taken together have brought you closer to what you need to do save our way of life. Finnius' abilities brought much of this about. Now through the Fire Lord's actions, Finnius has used all his powers and will remain hidden until his daughter can find him. Without the druid, you and Maecha will find it harder to defeat the Fire Lord, but it can be done. He was one of the keys to Akir's prison. The Awen Crystal was the second and the Fire Lord has that. He only has to take Imbas Skye from Maecha and he will be unstoppable."

"Is Maecha safe?" Kelan hated to ask, but needed to know.

For the first time, the Princess showed fear on her face. "You cannot feel her?"

"She…I or one of us has severed the tie and I fear she has betrayed me," Kelan admitted.

"Do not let your fear overrule your heart, Kelan. We know what you have suffered and how hard it is for you to love, but feel for Maecha and you will know the truth."

Frustration filled Kelan. "I have, my lady, and I feel nothing. My duty is here."

The Lord interrupted, "Your duty to your bond will always come first. This is a test for both of you. You must have faith in your love for one another and know that you will each be true. We must not always assume that what we see is actually the truth."

Kelan bowed his head, feeling like he had just been chastised for something he didn't do. He wasn't the one who was kissing another. Could there have been a reasonable explanation? "I will try to remember that, but right now I am concerned for

289

your well-being. What are these mages?"

"They encompass the power of the Fire Lord and defeated the Faery Folk. Their magic is powerful and tinged with an evil so dark, that just being around them is enough to kill someone. They fight in this world and in the world of dreams—killing their victims before they even know they are there. Defeat the beast who created them and the mages will dissipate."

"And you think something has happened to Lon?"

The Princess of the Otherworld held up her hand and a clear crystal orb lay on it. "Watch," she said.

Kelan peered into the orb and saw hundreds of villagers huddled together in Tara. He saw Finnius being taken by a group of men somewhere into the castle. He clenched his fists as he watched Cairpre smiling about Finnius' demise. Then he saw a very large man holding onto Lon and disappearing. The ball cleared.

"Now you must find Lon. He is here in the Otherworld. The Fire Lord was the one who had turned him into a monster. The Fire Lord fears Lon for the blacksmith holds the power of fire and steel. Free him and rid us of the beast, Althar, who captured him. He is a servant of the Fire Lord and fears nothing. Remember, Maecha is the only person who separates the Fire Lord from his ultimate power."

Kelan's jaw clenched at the thought of Maecha having such a powerful enemy. He still had much that he could do, and he had a kingdom to save. "I will not fail you."

The Lord of the Otherworld came forth, his black robe flowing around his body. "He has the Awen Crystal of the Otherworld, Kelan. The Princess took what is left of our powers and spread them between you and Maecha. Use the power wisely for it must be returned to the Otherworld. You must get the Awen Crystal back."

Kelan bowed and turned to walk away. Each-Lúath was there. Kelan meant to dismiss him, but Each-Lúath said, "The

Fian will accompany you. We are the protectors of the Otherworld and no other harm must come to it. We are yours to command."

His voice was strong and hard, so Kelan said, "I accept your help. Let us go and find Lon." He turned back to the Lord and Princess. "What about your safety?"

The Lord and Princess spoke in unison, "We are safe in here and a few warriors will stay behind to make it so. Go on your way. The Fire Lord has assumed a human form and he is near those you love. Go!"

Kelan felt a surge of panic and searched his mind and heart for Maecha. She was not there. He would fulfill his duty and return to her.

Kelan, Each-Lúath, and four of his men ran back through the main doorway to where all the injured and dead Faery Folk lay. Along the cavernous walls, there were various tunnels that led to different sidhes of the Otherworld.

"Which way?" one of men asked.

Kelan thought of the power of his crystal, and how he and Maecha had watched all the scenes happening along the crystal walls, when they first met the Lord and Princess. The visions were part of the power of the Awen Crystal. He clasped it in his hand and envisioned Lon. He didn't know if he was still alive, but he pictured his face when he had first lifted it up to Maecha. His hair was blond, and his brown eyes were large and filled with gratitude. Then he thought of him again among the fighting fields outside of Tara, when his eyes had raged red like the fires of a blacksmith. Yes, he did understand the power of fire, and hopefully that would help them take down this Fire Lord.

Kelan heard the banging of metal in his head, and saw an image of Lon tied up against a wall, his face singed and in pain. "This way," he said running toward a tunnel on his right. The warriors followed without question.

The tunnel was dark and narrow. The light of Kelan's

Awen Crystal led their way, and it grew brighter as Kelan felt they were getting closer to Lon. They approached a large opening and the smell of burnt skin and sulphur made Kelan pause. He signaled for them to unsheathe their weapons and approach with care. Two men crossed to the other side of the opening. From where he stood, Kelan could see a large platform that had burned down to embers. The putrid scent came from that source. Across from him, one of the men signaled and pointed. At Kelan's nod, they ran into the opening. The platform was empty, but they saw Lon on the other side of the cavern. A fiery prison separated them and he was being held against the wall by flaming shackles. His face was burnt and his body shook. That was the sound of steel that he heard earlier. The heat was molding Lon into a metal corpse.

"Lon!" Kelan yelled, urging him to come back to them.

Lon opened his eyes and flames shot toward them. The men jumped out of the way. Kelan knew he could not touch the flames. Kelan remembered the surge of power that he had felt through the Awen Crystal. Maybe that could help him. He took hold of the Awen Crystal and thought of ice and water and frigid temperatures. Avoiding the memories of his failure to produce water at the Isle of Imbas Skye, Kelan held his hand up toward the prison. Nothing happened. Pushing all doubt from his mind, Kelan thought of Lon and the fact that he needed help. This wasn't about him anymore. It was about helping a friend in need. Thinking harder and picturing water and ice on his hands, he touched the flaming cell.

"Kelan!" Each-Lúath yelled, afraid that he would ruin his hands.

The leaping flames flashed and then went out like a dampened torch. The prison disappeared. Each-Lúath stepped forth and slapped Kelan on the shoulder. "That was impressive," he said.

Relieved, Kelan nodded in agreement, but they weren't

done. He approached Lon whose big brown eyes bore through him like flaming arrows. Kelan ignored them.

"Lon, it is Kelan. We are here to release you. I am going to free your legs."

Lon continued to stare, so Kelan placed his hand on Lon's left ankle. His skin sizzled and Lon screamed in pain and then passed out.

"That'll make it easier," Each-Lúath said.

Kelan did the same for the other leg and both hands. Each-Lúath and another man laid him onto the ground. Kelan placed his hand on Lon's forehead. Lon's body shook as steam rose from it. Moments later, Lon peered up at Kelan in recognition.

"My friend," Lon muttered, trying to sit up.

"Be still, Lon," Kelan urged.

"The Fire Lord escaped."

"We know. He has left the Otherworld. We were sent to take care of you and find the man who brought you here. Do you know who he is or where he went?"

"I believe he led the black mages to the Lord and Princess. Are they still alive?" Lon tried to ask, but his throat felt like he swallowed burning embers.

"They are safe, but I am not sure for how long. The Fire Lord's minions have been released upon the world, and the Fire Lord holds the Awen Crystal of the Otherworld. We must find this creature and destroy him."

Kelan and Each-Lúath helped Lon to his feet. After introductions were made, Lon said, "Tara has fallen to Cairpre. I have failed you and Maecha."

"You did what you could and saved many of our villagers from what I have been told. There is honor in that. Now let us leave this accursed place. I have men to kill."

They found Althar on the Isle of the Blessed, the enchanted land where no one grew old. Food and drink were always in abundance. Children frolicked all day and the adults loved all night. The sight of the apple blossoms ignited Kelan's memory of the place during his and Maecha's challenges. Kelan had disappointed her then and she almost lost her life, because he had been too caught up in the playful revelry of this land. But it had also been the first challenge that they passed, and the connection that occurred between them was one of the best experiences of his life. Perhaps he did owe her a chance to explain.

The absence of music and laughter brought Kelan back to his senses. He remained alert as they entered the palace. Gaia, the lady of the isle, whispered in Kelan's head. "We are hidden. Please help us."

Kelan whispered that he would for he knew what death and destruction would do to the isle. The hearts and soul of these people would not be able to withstand the stench and horror of war. Kelan had never recovered from his family being murdered and he would not wish that on another. He motioned for Lon and the others to follow him. They stepped into the open field where the standing stones reached for the sky. "The enemy is close, but I do not want to fight in the palace. We will wait for the mages to grow impatient."

As darkness fell upon the magical land, a heavy mist settled around the warriors. Lon lifted his head and his eyes bounced with fire. "They come."

Lon stood and the others moved behind him. Althar stepped away from a stone and entered the circle. Their matching eyes glared at one another. Althar held a long sword toward Lon. Lon held out his right hand and it elongated into a sword, with blades of fire protruding from each side. Althar's eyes widened, but he recovered quickly, his strikes like hammers on an anvil.

Lon stepped out of Althar's range to give his body time to adjust. The Fire Lord had drained much of his energy, and he owed what he did have to the spirit he had inhaled. "Did the Fire Lord create you to amuse his boredom?" Lon taunted.

"I do not care for talk. Fight like a man."

"At least that is what I am. You are nothing but a servant to the Fire Lord, just like his minions. Once I get rid of you, they will all disappear."

Althar laughed. "I cannot die. Your weapons are useless against me."

"We'll see about that." Lon launched into a forward roll and sliced Althar's sword arm on his way back to his feet.

He may be invincible, but he wasn't impervious to pain. The large warrior yelled, but kept attacking. When he saw that his sword attacks were useless, Althar released fire balls with one hand at Lon, while he sliced at his midsection. Lon absorbed the fire like Althar would.

Lon was a large man, but he was also very fast. He moved out of Althar's reach and then, just as quickly, would step in and land a slicing blow. Althar's body needed time to rejuvenate, but Lon wouldn't allow it. He began to slow down. Lon was tiring too, and knew he couldn't go on like this forever.

He had forgotten about his companions, and a glance around told him that they were in trouble. A couple Fian were dead and that meant that only four of them were left. There were about fifty of the black mages, who weren't dying.

Lon thought about the spirit of the Faery Folk that he had taken into his body. He already used much of it to keep on his feet, but if he could harness that power, what would stop fire? When Lon created a sword, part of the process was heating the metal to a very high temperature and then dipping it into a quenching tank. This would cool the metal quickly and cause it to harden. If he could get Althar to become a flame and then drench him with water, would he turn to steel? It was worth a try, but where would he get water. Kelan. Kelan explained how he opened his prison through water and ice.

"Kelan, I need you!" Lon yelled.

"I'm . . . a . . . little . . . busy," Kelan grunted in between deflected fire balls.

"Use water!"

"Water? What are you talking about?"

"Water, fire, get the picture? I'll tell you when."

Kelan thought about his hand on the prison bars. That put out the fire, but he hadn't been able to create a powerful flow of water. He glanced at Lon and could hear him taunting the Fire Lord's beast. Sparks shot out of its hair and arms. He was turning into a fire ball. Lon needed water fast.

Kelan rolled away from the mage and ran toward his friend. He grabbed his Awen Crystal and prayed to the Mother Goddess to grant him the ability that would save them all. Give me water, he prayed to her. Give me powerful water. He thought it ironic that the element he feared most would be the same one to save him.

"Now!"

He heard Lon and stopped running. He was close enough, but not too close to be singed. Dropping his sword, he held his hands toward the beast that was now an eight foot flame. He soon would burn everything in his path. Kelan prayed and thought of losing his family. Then he thought of Maecha and how, no matter what she had done without him around, he wanted to start a family with her. His hands felt wet and he could see something drip. The beast burned toward him. It was now or never.

Kelan roared and pushed his hands toward the flame. Water spewed from his palms like fountains and connected with the flame. There was resistance, but then the water overpowered it like a wave. Kelan didn't feel connected to himself anymore. It felt like his body and mind were being cleansed, washed clean of all that had tainted him.

Althar didn't have time to register surprise. His whole body was pummeled with the flow of water. He spun over backward. Althar pushed up onto his knees, but they remained bent in that position. His left arm hardened into a cold gray mass. He lifted his sword in his right hand. As he moved to launch it one last time at Lon, his face stilled into a grimace. His body now matched his sword. He was a blacksmith's nightmarish creation. One by one the screams of mages were heard and then silenced. They disappeared back to their depths, hopefully never to be seen again.

"You can stop now," Lon said next to Kelan.

He dropped his hands and the water stopped. Kelan looked at them, not sure if he was impressed or horrified. Thinking about it, he realized he felt really good.

Each-Lúath clasped him on the shoulder. "Yet again, I am impressed."

"How did you know it would work?"

Lon shrugged. "I didn't."

"You saved all of us and the Otherworld tonight," Kelan said.

"Kelan," a sultry voice called from behind him.

The men's mouths fell open. Gaia stood in her shimmering transparent gown with her hands held out toward Kelan.

Every curve in her voluptuous body called to him. Kelan remembered being wrapped up in her arms and wanting to stay there for eternity. She sauntered to him and they embraced. All the men groaned.

"You have saved us all. Please join us for a celebration."

With reluctance, Kelan pulled himself away. "I would love to, my lady, but Maecha needs me."

Gaia pouted, but acquiesced. "Will any of you join us?"

Each-Lúath smiled and grasped Gaia's elbow. "We would be honored. As Fian of the Otherworld, it is our duty to ensure your safety." He turned to see a group of beautiful young women standing by the doorway to the palace. Waving to Kelan, he then smiled at Gaia. "All of you."

"Are you sure you don't want to join them?" Kelan asked Lon.

"Oh, I do, but I have an obligation to fulfill first."

Cairpre strolled through the open arena inside Tara where many villagers were still housed in makeshift camps. There just wasn't enough room for them to live. He had wanted them to leave, but many were either too sick or didn't have a home to go to. Thanks to him, he thought. He had been a little too enthusiastic about his destruction. Leann's words scorched his mind. Was he flawed? He knew he had physical flaws, but he never believed that such a thing should prohibit a man from ruling. So was he flawed in his mind? Was he wrong to follow in the footsteps of a powerful god, who may have turned out to be a monster? People may have been sick, but at least they weren't being attacked. The crops would grow again and his men were out scouring the fields for lost livestock. They would survive and planting would begin. It was time that the people claimed their lives and started anew.

He thought of the power that pulsed through him since the Fire Lord had visited the other day. Cairpre was dying to use it, but feared that it would kill the villagers if he forced them to leave. Perhaps he could use it to rebuild parts of the land. The people would love him then. He could create fields of wheat and barley, increase the livestock. He wouldn't rule out of fear, he would rule with generosity—just like his father.

Cairpre shook his head. No, he would not be like his father. Although it would seem like a smart move, he had turned from him too long ago to make a change now.

His thoughts were interrupted by a villager who ran up to him. "My lord. My son has fallen from his horse and has broken his limb. I need the *bendrui* to heal him."

Cairpre's face flooded red. "She will not be able to help him. Find another." Only his men had known what he had done to Leann and he had made them vow to be silent.

"But she is the most skilled and he will be lame if it is not set right."

Cairpre turned on him. "The *bendrui* is dead! Dead! She can no longer help. Find another way."

"Dead? How?"

Cairpre rubbed his hands over his unruly hair. He blew out a breath. "She was killed for trying to free Finnius."

The man stepped back in shock. "What have you done? This is not what you promised."

Cairpre shoved him back. "Do you have food, water, shelter? Do not lose hope. The Fire Lord has been here and, when he returns, we shall have our just rewards."

The man nodded with reluctance and fear. He left to see who could help them now.

Cairpre headed out to the woods. He did not want anyone else to ask him about Leann's death. He was sure that everyone would know of it by the time he went back. And they would blame him. What other choice did he have? Leann had betrayed him and helped Finnius to escape, although he probably should have thanked her for getting rid of him. Who knew when his self-inflicted hibernation would end? He couldn't let this bother him. It was a sign of weakness and he refused to ever be weak again. Once the Fire Lord got what he wanted, then Cairpre would have unlimited power and he could rule under his own name.

"And what will that power have cost you, my son?"

"Go away! I do not wish to speak with you!"

"Oh, but I wish to speak with you," she said. Her body transformed into a powerful lady in leather warrior garb with a sword sheathed at her side.

Cairpre unsheathed his sword and pointed it at her.

With a wave of her hand, the sword flew into the trees. "Foolish boy. I thought to win you over with love and understanding. But now I see that you have no respect for yourself or others."

She glided toward him and Cairpre stepped back. Deirdre's eyes turned sad. "Fine, then you will listen. Do you think I wished to die giving birth to you? I had my whole life ahead of me as a wife, queen, warrior, and mother. I did not wish to leave any of you. But it was the will of the Mother Goddess and I did not have a choice."

"What does that have to do with me now?"

"*You* have a choice. Do not turn your back on your father or your sister any longer. The Fire Lord is using you. He will betray you as he has done to all the others who have followed him."

Cairpre fisted his hands. "I don't believe you!"

"Then see for yourself." She opened her hands and a vision of Akir letting Circenn die flashed through his mind. Then another vision of the Fire Lord attempting to take his sister's sword from her slammed into his mind.

Cairpre's singed eyes shimmered with unshed tears. "But why? Why would he do that? Circenn only did what he asked. He was supposed to give him his own power so he could rule."

"Cairpre, the Fire Lord manipulates others into doing what he needs and then he destroys them. That is why he was locked away so long ago. He is a danger to everyone. You must help destroy him."

Cairpre roughly rubbed his hands over his face. He shook his head and turned to face the mother he had never known. "You are lying. You only show yourself now to get your way. Plus, the sword will be mine. It should have always been mine!"

"You used to see me all the time." Cairpre had a vision of himself running through the woods chasing a beautiful spirit. His breath caught at the memory. "But then you got these ideas in your head that the Mother Goddess didn't love you. She has always loved you as I have. Finnius loved you and now you have turned hard and shoved him away."

"And what about my father, eh, dear Mother! Where was his love, his understanding? The only reason why Finnius paid any attention to me was because my father ignored me to coddle his daughter and that whelp, Kelan. Father cast me aside when he came along. How could I compete? How can I compare with any of them when I am so physically marred?"

Deirdre moved closer. "I know that you hurt, but what you are doing is not the way. Our land is in danger and I have been asked to speak with you before the Fire Lord finishes what he has started in Tara. His vengeance goes beyond destroying your sister. Once he has her sword, he will use its power to avenge all the wrongs he feels that the gods and goddesses have done him, and he won't care who or what he destroys in the process. You must make your decision before it is made for you. I love you, my son, and I'm always with you for guidance. Choose wisely."

She faded and left Cairpre more alone than he had ever been in his life.

Chapter 32 - Eire

They sailed upon the morning breeze. Tears welled in Maecha's eyes as she thought about those left behind. She grieved for the death of Cruithne's sons. With all her knowledge and supposed power, she still could not prevent the tragedy. Scathach had said that sometimes knowledge did not come when it was needed most. Happy tears dropped as Maecha thought of Uatach, whom she considered as a sister. They had grown close and she wished her love and happiness in her new life with Fidach. But her heart grew heavy, and a large lump formed in her throat as she worried for Kelan. She knew that he was a skilled and cunning warrior. It was the lack of his presence, both physical and emotional, that hurt the most. She didn't feel him now, when his assurance and comfort would carry her through the rest of her journey. It was his faith in her that made her strong. Knowing that he was there to back her up made her brave. She felt like a coward. But then she thought about the Fire Lord and the beast he had conjured up to kill her. She had done that without Kelan, but she also had the help of her friends. You didn't have to fight alone to be brave. And while she may not have needed Kelan at that moment, she needed him as much as her own heart. He was a part of her and she would make sure they found their way back together.

Cormac joined Maecha at the bow of the boat. She no longer had to look up at him. He seemed to be bent with age. He still cradled his arm and carried a cloth with him to collect the phlegm that he constantly spit up. Maecha tried to ignore the fact that some of it contained blood. Leann was gone as was Finnius.

She would have to depend on one of the other druids to heal him. She just hoped she was in time. Maecha knew that Cairpre's betrayal weighed heavy on him. Maecha's heart burst with pain for her father.

She took his hand. "What will you do?"

Cormac's eyes reflected the storm clouds that formed overhead. "I will do what I must, Maecha. If he has done what everyone has said, then he will have to pay for his crimes. I only hope that he gives me a reason to forgive him. I would, Maecha." His sad eyes held hers when she raised her eyebrows. "It is not easy to turn away from your own child. You will know someday. I can only hope that there is some good left in him."

Maecha thought of the last time she saw Cairpre and remembered his threats to her. No, she didn't think her brother would change, but she couldn't break her father's heart.

Osgar called to Cormac, "A storm approaches. We should head below and ride this one out."

"You really must have a word with Manannán, Father."

Cormac's eyes twinkled. "And why is that?"

"He has a mind of his own and, although it may have been right to send us to Scathach first, we need to get home as soon as possible. I heard you and he are friends."

Cormac laughed. "I'm not the kind of friend that he would listen to, although he did help me before I wed your mother. It was after I had trained with the druids and was given the sword of my father as well as his other gifts. There was war and strife in our land and it was dangerous traveling with a warband, so you could imagine the danger I faced traveling alone. Having heard about the queen's desire for a king, I had set off toward Tara. The sky had been bursting with stars and I had settled down to sleep along a sandy beach, allowing the waves to lull me to sleep. Just as I was about to enter my dreams, I heard the distinct sound of a dagger being drawn. I would have been a dead man if it wasn't for the sea god, Manannán. The blade nicked my throat before I reacted, but then in a blur my attacker was thrown into the sea. I jumped up, prepared to defend myself and there, on a magnificent white horse, sat the sea god. He laughed like he had just told a joke instead saving my life.

"With a wave of his hand, he sent a goblet flying toward me. As I grabbed it from the air, he spoke these words to me: 'With a lie this shall break into four pieces; with a truth, it will come back together again.' Then he was gone."

"What did that mean?" Maecha asked.

"It meant that with this goblet, I would know if someone who called themselves my friend was truly so. There have been many times over the years, when the goblet has proven its worth for both friend and foe."

"But why did mac Lir give you the goblet?"

Cormac sighed. "That I do not know. I think that perhaps he enjoyed having some laughs at my expense, but he is also a generous god and gives as he sees fit. Come, let us go below. I do not think it will last, but we do not want to take a chance."

The unsteady rocking of the boat had caused Maecha's stomach to roll over on itself. She hadn't felt that way the first time they had traveled through a storm, but she felt the bile rise to her throat and hoped she could keep her food down.

They never made it below. The boat rocked with the crashing of the waves and glints of fire sparked across the air.

"The Fire Lord!" Maecha hissed. "We need help now, Father!"

They held on to the edge of the boat.

Cormac choked on the sea water, but he yelled as best he could. "Manannán! I call you to save my daughter if you cannot save me again!" Cormac was flung from the edge and fell back onto the deck.

"Father!" Maecha called and let go of the side to let the flow of water push her toward him. She grabbed him and held onto the railing.

Manannán mac Lir flew up into the air on his sea horse, spraying more water over them. His face was stern and there was nothing of the jovial god in his eyes when he addressed them.

"Get below! Akir does not want you to make it home. I will send you back very quickly." He looked at Maecha. "He will not stop; no deception is too small for him. Beware." To Cormac, he said, "I gave you that goblet because the light of the goddess flowed in you and I knew then and there that you would play a hand in this prophecy. Use that goblet well and pass it on to those deemed worthy. Good luck, old friend." He dove into the sea.

Maecha pulled him across the deck and down below.

Akir appeared on the deck and pulled out the Awen Crystal. He yelled into the storm. "Show yourself, Father!"

Manannán rose from the frothing waves on his sea horse. Thunder crackled around him and lightning sizzled across the sky.

Manannán stared at his son, love long gone. "You have gone too far!"

Akir shook his head. "Ha! That could have been said for you sending me down into that black hole to live out eternity."

"I was only one of the many gods who agreed that you needed to be punished. What you did was unforgivable, and the fact that you can't admit it just proves how right we were. It will happen again if you do not leave immediately."

The waves crashed against the sides of the boat threatening to split it in half.

"You do not scare me anymore." Akir lifted the Awen Crystal and it turned black in his grasp. With his other hand he blasted a flame toward Manannán. A wall of water rose straight up and staunched the flames. Akir tried again and again, but the wall would not budge. Fire burst from his eyes, shot from his fingers, and surrounded Manannán. The wall of water encircled him and Manannán yawned.

"What, that's it? You steal the sacred Awen Crystal of the

Otherworld and that's all the power you have? You are done, Akir. You will no longer be allowed to play outside."

Manannán created a whirlpool in front of the boat. He could not chance allowing Akir to get to Eire. He would save the humans, but his son had to be destroyed. Whatever power the god of the sea used had to be for the greater good, and the person who destroyed a god had to do it with the best intentions and to save others. Manannán raised his trident to hurl at Akir. The crack in the air surprised him. Akir raised his hand toward his father and spoke: "Through the fire, through the flames, destroy the one who is to blame." The shock of the bolt shoved Manannán over the back of his sea horse.

Akir laughed as his father sank down toward the bottom of the sea.

"That should numb him for a while," Akir said to no one. He had just stunned the god of the sea. It was a long time coming and he had enjoyed it.

Just then an enormous gust of wind lifted the boat and set it forth toward Eire at a god-like pace. Cursing his father and all his power, Akir disappeared. He would be at Tara to welcome the family home. He would definitely welcome Maecha and give her the surprise of her life. The sword would be his, but so would Maecha.

The sky cleared and the sun showed its pretty face. A sun shower fell on the boat as everyone stepped up on the deck. If one had the inclination to look closer, they would have seen the grieving and worried tears of Aiménd falling to the earth.

Less than a day from when they left Alba, they landed at the cliffs of Eire. Nothing seemed to have changed to Maecha and yet she had changed enough for a lifetime. She steadied herself on the beach and felt the heart of Eire beat into her soul. Yes, she was home, but her land was hurting.

They rode along the bare fields of Tara. Their eyes were

306

assaulted by the destruction and desolation that surrounded them. Houses were burnt to the ground, animals and villagers struck down next to one another. The vultures showed no preference. The scent of death and decay invaded their nostrils until they had to breathe through their mouths to avoid gagging.

As they neared Tara, the scouts returned claiming there were no signs of the enemy. The solemn band of warriors followed their leader home. They could see the east side of Tara rising on its hill. The main wall that had protected their home for centuries was a pile of crumpled rocks. The sounds of laborers building gave her hope that some of the destruction was being repaired. Maecha looked forward to making her brother suffer like so many of their people had.

King Cormac slowed his horse and Maecha could see him observing his home. Maecha watched as Cormac shut his eyes and held his hand to his heart, like that was all that kept it from falling apart. She placed her hand on her father's arm. He tapped it and the look of despair disappeared from his eyes. Maecha knew what it cost him to be outside his walls, and she felt pride when he straightened his back and prepared to take back his home. But Cormac surprised her when he motioned for her to go before him.

"Father, you need to call to the guard to open the gate. They will open it for you. You have been king too long for them not to obey."

When Cormac touched her face with his thick fingers, they felt like sand paper against her soft skin. "It is not me that they need to obey any longer. I pass that honor to you."

Maecha's face paled as she felt a bolt of energy surge through her Awen Crystal.

"What is it?" her father asked.

"I felt a great deal of power flow through my crystal."

"That is a sign from the goddess."

"Perhaps, but it is something more. They have given their

307

power to me to protect it. The Otherworld is in dire trouble. I only hope that Kelan is all right."

"Kelan has always been able to take care of himself. Your duty right now stands before you. Give him something to come home to."

Maecha smiled.

Osgar, Goll, and Caoilte positioned their horses behind her. Cormac moved back next to Osgar. Treasa and her women warriors formed a semi-circle at the rear. Maecha stood in her saddle and turned toward them. They all bowed their heads to her. She couldn't stop the tears from falling. She gazed at her father once again and saw that the decision had been made. So be it.

"You have all proved your loyalty to your king well beyond anything that I could have expected. You took a chance on a young girl and still supported me when I acted like one." She put her hand up to stop Goll from disagreeing with her. "I say what I see, and right now I see the best band of warriors that Tara has ever known." She pointed to the decimated wall of Tara and continued. "Now beyond those beaten walls are villagers and brave warriors who need us to help them. This is what we traveled across the sea for, trained with Scathach for, and saved my father for. I will be forever grateful to all of you."

Wiping her face, she turned toward the gates of Tara. "Open the gate!" Maecha yelled.

Those words echoed through Maecha's head as she realized that the last time she said them, she had been heading out to fight her brother. Now they were brought full circle to fight him within their own kingdom.

"Who calls to enter?" one guard yelled down.

Maecha almost turned her head to make her father take back his crown. Fear of what this would do to him haunted her. Would he lose his will to live? Maecha wouldn't let that happen. He would always be seen as the greatest king to rule this land and she was sure he would advise her.

Warrior, queen, lover. Maecha was all these and would be more. She sat proud in her saddle and called, "Maecha Ruadh mac Art, Queen of Tara, daughter of Cormac mac Art, son of Conn of the Hundred Battle, and Queen Deirdre of the Sun Kingdom."

They did not open the gate. Upon hearing her voice, villagers swarmed from a hidden part of the castle and surrounded her and Cormac, begging to be saved from Cairpre. They gave what comfort they could, but nothing could be done until they were within Tara and Cairpre had been removed. Maecha sensed her father's sorrow turn to anger. Gazing toward the guard's tower her heart lurched as she watched the spirit of her mother linger along the walls, carrying a bundle in her arms. Maecha smiled and closed her eyes. Her mother handed her the bundle she carried. "Treat it with care," she heard her mother say. Curious, Maecha put the bundle on her lap and opened it. A perfectly round face with green eyes peered up at her. The child puckered her lips and smacked them like she was throwing kisses. Maecha's mother laughed and the world brightened with her happiness. When Maecha looked up again her mother was gone and she felt a flutter in her stomach.

Maecha placed her hand on her middle and swooned slightly. Treasa was at her side, grabbing her arm. She glanced at her waistline and whispered, "What ails you, Maecha?"

"I'm not sure that it's an ailment," Maecha said.

"You must be very careful. Do not risk anything happening to the baby," Treasa whispered.

"You know?" Maecha whispered back.

"I've known for a while. Your body will only protect that small being so much. Stay out of harm's way."

Maecha's laugh was bitter. "That's easy for you to say."

Other villagers who had remained around the walls of Tara now came forward, begging for food and safety. They pulled at Cormac's legs. Some yelled at Maecha for leaving them in the hands of her horrid brother. They tried to push the other horses away to get closer to her.

Treasa barked, "Protect the queen! She must not be harmed!" Goll, Caoilte, and Osgar moved in closer so that they surrounded Maecha.

Maecha raised her hand. Everyone's eyes had been on the king. Now they shifted to the daughter.

Maecha scanned the starved faces of her people. Her people. She was Queen of Tara and she would lead in the same benevolent and caring manner as her father.

She raised her eyes toward the inner gate. "Cairpre!"

"Here I am, sister of mine!" Cairpre stood on the turret in full battle gear. He wore the same helmet that he stole from their father's armory, the very same helmet that belonged to the son of Cruithne. The villagers backed away, not wanting to get caught in what was sure to be the battle for sovereignty. Maecha brought her horse next to her father and the multitude of warriors who had traveled to Alba stood behind her.

"Why, Cairpre?" Cormac called out to him.

Cairpre sneered at his father. "Why? You need to ask?" Then he spat at his sister, his anger flaring. "Why her?"

"It is the way of the goddess. Maecha is next in line. She is Queen of Tara."

"Over my dead body."

"That can be arranged," Maecha said.

Cormac placed a hand on Maecha's arm. "Enough blood has been shed. Let us handle this in peace."

Cairpre's attention was distracted by something next to Cormac. Maecha followed his gaze and saw the outline of her mother next to their father. She noticed that his face softened, but then he grabbed his head. Shaking it, he spat, "There can be no peace until I am king. I have the power to rule and a new time has come upon us. Join or die!"

He turned away from his only family. Deirdre shook her head sadly and disappeared. The decision had been made.

"I'm sorry, Father," Maecha said.

"I am disappointed, but I must say that it was what I expected. Let us make camp here and come up with a plan."

Chapter 33 - Catskills

Spring brought warmth to the Catskill Mountains as Natalie celebrated earning her first karate belt. The dojo's frame and walls had been built, and Vince, Travis, and Bentley worked long hours wanting to get it finished before summer started. Michaela worked with Ben and other police officers at the station to determine which troubled kids would benefit the most from spending some time out in the fresh air. So far there were about twenty of them. Michaela would be busy.

But that wasn't what had taken up most of her time lately. She and Natalie had spent numerous hours reading Irish histories, working on Natalie's energy flows, and traversing the dreamworld.

This morning they had both woken up excited and, after finishing their morning run, were sitting at the table with all the guys to eat breakfast.

"So what did you dream about?" Travis asked. He had grown about four more inches and took every opportunity to show off the muscles he'd developed from hammering and carrying material around all day. Natalie and Travis were close and they often spoke about the dreams they had.

"I dreamt about the cottage by the water again, but this time the door was open and I was able to go in," Natalie began.

"Wow, did you see anyone?" Travis asked forgetting about the large mound of scrambled eggs and sausages on his plate.

"I did. I stepped over the threshold, and I saw a woman bent over taking biscuits out of the oven. Her hair was long and blond and she moved graceful like a dancer. When she turned to place the pan on the counter, she saw me, and almost dropped the biscuits. Then she laughed and she sounded like sparkling water. She spoke to me, but I couldn't understand her."

"That's a bummer, Nat. What did you do next?"

Natalie took a sip from her chocolate milk and continued, "I didn't know what to do. We just stared at each other. Then I saw Michaela at the table."

"Michaela?!" Travis interrupted. "How did she get there?"

Michaela laughed. "I dream traveled with Natalie. I knew that she was trying to find out more about this cottage, so we went in together."

"Cool, go on," Travis said completely engrossed in the story.

"The lady held her arms open like she wanted to hug me. I glanced at Michaela and she said to go to her, because she is my mother." Tears shimmered in Natalie's eyes and they spilled over her freckled cheeks. "I just don't know what she said. It was in another language and it's probably important."

Travis patted her hand as Michaela said, "I know what she said, Natalie."

Natalie perked up. "You do, but how?"

"In addition to all the obvious changes when I came back from ancient Ireland, I found that I could understand Gaelic, which is the language your mother had spoken to you. She and Finnius are your parents. Her name is Eithne and she had traveled with Finnius to this world when she was pregnant with you. She was lost in New York City and Ricky Cartillo found her."

"But I thought he killed her? How did she get away?"

"I do not know the answers to those questions." Michaela hesitated and looked at Travis, Bentley, Vince, and then back to Natalie. Max, who had been staying with Shannon in their apartment, had been brought up during her last visit. He was snoring on his bed by the large window. They had become a unique family, and what she said next would affect all of them. "All I know is that she said it's vital for you to come to Ireland and find her. She can't come to you. She has very little knowledge of this world, and has been able to get by because some still speak Gaelic in the part of Ireland where she resides. But time is running short for her."

"What do you mean?" Natalie whispered. Would she lose her mother so quickly after just finding her? There were so many questions racing through her head, she couldn't keep them all straight.

"She seems to be struggling with the same kind of daydreams and loss of energy that you have been experiencing. There's only so long that someone can stay out of their time and she has stayed much longer than has ever been done. She needs to get back home to her time." Michaela placed her hand on Natalie's arm. "Baby, she wants to take you back with her."

That night Michaela spoke to Shannon on the phone.

"How about if I get an associate to take my clients for a few weeks so we can get Natalie settled?" Shannon suggested.

"I don't want your business to suffer, Shannon," Michaela said, even though she really wanted her sister there. "What about Ben?"

Shannon hesitated. "Well, we were going to tell you when we came up, but there's been a development concerning Ricky Cartillo."

Michaela sat down on her bed and took a deep breath. Max hopped up and snuggled next to her. "What is it?"

"Apparently, Ben's brother has had a few problems with the law and has come home to stay with their parents. He told Ben that he connected with a burly guy who has multiple burn scars on his face, who was looking to sell a large amount of drugs."

Michaela gasped.

Shannon continued, feeling it was best to get it all out. "Ben's brother, Nate, was pretty shaken by the guy's appearance, and when this man found out that Nate and Ben were related, he wanted Nate to set Ben up."

"Is Ben safe? Are you safe?"

"Yes, we are fine and actually packing. Nate is terrified and told Ben everything. The SWAT team went to Boris' hideout, but he was already gone. He must have known that Nate would snitch."

Michaela rubbed Max's head to keep a sense of calm. "So Boris is still alive and somewhere in New York City."

"For now, Michaela. Ben is taking a leave of absence and coming up with me. He's afraid that Boris might try to tie up some loose ends."

Michaela knew that when Ricky and Boris disappeared, there was always a chance that this nightmare would return. She thought of Natalie. That girl was surrounded by danger.

"Fine. Get here as soon as you can, Shannon. Bring your passport; we're going to Ireland. Natalie must be kept safe and it's time to end this."

Chapter 34 - Eire

The warriors set camp near the trees and sat around the fire for their evening meal. In the morning, they would fight to take back their home. Maecha felt worn and sad. She missed Kelan's strategic thinking and his warmth. She felt for him, but there was nothing. It was like their bond had never existed. How could they be so close to one another and not feel each other? Of course, she didn't know how far the bond stretched, so perhaps it was only normal that she would not be able to sense him. The fluttering in her stomach continued. With all the fighting that they had been involved in, she had ignored the fact that her monthly flows had ended. She must protect their child and give Kelan a reason to come home.

Maecha heard some cheering and left the fire to see what the excitement was about. Standing in the midst of her warriors was Kelan. She touched her Awen Crystal. It didn't feel warm and it still pulsed with that pale yellow light. Was he still mad at her? She would make up for it.

Everyone parted when they saw Maecha hurrying toward them. Kelan turned to her and their gazes held. His eyes looked different, darker. She took in his long-sleeved black tunic and pants. His hair was tied back in its usual manner and she could see the rope that held his crystal. But she didn't feel him.

He smiled at her. She approached and tried to ignore the hesitation that she felt within. "Your eyes," she said.

"We've been separated for what seems an eternity and all you can mention are my eyes?" he responded. "What about them?"

"There are specks of black in the green. I've never noticed it before."

"Perhaps you are looking at me in a new way," he said, touching her face.

"Perhaps."

He kissed her. Maecha felt shocked by his energy and was overwhelmed by the anger in it. His thoughts and feelings were still blocked, but his need for her was strong. When he released her, everyone cheered. She wavered from the blackness of it.

Goll, Caoilte, and the others slapped him on his back to welcome him home. "You must tell us of your adventures in the Otherworld," Goll said.

"Yes, in time, but now I have other business to attend to." He touched Maecha's arm and she felt a shock. She pulled away and felt a wave of nausea.

"What is it?" Kelan snapped.

She touched her head. "It has been a long journey and I am tired. Cairpre will not surrender and we need to formulate a plan to bring the fight to us. I was just thinking how I missed your strategic planning."

"Can that wait until the morrow? I have missed you."

Treasa put her arms around Kelan's shoulders in the friendly yet flirty manner they had grown accustomed to. He raised his brow. "Yes?" he asked.

"Surely you can spare some time with us, Kelan. I especially have missed you," she said.

Kelan wrapped his arm around Treasa's waist and pulled her closer. "Perhaps another time, my lady."

Kelan's formal tone with Treasa surprised Maecha, but she didn't have time to think on it. "Excuse me." She ran toward the trees.

Kelan moved to follow, but Treasa stopped him. "Leave her to me."

The others grabbed Kelan and pulled him toward the fire to hear his tales. He had no choice, but to go along. He stared hard after Maecha wondering if he was too late.

Maecha knelt by a tree and spewed up her evening meal. Treasa knelt next to her and pulled her hair back away from her face. Maecha tensed, but relaxed when she saw who it was.

She wiped her mouth with a cloth and leaned back onto her heels. Caught between a sob and a sigh, Maecha said, "Why couldn't it have waited until after this battle? No harm can come to this child, Treasa."

"You carry your destiny, and I feel very strongly that this cannot be known outside of those very close to us. If the Fire Lord or Cairpre finds out, then you will be in even more danger."

"I must tell Kelan."

Treasa grabbed her arm as Maecha started to walk back toward the camp. "The chances of a child living, especially in your situation, are very slim. It may be wise to keep this just between us in case you do not hold the child."

Maecha watched Treasa. Her face was full of concern, but Maecha noted a hint of suspicion.

"What is it, Treasa?"

"I do not know, but keep your mind open to deception. Something about Kelan didn't feel right. What did you feel when he touched you?"

"I felt nauseous, but, if I have a child in my womb, then that would be expected. And his eyes looked different to me. Do you think something happened in the Otherworld to change him?"

"I do not know, but we must keep watch to see if we need to help him. And it may be dangerous for the babe if you lay with Kelan. Make an excuse to wait."

"All right, if you think that is best for the babe."

"Yes, I do."

Cairpre lay trapped in his dream.

"I am here. Now is the time to prove your allegiance to me," the Fire Lord said.

"I am ready, but—"

"But, what?" Akir asked, losing patience.

"I have heard that Circenn was killed and you were there. Why did you not save him?"

"It was his own stupidity that got him killed. Your sister has some interesting powers. She knew what he had done. I couldn't risk showing myself with the Goddess Scathach right there. But that doesn't matter anymore. You have been the most loyal. Start the battle and I will do the rest."

"Yes, my Lord," Cairpre grumbled, but he sweat with worry.

Maecha had fallen asleep early the night before and hadn't had a chance to speak with Kelan again. The night had been restless with nightmares of giving birth to the Fire Lord's child. Images of Kelan dead or dying tormented her. When she awoke she found Kelan standing next to her holding Imbas Skye. Her stomach lurched, but she wasn't sure if it was from the babe she carried in her womb or Kelan holding her sword—something he had never done before.

"What are you doing?"

Kelan looked at her and, for a moment, she thought his eyes were black. Then they switched to the same green she had noted yesterday. Treasa had been right, there was something wrong with Kelan. She reached out for him and mindspoke, *"I missed you."*

Not reacting, Kelan sheathed the sword and placed it on his side of their bed. He pulled her to him and kissed her neck. "I was just admiring your sword and now I want to admire you."

He nuzzled her, but Maecha pulled away, upset that he hadn't responded to her connection. "I have not been able to feel you in my dreams or mindspeak with you. Are you still angry at me over Fidach? There was nothing between us."

Kelan rolled on top of her and kissed her breasts. "I know there was nothing between you. It is in the past. Let us make up."

Maecha didn't know why, but she felt disgusted by his attention. He pawed at her like an animal. "Kelan, stop!" she said, pushing him away.

"What is it now?" he asked, impatience showing on his face.

"I haven't had a chance to speak with you. I was not myself last night."

"And now you are fine, so let us show one another our love." He kissed her hard and again Maecha shoved him away.

"I want to know what happened in the Otherworld. Are the Lord and Princess safe?"

"All is well. They are safe and life goes on."

"And what of Lon? Is he well? Finnius had told me that he was captured. I didn't see him last night."

Kelan's face clouded over and he shifted away from her. "Lon did not make it."

"What?" Maecha touched his shoulder. "How?"

Kelan jumped up. "What difference does it make? He's gone and I'm here and yet you have not shown me how much you care!"

His words scorched her soul. She stood, her angry stance matching his. "I did not mean to imply anything, and I apologize if I have not given you more of a welcome. So much has happened and I need your support. Let's break fast and plan how we will get rid of Cairpre. Then we can worry about what is going on between us." She started to walk out of the tent.

"Maecha?"

"Yes?" She stopped and turned.

"You forgot your sword." He held it out for her. When she grasped it, Kelan held on. Again Maecha saw the shift in his eyes, like something fought within to overpower him.

Kelan let go of the sword and then pulled her into another embrace. He kissed her gently on the lips. "Something to look forward to." Maecha's Awen Crystal glowed brighter.

Maecha felt something in her gut loosen and she smiled. Why would she not feel safe around her soul mate? "Yes, for later."

A horn sounded and they ran outside. Cairpre had opened the gate, but not to let them in. Standing on the partially built walls, Cairpre wore the Picti helmet and again Maecha felt her fury rising at his lack of respect. She didn't know whether it was to mock his father or her, but it didn't matter. The time for mercy was over. She had a home to fight for and she would do just that.

Running back into her tent, Treasa helped her into the leather armor that had been her mother's. She prayed to the Mother Goddess to give her victory this day, not only to prove the rights of sovereignty, but to punish her brother for his lack of faith in it. His betrayal had weakened her father to the point that he could barely lift a sword. She wanted her father away from the battle, but he said he would come forth on his horse to support her. Unbeknownst to him, she had asked Osgar to protect her father. She needn't have asked; he would have done it anyway.

"Be careful," Treasa whispered in her ear as she finished wrapping Maecha's arm.

Kelan appeared next to her with a white horse. "Where is Octar?" she asked.

"He has a lame shoe. This one will suffice."

She didn't comment on the tunic that covered his arms. For as long as she had known him, he had always worn sleeveless shirts, so as to not hinder his movements. She also noted that his flail was missing, but perhaps he lost it in the Otherworld.

"Kelan, I need you to lead the band on the right," Maecha said.

Kelan did not move, but stood rigid on his horse with his sword unsheathed. "No, I will stay with you."

Maecha looked at him in exasperation. "I thought we cleared this up. I can take care of myself and will be well protected by those around me."

"Send Treasa."

"She has her women warriors."

"Then send Caoilte or Goll." Kelan took her hand and added, "I am only worried for your safety, Maecha. It was hard being away from you and not knowing if you were safe. Your safety is my utmost concern."

Maecha was torn. She could sense that she and Kelan were still on shaky ground, and she understood his fear for she had felt the same way. Sensing his stubbornness, Maecha sent Goll.

"Father!" Cairpre called from the turrets of the *rath*. "I give you one last chance."

"It is not my place to say. Maecha is the Queen of Tara now."

Cairpre spat toward them. "Then I will not waste my breath." He raised his sword to attack. Having locked the men still loyal to Lon down in the dungeons, Cairpre led his men to finish what should have ended months ago.

Filled with rage, Cairpre rode straight for Maecha. Kelan moved his horse in front of her and Maecha yelled, "Move out of the way!"

Kelan swung his sword toward Cairpre and he deflected it well enough. Cairpre had always feared Kelan, but he seemed fiercer and Cairpre wanted nothing to do with him.

Cairpre turned toward his father, wanting to destroy the man who never had time for him. This man cast him off, because the goddess didn't deem him suitable to rule. He had two strikes against him—being born a male and born with a limp. Then his sister had to burn his eyes, which made him appear even weaker. Cairpre would have become even angrier, but the vision in front of his father stopped him. His mother rode on a brilliant white mare. Her hair glittered in the morning sun. She leaned over his father, and he watched as she placed a soft kiss on Cormac's cheek. Cormac closed his eyes and nodded. He put his sword away. Deirdre turned to Cairpre and blew him a kiss.

"I will acquiesce for you, Mother, but I will be back to finish him." Cairpre fought his way to his sister.

Maecha fought next to Kelan. She waited for the sense of unity she usually felt when fighting with him, but it did not come. She knew he was there, but not what he was doing. When they fought together, she usually had a mental picture of what their attackers were doing, and she could anticipate what Kelan's next move would be. She would move with him, so that they could always protect one another's back. Their bond was broken. A feeling of evil threaded its way down her neck and threatened to choke her. The Fire Lord was here, she knew it. Maecha scanned the area to look for the man who had caused so much of this war. She couldn't find him.

Suddenly, Finn reared up onto his hind legs. Maecha flipped off his back and landed on her feet. She saw a deep burn on the back of her horse.

She yelled to Kelan. "We are being attacked by fire! The Fire Lord is here!"

He jumped off his horse and stood next to her.

"Why did you leave your horse?"

"To stay closer to you," he said.

"I would have ridden behind you. We are more vulnerable on the ground."

Several warriors attacked them in unison, and it took all of Maecha's concentration to keep them at bay. She blocked a vicious blow toward her head with her *ton-fa,* and the eye of her sword seared a hole through her enemy's heart. As she turned to protect herself from the next onslaught, Maecha noted Kelan staring at her, not fighting.

She yelled at him. "What is wrong with you? You're going to get killed!" That would have been true for any fighter, but no one seemed to come near him. When Maecha took a closer look, she realized that he wasn't looking at her, but at her sword. He had been watching the eye blast its attackers.

Maecha stormed up to him and slapped him across the face. "Kelan! Fight!"

Kelan eyes blazed red for an instant and he grabbed her wrist. "Never do that again."

"What is wrong with you?" The scream of her enemy forced Maecha to turn away from her soul mate. She stepped out to her left and rammed her dagger into a man's midriff just under his tunic. Then she whirled around and sliced through the warrior behind him. She lost sight of Kelan and fought to stay alive.

Treasa and her band of warriors battled their way to Maecha. Treasa knew Maecha's vulnerability and the others were too involved in their own battles to protect her. She had seen Maecha get thrown from her horse and Kelan jump off with her. Treasa hoped that Kelan was protecting her.

When she saw Kelan alone, she rode up to him. "Where is Maecha?"

He glanced at her in a casual manner and said, "Fighting her way to Cairpre, I would imagine."

Treasa fumed. "How could you let her go after him in her condition?"

Kelan grabbed her leg. His face turned stone cold. "In what condition?"

Realizing her mistake, Treasa attempted to ignore his question. "I must find her." She lifted her reins, but Kelan didn't let go. "Release me."

Kelan stepped closer and Treasa could see that the green of his eyes were now lined with red. "Not until you tell me what is going on with Maecha."

"You are not Kelan," she said and raised her sword to slice through his arm.

Kelan moved back faster than any man would have been able to. He raised his arms and the ground began to rumble. Fire demons shot up through the earth in front of Treasa. She turned her right side to them and protected her body with her shield. The heat from their flames burned her skin, but she held on. Instead the eye of her shield pummeled the demons with ice. They scattered and she used the opportunity to fall back. Kelan was gone.

Treasa trampled her enemy with her horse and rode toward Goll and Caoilte. They were on foot and surrounded by two rows of men, clamoring to get to them first. Treasa's horse kicked through the rear, and she hacked at bodies with her sword until the circle had been broken.

"Maecha is in danger! We must help her. The Fire Lord's demons have arrived and I think Kelan is possessed by one of them."

Not needing any other explanation, they grabbed three horses and rode away from Tara to the flat field that was scattered with the dead and the living who tried to fight over them.

Once again, the ground shook and warriors the size of two men uncurled from the ground. Their arms were fiery swords, and their eyes shot flaming arrows.

Goll yelled the ancient battle cry of his people and stormed toward one warrior. He swung his ironwood hammer into the enemy's arm. It was like hitting steel, but Goll didn't flinch. With the strength of the gods, he swung his axe like he was chopping wood and hit both sides of the monster. With each assault, the steel flew away until Goll smashed the demon. It fell to the ground where it burned a hole the size of a large boulder.

From his horse, Caoilte launched dagger after dagger at another demon. The force of the impact pushed the demon back until it tripped over a dead warrior. Treasa blasted the demon with the blue eye on her shield, and it burst into a towering flame and then vanished.

No one had heard Osgar join the fight, so they were all surprised when they heard an anguished cry. As if in slow motion, they turned to see Osgar with his sword in the air and another demon's blazing sword protruding from his side.

"No!!!" Goll yelled and, together with Caoilte and Treasa, they chopped the demon into useless pieces. But it was too late. Osgar gasped and fell to the ground.

"The king," he whispered. "Protect Cormac."

Kelan joined Maecha once again. The fighting had slowed down with heavy injuries on both sides.

From the corner of her eye, Maecha watched Cairpre head toward her. "He's mine."

"As you wish," he said positioning himself next to her.

Cairpre slid off his horse and limped toward his sister, his sword pointed right at her heart. She lifted her sword and tapped his. As they fought, their swords clashed and sang the ancient battle song. Cairpre thrust his sword at Maecha at the same time a bolt of energy hit her sword arm. Stunned by the pain, Maecha dropped her sword.

"No," Maecha gasped and lunged for it just as Cairpre did the same. Maecha grabbed the sword, but Cairpre pushed her off balance. She rolled onto her back and, as he launched his body on top of hers, she kicked out her foot striking his belly, and throwing him over her head. Cairpre landed flat on his back, but sat up to defend himself. Maecha kicked him square in the face and his head snapped back. She jumped in the air to make space and kicked him in the chest. When she lifted her sword to stab him, Cairpre raised his hand, which released a powerful force throwing her back. Kelan caught her. Pain seared through Maecha's soul and she attempted to break free from his grasp.

Cairpre felt the Fire Lord. First, he was in his head, but then he felt his presence and knew he was very near. He wondered why Kelan didn't attack him, but was glad of it. Kelan. He looked at him again and noted that instead of fighting, he still held Maecha. And his eyes. They were as black as the hole where the Fire Lord had crawled out of. The Fire Lord. It was not Kelan! The Fire Lord had come to help him. In that instance of recognition, Akir shoved Maecha away from him. A flash of fire scorched Maecha in the back. She screamed. Cairpre whipped his sword at hers and Imbas Skye flew out of her hands.

It fell to the ground and the Fire Lord picked it up. As he held it, his hair turned back to his sandy brown shade, while the rest of his body and clothing returned to normal. He wiped some dust from his arm and smiled at the shocked look on Maecha's face.

"Isn't this interesting? You are caught between your two worst enemies and no one is here to help you."

"Give me back my sword and I'll show you what I'll do," Maecha sneered.

"So nasty. I know it is hard to give up. I have been waiting two hundred years just to touch it again. And now it is mine."

"You did not take it from me."

Cairpre stepped in, and said, "That sword is mine. I rightfully took it from her. I own its power now!"

The Fire Lord noted Cairpre's agitated state and was annoyed by it. "You have fulfilled your purpose and have the power that you craved. Now the sword is mine, so that all may pay for what was done to me. I shall have my revenge."

Cairpre sneered and lunged for the Fire Lord. With all the strength she possessed Maecha flipped her *ton-fa* at the Fire

327

Lord's arm to disengage her sword from his hand.

With a swipe of his hand, the Fire Lord tossed Cairpre to the side and thrust Imbas Skye through Maecha's chest.

Kelan felt the burn and then the most intense pain in his chest. He faltered and Lon caught him.

"What ails you, Kelan?" he asked. They had just come upon the oak tree that would lead them out of the Otherworld.

Kelan yanked out his Awen Crystal. Maecha's crystal was bright red. "NO! NO!"

The triumphant laughter of the Fire Lord pounded in his head. He pushed it all away. The past could not be changed, but he had vowed to save Maecha and he would. He loved her with everything that was inside him. All his doubt, fear, and bitterness evaporated from his heart.

Kelan raised his hands and called to the great Mother Goddess, "Goddess show me the way!"

A brilliant light consumed him and Lon. When he could see again, Kelan was on the outskirts of the battle. Maecha's essence glowed like a faint beacon. He ran. Lon rushed ahead of him killing anyone in his path.

Maecha staggered back from the pain, fearing the worst for her unborn child.

"Give me the sword!" Cairpre yelled and jumped at the god he had thrown everything away for.

Akir swatted him away. "This is rightfully mine. I destroyed its owner."

"You swore to give it to me!"

"I grow tired of your complaining, Cairpre. Move out of my way, so I can finish your sister. Or would you like to?"

Cairpre turned and saw Maecha kneeling on the ground. Then he saw his father running toward them. There was nothing feeble about the old king now, Cairpre thought. Which child was he trying to save? Did it matter anymore? All that Cairpre worked for, had given up, was being ripped from him yet again. The Fire Lord raised his hand to launch a fire ball at his father. The image of his mother's face shattered in front of him. Regret and shame filled Cairpre. He had betrayed all of them when he was needed most. Everything he had done to gain power was through deceit and cowardice. Hundreds of people had died by his hand, by his orders; he had killed Leann and Finnius' power was gone. Those who had loved him were no more. When Cairpre stared into his father's face, he saw love and concern, even though he had been betrayed. His father loved him and that was all Cairpre needed to see. He had come for his son.

Cairpre sprinted forward on legs fit for an athlete and launched himself in front of his father. The fire ball seared through his middle and he collapsed to the ground.

"Cairpre!" Cormac yelled and fell to his son.

Cairpre felt like his insides were melting. He was surprised to find his father holding him. Grabbing on to his father's tunic like a lifeline, he pulled him closer. "I . . . am . . . sorry," he gasped, wanting to say more.

"I am sorry, my son. Just hold on. We can find a druid to save you and we can start over again," Cormac said trying to will life into his son.

They felt her presence at the same time. Deirdre hovered over both of them, tears of joy and sorrow glistening in her eyes. She spoke, "Let me take him before the Fire Lord consumes him. He will be with me."

Cormac stared at the beautiful vision of his wife and said, "Take me with you, my love."

Deirdre touched his cheek. "Soon, my dear, soon, but first look to your daughter."

She and Cairpre disappeared.

Akir raised Imbas Skye to remove Maecha's head. She could only stare at him with disbelief. Her baby. She had to protect the child who would save their world. With her last bit of strength, she lifted her *ton-fa* to block the blow that was sure to come. Suddenly, Lon's broadsword knocked Imbas Skye back.

"You!" Akir yelled.

"Who were you expecting? I waited years to destroy the bastard that took my life away. By the way, that deformed beast of yours and his mages have been destroyed." Lon whipped his sword inches from Akir's face. "And now it is your turn."

Akir ignored him wanting to finish Maecha. That was all that mattered now. It was a shame that he didn't get to lie with her, but having that sword would be enough. Once again Lon blocked his sword, but this time he kicked Akir in the chest and the Fire Lord flew back over numerous dead bodies. Lon's eyes swirled with the fires of his ancestors.

He raised his sword and waited for the man who had ruined his life. "Let's finish this," Lon said.

Akir had had enough. "You can finish this on your own. I have better things to do than fight a sore loser. Get over it." Akir waved his hand at Lon and the warrior was surrounded by flaming monsters. "That'll hold you for a bit," he said and went back to destroy Maecha.

Cormac reached Maecha at the same time that Kelan did.

Without a word, Kelan fumbled in his bag to remove the tooth of the green serpent.

"Kelan, is it really you?" she panted.

"Yes, it's me. Just hold on, Maecha. I will save you."

She pulled him down toward her. "I carry your daughter. Our child is within me. I don't want to die. I don't want to lose her."

A new kind of pain stabbed his heart—one filled with determination to fight for more than himself. Kelan kissed her hand. "You will not lose her. Both of you will survive and we will be a family."

Kelan took out his knife and scooped the marrow of the tooth and rubbed it on Maecha's wound. It began to close, but then it stopped and Maecha continued to bleed. The poisoned wound in her arm also bled as the life drained out of her.

"She's mine!" Akir yelled.

Kelan heard the Fire Lord at the same moment his back exploded in pain.

The tip of Imbas Skye protruded through his middle. Then it was yanked back.

The Fire Lord's laughter split his ears. Kelan held forth his forearms and called out, "Mother Goddess! I beg you to spare her, so that she can fulfill the prophecy!"

The spirit of the goddess lifted from the eyes tattooed on Kelan's forearms and swirled through the air above him. Her beauty and power were hard for human eyes to bear. She lowered next to Maecha and the goddess' brilliance covered them both. "Go, Kelan and fulfill your duty," she spoke in his mind. He bowed and understood that they wouldn't be together.

He kissed Maecha on the lips and with a last battle cry, Kelan ran toward Akir who still wielded Imbas Skye. He plunged the tooth of the green serpent into Akir's heart. Akir gasped and grabbed his chest. He tried to hold onto the sword. The spirits of Imbas Skye flew out of the tip and surrounded him. The one who had defeated him two hundred years ago removed the sword from his hands and lay it down next to Maecha, who shimmered in the Mother Goddess' love. Akir collapsed. Kelan removed the Awen Crystal from Akir's neck and fell back next to Maecha.

Kelan placed the crystal around her neck. Then he took her hand in his and fell back next to her. His eyes closed. The spirit of the Mother Goddess entered Maecha on her last gasp for breath. She spread her love and life within her. The wound in Maecha's chest closed. Her arm healed. Maecha opened her eyes and saw her father, tears streaming down his face. She felt the cold hand in hers and sat up to see Kelan strewn next to her, a gaping wound in his midsection.

"No," she cried. She leaned over him and her tears fell on his face. "I love you, Kelan. Do not leave me." She kissed his lips and the goddess' spirit filled them both.

The goodness of the earth, sky, and sea encompassed them as their spirits rose from their bodies and entwined above them. They were one, married in the spirit of the goddess. They had fulfilled their prophecy and sacrificed themselves for the love of the other. The golden glow of their love entered back into their bodies and slowly they revived, opening their eyes with wonder. Kelan pulled Maecha to him. They looked down at their crystals and saw that all three were brilliant. The prophecy was complete and the time for the next step, protecting their unborn child, was upon them. Maecha removed the Awen Crystal of the Otherworld and held it up toward the sky.

"You did well," the Lord and Princess spoke in their minds and the crystal disappeared back to the safety of the Otherworld.

Her father helped Maecha stand.

"Where is Cairpre?" she asked.

"He sacrificed himself for me," Cormac said, his eyes filled with tears. "Your mother's spirit took him so that he will be with her. In the end, he was worthy."

"Then he has redeemed himself," Maecha said.

A yellow light flashed and the Sun Goddess Aiménd appeared with Manannán mac Lir on a winged horse. The spirits of Imbas Skye returned to the sword as Akir's parents stood by his crumpled body. They clasped hands and Akir's body lifted into the air. His black spirit separated from his body and Manannán blew it to different parts of the world, so that it could never grow strong again. With the power of the sun, his mother burned his body to ashes.

Manannán spoke to Kelan, "We thank you for fulfilling your vows to the Otherworld and the Mother Goddess. Without your bravery, the prophecy would have been destroyed."

"It has been my honor," Kelan said and bowed.

Aiménd addressed Maecha. "The power of the goddess is within you. Thank you for bringing my love back to me. We can be together now."

Maecha nodded. "I am sorry for your son."

Aiménd touched Maecha's cheeks and they turned red with her warmth. "It had to be this way. He was lost to us a long time ago, but I will live with regret. Love your child unconditionally and show her an honorable path. Only then will your family circle be complete. Do not make the same mistakes we did." The sun goddess stepped back and let her sea god lift her onto Enbarr.

"Until we meet again," Manannán called and they flew away.

The clouds disappeared and the sun glowed bright upon them all.

"Maecha!" Treasa called.

With all that happened, Maecha had forgotten about her friends. She saw Goll carrying Osgar.

"Oh, no!" Maecha called and ran to him. Goll laid him gently on the ground. "Is he dead?"

"Yes," Goll answered.

Caoilte stood next to Treasa, unabashed tears streaming down his face.

"We were fighting those blasted demons and Osgar saved us by attacking one at our backs," Treasa said. She noticed Kelan and withdrew her sword.

Maecha held her arm. "It's all right. The Fire Lord is dead. This *is* Kelan."

Treasa's face brightened. "You could use the marrow."

Kelan's face tightened as he knelt down next to the fallen warrior. "I'm afraid I used it to save Maecha and the rest to destroy the Fire Lord."

Cormac knelt next to his oldest friend and bowed his head. "He died with honor."

Before anyone could say anything else, the sky darkened and bolts of lightning flashed above Osgar. They all fell back.

Scathach approached. She wore the regalia of the goddess that she was, her tunic and leather skirt studded with gems that sparked with her anger. Everyone shifted as she made her way to her long lost love. It was only then that her anger softened and her heart showed on her face. Tears fell from her eyes.

Scathach said to Maecha, "You have made your mother proud."

"Scathach," Maecha started, but stopped because no words could soothe what pain she knew was in the goddess' heart.

Scathach bent down and lifted Osgar into her arms. "You have done well, my love; you have sacrificed for another. Now it shall be as it should have been."

The sky opened up with the torrent of lightning and thunder. Scathach's body glowed white as did Osgar's. With one last power surge from the sky, she brought her love home.

Once again the sky cleared, and they were left reeling from the events of this momentous battle. "He will live on at the Isle of Imbas Skye," Treasa said and she grabbed each of Goll's and Caoilte's arms to pull them away. "Let's give them a moment."

Lon helped Cormac stand and led him home.

Kelan strode up behind Maecha and wrapped his arms around her waist. He rubbed her belly, round with their precious child. "She will be determined and willful like her mother," he said.

Maecha faced him and wrapped her arms around his

neck. "And a brave warrior, like her father."

Kelan kissed her. "And she will be loved and cherished by both."

"Yes, she will," Maecha said and they walked back to the halls of Tara to prepare for the child that would save them all.

Book Discussion Questions

What is a favorite memory that you have of your mother or father when you were little?

How do you think children's upbringings differ from modern society compared to ancient civilizations?

If you thought you lost your spouse and were given a second chance, what would you change?

Would you want to know the future? What if you knew about it, but couldn't change it?

What do you hope happens in the third book? Who is your favorite character?

What do you think about time travel? Do you think it is possible, or is actually happening now?

What do you think of the different perspectives of reality, as when Ben thinks that dreams are just dreams? Are they actually something much greater, and are there other dimensions to which most of us do not have access?

What constitutes loyalty and why is it such a major theme in this book? What about Michaela's loyalty to her family and the betrayals of the sons to their fathers? Is Cairpre wrong for believing in a different god and wanting to force that belief on others? How does that relate to our modern world?

What do you think about giving up what appears to be the "right" (or expected or normal) path, and then having a whole new path open up? Is this faith, destiny, following your instincts, or something else? (For example, Michaela inheriting the house in the Catskills where the new dojo is opened and troubled children will be helped, rather than sticking with the dojo in the city.)

Do you think the stable sister Shannon is jealous of the dreaming and time traveling that her sister does? She mentions how dull her life seems by comparison, being the anchor, the one who stays put and is always there (loyalty, again). Which sister would you rather be?

How do you feel about a woman in a position of real power leading her people? Is age a factor? In societies where childbearing (especially heirs) is prized, and when life span was much shorter, age may be a necessary factor, but what about wisdom and experience – could there be a real leadership role for older women?

Do you think that being prepared from birth (including lineage and station) for a particular destiny makes it easier for the person to assume her position, and easier for the people she is to lead to accept her – as in she has the right (lineage, education and training) to lead?

How do you feel about a leader also being a warrior, trained physically as well as mentally and emotionally in that track and way of thinking? Do you think that if a leader were trained in another philosophy, it would make a difference in her or his decisions? Would those decisions work (keep their people safe) in a world where other leaders were more or only of the warrior mentality? Is a leader shaped by the times, as well as by their culture, training, and education?

What do you think of the concept of royalty? Do you think it is possible (and therefore legitimate) that ancient gods and goddesses really did start (create or give birth to) certain lineages? In this case, wouldn't it make sense to track the lineage through the mother? (Old saying—you always know who the mother is). How did societies change when patriarchy took over, how were women 'protected' to assure a father's parentage, and how did that concern rule women's lives?

How do you feel about divinity (of any description) being part of a 'legitimate lineage' for power? How many cultures have used this measure and belief? Is this belief still alive in certain countries of the world? When did this measure change, and how, or has it changed?

What 'divinity markers' do we use in our modern world to choose leaders – such as education, upbringing, religious practices and beliefs, 'connections,' mastery of money, ease of speaking, 'position' in society, appearance, presentation, etc.?

Also by Janine De Tillio Cammarata

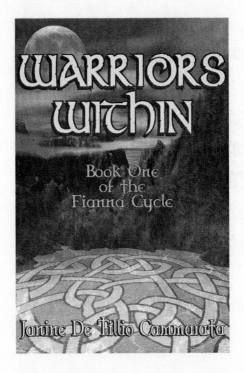

WARRIORS WITHIN:
Book One of the Fianna Cycle